When he moved — — fingers gripping his bicep like a vice. The restraint snapped his tenuous control and he rounded on her. Grasping her shoulders, he backed her against the wall. Confusion surfaced when she offered no resistance. He knew from experience she could lay him out flat in one move if she wanted. So what was her game?

Hands flattened against his chest, she lifted her face to his. He swallowed hard at what he saw. Earlier she'd turned away from him. Now the heat in her gaze was pure invitation.

Closing his eyes against the temptation did nothing to stop latent desire from rising up to engulf him. Things had been explosive between them in the past. He discovered nothing had changed when his body hardened in response.

Desperation tightened his grasp. "What do you want from me?"

Her fingers curled into his shirt, nails scraping his chest through the silk material. "I don't know," she whispered.

Opening his eyes, he locked his gaze with hers and was surprised to see there was some truth to her words. Uncertainty was mixed with an intense hunger that matched his. Shallow breaths feathered his chin, raising his response level past rational thought.

He slid his hands up to frame her face and lowered his head. "Is it this?"

Giving her no chance to answer, he covered her mouth with his. He swept his tongue inside and there was nothing tentative about his possession or her response. She tasted better than he remembered; a unique blend of sweet and spice that could never be replicated.

Breaking the kiss, he rasped, "Tell me, Eva. Is that what you want?"

"Yes," she breathed.

# Praise for Stacey Joy Netzel's other work

"Stacey has an exceptional way of making her characters come alive both on the page and in the reader's heart."

~ Karen, LovesToRead, about **SUMMER SCANDAL**

"I always love to read books by Stacey Joy Netzel and [**VOW OF TRUST**] is no exception. You can read this one alone or the whole series. Enjoy!"

~ Cheryl, Amazon Reviewer

**ILLUSION OF TRUST**: "Stacey Joy Netzel has a talent for creating characters that bring the story to life...dialogue is both sharp and spicy. The story is intense and is filled with unexpected twists."

~ Rosemary, Amazon Reviewer

"The story of Alex Reily returning to his hometown after 9 years away (3 of those years in prison) had a lot of plot twists that really kept [**SPRING DREAMS**] interesting! Santa Butch is back and up to his matchmaking ways, and seeing Alex and Emma's relationship grow, and how Alex changes and grows with it, makes for a wonderful story."

~ Elizabeth, Amazon Reviewer

"I thoroughly enjoyed [**SAY YOU'LL MARRY ME**] as I did the previous nine in the [Welcome to Redemption series]. I just hope there are more to come. All of the characters were perfect from the other book's in this one and Joy and Logan were great!"

~ Dale, Amazon Reviewer

*Stacey Joy Netzel's Other Titles:*

ITALY INTRIGUE SERIES
   ***Kidnapped*****
   ***Betrayed***
   ***Conned***
   *2012 Write Touch Readers' Award Winner, as *Lost in Italy*

COLORADO TRUST SERIES
   ***Evidence of Trust***
   ***Trust by Design***
   ***Trust in the Lawe***
   ***Shattered Trust***
   ***Dare to Trust***
   ***Vow of Trust***
   ***Illusion of Trust***

WELCOME TO REDEMPTION SERIES
   ***A Fair to Remember***, Book 2
   ***Grounds For Change***, Book 4
   ***The Heart of the Matter***, Book 6
   ***Hold On To Me***, Book 8
   ***Say You'll Marry Me***, Book 10
   (books 1,3,5,7,9 written by Donna Marie Rogers)

ROMANCING WISCONSIN SERIES
   ***Mistletoe Mischief*****
   ***Mistletoe Magic*****
   ***Mistletoe Match-up*****
   ***Mistletoe Rules***, short ebook bonus story
   ***Autumn Wish***
   ***Autumn Bliss***
   ***Autumn Kiss***
   ***Autumn Glimmer***, short ebook bonus story
   ***Spring Fling***

***Spring Serendipity***
***Spring Dreams*****
***Spring Spark***, short ebook bonus story
***Summer Scandal***
　*2010 Write Touch Readers Award Winner in previously published anthology
　**2017 Write Touch Readers Award Winner

STAND ALONE ROMANCE TITLES
　***More Than a Kiss***, contemporary romance
　***Chasin' Mason***, contemporary western romance
　***Ditched Again***, high school reunion novella
　***Dragonfly Dreams***, Christmas novella
　***NINA***, Beach Brides multi-author series novella

PARANORMAL ROMANCE TITLES
　***If Tombstones Could Talk***
　***Beneath Still Waters*** (Part One)
　***Rising Above*** (Still Waters Part Two)

# BETRAYED

Italy Intrigue Series – 2

BY
STACEY JOY NETZEL

BETRAYED

Copyright 2016, 2nd edition, *BETRAYED*
Copyright 2013, 1st edition, as *Run to Rome*

**\*\*\*Previously Published as *RUN TO ROME*\*\*\***

This is a work of fiction. Names, characters, places, and incidents are either the product of the author's imagination or are used fictitiously, and any resemblance to actual persons living or dead, business establishments, events, or locales, is entirely coincidental.

All rights reserved. No part of this book may be used or reproduced in any manner whatsoever without the written permission of the author, except in the case of brief quotations embodied in critical articles or reviews.

Cover design: Anna © Cover Couture

ISBN: 9781939143655
Print Edition

# Acknowledgements

Anyone who's read the acknowledgements in **KIDNAPPED** (previously titled *Lost In Italy*) knows the idea for that book came from the incident where my favorite brother and older sister left me behind alongside Lake Como. Fourteen years later, the same brother (he's my only brother) offered to take me back to research book two, but this time he did not leave me standing all alone at the lake. Instead, he drove me along the approximate route my characters would travel, and then he abandoned me each day while he went to work.

I can't complain, though, because I thoroughly enjoyed my time spent exploring the beautiful city of Lucca. So, thanks goes to him yet again, but for much better reasons this time around. Love ya, Troy!

My second thank you goes to Emilio Bertoncini, for a wonderful day hiking in the Garfagnana region of Tuscany, for sharing the amazing city of Sillico, and for setting up a meeting with Sovrintendente Capo Fabio Martinelli of the *Polizia di Stato*. (*Sovrintendente Capo* = Chief Superintendent) Emilio was a wonderful host and translator, and an even better storyteller. **BETRAYED** wouldn't be the same without his help, and I appreciated meeting him and his family.

Next I must offer a special thanks to Miss Luna Bertoncini, who gave up her 'bed' on the couch in their living room so I could conduct my interview with Sovrintendente Capo Martinelli. I promised this beautiful little girl who practiced some of her English on me that I would mention her to make up for me keeping her up past her bedtime. "Thank you, Miss Luna!"

Sovrintendente Capo Fabio Martinelli receives thanks for being gracious enough to give up his evening to answer this American's questions. I may not have gone the route I first intended with the plot, but his input and expertise helped me figure out the new direction.

I feel I must mention Dion and Perry, two of my brothers coworkers who made a great trip even more memorable—especially the bike ride around Lucca's walls on Halloween night. And Davide, I'm still drinking tea after dinner instead of wine.

My awesome brainstorming crew, Donna, Virginia and Lily—thank you for the plot discussions over yummy cups of chai tea. Thank you to my son, Cody, who's always willing to listen to a crazy idea when I need to voice it out loud, Natalie G. Owens and E.C. Adams for their help with all things Italy and their translation skills, and to my wonderful editor, Stacy, who always makes sure I work hard to write the best book I can.

Last but not least, thanks to my husband, Wayne, who didn't voice one word of complaint when I asked to go to Italy and left him with the kids for almost two weeks over his 40th birthday. Love you, dear!

~Stacey

## Dedication

To KIDNAPPED's (*Lost In Italy's*) biggest fan…

Danielle

Thank you for all you do for authors ~
your enthusiastic support always makes my day!

## Prologue

*Thirteen years earlier...*

RICHARD SANDERS SCANNED the first of the three letters laid out on his small, utilitarian table. He'd always had neat handwriting, but this one he'd printed with meticulous care to make sure not a single word was out of place.

Sounds echoed behind him—the occasional shout, the heavy clang of steel on steel, footsteps and music blending into a discordant cacophony of background white noise that he consciously tuned out.

He'd prepared a year for this letter. Made sure the correspondence leading up to this particular missive included the clues essential to unlocking the mystery—if the reader understood there was a mystery to unlock. To the casual observer, or prison guard monitoring his mail, it was nothing more than a letter from a father to a daughter. Only a trained eye would understand one mistake could unravel the entire code.

Satisfied with his efforts, he addressed the envelope, inserted the letter and left it unsealed before setting it precisely on the corner of the metal table that comprised his work station.

The second letter was for his son. The boy had become a man

much quicker than most, but he'd had a knack for the game that Richard hadn't been able to resist nurturing, molding, refining. They never spoke of the past during their infrequent visits, and after avoiding incarceration himself, his son had insisted he'd left their life of crime behind.

Sources confirmed he'd hired on with a legitimate courier company, though recently, he'd taken a side job that hadn't exactly adhered to the full letter of the law. Knowing his son could potentially still be swayed in his favor could prove beneficial in the future. For that reason, he would receive the information about the key.

Once the second letter was addressed, he stacked it on top of the first. His gaze reluctantly tracked to the third piece of paper as he sat back, but from the corner of his eye he noticed the first two weren't lined up and sat forward once more. With the quarter inch overlap between the envelopes corrected, his attention returned to the lingering order of business.

The words on the page had etched into his memory since the first time he'd read them, yet he still ran his gaze over the flowing script as he picked up the paper with a steady hand.

*Dearest Richard,*

*I am sorry. I never meant for our family to be torn apart like this, I simply wished for the life we could've lived had we made different choices. The Bible may have led us to great rewards, but it would have been at the cost of our children. For their sake, I felt it was time for me to make the right choice before we lost Benjamin and Rachel the way we lost Halliwell. I only hope someday you will find it in your heart to forgive me, and we can be a family once more.*

*Yours Always,*
*Lia*

He'd received the letter through his lawyer almost a year earlier, after federal agents had taken him into custody with a mountain of evidence to seal their case. At first, his wife's betrayal had been too surreal to believe. During the trial, the truth had sliced deep and begun to fester. Not even her own arrest and conviction had managed to flush out the wound.

Forgiveness was not in the cards; not when he knew the real reason for her duplicity.

His fist clenched on the paper that had previously only born two worn creases where it folded into thirds. He hadn't responded to her letter, hadn't spoken to her since the trial, and didn't plan to again.

"Sanders."

His heart skipped a beat. Outwardly, he gave no indication the abrupt voice at his back had startled him. He relaxed his hand and set the crumpled letter on the table before turning to face the sandy-blond, slightly pudgy uniformed guard with a smile.

"Johnson." He picked up the letters as he rose to take the four steps to the closed cell door. "How are Laura and the kids? Are they feeling any better?" Though a quick glance confirmed no one within earshot, he still lowered his voice. It was imperative he maintain the trust and friendship he'd cultivated with the forty-two year old officer since his arrival.

Johnson conducted his own security check before nodding. "No one's puked since yesterday morning. Finally got some sleep last night."

"Good for you."

"Yeah, I needed it." He looked around again, then dropped his gaze to the envelopes in Richard's hand. "You need those mailed?"

He'd prefer to put them in the mail slot himself, but Johnson was the only one he trusted enough to do the job for him. "I'd appreciate it," he said, passing them between the bars. "It's Rachel's eighteenth birthday on Monday."

The guard lifted the unsealed flaps for a cursory glance as protocol required. He returned them for Richard to seal. "You hear from Halli yet?"

His smile faded as he licked the dried glue and closed both

pieces of mail. "No. Don't expect I will either. Those bridges were burned a while ago."

"Bridges can be rebuilt, man. Keep the faith."

A buzzer sounded throughout the cell hall, indicating the dinner hour. Three hots and a cot had been budgeted down to breakfast at seven a.m. and early dinner at three in the afternoon. On the flip side, his bed was a step above a cot, and he had a TV and cable.

Johnson held up the letters before dropping his hand to his side. "I gotta go see the warden before I head home, but I'll make sure these get out today."

"Thank you."

Richard watched the guard walk away. Once those letters were delivered, he'd be one step closer to making sure his disloyal wife never got her traitorous hands on the reason he was serving a fifteen year sentence in this maximum security Ritz of a prison.

## Chapter 1

*Present Day*

HE SUCKED HER lower lip between his teeth for a soft nibble before giving up all pretense of gentleness. Her back made solid contact with the door of his hotel room as it slammed shut. An expected jolt of pain to her head was tempered by the cushion of his large hand as he cradled the back of her head. His mouth opened on hers, his head angling as he pushed his tongue inside with no pause for permission.

A moan of approval vibrated in her throat, and she surrendered to the aggressive possession. It'd been like this from the moment they first touched at the villa. At the beginning, she assumed danger had heightened the combustible sexual energy that pulsed between them. Now she knew it was so much more than that.

Her former Italian lover had nothing on this hot blooded American, and she was helpless to resist. She didn't want to resist. Because even with his left arm confined in a sling, his free hand slid down to caress her body in ways she shouldn't allow without making him pay for dinner first. At the very least.

But whenever he was near, she came alive. The high of getting justice for her murdered father had faded much too fast, and this man counteracted her growing sense of unease. He made her feel again, filled the gnawing hollow chasm expanding within her chest.

His palm flattened on her ribcage and eased upward. Her body was on fire, every cell tingling with elemental awareness. Panting for oxygen, she arched her back, bringing their hips closer while allowing him access up top. He gave a low growl, his palm brushing over the front of her midnight blue, silk dress, and her nipples tightened beneath her black lace bra.

She lifted her leg to rub along the outside of his thigh. The rough denim of his jeans created a sensual abrasion against her sensitive skin. He trailed wet kisses down her neck, his labored breath sending shivers along her spine with each steamy puff. The shivers raced back up when he grasped her knee to pull her body tighter against his leg.

The exquisite pressure at the juncture of her thighs made her gasp. He chuckled and drew her mouth back to his for another mind-numbing kiss. Keeping her leg high, his hand slid beneath the flared skirt of her dress and skimmed along the underside of her thigh. When he reached the edge of her sheer black stockings and fingered the tiny metal clasps of her garter, his fingers tightened on bare skin above the lace.

"For me?"

"*Sì*."

"Aw, hell," he groaned. "We're never gonna make it to dinner."

The rough rasp of his voice told her he was equally affected. So did his body. *Va benisimo*. Again, she whispered, "*Sì*."

She'd dressed with the intent to seduce him beyond control, needing the mind-numbing peace of physical release. The stockings and garters made her feel feminine in a way she'd never dared indulge before him, ensuring she'd get exactly what she wanted tonight.

His hand moved higher, blunt, calloused fingers digging into her flesh as his mouth possessed hers once more. Without warning, he bent at the knees and lifted her, spreading her legs to straddle his hips, supporting her weight with one strong arm. She grabbed for his shoulders to keep her balance.

As if the bulk of the bandages beneath his shirt weren't reminder enough, his breath hissed through his teeth as pain tightened his features.

She quickly shifted her hold to the back of his neck. "Put me down."

"I'm okay."

"You'll hurt yourself more. The doctors will—"

"*Shhh.*" He pressed his lips to the hollow at the base of her neck. His tongue pressed against her wild pulse as he strode across the room with sure strides.

On the way to the bed, his mouth descended to the curve of her breast exposed by her plunging neckline. Anchoring her fingers in his dark blond hair, she pressed closer, lifting herself ever so slightly. He murmured approval, nuzzling aside the silky material of her dress to lave his tongue across her skin.

Her stomach clenched in anticipation of his hot mouth closing over—

"*Gallo!*"

Evalina startled in her chair, the sound of her last name bellowed across the police station jerking her back to reality. Her gaze flew from her spiraling screensaver to the grim expression on her Commissario's face. Mortified to find herself slightly short of breath and tingling in places that should *not* tingle at work, she quickly crossed her arms over her chest and sat up straight.

"Yes, sir?"

"My office. Now."

"Yes, sir."

Evalina did her best to banish the lingering memory of the one man who'd ever truly gotten under her skin. She'd relived that night too many times in the past nine months, damn it. Mind-numbing peace. What a joke. It hadn't worked when she caught her father's killer, and it certainly hadn't worked when she'd slept with the American.

The past was in the past. Allowing it to surface only served to remind her of what she'd never have again. Not that she wanted it, mind you. Involvement, no matter how brief and shallow, only led to heartache.

Shoving to her feet, she checked her navy polo and smoothed her palms over the front of her tan khakis. A few of her fellow officers at the Milan interagency office followed her progress across the room, but knowing their rapt attention had nothing to do with worry, she kept her gaze fixed straight ahead.

She didn't want their concern anyway. No distraction was the key. No family. No friends. Not even a partner these days. Work filled her days—and many of her nights so she could avoid the night version of her earlier daydream. But beyond the job, her life was completely empty.

Conflicting emotions rose up, as they always did with even the briefest thought of the sister who wanted nothing to do with her. They hadn't spoken in almost five years.

Then there was her deceased partner, Nino Da Via. Losing a partner in the line of duty was never easy, but him being a dirty cop made it worse. She knew that made no sense. His intent to kill her should've made his death easier to come to terms with, but lately she couldn't shake the feeling of being completely adrift. Lost.

Evalina mentally stuffed Carina and Nino in the Unwelcome file next to her earlier unsettling memory, and stepped into her superior's office.

"If you're looking for the Perini report, I'll have it on your desk before—"

"Close the door," he interrupted without looking up.

Her stomach gave an uneasy flip as she shut the door with a quiet click. Seeing as a closed door had never only taken a moment, she took a seat opposite Commissario Marino and studied his face while he continued to write.

Craggy was the word that came to mind. He'd acquired more lines around the eyes, and the grooves bracketing his tightly pressed, downturned mouth had deepened considerably. Her eyes widened slightly as she wondered when he'd started to grey at the temples. For someone whose very life depended on her noticing the slightest detail, how had she missed that?

*Dio mio.* Evalina fingered the crease she'd ironed into her khaki pants at three a.m. More sleep-depriving thoughts to prey on her mind. The next two weeks were going to be hell.

Commissario Marino set his pen down and lifted his blue gaze. "The Perini report can wait."

"I'd rather finish it before I have to leave."

"Do you have any specific plans for your time off?"

"Just some alone time with me, myself and I."

His jaw tightened. Evalina ignored his visible annoyance. Her 'time off' was as appealing as a hole in the head, so why bother pretending enthusiasm? Hour upon hour to think about what the hell she was doing with her life made her itchier than a dog with fleas.

And they'd given her no choice in the matter. After she'd screwed up on her last two undercover assignments, she'd been put on probation, then forced to take two weeks of her vacation. It felt more like a suspension, but Marino assured her she would have a job upon her return. Either way, happy Monday.

Staring at her superior, she wondered if she was in danger of burning out, or had she missed her mentor's physical changes because she hadn't been around the office?

*That's it,* she rationalized with relief. *I haven't been around enough to notice.*

In the silence, Marino heaved a sigh. "As of right now, your vacation is cancelled."

Evalina sat up a little straighter. "It is?"

Her eagerness earned her a sharp glance as her superior extracted a file from atop a tall stack on the right hand side of his desk. "I received a call from Magistrate Baroni about an hour ago. The DAC has requested your help on a case."

The *Direzione Centrale Anticrimine* specifically requested her? *Why?*

She managed to keep the questions to herself, unwilling to jeopardize the opportunity to evade two whole weeks alone with her thoughts.

"At sixteen-o-five p.m. this afternoon, an international courier will land at the Malpensa airport from New York's JFK airport," Commissario Marino continued. "Based on information we've gathered, he'll be meeting with Dante Fedorio of the Fedorio group in Novara."

"I know the name. Why is this a concern?"

"The Fedorio group has been under investigation over the past year for a number of activities—money laundering, transportation of stolen goods, procuring and selling illegal weapons."

The city of Novara was centrally located, a perfect place to set up shop along the commercial traffic routes stretching from Milan to Turin, and from Genoa to Switzerland.

"Mafia?" That would explain the DAC's involvement. Their jurisdiction covered all major and organized crime investigations.

"They have had dealings with the northern families in the past, but essentially run their own organization. We need you to get close to this courier and confirm the true nature of his business before he leaves the country. He's scheduled to depart the following morning, so time is of the essence."

Less than twenty-four hours inside their borders. Considering whom he was meeting with, it was a definite red flag.

Evalina had a quick flash of the morning's newscast. "What about the volcano erupting in Iceland?" she asked. "Any word on when air travel may be affected?"

The Commissario shook his head, lips pressed tight. "Flights won't be cancelled until absolutely necessary. We cannot depend on Mother Nature to do our job."

Her superior's rebuke put her on the defensive. "What's so special about *this* courier?"

"He is the son of a federal prisoner in the United States. Interpol believes—"

"Interpol is involved?" Evalina asked in surprise.

"Yes." Tossing her a brief frown for the interruption, Marino continued, "They believe this courier is reactivating connections within our country in preparation for his father's upcoming release from prison. It's an interagency investigation, and we've been tasked with confirming this man's intentions."

She conveyed her understanding with a brisk nod. Now that she was armed with some details of the assignment, her earlier curiosity refused to be contained. "Why me, sir? Considering how adamant you were about my time off, surely there were other female agents who could do the job?"

"You won't be alone on this assignment." His gaze shifted behind her as he lifted a hand to motion someone into the office.

Evalina swiveled in her seat and received a nasty jolt that would've knocked her from the chair if she wasn't adept at concealing her emotions. The last time she'd seen Europol agent Antonio Butelli was nine months earlier when they closed the case against her father's killer. Butelli looked completely different from his former undercover persona, but even so, the sight of him shattered the lock on memories she ruthlessly suppressed except when caught unaware by a rogue daydream.

Summoning her undercover face, she met his cool blue gaze. "Antonio."

He inclined his head. "Evalina. Good to see you."

She didn't return the sentiment and noted he'd also reverted to their formal names instead of how they'd known each other while undercover. She preferred the formality. Her mind whirled, wondering why Europol had sent him. Last they'd interacted, he worked internal affairs. In addition to the probation, was she now under investigation, too?

"You and Ispettore Butelli have been handpicked because of your personal history with the courier."

Suspicion and memory collided. Antonio's face remained impassive, but for a millisecond, a flicker of sympathy darkened his eyes. Her stomach dropped as she faced her Commissario's rigid features.

*American courier.*
*Antonio.*

*Personal history.*

Commissario Marino withdrew a photograph from the file in front of him and slid it across the desk. "Not only does it appear the father may be attempting to reestablish the lines of communication with his former associates, but the mother went off-grid less than twenty-four hours after her own release from prison a few days ago."

Evalina didn't need to see the passport photo in front of her to confirm the identity of her target. Suddenly, even a suspension sounded pretty damn good.

## Chapter 2

BENJAMIN SANDERS THREADED through the crowded baggage claim of the Malpensa International Airport, thankful to be carrying his only luggage. One didn't need much more than a change of clothes and a toothbrush when the length of their stay comprised less than twenty-four hours.

Numerous overhead monitors displayed news of the volcanic eruption in Iceland. Eyjafjallajökull was spewing lava and shooting ash thirty thousand feet into the air again, threatening to create havoc for any country in the path of the soot-laden Jet Stream.

He didn't need to understand Italian to translate the pictures of stranded people after the previous eruption had closed European airports for over a week. Thankfully, the next few days were forecasted to be clear, so he would have no problem making his return flight in the morning. The prospect of being trapped in Italy rated just above getting shot and well below a root canal with no anesthesia.

His canvas, Quicksilver weekend bag bumped against his hip as he side-stepped a pair of business men too intent on their own destination to watch where they were going. Breaking free of the thick throng milling about waiting for luggage, Ben strode toward the exit to locate a taxi. He'd considered renting a car, but decided dealing with traffic and the confusing one-way streets after the long flight might not be such a good idea. Besides, it wasn't like he planned to sightsee at all. Once he collected what he'd come for, he was going to check into his airport hotel and sleep until his wake-up call.

"Ben!"

The unexpected sound of his name halted his steps, and he swung around to see the pretty redhead who'd been seated next to him on the plane.

Alisa, as she'd introduced herself, was twenty-three; eight years his junior, but much more sophisticated than her age suggested. After a few casual comments during take-off, they'd fallen into easy conversation. She'd provided a very pleasant distraction as he encouraged her to tell him about her life in Maine and her current trip to study abroad for a semester. There'd been some harmless flirting as well, but he hadn't expected her to seek him out after they'd landed.

"Alisa."

"I'm glad I caught you." She moved close and extended her hand to rest against his chest, a slip of paper between her manicured fingers. Her lashes lifted only enough for a glimpse of her hazel eyes. "I was thinking...if you wrap up your business early, give me a call. We could meet for drinks later...or something."

He removed his hand from the strap of his bag to take the note while noticing she'd removed her sweater. From the plunging neckline of her dress to the husky seduction of her tone, the woman had given up subtlety in favor of blatant invitation. He shifted his gaze to scan the phone number and hotel name scrawled on the paper as he considered her offer.

*Armani Milano.* Sounded expensive. Anything with the name Armani was bound to be high end, and better than what he had booked for the night. Not to mention, she'd certainly keep his mind off the reason he really hated this country.

He'd left nine months ago and done his damnedest not to look back. Tried to forget the ordeal he and his sisters had gone through on their vacation turned nightmare. Forget the beautiful undercover cop who'd saved his life and then stomped all over his heart with her sexy stiletto heels.

He'd been relatively successful at the the first. The second, not so much.

*What the hell*, he thought with a mental shrug. He'd been a frickin' monk since his last trip across the ocean. Maybe No-Strings Alisa was just what he needed to get over the memories that tortured him almost daily.

Ben dropped his gaze to her freshly glossed lips. They curved into a sensual smile, and he returned it as he stepped back. While pocketing the invitation, he murmured, "I'll see what I can do."

"I hope so."

A series of loud beeps preceded the rumblings of the nearest luggage carousel. She spun around, cast him one last sultry look over her shoulder, then sashayed toward the arriving luggage. As he watched those long, shapely legs walking away, from the corner of his eye he noticed one of their fellow passengers on his cell phone nearby. The smirk on his face as he also monitored the redhead's departure told Ben he'd witnessed their exchange.

There had been a point on the plane he'd swore the guy was listening to him and Alisa from his seat directly behind them, but a glance revealed he was simply reading his Italian newspaper. An attempt to engage him in conversation later earned Ben a few accented words before the guy rose to go use the bathroom.

Once again, his curiosity was piqued, so he headed toward the man, sizing him up as he went. His dark hair, the accent, and newspaper all suggested Italian nationality. He was maybe an inch or two shorter than Ben, well dressed in jeans, a sweater over his Oxford shirt, and a nice pair of leather boots. Other than a black jacket fisted in his other hand, no carryon luggage in sight.

The guy glanced over and their eyes met. His expression sobered as he gave Ben a brief nod, then turned for the exit.

No checked luggage either? Since he was headed the same direction, Ben followed him outside, but the man was in a taxi and gone before Ben cleared the doors. He frowned, then forced himself to focus on his own business instead of some random guy from the plane. The goal was cut and dry. Get the Bible his father had shipped to his old college roommate in Italy just before his incarceration thirteen years ago, and get the hell out of Dodge.

Despite a sign indicating the taxi stand further on, there were three vehicles parked along the curb with the taxi lights on top. The three drivers stood in front of the middle car, one of them talking rather enthusiastically, hands gesticulating a mile a minute. The short, heavier-set one flicked a glance in Ben's direction, his gaze sweeping down over his worn jeans and practical boots before ignoring him completely.

The third man cast his own glance, then excused himself and faced Ben. Tall, dark, and better groomed than the others, he raised his eyebrows in a gesture of universal inquiry. When Ben nodded, the driver moved to the third taxi and opened the door of the black sedan.

"*Salve, signore.*"

The man looked familiar…and yet he didn't. A prick of unease tingled along Ben's spine, though he had no idea why as he returned the greeting. "*Salve.*"

"*Dove?*"

After his last visit, he knew enough of the language to get by, and told the driver where he wanted to go. "Novara. The Fedorio building?"

"Ahh, *lei è americano, parla italiano?*"

"*Un pò.* Very little."

"*Va bene.* No problem. We speak English…no?"

He was tired, and English would be easier, so he gave the Italian a grateful smile. "*Grazie.*"

"Very good. Now we go to Novara."

Ben slipped his canvas bag from his shoulder and paused as he stared at the taxi. Maybe that was it—the vehicle was identical to the one he and Rachel had been forced into nine months earlier. Shaking off the recollection, he slid into the back seat.

The driver closed the door before hurrying around to slip behind the wheel. His gaze briefly met Ben's in the rearview. "My name is Antonio."

"Ben."

"You travel with very little, *signore.*"

Ben shrugged noncommittally.

"You do not stay with us long?"

As he voiced the inquiry, Antonio checked his side mirror and shot out into traffic. Horns blared and tires screeched. Ben grasped the door handle and braced for impact. When they simply continued on their way, he took a deep breath to relax his fingers, then rubbed his palm on his leg. He was no stranger to aggressive driving, but usually he was behind the wheel. It was a bit unsettling being at the mercy of someone else's confidence.

"Only long enough," he replied to the Italian.

He gripped his thigh to halt the sudden drumming of his fingers. Immediately, his left foot started tapping. When they cleared the airport grounds in a single hair-raising minute, Ben gave up trying to control his nervous tics while studying the driver in the review mirror.

He couldn't shake the sensation that he knew the man, yet nothing about his dark hair, brown eyes, fashionable glasses, or neatly trimmed mustache jogged Ben's memory.

They sped along the autostrada, skirting the larger metropolis of Milan on their way toward the neighboring town of Novara at a speed even Ben would've hesitated to push. The man's competent driving skills made him conclude past experiences in this country were affecting his nerves too much. In his impeccably pressed uniform, Antonio was just a typical Italian guy doing his job.

The man's eyes met his in the mirror before returning to the road. "Have you visited *Italia* before, *signore?*"

"Please, call me Ben," he invited, stalling his response. He didn't want to think or talk about his previous visit.

Though he cast another questioning glance in the review mirror, Antonio then remained silent while checking his side mirrors. He gave no indication that he was offended by the lack of a reply. Ironically, his professionalism made Ben feel rude.

"This is my second trip."

"Ah, *va bene*. And the first? Did you find pleasure in our beautiful country?"

*Only one part of it. Only for one night. One short, gratifying, unfulfilling night.*

With a quietly muttered, "Not really," Ben turned to stare out the right hand window. Rude suited him all of a sudden.

After a few minutes of silence, his chatty driver said, "There is some concern the volcano in Iceland will close our airports again."

His muscles tensed at the thought of his return flight cancelled. Once the airport closed, who knew how long before they'd reopen. If it was like the last time, it could be days before officials deemed the skies safe for air travel.

"I'll be gone before that happens." Still, he leaned sideways, squinting at the bright sun and wide expanse of blue sky. Hard to believe an act of nature almost two thousand miles away could wreak such havoc.

They reached the Novara city limits in ten minutes. Navigating the afternoon traffic took another ten. When the car halted in front of a glass office building taller than most of its older neighbors, he opened his door at the same time Antonio opened the driver's side.

Taking in the large, silver block letters that spelled out *Fedorio S.P.A.* on the side of the building between the first and second floor, he slung the strap of his canvas bag over his head to rest diagonally across his chest once more. Bag secure, he withdrew his wallet and turned to the taxi driver.

"I may need a ride to my hotel when I'm done with my business here. Would you—"

"*Sì.* I am pleased to wait."

"Thank you. If I'm not back in thirty minutes, assume I found another ride." He handed Antonio some American bills that more than covered the cab fare and his wait time.

When a break in traffic allowed, Ben crossed the street, and then passed through the revolving glass doors into the lobby.

The next few minutes would be interesting. Dante Fedorio knew he was coming, he just didn't know the real reason why.

In the quiet moments, Ben himself wondered once or twice on the plane why he still found it impossible to say no to his mother after all these years. Probably because her plea about righting past wrongs had contained enough sincerity that he'd decided to give her the benefit of the doubt. By all appearances, prison had completely reformed her.

He stopped to sign the electronic register at the front reception area. The blond woman behind the desk asked him to wait, and his fingers began to drum the elevated desktop. Flattening his palm against the cool, gray marble, he fisted his other hand on the strap across his chest.

His first glance around the understated elegance of the lobby was for pure distraction. A double-take swung his entire body to the left as his gaze zeroed in on the petite female headed for a bank of shiny, steel elevators. His pulse skipped before revving out of control.

Lush curves. Small waist. Long, dark curls that he knew were softer than silk.

The unexpected need for answers carried him across the lobby floor before he could consider the wisdom of his actions. Shouts behind him registered dimly, but he kept focus on the woman three strides ahead.

## Chapter 3

EVALINA SHIFTED IN her seat to glance at the neighboring tables crowded on the sidewalk not far from the *Piazza della Repubblica,* and the *Duomo di Novara.* Better known to the locals as cathedral of Santa Maria Assunta. The breeze was cooler in the shade of the building and she suppressed a shiver. Antonio had it easy, sitting in the taxi cab outside the Fedorio building. How had she drawn the short end of the stick?

"I'm telling you, I don't think this will work."

"I'll be sure to drive by nice and slow." Antonio's voice carried through the tiny earpiece hidden by her long curls. "There's no way he'll miss you."

How could he? Between the four inch stilettos and skin-tight dress she felt like a *battona* looking for work. She'd already gotten a month's worth of wolf whistles and come-on lines, and she'd only been sitting at the outside café table for a half an hour.

"And if he doesn't ask you to stop?"

Two men walking past cast her toothy grins. *"Che belle gambe!"*

Antonio's chuckle echoed in her ear while she scowled in disgust. Tugging her skirt down for the hundredth time, Evalina gritted her teeth and lowered her chin toward her exposed cleavage. "Shut up."

"What's the problem? You didn't seem to mind dressing the part when working the Lapaglia case last year."

Normally, she didn't mind pushing against her comfort zone when undercover. It was *who* she'd dressed for that bothered her now. She hadn't expected to ever see Benjamin Sanders again.

"I thought you and Sanders had a connection?" Antonio's curiosity read loud and clear.

"You listen as well as Marino."

"Don't forget, I saw him take a bullet for you. And that was before he knew you were an undercover cop. How do you explain that?"

"Stupidity."

"Nothing is ever that simple. According to your file at Europol, you two had dinner after he was released from the hospital."

*Dinner*. There was a word for it. Ignoring the fact Europol kept a file on her, she sipped her espresso and carefully placed the small cup back on its saucer. Obviously, Europol didn't know everything, or she wouldn't be sitting here waiting for an afternoon trick.

"So, what happened?" Antonio nudged.

"I wouldn't tell my friends, why would I tell you?"

"You have no friends, Eva."

Her fingers crumpled the paper napkin next to her cup.

"*Perdonami*," Antonio added stiffly. "I shouldn't have said that."

"As if I care."

Now, if only saying the words out loud made them true.

Silence fell between them, which unfortunately, gave her time to think. Antonio had left his mic on when he'd first met Ben at the airport and for the ensuing ride. The sound of the American's voice after the past nine months had rattled her. Stirred emotions better left buried—even through the electronic earpiece.

She wondered how much longer before he exited the building three blocks away?

How much longer before he slid into the back of her new partner's car again?

How much longer before she found out just how much he hated her?

"Do you think he knows?" she asked Antonio.

"Sanders? He seemed a little edgy, but he gave no indication he recognized me."

"I meant about the Fedorios," Evalina clarified. "And his father's illegal dealings with them?"

"His parents were convicted for crimes committed in the United States, so our suspicions are not substantiated. *Yet.*"

True. She discovered she hoped Ben didn't know. Hoped he was one of the good guys. She took a deep breath. "Got a file on everyone, do you?"

"Almost."

"Then let me ask again, do you think he knows?"

A group of teens exited the café to sit at a nearby table. They were talking so loud she barely heard her partner's clipped reply.

"I don't care. I'm just here to do a job."

"Nice." Evalina picked up her phone so it wouldn't appear as if she was talking to herself. Pressing it to her ear, she spun on the small, hard chair so her back was to the noisy kids.

"You don't want to know what I think," Antonio warned.

"Yes I do." Especially since he'd seemed to respect Ben for his refusal to give up in the face of Alrigo's brutality nine months ago.

After another moment of silence, his resigned voice came across the line. "The man grew up helping his parents cheat, steal, and con people out of hundreds of thousands of dollars. Probably millions. He's maintained contact with them during their thirteen years of incarceration, and then the moment Lea Sanders is out of prison, she disappears and he's on a flight across the Atlantic."

So much for respect.

"He was never prosecuted even though he was old enough when his parents were arrested," she pointed out. "And what's wrong with a child staying in contact with their parents?"

What she wouldn't give to speak with *hers* one more time.

"Nothing," Antonio replied. "Unless the mother is a cousin of the Fedorios and the father was Dante Fedorio's college roommate during his two years in the States at Ohio State University."

Disappointment and an odd sense of betrayal stiffened her spine. "Really?"

"Yes. Now you tell me if you think Benjamin Sanders knows what the hell he's doing."

Experience told her that answer. Not that it mattered to her, though. She didn't care. Couldn't afford to care. When she cared, people got hurt. Including herself.

She forced herself to relax. Seconds ticked by. Minutes. She distracted herself by rehearsing her cover story while tossing biscotti chunks to some pigeons strutting along the sidewalk.

*On vacation. Meeting a friend. Cell phone rings, friend cancels...how about that dinner we never got around to last time?*

Oh, Antonio was going to love hearing that line.

She shook her head. Ben would never buy it. Marino should've listened to her.

"What if he doesn't ask you to stop?" she repeated, almost hoping he wouldn't.

A soft snort preceded the *ispettore's* reply. "I saw the dress you're wearing. Believe me, he'll ask."

Her partner sounded so sure. He didn't know shit.

## Chapter 4

BEN GRABBED THE edge of the steel door sliding shut and slammed it back into the wall. "Evali—"

Already in mid-turn, the woman jerked backward. Her startled gaze met his, her breath sucked in on a gasp.

*Not Evalina.*

Disappointment flooded his body and he slowly straightened, pushing away from the elevator. He should've seen it. Too tall. And now that he saw her face, he noticed her eyes didn't have that distinct whiskey color that still haunted his dreams.

"I'm sorry. Ah…*'scusa.* I thought you were someone else."

She remained frozen in the corner as the door silently slid closed between them.

Wow. He stood in stunned silence until two security guards dressed in all black arrived. They rattled off angry words faster than his limited knowledge of the language could translate.

He held up his hands, palms out. "Relax guys. I thought I saw someone I knew, that's all."

One turned and walked away, and the other motioned for Ben to follow the first. *Great.* He'd screwed up royally. God, when was he going to get that damn woman out of his head? He had to focus on the matter at hand because, realistically, the chances of seeing her during the few hours he planned to be in the country were a million to one.

The guards led him through the lobby where he cast a smile of apology toward the receptionist. She smiled back and his tension eased. It returned two-fold when the first guard stopped in front of a second bank of elevators. He was the bigger of the two; dark haired and burly, his thick biceps stretching the material of his black polo. If necessary, Ben figured he could take the smaller man behind him, but this brute would be a challenge.

"You know, I did sign in at the front desk," he said, wishing for a set of stairs instead. "Do we really need to do this? Mr. Fedorio is expecting me."

Saying the name that graced the side of the building got him nothing but more silence as the doors opened. Guard number one stepped in. Guard number two made the *after-you* motion again. A slight shift parted his unbuttoned jacket. One glimpse of the man's concealed weapon convinced Ben to do as instructed. He didn't relax when the armed man didn't join them in the elevator since he'd bet his life the man behind him was equally equipped.

The number seven was lit on the control panel. That brought a bit of relief, but then he fought the urge to laugh at the absurd response. Down didn't automatically mean bad and up good.

His uneasy stomach told him the elevator had come to a stop a second before the muted ding signaled the opening door. He stepped forward, glad to be free of the confining space.

Compared to the understated elegance of the lobby, the interior of the seventh floor was absolute luxury from the Italian marble beneath his feet to the leather chairs in the waiting area. It confirmed what he already knew; the Fedorio Group had money with a capitol M.

Which explained the security, but not specifically why *he* now had a personal escort. So he'd run through the lobby. Big deal. It wasn't like he'd tried to steal one of the half-million dollar paintings hanging on the wall to his left…*and* his right.

Some kids had art history at school; his mother had taught

him how to estimate worth and spot forgery tells in thirty seconds flat. He'd bet these were real, but that still didn't warrant the presence of the muscle behind him.

All he wanted was to get the Bible and be on his way back to the U.S. Except the executive waiting area was empty, and as silent as his unwanted companion. Stuffing his hands in his pockets, he made his way over to the window, noting the cab still parked across the street, seven stories down. Off to his right was the door for the stairs he'd have rather used for the journey up. He preferred the illusion of an exit that an elevator did not convey.

A muted noise across the waiting area brought him around to see a tall brunette step through the doorway of an office behind the sleek receptionist desk. The elegant woman left the door ajar and crossed the room, her fashionable heels tapping the marble with each step.

She offered a polite smile. "Signor Sanders?"

He nodded.

"Signor Fedorio will see you now." The woman's gaze shifted to the brute guarding the exit. "*Grazie*, Angelo."

Ben watched the dismissed man enter the elevator and steeled himself for the upcoming meeting.

The gentleman behind the desk stood as his assistant announced Ben's entrance into his office and closed the door behind her when she left.

With a full head of close-cropped silver hair, Dante Fedorio was as well dressed as his offices. Ben's keen gaze noted the superior fit of his suit, diamond cufflinks, and as he stepped around to offer a handshake, the fine Italian leather dress shoes.

His jaw tightened. It'd been years since he'd taken stock of a man's net worth in a single glance. His mother's request and father's letter had him reverting to old habits. He'd had no problem leaving the con behind the day they'd been arrested, yet here he was, back in the thick of things.

*For the family*, he reminded himself. It'd always been for the family.

"Benjamin, I am pleased to finally meet you."

"Likewise. My father spoke of you often."

Dante's smile revealed the man still considered Richard Sanders a friend. They shook hands before Ben cast his gaze about the office. It was equally well appointed with its plush charcoal carpeting, black leather chairs, and a built-in bookcase full to the brim with expensive looking volumes behind the mahogany pedestal desk. The muted sound of running water had him searching until he located a three foot water fountain in the far corner. He took his time admiring the view through the floor to ceiling glass that made up the wall opposite the door.

Noticing his attention, Dante silently invited him forward with a sweep of his hand. Despite his nerves urging him to get on with the meeting, Ben crossed the room.

The man pointed to a domed building maybe a half dozen city blocks away. "The *Basilica de San Gaudenzio*. It is the highest point in the city. Beautiful, is it not?"

"Very. This is an amazing view." He looked beyond the city to the lush green and brown countryside beyond. No vineyards in sight, but lots of farmland. Fedorio pointed out a few more items of interest before moving toward his desk.

"How is your father?"

Ben turned around to face him.

"Any attempts I have made to communicate with him were unsuccessful," the man explained. "Your government is especially protective of their criminals."

"Dad's a special case. Family and legal team only." A fact he was thankful for. His success today hinged on Dante not having talked to his father since Ben had called from the U.S. "But to answer your question, he's doing well and looking forward to his release next month."

"That is good. Too many years have passed." The older man backed up to lean against his desk as if settling in for an extended chat. "And my dear cousin? She is also well and anticipating an early release?"

Ben lowered his bag from his shoulder as he moved to sit in

one of the chairs facing Fedorio. He worded his response carefully after the older man's thinly veiled derision. His mother had been right about with whom her cousin's sympathy lie, reiterating the importance that the Italian not find out she had initiated this trip instead of his father.

He leaned back in his chair. "Last I spoke with her, she said she's looking forward to when the family can get back together again." Technically, it wasn't a lie.

"Lia? All about family? That is refreshing."

"Prison has changed her. She hopes for a reunion with this side of the family after she and dad are both released and their probation is over. She wants to revive her Italian heritage to share with us."

"I should very much like to see my friend again. And I would love to meet your sisters."

Dante's pointed omission of his blood cousin had Ben debating how best to broach the subject he needed to address.

The man tilted his head slightly, shrewd eyes locked in steady regard. When his brown gaze dropped, Ben realized his right knee had started a rapid bounce. He sat up as Dante straightened and retreated to his executive chair. Seated at his desk, the Italian braced his forearms on the green leather surface and linked his fingers together in front of him.

"You did not come all this way to speak of unlikely family reunions, did you, Benjamin?"

"No," he admitted, not surprised at the perceptive question.

"Then tell me, what can I do for you?"

Straight to business—he was fine with that. The sooner this was over and he was on his way home, the better. "My father sent you a box just before his arrest."

Dante remained poker-faced.

"I have the key for that box, and the request to retrieve it."

Steel-grey eyebrows arched in silent inquiry.

Ben withdrew the letter he'd carefully prepared and rose to hand it over. The Italian examined the envelope, paying particular attention to the carefully copied postal service stamp in the upper right corner dated less than a week earlier before turning it over to remove the letter. Ben remained standing to avoid the nervous tic in his leg revealing too much. The man was suspicious enough, and he was rusty from years of playing it straight.

Dante's gaze scanned the paper before returning to Ben. "Richard advised he would personally retrieve his possessions upon his release."

"Unfortunately, a monitoring anklet will make leaving the country impossible for at least a year, probably more. After that, his every move will still be documented during the probationary period."

Ben reclaimed his seat, but this time leaned forward to brace his elbows on his knees. "Look, I know we both know there are ways around that. Cut the anklet, get a new identity, but he doesn't want to live on the run anymore. My sisters and I have made lives for ourselves in Wisconsin. We've put down roots. Dad realizes how much he's missed over the past thirteen years, and he wants to make a clean start so we can be a family again. My youngest sister will be married soon, and he doesn't want to lose another five years."

In truth, those last sentences were his mother's words, not his father's, but they appeared to do the trick. The caution in Fedorio's expression receded.

From the side pocket of his overnight bag, Ben pulled out a second letter for his father's friend to read. He didn't miss the comparison Dante made between the two missives as they sat side by side on the desk top. He'd been very careful to make sure the first would hold up to the second and watched closely as the Italian picked up the much older letter.

This one was authentic, where his father had first told him about the box he'd shipped to Italy and where to locate the key that would unlock it. Not in so many words, but the expression on the older man's face told Ben he recognized the code embedded within the words. It also confirmed he was well versed in the way Richard Sanders used to operate. The mental note was filed for later.

"I understand his desire," Dante said. "Our years are advanced. The choices your parents made came at a heavy price."

"For all of us," he agreed. "But at least we can have a second chance."

"*Sì. Bene.*"

Brown eyes rose for a thorough appraisal. Ben met the man's probing gaze and managed to subdue the urge to fidget. After a long moment, the Italian rose from his desk and walked toward the bookcase that took up half the wall behind his desk.

From one of the shelves, he withdrew a small wooden box, no larger than his hand. When he approached and handed it over, Ben frowned.

"This can't be it." He turned the box in his hands. "It's not big enough."

"That is the item your father sent," Dante assured him.

"And you just happen to have it here? I didn't tell you why I was coming."

"After nearly fourteen years, I did not expect you to come for anything else. You are your father's son."

Ironic, considering he was here at his mother's request.

Leaning back in the chair, Ben reached deep into his front pocket for the skeleton key his father had revealed with the letter all those years ago. Hesitation over opening the box in front of the Italian was swept away by the possibility the man knew more than he let on. Since it could not possibly contain the Bible, he'd have to play whatever game his father had set up and refused to reveal to his mother.

The old-fashioned key fit inside the hole and one twist released the latch. Inside rested a piece of plain paper, folded twice to fit the small space. He lifted it out and saw a second, more modern key resting on the felt bottom. One that would unlock a padlock, or maybe a door. Removing that, too, he rubbed his thumb across the jagged teeth while unfolding the paper with his other hand.

An address. *What the hell?* He stared at the letters and numbers printed in his father's neat handwriting, then pinned his gaze on Fedorio. "This is it? You're sure he didn't send you anything else?"

"*Sì*. Nothing else."

The man held eye contact without revealing a single tell to indicate a lie.

Ben's fingers tightened around the key. *Sonofabitch.* His simple trip had just been extended to include Rome.

## Chapter 5

"IT IS NOT as you expected?" Fedorio asked with a hint of concern.

"No." Ben relaxed his fingers and stood to shove both keys and the paper in his front pocket again. "I was under the impression you were in possession of what I was sent here for, but that's not the case."

"Issues with your father are rarely as they appear."

"Truer words have never been spoken." He stooped to get his bag and settled the strap on his shoulder as Fedorio also rose. With the box in his left hand, Ben extended his right to the Italian for a firm shake. "It was nice to meet you. Thank you for your help."

"You must leave so soon? Let me extend an invitation to dine at my house this evening. We have much to talk about."

He lifted the box with a pointed grimace. "I'm sorry, I appreciate the invitation, but I can't."

The man appeared to consider for a moment before nodding. "I understand. Another time perhaps."

Ben returned the nod and exited the office. With a smile for the man's secretary as he deposited the box inside his bag, he headed for the elevators. A glance toward the windows had him switching direction for the stairs he'd noticed earlier.

He'd already reached the landing for the sixth floor when he heard the door open above him.

"Signore?" Fedorio called down. "Benjamin, please wait."

He paused and leaned over to look up. Fedorio hurried down the stairs toward him.

"*Per favore*...before you go..." He reached the landing and extended a book.

Ben accepted it, instantly curious about the worn, leather-bound tome. "What is this?"

"A gift for my friend. An old diary I discovered that will appease his love of history."

The yellowed page he opened to in the middle of the book was dated eighteen ninety-eight. Old was an understatement.

"I had intended to send it to him, but perhaps you could deliver it in person," Fedorio suggested. "I would not want careless handling to ruin such a treasure."

He closed the pages with more care than he'd opened them. "I will do that, thank you."

Fedorio nodded once more and ascended the stairs while Ben went the opposite way.

Curiosity and his own affinity for history had him reopening the diary in his hands. The flowing Italian script made it difficult to pick out any familiar words as he navigated the stairs, but just as he reached the fourth floor landing, he noticed that one of the passages had a few words that were darker than the rest.

His steps slowed as he lifted the book closer to his face, concentrating on the page. The letters of the marked words appeared to have been traced over to make them a shade darker. The words themselves seemed random, but he couldn't be sure since they were written in Italian.

Two pages later, he noticed the same thing, this time with five different traced words. Still taking care with the old book, he navigated the next two levels while noting the anomaly skipped one page, then seven, two, and four. A pattern, and yet not.

At the next landing, he stopped altogether and moved closer

to the window for better light. Experience warned this wasn't a random diary Fedorio had given him to transport back to his father.

Well, crap. Did he take the damn thing with him, or return it with a firm *thanks, but no thanks*? The last thing he wanted to do was become involved in one of his father's deals again, even if it was only delivering information.

He closed the diary with a snap that echoed in the deserted stairwell. As he stared outside while considering his options, he noticed the cab still waiting by the curb one story below. To hell with it. He lifted the flap of his canvas bag and slipped the book inside so he could take advantage of his a ride back to the airport before Antonio decided he'd waited long enough.

Ben started for the final set of stairs, but then a second cab parked further down the street caught his eye. He got a split-second glimpse of the figure leaning against the side of the vehicle before the man turned away and ducked into the backseat of the car.

The hair on the back of Ben's neck stood on end. He'd swear it was the guy who'd sat behind him on the plane from JFK. The same guy who'd exited the airport and gotten into a taxi *ahead* of him. His gaze narrowed in consideration. How the hell could he have followed him *here*?

He eased back from the window. The rational side of his brain said he was seeing things again, like when he'd mistaken that woman in the lobby for Evalina. He was tired, jetlagged, and his mind was playing tricks on him.

The paranoid side of his brain told him small-world coincidences such as this were orchestrated in his world, not situations of happenstance. He'd helped his parents with way too many cons growing up. Off the top of his head, he could easily see the two taxi drivers and other passenger collaborating to set up and rob the unsuspecting American. Cash, credit cards, identity. All three were worth their time, and it certainly explained why his driver was willing to wait so long.

Annoyed that he'd just lost his ride, Ben secured the strap of his bag over his head and crosswise on his chest as he took the remaining stairs at a fast clip. Much as he'd like to confront the men outside, he had no idea if they were armed, and he wasn't looking for a replay of his last visit to Italy.

In the lobby, he avoided the front doors and approached the receptionist. "Excuse me? Is there an exit this way? Ah—*uscita?*" He pointed in the direction opposite the main entrance.

When the blond nodded, he smiled his thanks and started for the exit. He hadn't even taken his second step when the guard Angelo appeared to block the way.

"Great," Ben muttered.

The guard jerked his head toward the lobby doors. Ben glanced over his shoulder to see the taxi still in place, and shook his head. When the frowning Italian stepped closer, he lifted his hands in surrender.

"Look, man, I don't want any trouble. I just want to go out *that* way. *USCITA. Per favore.*"

Angelo's eyes narrowed, shifting from Ben, to the doors, and back again. Still mute, he finally stepped aside and let Ben pass. The guard followed him to the back exit, and Ben nodded appreciation as he pushed open the door.

Outside the building, he did a quick spin and visual sweep, then stepped back to lean against the building. The seven hour time difference from Wisconsin was beginning to take its toll, spinning his mind as if he were caught in an episode of *The Twilight Zone.*

Man, he had a long night ahead of him. Exhaustion threatened, but he shoved away from the cold support at his back. First things first. He'd find himself a new taxi to the airport. Then, if there was an evening flight to Rome, he'd retrieve the Bible tonight, catch a flight back to Milan first thing in the morning, and still make his scheduled return at noon.

No, better yet, he'd change his ticket to leave right from the capitol city. It would be expensive to alter the routing at the last minute, but worth it to not have to fly all over the frickin' country.

Decision made, he used the shadows cast by the setting sun to head east and strode at a brisk pace along the busy sidewalk while keeping an eye out for the guy from the airport, or his friendly neighborhood cab driver, Antonio. He couldn't be sure they hadn't seen him leave out the back.

After about a block, the architecture changed, in both the buildings and the cobblestones now beneath his boots. Slightly uneven—they were worn smooth from hundreds of years of use. With growth and urbanization came the need to expand beyond the walls that had protected many a European city or town from attack in the past. The walls may have come down, but around him, the old city remained mostly intact.

If one took away the cars, scooters, bikes, street lights, and modern fashions, it was like stepping back in time a few centuries. A bit time and weather worn, but full of past culture nonetheless.

His determined stride slowed as he couldn't help but examine the interesting carved wooden doors, beautiful stonework in grand archways, and intricate iron lined balconies adorning many a second floor residence.

A tourist sign to his right pointed him in the direction of the Basilica which Fedorio had pointed out from his office window. Endless fascinating history so close, yet it might as well be an ocean away. The pang of regret caught him completely unaware. After the adverse events of his previous visit had allowed no time for sightseeing, it shouldn't have surprised him. Yet it did.

Maybe he didn't hate the *country* as much as he'd thought.

Maintaining a vigilant eye for his tail, Ben took the short detour that would lead him to the old church. He'd indulge his own love of history with a quick tour before hailing a taxi that was sure to be hanging around a tourist attraction.

A few blocks later, he reached the Basilica only to find it closed for renovations. Near the entrance was a stand offering tourist maps. He swiped one and scanned the page to see if anything of interest lie in the general direction he was headed. South of his current location stood the *Duomo di Novara*, and it appeared to be a major attraction.

The route would take him back to the same street the Fedorio building was located on, but so far he hadn't spotted anyone following him. Plus, it was a few intersections from the building. If the men were still waiting, they'd never see him from that far away.

He followed the signs noted on the map until he walked along a narrow street lined on both sides by stone columns and elegant arches. Numerous shops behind those arches displayed high fashion, shoes, jewelry, antiques and glassware.

His attention zeroed in on the one up ahead offering outdoor seating for its customers. The strong scent of espresso and pastries made his stomach growl and his mouth water. He could certainly use a dose of caffeine right about now.

Angling his body, he moved through the thickening crowd of pedestrians. A final glance at the map confirmed the Duomo located at the end of the street, so he folded the paper and stuffed it into a side pocket of his bag. When he lifted his gaze, it snagged on a bare pair of legs partially visible next to one of the stone columns supporting the arch in front of the café.

A man would have to be dead to keep his eyes from tracing the sensual line running from the pair of four inch stilettos to the tight skirt that ended high on the thigh.

He definitely was not dead.

His next step moved him past the column and brought the owner of those legs into view. His stomach dropped into a freefall when his gaze locked on her face.

*Evalina.*

Someone bumped into him from behind. He took an automatic step forward. *Twilight Zone?* Try the Bermuda Triangle. How else did one explain the sudden appearance of the woman who'd screwed him and then disappeared into thin air? He'd woken up that morning nine months ago, all alone in his hotel room. No note, no explanation, no goodbye.

His gaze narrowed. This time would be different.

He must've made some sort of noise or something, because

she turned her head and those whiskey-colored eyes he remembered so well widened in surprise. His feet carried him toward her while his gaze swept over her form-fitting dress and heels. She was more beautiful than ever. Her ability to captivate hadn't diminished one damn bit.

Something odd niggled on the edge of his brain, but then her voice blocked out any other thoughts.

## Chapter 6

"BENJAMIN SANDERS?" EVALINA exclaimed with a forced smile.

*You hear that Antonio?* Far as she knew, he was still waiting for the American's exit from the Fedorio building. As her partner's surprised *"What?"* sounded in her earpiece, Ben smiled in front of her.

It was not a warm, welcoming, it's-great-to-see-you smile.

"Evalina."

*Dio Mio.* In person, that deep American accent of his sent all sorts of delicious sensations scorching through her body. He looked good. Better than good considering the last time she'd gazed upon his handsome face, it had been a canvas of multi-colored bruises.

She rose to her feet to avoid a sore neck, then had to grasp the chair to steady herself for having moved too fast. Even in her heels, she still had to tilt her head back to meet his stormy blue eyes.

"I—wow." She sucked in air to eliminate the breathless note in her voice. "What are you doing here?"

That second part was as much for Antonio as the man in front of her, but her partner's reply was lost as Ben's chin dipped and his eyebrows rose.

"What am I doing here? That's the first thing you have to say to me after all this time?"

"I..." What could she say? Apologizing was out of the question while Antonio listened. She wasn't even sure she wanted to apologize, but if she didn't say something, any chance of getting close to Ben would be ruined. The way his gaze bored into hers, she knew it was a long shot to begin with, but she had to try.

"I'm on my way," Antonio told her through the earpiece.

"No!"

Ben's brows rose a notch at her abrupt statement. Willing another smile to her lips, she lifted her free hand to indicate the empty chair at her small café table. "Will you join me for a *café?*"

His gaze narrowed.

*Smooth, Gallo. Real smooth.* The man had a way of making her act like a total amateur. It'd been that way from the moment they first met, and the exact reason she'd been against this whole fake set-up from the start.

Suspicion in his expression gave way to consideration. He shifted, then checked his watch. The fidgeting reminded her there was a reason he was on foot instead of in the back of Antonio's cab, and it was her job to discover why.

Their gazes connected once more. Her traitorous heart skipped a beat when he opened his mouth to reply to her invitation.

All of a sudden he lurched and stumbled forward. She saw a brief flash of dark behind him, then his hands caught her arm and the table for balance. Her hold on the chair barely kept them both upright. When he straightened, steady on his feet again, his gaze swept over her.

"Sor—"

He broke off abruptly, eyes widening. His hand rose to sweep across his chest, and then he spun around with a curse. Before she could make any sense of the past few seconds, he took off running through the crowd.

Training kicked in. Evalina grabbed her purse with her gun and dashed after him. A couple steps in the stupid heels and she almost twisted her ankle. She ditched the stilettos and picked up speed while dodging the confused pedestrians milling in Ben's wake.

"Antonio," she barked as she ran. "Where are you?"

"Heading east on Via Fratelli Rosselli. I'll stay—"

"He took off, also headed east toward the Cathedral. I may not catch him."

"Not in those shoes you won't."

"I'm not wearing them!"

The impatient blare of a car horn echoed in her earpiece and from somewhere behind her.

"Do what you can," Antonio instructed. "I have to go around—there are too many people. Keep me informed."

"Copy."

Eva continued her pursuit and caught sight of Ben up ahead. She dodged a couple of tourists, but lost him again when he entered the crowded piazza. The cool, worn cobblestones beneath her bare feet were so smooth she had trouble gaining any ground while avoiding pedestrians.

When she reached the open square, she located the closest vehicle and climbed atop the hood to see what direction Ben had gone. Antonio might still be able to cut him off. Ignoring the strange looks cast her direction, she straightened to search the area, purse held in front of her in case she needed her Beretta.

Halfway across the piazza, Ben stood in one place, turning this way and that, head craned as if trying to see above the crowd.

"I have eyes," she told Antonio. "Sanders is in front of the Cathedral."

"Good. I'm almost there."

As she started to climb back down, Ben hopped up into the air. She paused and watched. When he made a quarter turn and did it again, she realized he was searching for someone. Her gaze swept the square. On the far opposite side of the piazza a dark figure darted from the crowd and disappeared around the corner.

Evalina frowned just as Ben turned in her direction. Even from a distance their gazes met as if magnetized. Instead of continuing his escape, he started toward her, his long strides eating up the distance.

"Hold back," she instructed her partner as she maneuvered to vacate the hood of the car without giving anyone a peep show. "There's something more going on here. He wasn't running from me."

"Are you sure?"

"*Sì.*"

She met Ben half way, but before she could say a word, he asked, "Did you see him?"

"See who?"

"The guy who stole my bag. The sonofabitch cut the strap when he pushed me."

In her mind, a split-second flash of the dark figure behind Ben by the café was followed by the man running from the piazza. Had to be the same guy.

Her downward glance confirmed the canvas bag that had rested against Ben's hip earlier was gone. He turned around for another glance at the piazza, and when she caught sight of a crimson-stained tear in his jacket near his waist, her pulse spiked.

"You're bleeding."

Had he been stabbed? One step forward brought her to his side. After tucking her purse under one arm, she lifted his lightweight jacket and torn shirt to assess the severity of the wound. From what she could see through the smeared blood, the cut started a little above the waistband of his jeans on his side, and extended toward his back at a downward angle. The moment her fingers grazed his warm, bare skin, he jerked away from her touch. He twisted to take a look himself before yanking the edge of his shirt down with a grimace.

"It's fine. He must've nicked me with the blade, that's all."

It appeared more than a nick to her, but she bit back concern he clearly didn't appreciate and dropped the issue to take advantage of the opportunity that had fallen into her lap. "What was in the bag?"

One hand went to his jeans pocket, the other to an inside pocket of his jacket. His gaze met hers, then shifted to the people moving past them. He bunched the tail of his shirt in one hand and held it against the cut on his back side, presumably to stop the bleeding. His other hand rose from his chest to rub the back of his neck.

"Nothing major. A change of clothes, toothbrush, razor. I still have my wallet and passport in my inside jacket pocket."

"So there was nothing else in the bag someone would want to steal?"

"Not that I'm aware of." That perceptive blue gaze returned to hers, once more full of shadows and suspicion. He lowered his arm and tilted his head. "You know, it strikes me that this is one of those small-world moments."

Small world...? Ah, as in them meeting like this. "It is," she agreed. The plan might work out after all.

He smiled as if enjoying a private joke.

Drawing upon her undercover experience, she managed to look him in the eye. "How crazy is it that we would meet up like this? I'm having dinner with friends."

His gaze lowered for a slow, tingle-inducing appraisal. Heat flooded her face and spread through her body.

"Is that what they're called these days?"

So much for working out. It didn't matter that she'd warned her partner about this very thing, Ben's disbelieving derision flipped sensual awareness to indignation in the blink of an eye. "I do not appreciate your insinuation."

"Then what's with the *professional* get up?"

His tone left no doubt as to his definition of the stressed word.

"Well, it certainly got your attention," she sneered without thinking.

He glanced to her right with a smirk. "It's got *everyone's* attention, Evalina. That's nothing to be proud of."

A soft beep in her ear preceded Antonio's, *"Scusi."* The *ispettore's* voice reminded her she walked a thin line. She had to steer the conversation back around to their advantage. Before she had the chance to form a non-defensive, *professional* reply, Ben stepped closer.

"But that was the point, wasn't it? To get my attention."

His question made her swallow hard, along with the fact that he towered over her as his gaze held hers with relentless intensity.

"I do not know what you mean. I told you I'm meeting friends."

"What happened to your shoes?"

The abrupt switch threw her off guard. He took another step forward. She retreated, mentally scrambling for an excuse while fighting the urge to look down at her bare feet. "I, ah..."

"You ran after me."

Her stomach sank. Her chest grew tight. How did she explain that one without blowing her cover? You'd think it was her first day on the job! If Antonio reported this back to the Commissario, she'd be demoted to desk duty in a heartbeat—*if* she was allowed to keep her badge.

Ben stepped closer. She backed up, clutching her purse in front of her. One bare heel scraped against stone, and then the rough surface of one of the columns supporting the piazza archways bit into her shoulder blade. He let go of the makeshift bandage at his side and reached forward to grasp her upper arms.

"The last time we were together, you couldn't get away fast enough. Why chase me now?"

"Release me." What was intended to be a demand came out as a whisper. He'd gotten so close she couldn't breathe. What the hell was wrong with her? She'd never backed down from a suspect in her life.

*You never slept with one, either.*

"Answer my question," he demanded.

Self-preservation kicked in and she lifted her chin to glare up at him. "Remove your hands, *signore*."

The new determination in her words only tightened his grip. "Why did you run after me?"

She fumbled for the zipper of her purse just as Antonio stepped up behind him from the right.

"Let her go."

Ben whipped his head toward her partner. She caught a glimpse of alarm in his expression before he released her and spun around. His broad shoulders blocked her view, so she stepped sideways in time to see Antonio ease his jacket aside to reveal his holstered gun.

The American's arm extended to keep her behind him as he glared at Antonio. "You need to walk away, buddy. You got my bag, but you're not getting anything else."

Evalina marveled at his obvious protection of her until his words registered. She frowned toward Ben. "You think *he* stole your bag?"

"If not him specifically, then one of the guys he's working with," he stated over his shoulder. "They're running a scam from the airport. Park a couple taxis out front, an inside man finds the mark, then they coordinate a tail to watch for an opportunity to relieve said mark of his possessions."

"Interesting idea, but no," Antonio said.

Her partner turned his gaze to Evalina and raised his eyebrows, silently asking how she wished to proceed. If someone had listened to her in the first place, Benjamin Sanders' unpredictability would've figured into the plan, and they might've had a chance of pulling off this whole screwed up situation. As it was now, there was no sense continuing, so she lifted her hands, shrugged, and sighed.

Ben's arm lowered to his side as he turned, his narrowed gaze shifting between her and the man he'd thought was a cab driver. Evalina waited, knowing it wouldn't take long once his attention returned to Antonio.

Comprehension dawned in those blue eyes even before the *ispettore* reached up to remove his glasses and retrieve his credentials.

## Chapter 7

AFTER THE PAST ten minutes with Evalina, Ben didn't need to see the badge the man flashed. Antonio the taxi driver was Antonio Butelli the undercover cop. The Italian had been blond last time Ben had seen him; no glasses, no mustache. Easy to see how he'd been fooled, except now that he knew, the similarities were glaringly obvious.

Next time, he'd listen to his gut instead of blaming his paranoia on the past.

Speaking of the past, he turned to Evalina. "Now you want to tell me what the hell is going on, or are you still sticking with your dinner story? Or maybe, the two of you have found true love since last summer?"

That idea soured his stomach far quicker than he'd ever admit.

All signs of nervousness disappeared when irritation flashed in her whiskey-colored eyes. "What is your business with Fedorio?" she demanded.

Given that she'd confirmed his suspicion while avoiding a direct answer, he took care to be equally forthcoming. "Dante Fedorio is my mother's cousin. Is it a crime to be related to someone in Italy these days?"

"No," she replied. "However, the brevity of your stay does not allow time for the expected familial socializing."

A spurt of surprise gave way to reason. If they'd gone through the trouble to set up this 'unexpected' meeting, then of course they'd know his travel schedule.

"Are you working for them?" Butelli asked.

Ben shifted his stance so he could watch both agents at the same time. "The only person I work for is myself."

"Couriers work for their clients," Evalina pointed out. "Transporting whatever is given to them, usually with no questions asked."

He never told her what he did for a living nine months ago. Too busy exploring each others' bodies, they hadn't gotten to the discussion part of the evening. And before that, there'd been the whole hostage situation. She hadn't shown any interest in his job then either.

Despite his best efforts, his attention dropped to her mouth. His blood warmed with the memory of how her lips felt gliding across his skin—

*No.* She'd left without a word in the middle of the night. He would not set himself up to be the schmuck again. "I see you've done your homework," he quipped.

"A basic background check is standard operating procedure."

What else did she know? The gaze that met his was so distant and impersonal, he gave in to the urge to strike back. *"*Oh, yeah? Did you run that check before or *after* you slept with me?"

Color rose in her cheeks, telling him the barb had met its mark. Unfortunately, he hadn't been able to keep the accusation from his own voice. And then he couldn't keep his mouth shut.

"I'm guessing *after* you snuck out in the middle of the night. I'm also guessing it was a little more than basic. Tell me, Evalina, if you'd known about my parents beforehand, would you have even shown up at my hotel that night?"

Her gaze faltered. His chest tightened just as Butelli jerked his hand up.

"Enough."

Ben transferred his attention to the agent's gaze. The man played undercover well, switching from friendly cab driver to interrogator with ease. Silently, he thanked the Italian for his interruption. The fact that Evalina saw him differently after finding out his parents were convicted felons hurt more than he wanted to admit. By the direction the conversation was headed, no telling what he'd have said. As it was now, he'd already revealed too much, and his anger would make it sound like he cared.

He mentally stiffened his spine, squared his shoulders, and put the past where it belonged so he could focus on the current situation.

What the heck was Dante Fedorio part of that Ben found himself under investigation after one fifteen minute meeting with the man? And if his fake cab driver wasn't part of a tourist scam, who had stolen his bag, and why?

"Tell us why you were at the Fedorio building," Butelli demanded.

"I'd be delighted to." Shifting his weight, he crossed his arms over his chest again. "After you tell me why you care." When the Italian's jaw clenched, Ben feigned surprised concern. "I'm not under arrest, am I?"

"That can be arranged."

"On what charges?"

"You fled the scene."

"I chased the guy who robbed me."

Butelli didn't blink. "So you say."

"Where the fuck else do you think my stuff went?" He extended his arms, revealing the obvious. Twisting toward Evalina, he fought a grimace from the pull on the sliced skin near his waist and asked, "Are you going to go along with this lie?"

Before she could do more than begin to shake her head, another thought occurred to Ben. He lowered one arm while pointing the other at her partner.

"Come to think of it, maybe you *did* take my bag. Last time she didn't know you were undercover, so why should this be any different?"

Butelli moved forward, but Evalina stepped in to cut him off. "Stop." Then she turned to Ben. "Both of you. Antonio and I are working together in every aspect of this case."

"Wonderful. Now that we've established there is an official case, let's talk about the fact that neither of you appear to care that I was robbed."

Her gaze drilled into his. "You said all you had in the bag was a change of clothes."

"Oh...I see." He nodded. "No big deal then."

"I did not—"

"Did this man you say followed you from the airport know of your destination?" Antonio interrupted. "The Fedorio group is well known within our country. That could be why you were chosen as the target."

Ben considered that possibility and did his best to recall if he'd mentioned anything to the flirty Alisa during their conversation that the man behind them could've overheard. "I never once said the name of who I was meeting."

"And you didn't pick up anything for the Fedorios that someone would want to steal?"

"No."

Technically, Dante had *given* him the diary, for his *father*. And the box with the key for the Bible was for his *mother*. Not a single thing *for* the Fedorios.

If the police weren't behind the theft of his bag because of their investigation, it appeared he'd been a victim of bad luck. He wasn't sure he bought that, but didn't really have time to think about it right now. The brief thought of his mother had reminded him he'd been headed back to the airport for a reason, and he still had the address and the key that'd been in the box.

He glanced at his watch to see it was already after six p.m. He had no clue of the latest scheduled flight to Rome, but he'd bet he was running out of time.

"Somewhere you need to be?" Evalina asked, eyes narrowed.

"It was a long flight," he said with a shrug. "I'd like to get to my hotel."

"To rest up for your return tomorrow?"

Maybe it was her flippant tone. Maybe it was just to get back at her for leaving him that night. Either way, he let a slow smile curve his lips. "If you must know, I have a date with a sexy little redhead I met on the plane."

His statement triggered no emotion. The woman who'd haunted his dreams the past nine months had found and locked in her cop persona. Either that, or she didn't care. He refused to let the latter possibility bother him.

She moved closer to Antonio and spoke in a low tone. "We should check in with headquarters. Anything he might have received from Fedorio is gone now anyway, so see what Marino wants us to do. I am going to find my shoes."

Ben shook his head, despite recognizing the irony of being annoyed that they didn't believe him when he hadn't told them the whole truth.

The agent nodded at Evalina's suggestion, withdrawing his phone to make the call.

"Am I free to go?" Ben asked.

"Remain here with Antonio," she ordered before disappearing into the crowd. She returned a few minutes later, hands empty, feet still bare. Apparently her shoes had disappeared like his bag.

Butelli continued his phone conversation in Italian, which left Ben and Evalina standing together. There was so much he wanted to say to her, and yet the safest topic of conversation would be the weather. He glanced sideways and noted she held her purse in front of her with both hands, feet planted firmly on the ground, shoulders back, spine stiff, chin at a mutinous tilt. Though the top of her head barely reached his shoulders, her intimidating stance reminded him of a cornered skunk.

Yeah...no go on the small talk. He shoved his hands in his front jeans pockets, absently noting the keys had warmed from his body heat as he turned his back to her and surveyed the busy piazza.

While watching people move through the old square, he ran his thumb back and forth along the jagged side of the key that'd been locked inside the box. The edges caught his thumbnail in one direction, and slid along the pad of his thumb in the other.

Tourists were easy to spot with their cameras. They stood in various groups, posed for clichéd pictures, and stared in awe at the building before them. The Italians were just as noticeable as they strolled the cobblestones without paying anyone any attention other than the occasional derisive expression for one of the many fashion faux pas committed by the tourists. He'd received a few of those looks himself. Glancing down, he figured it must be the boots—not that he cared what anyone in Italy thought of him.

Resisting the urge to glance over his shoulder at the rigid woman behind him, he tilted his head back and eyed the square tower that rose above the rest of the three story cathedral. It was not that tall, constructed mostly of red brick except where topped by a section as plain as the blond walls that faced the piazza. Not as impressive as the word *Duomo* implied, but what did he know? Further down, he could see a larger crowd near the front of the historical structure. Must be more to it on that end.

"What did he say?"

Evalina's question in English brought Ben back around to see Antonio had finished his call and rejoined them.

"Our orders are to remain with him until he boards his flight back to the U.S. tomorrow."

Ben's fingers curled around the two keys until the cut edges on the newer one bit into his palm. Another whole night in Evalina's company? That scenario was too dangerous on multiple levels. Not to mention, personal escorts screwed up his new plans, but telling them of his side trip to Rome wouldn't get him anywhere either. They'd want to know why.

He summoned a friendly smile as he released the keys and removed his hands from his pockets. "That's really not necessary. I have every intention of getting the hell out of here by tomorrow."

"And we will ensure you make good on that intention," Antonio said.

Annoyance threatened to wipe away his easy-going smile. "I haven't broken any laws."

"The Commissario is not inclined to give you the opportunity to do so, either. Due to your family history, he is not comfortable with you remaining on Italian soil."

Was he being kicked out of the country because of his parents, or his mother's cousin? If he thought about it, probably both. Then why the hell did they allow him inside their border in the first place?

With an arrogant flick of his wrist, Butelli extended his arm in a sweeping gesture for Ben to precede him. "Your taxi awaits."

"And if I refuse?"

"We will detain you for forty-eight hours and you will *still* end up on a plane out of the country. Unless the volcano shuts down the airports, then you can be our guest even longer." He smirked. "The choice to waste your time is entirely up to you."

They had absolutely nothing to hold him on. Back home, he'd call their bluff and walk away. But he wasn't in the United States, and he wasn't so sure of his rights here, or if the Italian would be willing to make things up just to prove a point. A questioning glance for help from Evalina got him nowhere.

"If you have nothing to hide," she reasoned, "why do you resist?"

"Because I'm being treated like I did something wrong when you know damn well I didn't."

Her gaze shifted from his.

"You are not handcuffed, are you?" Antonio interjected.

"Might as well be."

The agent reached into his pocket and Ben stiffened. Instead of pulling out a set of cuffs, the man extended the money Ben had paid him outside the Fedorio building. "Relax, *amico*. Consider us your chauffeurs, courtesy of the *Polizia di Stato*."

Ben pocketed the bills as he gave a short laugh. "This is bullshit and you both know it."

"We have our orders. Don't make the situation more difficult than it needs to be," Evalina advised in a clipped tone before starting across the piazza in her bare feet.

Antonio stood his ground, clearly alert and ready should Ben decide to make a break for it. Good God, he may be stupid when it came to some things in Italy, but he wasn't that much of an idiot. Not to mention, the Bible his mother wished to return to its rightful owners wasn't worth the trouble of sitting in an Italian jail cell for two days.

After a long moment, he blew out a frustrated breath and followed Evalina to the car. She got in the front passenger side and he slid into the back with a brief wince before pulling the door closed behind him. As they departed, Antonio's reflection in the review mirror mocked his inability to recognize the man's features earlier.

He dropped his gaze and twisted slightly to check the cut on his side. It stung like hell, but since it'd mostly stopped bleeding, so he turned his attention to the scenery passing by at a much slower rate than on his trip into Novara.

So, no Rome. Without being too obvious, he withdrew both keys from his pocket. The antique skeleton key was twice as long and double the thickness of the newer silver key. That one he slid back into his pocket. He didn't imagine he'd need it again now that the box was open and lost along with his bag. The other he discreetly tucked into a small pocket he'd sewn into the inside lining of his right boot. A habit that remained from the old days that came in handy every now and again.

His mother would be disappointed when he showed up empty-handed, but not all was lost. The Bible had waited for thirteen years, a little longer wouldn't hurt. Seeing as Halli and Trent had no problem entering the country over the past nine months, he'd see if he could talk them into retrieving the book on their next trip to the new villa they'd purchased together on Lake Como. His movie-star future brother-in-law was the better bet. Truthfully, probably his *only* bet. Because no matter how belatedly noble their mother's intentions, if his little sister got wind of any connection to their parents, he'd be in deep shit.

Speaking of his sister...

Ben leaned forward toward the agents in the front seat. "How come I get the special treatment? Halli's been back here twice and no one's met her at the airport."

"Difference is, we like *her*," Antonio stated.

Evalina shot her partner a quelling look. "Your sister does not maintain contact with your parents," she informed Ben. "Nor does she arrange meetings with the Fedorios and depart less than twenty-four hours later."

Something told him his length of stay was the smaller part of the equation, and once again, everything circled back to his mother's cousin. Not that they'd tell him why.

Avoiding that question, he sat back and asked one that had a chance of being answered. "You going to tell me where we're going? Or is that a big secret, too?"

Antonio's gaze flicked to his in the mirror, then returned to the Autostrada. "You have a reservation at the Hotel Cavalieri, correct?"

"Yeah."

"That is our destination."

"I get to stay at my own hotel?"

"As you pointed out, you are not under arrest. You may proceed with whatever you had planned for your evening, so long as we accompany you."

*Hmm.* He could work with that. Not that he planned to go on the run to Rome—being chased through Italy by the police was not a good plan in any book. But as for other matters... His gaze transferred to Evalina's stoic profile. "In that case, you should know my plans have changed since landing. I'll be staying at the Armani Milano tonight."

Antonio gave a low whistle as he checked his mirrors to change lanes. "From a Best Western to the Armani? Tell us again how you do not work for Fedorio."

Ben didn't bother to repeat a denial they wouldn't believe.

Evalina's eyebrows rose as she exchanged glances with her partner before turning her sharp gaze to the back seat. "You're not paying that with the salary of a courier."

He eased back in his seat while giving her a slow smile. "Who said I was sleeping in my own room?"

Whiskey darkened to cocoa before she faced forward once more. Long, dark curls fell forward to shield her face. Showing her that her rejection nine months ago meant nothing to him was all the more satisfying when it actually garnered a reaction from her. He leaned his head back against the headrest and closed his tired eyes.

Tonight could be fun in more ways than one.

## Chapter 8

PRIOR TO REACHING the hotel, Ben punched in the number written on the slip of paper he'd withdrawn from his pocket and made the call. After four rings, he heard a breathless, "Hello?"

"Alisa, hi. It's Ben."

Silence greeted him. He hesitated reminding her of where they'd met with Evalina listening in the front seat. That would defeat the whole point of calling while still in the car.

"Ben. Hello," Alisa finally replied. "This is a nice surprise."

He picked up on an odd note in her voice. "Everything okay?"

"Yes, of course. I, um…I wasn't sure I'd hear from you." Her soft, sultry laugh oozed over the line. "I mean, I'd hoped, but…"

A voice echoed from somewhere in the background. Muffled, but still clear enough to recognize as male.

Lowering his voice, he asked, "Is someone with you?"

"What? Oh, no. That's the television. I'll turn it down."

He imagined her aiming the remote at the TV as she continued.

"So, if you're calling me, does that mean…?"

"I'm on the way to the hotel right now," he told her. "I'm all yours for the rest of the evening."

In the front of the vehicle, Evalina shifted in her seat to snap a few sentences toward Antonio in Italian. Then she swung her attention out the passenger side window, and Ben grinned at her obvious annoyance.

"And who might that be?" the redhead on the other end of the phone inquired.

"That would be my…chauffeur."

"Oh, wow. That's nice."

His lips twisted in a wry smile. "Not really. What do you say we meet at the bar about eight-thirty?"

"I've got a better idea," she replied, her tone low and sultry. "I haven't eaten dinner yet, so why don't we order in?"

Unfortunately for him, and her, after seeing Evalina again, the straightforward approach had the opposite affect than he guessed Alisa anticipated. And despite what he'd told Evalina, after some drinks and flirting at the bar, he fully intended to return to a room of his own—alone.

For the sake of his audience, he put a grin on his face that reflected in his voice. "Room service? Mmm. I like the sound of that. I'll see you soon."

He finished his call as the sedan slowed. Antonio made a right turn before braking for a sudden stop. Ben slid his phone back in his pocket when Evalina exited the car, slammed the door, and strode down a narrow side street lined with shops. His gaze was drawn to her natural grace and the sensual sway of her hips in the short, tight dress. Heat coiled through him. Why the hell did she stir arousal whereas a sure thing with Alisa barely warmed his blood?

He averted his attention from Evalina's petite figure before erotic memories began to surface. Storefronts of glass revealed clothing, shoes, bags, and various other items of fashion, and her bare feet made it unnecessary for him to ask her destination. He was also reminded he had no change of clothes to replace the ripped, bloody shirt on his back.

Catching Antonio's eye in the rearview mirror, he slid across the back seat. "I need to replace my stolen clothes."

He exited without waiting for the Italian's response, but wasn't surprised when the man appeared behind him less than a minute later. Ben went inside the first store he saw with men's clothing and picked out a black silk shirt, underwear, socks and a ridiculously priced pair of jeans. A brown leather overnight bag replaced his canvas one and doubled his already exorbitant charge card receipt. After stuffing his items inside, he passed his shadow lurking by the door and returned to toss his purchases in the back seat. Having sat enough, he lounged against the side of the car while they waited for Evalina.

She rejoined them a few minutes later, dressed as if she'd stepped off the page of a fashion magazine featuring casual weekend-wear. Low-heeled, black leather boots encased her calves over dark, skin-tight jeans. The splash of color in her bright pink shirt surprised him, but she reverted to the classic Italian look with a black jacket and a filmy gray scarf draped carelessly about her neck. She strode along the cobblestones as if she owned the street, the epitome of fluid sophistication.

Those luxuriant curls lifted and bounced about her rigid shoulders with each step. Her bold confidence only emphasized the fact that Alisa tried too hard. Hell, even with most of her skin covered up, the Italian in front of him was sexier than any woman he'd ever met.

With a frown, he straightened from the vehicle and opened his door to get in. Thoughts like that were exactly what had screwed with his head the past nine months.

On the drive to the hotel, he knew somehow he had to get the woman out of his mind for good. He rubbed his chin as he watched the buildings scroll by. Maybe the redheaded Alisa was yet another key in this day of dilemmas.

Antonio drew up to the front doors of the *Armani Milano*, and Ben wasted no time grabbing his new bag while opening his door. "Thanks for the ride. I'll see you two in the morning."

Once on the sidewalk, he shut the door on their rapid exchange of Italian. The front passenger door swung open, and then Evalina joined him on the sidewalk.

"Eva will accompany you inside," Antonio called out.

"Wow, you guys really don't trust me, do you?" When the question was met with silence, he shrugged with forced indifference. "Fine. Suit yourself."

Then he caught the door before she could close it and dipped his head to look at Antonio. "You sure you want to send her? She doesn't usually stay the whole night."

The Italian side-tilted his head toward Ben and cocked an eyebrow. "Perhaps you did not satisfy her."

He straightened with a laugh. Oh, he'd satisfied her quite well. More than once.

"*Basta!*" Evalina jerked the door from his grasp and slammed it shut.

Pleased at her heated reaction, Ben slung the strap of his new bag over his shoulder, hooked his thumbs in his jeans pockets and strolled toward the hotel. The rapid click of boot heels told him his new, smaller shadow followed. Two doormen stood outside and both opened the doors as they approached. Ingrained courtesy had Ben stepping aside for Evalina to go first. Once inside, he took a moment to appreciate the sleek, modern lines of the elegant lobby. Not that he really cared, but the beauty inside was the only thing that had any hope of diverting his attention from the woman in front of him.

Until he moved ahead of her again and saw the tall, slim figure at the front desk speaking with the formally dressed hotel clerk. The red hair made his stomach sink.

*Alisa.*

She slipped something the employee handed her into a small hand purse, then glanced toward the doors. When she spotted him, she pivoted with an inviting smile and leaned sideways against the check-in counter.

She'd freshened up. Probably showered and redid her makeup and hair in addition to changing her dress. This one was black, but equally feminine and seductive. She appeared ready for a night out, and even though he was exhausted, he hoped she'd decided against room service.

Fully aware of Evalina's presence in the background, he hurried forward while positioning his bag over the bloody stain on his shirt. Working on the fly since the piazza, in the car he had devised a new plan to leave his escorts outside, book his own room, then call his date with his apologies. Now, with her waiting at the desk and Evalina accompanying him inside, he was fast running out of options.

"Hey," he greeted the redhead. "Change your mind about meeting upstairs?"

"Why do you ask that?"

He swept his gaze over her dress.

"Oh, no, I just threw this on for comfort." She fiddled with the sparkly little bag in her hands. "The thing is, Daddy booked me a suite with plenty of room for two, so I thought I'd save you some time and mon…ney…"

She trailed off when Evalina appeared at his side, close enough to signify they were together. Ben caught a hint of her perfume from earlier in the piazza. A second inhale strengthened the exotic scent and memories shot forward to mess with his senses.

Alisa straightened from the counter, her hazel eyes swinging from him to the petite Italian cop. "Who's this?"

He shifted away from Evalina and opened his mouth to reiterate the chauffeur explanation, but she beat him to the punch.

"*Salve*," she greeted, all business in her tone. "You are Alisa?"

The redhead's puzzled gaze shot to Ben's before returning to Evalina as she voiced a cautious, "Yes."

"My name is Ispettore Gallo, and I am with the *Polizia di Stato*. Signor Sanders has been asked to leave our country, and it is my duty to ensure that he does."

Hazel eyes widened in alarm. He wasn't sure if he wanted to thank Evalina or throttle her when his date blanched and took a hasty step back. One hand gripped the counter, her knuckles snow-white.

"You're a police officer?"

"*Sì*." Evalina flashed her badge with practiced ease.

Alisa visibly swallowed hard. "Am I in trouble?"

Evalina's stern expression softened in the face of her obvious apprehension. "No, of course not. Our concern is only with Signor Sanders."

After an initial show of relief, confusion wrinkled the younger woman's pale forehead. "Is he under arrest?"

"No."

"Then why does he have to leave? What did he do?"

Ben leaned an elbow on the counter and angled toward Evalina. "You know, I'd love to hear the answer to that question myself, Ispettore Gallo. Why must I leave again?"

Alisa swung her gaze to him. "She hasn't told you?"

"Not exactly." He shrugged. "I suspect it's related to my local family ties, but no one seems inclined to fully explain to me how or why that's an issue."

"I am not at liberty to discuss the situation," Evalina stated formally, avoiding his gaze.

Ben rolled his eyes and shook his head. The redhead cast a quick glance toward the hovering desk clerk, then her gaze bounced back and forth between him and his tight-lipped escort.

"Is he dangerous?" she asked Evalina in a hushed tone.

He maintained his relaxed pose with effort as he waited for that answer. Evalina turned narrowed whisky eyes his way for a brief moment, and the tension in his muscles increased. Indefinable emotion flashed before she gave a barely perceptible shake of her head.

"We do not consider him to be, no."

Alisa appeared to relax. "So…he's in your custody, but not under arrest."

"*Sì*. That is correct."

Since he assumed she was trying to scare the younger woman away, her response surprised him. She could've easily used that question to her advantage. In fact, he wished she would have.

"Do you have to stay with him all night?" Alisa asked.

Ben noted the color high on Evalina's cheeks. "That's not the *Ispettore's* style. Is it Eva?"

Alisa's brownish-green eyes narrowed slightly at the sudden familiarity his use of her first name implied.

Evalina kept her gaze on the redhead as she replied, "*Signor* Sanders is free to spend his evening however he wishes, so long as he remains within the hotel. My partner and I will escort him back to the airport in the morning."

Alisa nodded. He was glad it seemed to make sense to someone, because he still didn't quite get it. He watched her study the black sequined purse in her hands and it dawned on him she was probably rethinking her invitation. *Good.* It gave him a perfect out without conceding anything in front of Evalina. If fact, he'd appear the gentleman next to her cold superiority.

"Listen, Alisa." He lowered his voice in gentle understanding. "I won't be offended if you've changed your mind."

Her fingers tightened on her purse, indecision evident in her expression. One more glance at Evalina, then she shook her head. "No. You know what? You struck me as a nice guy on the plane, and you still do now." She gave him a tentative smile so unlike the seductress of earlier. "Have you done anything illegal?"

After a beat of disbelief, he replied in a low monotone. "No."

Her smile widened, giving him a glimpse of the woman in the airport. "Then I trust her judgment *and* you."

*What the hell?* Backed into a corner, he lifted his eyebrows and tried one last time. "You're sure? Jetlag is catching up fast. I may not be the best company."

"I'm sure. And like I said, my suite is huge. Way too much room for just me."

"*Scusa*," the man behind the desk interrupted. "If you wish to add a guest to your room, I require passport information."

"Of course. Room two-twelve."

"*Sì*." His expectant brown gaze shifted to Ben.

He reluctantly handed over his documents so the man could enter his information. After some quick keystrokes and a pass through the scanner, he slid the passport back across the desk.

Alisa sidled up next to him and hooked her arm in his to pull him forward. "I'll have him back to you in the morning," she told Evalina while steering him toward the elevators.

He went with her, swept along on a wave of his own making that he was now powerless to stop. Not to mention, he hadn't been kidding about the jetlag.

"Ben."

Evalina's warning tone swung him around to walk backwards.

"Do not leave this hotel."

He gave her a tired smile that he hoped came across as cocky. "Believe me, I'm not going anywhere tonight."

## Chapter 9

Evalina took a deep breath and counted to ten as the elevator doors slid closed on Ben's infuriating grin. He hadn't exaggerated; the woman was beautiful. Compared to her own petite, curvy figure, the redhead's tall, slim stature was the perfect complement to his height and dark blond hair.

She knew she had no right to be upset. She had run out on him in the middle of the night, so him hooking up with some girl he met a few hours ago on the plane shouldn't bother her for even a second.

But it had been eating at her since he'd announced he had a date for the evening. Because it made her wonder what she'd been to him back when they'd been together for that one time. Nothing more than a convenience? The closest warm body? When he'd first come on to her at Lapaglia's villa, he hadn't known she was an undercover cop. Would he have slept with her then, even while he believed she held him hostage?

When they'd gotten together *after* everything was over, she'd thought there was more between them than that. Apparently not.

*Then why did he take a bullet for you?*

Memories from the previous summer flooded back. Ben lying on the floor of the boat, chest bleeding. Similar panic had assailed her when she saw the red stain on his shirt in the piazza and thought he'd been stabbed.

She didn't want to care for the American. Couldn't afford to care for him. Not then, and not now. So, just like when she'd walked out of that hotel room, she ignored her heart and focused on the job. Lifting her hand to key her mic, she paced away from the front desk and slipped back into her native tongue.

"Antonio? Are you there?"

"Copy."

"I just met this Alisa woman Sanders mentioned in the car. They're on their way up to her hotel suite right now. I don't like it."

"Are you speaking professionally or personally?"

Indignation slowed her step. "Professionally, of course."

"Just checking."

"Well don't."

"Your past with the man affects your objectivity. Back in the car—"

"My past with the man is precisely *why* I'm on the case," she reminded. "I don't appreciate you questioning my judgment."

"*In the car*," he repeated impatiently, "it was clear to me the guy wanted to get a rise out of you. It was equally clear he succeeded. I need to be sure you can put your personal feelings aside here. The job comes first."

Considering her thoughts a moment ago, his concerns were valid. It didn't mean she appreciated him pointing them out. "You think I don't know that? I managed when I took down the man who murdered my father, did I not?"

"Yes, you did. But since then, you've been operating on the edge."

"I have not—"

"I've seen your case files. I know you're on probation."

*Damn.*

"You barely held it together back in the piazza with him. I also heard your voice earlier when you saw he'd been hurt."

Her steps halted as her stomach plummeted. Yes, he was

right, and apparently he was watching her every move. If she wanted to keep her job, the last thing she needed was Antonio thinking she carried some sort of torch for Benjamin Sanders. *She* was the one who'd chosen not to continue any type of relationship, not Ben.

She took a deep breath and blew it out silently with measured control. "I assure you, what happened between me and Sanders is in the past. There are no personal feelings to warrant your concern."

"If you say so."

Disbelief still echoed in his words. She relaxed her clenched jaw to avoid sounding too defensive. "I do."

The mic picked up his soft sigh before he said, "*Bene*. Then tell me, what about this woman bothers you?"

"I told her I was with the *Polizia* and that Sanders has to leave the country. She appeared nervous, asked a few questions, but still took him to her room."

"Perhaps they knew each other prior to the plane?"

"I don't know, maybe. But we should look into her."

"I agree. Get me a full name for Interpol."

She retraced her steps to the front desk and commanded the attention of the attendant while extending her badge across the polished marble counter. "That woman who was just here. What is her name?"

The man leaned forward to scrutinize her credentials. "One moment, please."

Evalina reined in her impatience when he disappeared. True to his word, he returned a moment later with a second impeccably dressed gentleman. This one introduced himself as the manager and took his own turn reviewing her badge.

"How may I be of service, *ispettore*?"

"I need information on a guest registered with your hotel."

The front desk attendant pointed to the computer screen and the manager nodded while donning a pair of reading glasses. "Suite two-twelve is registered to Signorina Alisa Marshall."

"And she is a citizen of the United States?"

"*Sì.*"

"I'll need a copy of her passport and use of your business center."

After a few keystrokes, an unseen printer processed the requested information. The attendant handed over the sheet of paper and she took a moment to verify the picture before reading the residential address in the state of Maine for her partner.

She turned her attention back to the manager. "Can you confirm who booked the reservation?"

Two clicks of the mouse had him lifting his chin to peer through the bottom half of his glasses. "It was confirmed through our website, so the only information we require is the guest's name."

"And when was it booked?"

"Yesterday."

Evalina frowned at the last minute arrangement. If it had been booked by the girl's father as she'd indicated, wouldn't he have his daughter's travel details finalized well ahead of time?

A low click in her ear preceded Antonio's voice over the com system. "Check the credit card."

"Is the credit card on file in her name?" she asked the manager.

"*Sì.*"

The original employee stepped forward once more. "Signorina Marshall presented her own card upon arrival earlier. The reservation was held with a different card."

She looked back to the manager, who maintained his position in front of the computer. "Does your computer retain that information?"

This time he clicked three times before replying. "The original card was in the name of Signor Nicholas Marshall."

"I'll confirm the relation on that name," Antonio commented in her ear.

Evalina concentrated on the men in front of her. "How many guests in the room?"

"The suite is registered for two guests."

She pinned her gaze on the one who'd entered Ben's passport information. "Including Signor Sanders?"

He leaned closer to the computer, his dark gaze transferring to the screen. "She only requested one key card at check-in..."

"Then the addition of the *signore* resulted in an increase from one registered guest to two?"

The attendant shook his head. "No. It appears the reservation was always for two."

Ah, *now* they were getting somewhere.

## Chapter 10

BEN FOLLOWED ALISA into the suite and closed the door as he swept his gaze over the modern furnishings. Sleek and simple, they were less lavish than he'd expected. On the other hand, the living room alone was bigger than his apartment back in Wisconsin. The lights of neighboring buildings winked through the slit in the curtains of one window. The other floor-to-ceiling coverings were closed to the night.

On his right, a curved staircase rose to a second floor where the bedroom must be located. He brought his attention back front and center as his young hostess stepped toward him with an inviting smile.

"Would you like a drink before your shower?" She stopped in front of him and peered up through her lashes.

"Alisa…"

"I'll order room service. It'll be here by the time you're done."

Her fingers found the top button of his shirt. He let his leather bag drop to the floor, then reached up to grasp her hands in his. "Stop."

She looked up in surprise. Her smile faltered and her eyebrows drew together.

"This isn't going to happen." He offered a gentle smile of his own while easing her back a step to lower their hands and let go.

For a moment, he thought he glimpsed relief in those hazel eyes, but then her lashes dipped and her bottom lip protruded in the slightest hint of a pout. "It's not?"

"No. And I'm sorry, I owe—"

Her soft gasp cut him off. "Is that blood?" She retreated further, hand over her mouth, eyes wide as she stared at his side.

"It's no big deal," he assured her.

"What happened?"

"My bag was stolen. The bastard cut the strap and his knife sliced through my clothes."

She jerked her gaze to his. "Oh my God."

He held up a hand at the tremor in her voice. "It's okay. It barely hurts." Unless he started thinking about it. Like now.

"Is that why the cop was with you? Do you know who did it?"

"No clue, and Evalina's completely unrelated." He sighed as a wave of exhaustion swept over him. "The truth is, she and I have a history, and I wanted to piss her off by coming up here with you."

Her gaze met his and understanding dawned in her eyes. "That's the only reason you came up, isn't it?"

"Unfortunately, yes."

"So, you were just using me?"

"Pretty much, yeah." He picked up his bag and slung it back over his shoulder. "Again, I'm sorry. I'll leave and get my own room."

When he turned and reached for the door, she darted past him to block his exit. "No, please—you don't have to go."

He blinked in surprise, but let his arm fall back to his side.

"I don't like being alone," she said in a rush. "My brother Nick was supposed to join me, but he was delayed on business."

She bit her lip, her delicate eyebrows drawn together in a sudden frown as if she hadn't intended to say so much. She took a deep breath, and when her lips curved into a tremulous smile, she looked more like a girl than a woman.

"Please. Stay and keep me company? Even if you're sleeping, I'll feel better having someone here with me."

Those green-brown eyes beseeched him and, honestly, he was too tired for another round of verbal sparring with Evalina downstairs. Giving in was so much easier.

"All right."

Her entire stance relaxed as she smiled. "Thank you." Then she turned him around and pointed to the right. "Shower's that way, up the stairs. I'll pour you something to drink and order us some dinner. By the time you're done, we'll eat, and then the bed is all yours."

He'd take the couch, but didn't bother arguing that point now.

"Brandy, scotch, or whiskey?" she asked on her way across the room.

"Whiskey."

Halfway up the stairs, he paused and commented on something that'd been bugging him since the lobby. "You're awfully trusting with a complete stranger."

"I thought we'd become pretty good friends on the plane." From the bar, she tossed a friendly smile at him over shoulder. "Besides, there's a cop downstairs who knows exactly where you are and who you're with. I think I'm pretty safe."

Good point. He continued upstairs into the loft bedroom before it dawned on him that she'd invited him to her hotel well before Evalina entered the picture. His big brother instincts kicked in and he decided to have a talk with her during dinner about making smarter choices. Something her father or brother should've already done instead of spoiling her.

After tossing his bag and jacket on the bed, he unbuttoned his shirt and stripped it off. Twisting to get a better look at his side made the dried blood pull the edges of the wound. The slash spanned a good three inches, and though it wasn't very deep, it would probably scar.

Wonderful. A second memento for his second trip to Italy.

He lifted his hand to run his fingertips over the puckered circle of skin from when he'd been shot. Both times he'd been with Evalina, but thankfully, this time didn't involve a hospital and surgery.

He glanced toward the bathroom, wondering if he'd find a first aid kit in there as he emptied his jeans pockets out of habit. The skeleton key and notepaper came out together. The key he slipped into a side zipper pocket of his new leather bag. He hesitated with the paper, then sat on the bed to dig his phone from his inside jacket pocket.

Like on his previous trip overseas, he'd made sure his phone would have international calling and internet access. Once he plugged the address his father had written on the paper into his maps app, he thumbed the search button.

A sound on the stairs jerked his head up and he quickly slid the phone and paper under his bag. Damn, he hadn't expected her to bring the drink up to him. Rising to his feet, he purposely reached for the button of his jeans just as Alisa appeared at the top of the stairs, a glass of amber liquid in one hand.

The color reminded him of Evalina's eyes.

"Here you go." Alisa extended the tumbler, her gaze trained on his bare chest as he accepted the whiskey. "Dinner will be here in about forty-five minutes."

"Thanks." He took a sip, waiting for her to head back downstairs.

Instead she stood there, as if waiting for something as well. Her attention shifted to the bed, then returned to his chest. She shifted her stance, then clasped her hands together in front of her. Was she staring at his scar, working up the courage to ask for the story he didn't want to tell? When his pulse thrummed faster, he lifted the glass in his hand and downed the contents in one swallow.

Alisa's gaze widened while the alcohol burned down his throat and into his stomach, igniting a fire along the way. He handed the glass back with a shrug and a wry twist of his lips.

"It's been a long day."

She nodded, fidgeting with the empty glass now.

When she still didn't leave, he said pointedly, "Getting longer by the minute."

She jerked her gaze up to his. A sheepish grin curved her mouth. "Sorry, I'll leave you be."

His gaze followed her down the stairs until she was out of sight. Something about her felt off, he just couldn't put his finger on it. With a little shake of his head, he turned back to the bed and retrieved his phone.

The search results indicated *no address found*.

He checked the note again, making sure he hadn't transposed a number or letter, or spelled the street wrong. Over the next fifteen minutes, subsequent searches of alternate combinations resulted in the same response, so the paper joined the skeleton key in his bag until he had time for further examination. It was very likely his father had coded the address, in which case he'd have plenty of time to decipher it for Trent on his flight home.

Eying the bed, the thought crossed his mind to skip the shower and dinner and just sink down onto its inviting surface. But that wouldn't do when he planned to take the couch downstairs.

He did drop down, but only to a sitting position so he could lean over and untie his boots. Once the laces were loosened, he sat up to toe off first one, then the other. A sudden wave of dizziness made him brace his hands on his knees. Closing his eyes didn't help. When he opened them again, the room swam out of focus and started to spin.

*Whoa.*

He shoved his bag aside and eased back on the bed. His hands and feet seemed to weigh a hundred pounds each. Darkness edged his vision. The disorientating whirling persisted and as he began to lie down, the room faded to black.

## Chapter 11

EVALINA REACHED FOR the photo copy of the passport she'd just faxed, then cleared the browser history of the business center's computer. Now she'd go wait with Antonio in the car, parked across the street. It was going to be a long night, even with them napping in shifts.

The sight of Alisa Marshall stepping from the lift with a dark-haired man made Evalina shrink back behind the privacy wall. The man looked about thirty and of her own native descent. If he was the Nicholas Marshall whose credit card had originally held the reservation, there was no hint of family resemblance between his dark, wavy hair and the redhead. Then again, her own sister had inherited their mother's genes and sported straight blond hair compared to her near-black curls.

He held a cell phone to his ear, and lagged behind with a dark gray pull-behind suitcase while the redhead strode across the lobby toward the doors. Evalina snapped a quick picture with her cell before shifting her attention back to Alisa.

The woman had been so determined to get Ben up to her room, where was she going less than forty minutes later? She hadn't changed from her black dress, but instead of the sequined clutch, she carried a black shoulder bag.

To most, she'd appear casual and nonchalant, on her way out for a night on the town. But Evalina noted the rigid set of her shoulders and the nervous glances she cast in each direction, especially when she drew even with the front desk.

After a slight pause, the woman's tension eased and she lifted her hand to adjust the strap of her bag as she continued out the door. When the man with the suitcase strode forward without any further hesitation, Evalina wondered if the strap adjustment had been an all clear signal.

But all clear from whom? Her?

And where the hell was Ben?

She keyed her mic for Antonio as she eased out from behind the privacy wall. A few clicks of her thumb on her phone and she forwarded the picture of the guy to her partner. "The woman who just exited the hotel is Alisa Marshall. In a moment, you'll see the man I just sent you a picture of. He exited the elevator with her, but I'm not one hundred percent sure they're together."

"Where's Sanders?"

"No sight of him. You stick with her. I'm going to head up to the room."

"If these two are working with him, he's long gone."

*Probably.* She ruthlessly shoved aside her disappointment and ignored his prediction. "If we lose the link, switch to text and keep me posted."

"Copy that."

The earpiece went silent and she returned to the lobby to find the manager covering the desk. "I need a key for room two-twelve please."

Indecision filtered across his expression before he nodded and configured a duplicate card. As the lift rose to the second floor, her pulse beat with dread at the thought of finding the room empty. She refused to examine the reason why beyond the affect it would have on her job. A simple one night surveillance and get the guy back on the plane was not something she could afford to mess up.

If she'd kept him in sight, she wouldn't be screwed right

now. Then again, Antonio had totally called it earlier, so it was his fault for insisting *she* be the one to go inside with Ben. He wouldn't have given a damn about watching Ben flirt with the woman—or going up to the room with them for that matter.

*No*, she thought as she stepped from the lift into the dim hallway. Losing the subject of their assignment was her fault, not Antonio's. She'd insisted to her partner she could keep this about the job, it was about damn time she proved it. If she ever found Ben again, he'd see just how professional she could be.

Outside the suite's door, she heard a soft click in her ear, then Antonio's voice. "Evalina?"

"Go."

"She left on foot, but about two blocks away, the man with the suitcase pulled up in a blue Alpha Romero. They are together."

"Any sign of Ben?" She cringed for having used his first name, but Antonio either didn't catch the slip or thankfully overlooked it.

"None. You?"

"I'm about to enter the room now."

"I should come back—"

"No. I'm fine. Don't lose them. If Sanders is gone, they could lead us back to him."

A swipe of the card key turned the light green, and she drew her Beretta before cautiously opening the door.

"They're on the move, so I'm probably going to lose you," Antonio advised. "Watch your phone."

Evalina keyed her mic twice to indicate she understood as she entered the suite, then eased the door closed as quietly as possible. She moved past the small foyer, into the huge living area. Dead silence greeted her.

*Dio mio*. Not looking good.

She did a sweep of the downstairs, found nothing, and approached the curved staircase to the second floor loft area. Weapon extended, she ascended the stairs simply to follow protocol. Antonio was right; Benjamin Sanders was long gone. In weak moments, she'd wondered about leaving him all those months ago. His disappearance now confirmed she'd made the right choice.

Four steps from the top, her eyes drew level with the loft floor. A pair of boots lying on the floor froze her in her tracks. Her finger tightened infinitesimally on the trigger. She recognized those broken-in, scuffed boots. Drawing in a shallow breath, she continued up the final stairs, sweeping the room as it became visible.

Her gaze made it no farther than Ben's large body sprawled atop the king-sized bed. He appeared to be sleeping, but knowing the redhead and the man were together shoved her heart into her throat. Gun trained on the bathroom doorway until she could clear the room, she quickly crossed the plush carpet to the bed. She felt for Ben's wrist until she could apply pressure to the pulse point as she'd been trained in her emergency medical courses.

A steady beat eased the vice-grip on her chest.

Gripping her weapon in both hands once more, she crossed silently to the bathroom and quickly determined it to be as empty as the lower level. Tucking her gun into the rear waistband of her pants, she returned to the bed and the sleeping American.

He hadn't left. Joy swept through her before she could gather enough common sense to suppress the ridiculous emotion. With Antonio following Alisa, she'd better see if she could get some answers on her end.

"Ben. Wake up. Benjamin."

He gave absolutely no indication of hearing her and she sighed. He'd been a sound sleeper the night they'd spent together, too. Add in jet lag, and she wasn't surprised by his lack of response to her voice. His chest rose and fell with each deep, even breath he took.

Her gaze swept over his bare skin and stopped cold on the healed bullet scar. Forcing her attention to move on, she noted his solid muscles and trim physique hadn't changed one bit since she'd last had her hands on him. Completely negating her silent assertions of professionalism, she fought the urge to touch him now.

Dried blood remained on his skin where he'd been cut. She frowned slightly, taking in his unbuttoned but still zipped jeans. With his boots on the floor, and shirt off, she assumed he'd been on his way to the shower before passing out on the bed.

Is that why Alisa Marshall had left? He'd fallen asleep, and she went out to find herself another good time?

She shook her head. The mysterious Italian with the suitcase negated that theory, and a sudden heaviness in her gut told her there was much more going on here.

Raising her voice, she commanded, "Benjamin Sanders, wake up."

He still didn't stir. She braced a knee alongside his hip to lean over and shake his shoulder. His bare skin warmed her palm and she stilled. Stared at his mussed hair, blond-tipped lashes resting against his cheeks, the shadow of a day's growth of whiskers on his jaw. Memories flooded back, all the more vivid with the live version of him sprawled out before her and his unyielding bulk beneath her hand. A wave of heat coursed through her entire body and settled low in her belly.

She drew back as if she'd been burned and shoved away from the bed. Damn the man. Even asleep he was beyond tempting. Better to leave him alone than have him wake to her drooling over his body.

Desperate for a distraction, she dug her cell phone from her jacket pocket. No new messages, but she had one for Antonio.

*Sanders is here. Sleeping off jetlag.*

After another glance toward the bed, she paced to the stairs and retreated to the lower living room. No more than she grabbed a mineral water from the fully stocked mini-bar, her phone vibrated in her hand.

Seeing as Antonio was driving, she wasn't surprised by the incoming call. "Gallo."

"Color me shocked."

*Me, too.* "I'm letting him sleep. Makes it easier to keep him in one spot until his flight."

"Good point. And these two? Any clues around as to how they fit?"

"No."

"Do you think the three of them could be working together?" Antonio asked.

"The girl was very nervous when I introduced myself. She certainly wasn't expecting to see me," Evalina mused, considering that angle. Then she shook her head even though he couldn't see her. "But wouldn't Ben have warned her when he called from the car?"

"He's the decoy. He didn't tip her off to keep it authentic, and now he stays back so they can finish the job."

It didn't quite add up for her, but she gave Antonio a vague, "Maybe."

"I'm going to stick with them and see if they lead me anywhere. You stay there and work that angle when Sanders wakes up."

"Okay. Keep in touch with any developments."

"Will do," he promised. "*Ciao.*"

She hung up and pocketed her phone. After a glance up the stairs, she spun on her heel to examine the suite now that she had time on her hands. There was nothing much to investigate, but she pretended there was simply to keep her mind off the man lying on the silver-gray bed upstairs.

Beneath the well-stocked bar, she found a trash bin. Inside were a couple of tissues, an empty plastic bottle, and the torn wrapper from a sample packet of an American pharmaceutical sleep aide. She removed the torn garbage and read the ingredients and warning on the label. Her gaze shifted to survey the surface of the bar and spotted the faintest hint of white powder edging the corner.

On a serving tray, two of the six glasses sat right-side-up. The first had contained a drink—alcohol by the smell of it, but the second was dry inside. She lifted it to inspect the bottom and found a tiny bit of white powder still clinging to the edges. Add alcohol and jetlag...

She looked back over her shoulder at the loft, then rose and rushed back up the stairs. Was Ben sleeping, or had he been drugged?

## Chapter 12

THE SOFT TOUCH against his side bordered on ticklish. Warm liquid trickled over his skin, then a sharp sting made him flinch as he sucked in a quick breath. Ben opened his eyes in time to see Evalina glance up from where she sat beside him on the bed. Their eyes met for only a split second before she turned to dip a cloth in a bowl of water. In that split second, he imagined he'd caught a glimpse of concern and relief.

A serious wave of déjà vu hit hard when she gently swept the washcloth across the cut on his side. The scene was like a replay of nine months ago, when she'd taken care of his injuries inflicted by his captor, Alrigo Lapaglia. Same as then, he didn't relish the feeling of helplessness. This time, he wasn't handcuffed, so he moved to sit up.

His head protested at the same time she did. "Lie still."

Closing his eyes, he dropped the couple inches back to the bed. Despite following orders, his head continued to pound. He raised his hands to his temples with a low groan. "God, I feel like I've been drugged."

"You didn't take something to help yourself sleep?"

He opened his eyes again to peer at her. "No, I didn't take anything—I had no need to. I did have a drink, but…that was it."

This time, she held his gaze, as if searching for the answer in his eyes. "It appears something was added to your drink to knock you out. Your pulse was steady, and you showed no other signs of an overdose, so I let you sleep it off instead of calling for emergency services."

Vaguely, he recalled downing the glass of whisky Alisa had given him, searching the address on his phone, and then feeling woozy as all hell. After that, everything was blank.

"Do you remember anything?"

"Nothing. How long have I been out?"

"Almost eight hours."

He swiveled his head toward the windows, but the drapes were drawn tight.

"It's just after five a.m.," she supplied.

"Where's Alisa?"

"Gone."

He tried to make sense of everything Evalina was saying, but his brain wouldn't work. And then the warmth and gentleness of her ministrations on his torso added to the confusion swirling through him. He lowered his left arm while grappling blindly with his right for one of the pillows that must be somewhere nearby.

Evalina rose, set the bowl aside, and started to reach over him, above his head. She'd removed her jacket, and the shimmery pink fabric of her short-sleeved top clung to her breasts. God, if she got any closer, the scent of her that'd been torturing him since the piazza was going to inundate every bit of his senses. Senses that weren't strong enough to handle her proximity right now.

He met her reach half way, grasping her wrist to halt her forward movement. She jerked away from his hold and took a step back. The extra space allowed him to swing his legs over the edge of the mattress and sit all the way up this time. And he paid for the too-sudden movement. Another wave of dizziness nearly toppled him off the bed.

She rushed forward to catch him, muttering in Italian. He was pretty sure he heard a word that would translate to *idiot* in English. Sitting there with her supporting at least half his weight, he had to agree with her.

Once his head stopped spinning, he lifted a hand to push her away. "I got it."

Again, she moved back, but only far enough to give him some breathing space. Moving much more cautiously, he straightened, then rose to his feet. The slightest sway had her reaching out to take his arm. He accepted her help, gripping her shoulder to steady himself before taking a step forward.

"What are you doing?" she asked with exasperation. "You need to lie back down."

"I *need* to use the bathroom." He cocked an eyebrow in her direction. "You're welcome to come help me in there, if you'd like?"

Color flooded her face as she released his arm. He headed into the bathroom before he could miss the warmth of her touch. After answering nature's call, the sight of the shower made him hesitate to zip his jeans. He was long overdue, and a cold one would go a long way in clearing his fuzzy mind. Removing some other thoughts from his head would be a bonus.

"I'm gonna take a shower," he called out to Evalina.

He didn't wait for her response before stripping and stepping under the bracing spray. A minute of cold water did the trick, and then he cranked the handle to hot. Half way through, his thoughts began to catch up to events. The direction they took had him rushing to rinse suds off.

That's why Alisa had brought the glass of whiskey up and waited for him to drink. Not because she wanted to seduce him, or ask about his scar, but because she wanted to be sure he swallowed every last drop. He really was an idiot.

He wrapped one of the soft, fluffy towels around his waist as he hurried back to the bedroom without bothering to dry off. The loft was empty, and a quick glance over the half-wall confirmed Evalina was downstairs. Good. His jacket lay on the foot of the bed with his new leather overnight bag. Snatching it up, he went for the pocket with his wallet and passport. Relieved to find both items, he searched his wallet and found nothing missing. Frowning, he tossed them onto the bed next to his phone.

If not for his money, why had she drugged him?

He removed the newly purchased clothes from his bag, then a flash of comprehension had him scrambling for the side zipper pocket. Finding it empty of both the skeleton key and the address his father had left him, he had his answer.

"*Sonofabitch.*"

The expletive came out louder than he'd intended, and didn't relieve his anger one bit. He sat on the bed, leather crushed between his fingers as he fisted his hands in impotent frustration. Another thought dawned on him, and he leaned over for his right boot just as Evalina rushed up the stairs. He sat up and their eyes met as she slid to a halt.

"Sorry. I thought..."

He knew what she thought even though she didn't finish the sentence. Her running to take care of him like he was some sort of helpless invalid grated on his ego.

"I'm fine," he ground out.

Ignoring her, he felt inside his boot for the little hidden pocket. The moment his finger touched the cool metal of the key, he breathed a silent sigh of relief and thanked God for old habits from his youth dying hard.

Let that deceitful little con artist Alisa have the address—it was wrong anyway. At least he still had the key for when he figured out the code. Next order of business, find out what the hell his mother had gotten him into.

Tossing the boot back to the floor next to the other one, he glanced up to find Evalina watching him. The sight of those darkened whiskey eyes moving over his wet chest sent a shot of heat straight to his groin. Despite their past, the sizzling attraction hadn't dimmed a bit. He saw her swallow hard at the same time he did.

*Get dressed* common sense shouted above his libido. In this moment, that was imminently more important than talking to his mother. He reached for the package of boxer briefs lying with his clothes. Evalina's gaze tracked his movements and a second later, she whirled around. He ripped open the plastic, but before she could retreat back downstairs, he asked, "How'd you end up in here with me?"

She paused with her foot on the first stair. "I saw your date leaving the hotel and got curious."

He almost laughed. Curious? More likely, she ran up to the suite thinking he'd ditched her and Butelli. Ben tossed the towel on the bed and stepped into his underwear.

"How long after we came upstairs did she bail?"

"Bail?"

Her over the shoulder glance caught him in the middle of pulling his boxers on. He found himself grinning when she blushed again, her face matching the bright pink of her shirt as she turned her back to him once more. So different from the woman who'd exerted her power when he was a hostage, then ran those sassy lips all over his body when they slept together a few days later. The specific memory of her riding him threatened to take over.

Heat roared through him. With effort, he shut the memory down and reached for his new jeans. "Bail means leave. How long after did she leave?"

"About forty minutes. And she wasn't alone."

Ben paused. "What?"

She turned around, now seemingly unconcerned as he hiked his jeans up over his hips and fastened them before reaching for his shirt.

"There was a man with her in the elevator," she revealed, leaning her butt back against the loft wall with her arms crossed over her chest. "He stayed back to make it look like they weren't together, but Antonio followed Alisa, and she met up with this man three blocks from the hotel."

So, he hadn't been imaging things on the phone when he thought he heard a man in the background. Probably the brother she'd mentioned. *Nick.* He couldn't believe he'd fallen for the

TV explanation. He recalled her nervousness when he tried to leave. She hadn't been afraid to be alone, she'd just been desperate to get him to stay.

"What'd he look like?"

"Tall. Dark. Looked Italian, but Antonio found out through Interpol he's her brother."

Yep. His tail from the plane and likely his thief in the piazza. Picturing him and Alisa, he'd never have guessed they were related. Which was perfect for them, wasn't it? And by all appearances, the brother and sister con-duo had specifically followed him from the States. He gave an inward sigh; for that, there could only be one reason.

Giving his dear mother the benefit of the doubt appeared to have been a mistake. Wasn't he the fool?

He slipped his arms in the sleeves of his new black silk shirt, adjusted the material over his shoulders, fixed the collar, and began buttoning. "Where'd they go?"

There was a brief hesitation when he thought she might not answer, but then she said, "South. Antonio lost the vehicle outside the city of Bologna. He's searching for their plates using the Tudor traffic cameras on the Autostrada."

Once she'd said south, Ben didn't need a traffic camera to know exactly where they were headed.

"Antonio seems to think the three of you were working together," Evalina added.

"Antonio's full of shit," he retorted.

That got him a laugh. When he glanced up, she sobered quickly and held his gaze. "What did they want?"

She'd seen him checking his stuff and heard his aggravation a few minutes ago. *Nothing* wasn't going to cut it when he assumed she'd searched his things while he was passed out. She was a cop; he was apparently a suspect in whatever the hell she was investigating. She'd have been stupid to *not* take the opportunity.

"It doesn't appear they took anything, but I'm guessing that's the whole point. With access to my passport information and ID, they now have all the personal information they need."

Her eyebrows rose, and she turned to look down into the lavish suite. "All of this for identity theft? They could've hacked a computer for that."

"I've never done it before, so how would I know?"

Her expression clearly said she didn't believe his explanation. Tough shit. He retrieved his dirty clothes from the bathroom and began packing his bag. He'd be on a plane soon and wouldn't have to worry about what she believed.

"I don't think you're guilty of anything, you know. I'm just doing my job."

The quiet admission made him pause. First of all, it was so unlike her not to be in his face demanding answers right now. But worse, he wanted so badly to believe she believed in him. Except that would be the second stupidest move he'd ever made. The little leap of hope in his chest reminded him if he wasn't careful, he could be in danger of repeating the first.

She sighed behind him. "What's really going on here, Ben?"

As an afterthought, he added the hotel stationery and pen to his bag, zipped it shut and picked up his phone. Then he turned around to tell her the truth. "A really sucky string of bad luck."

Frustration darkened her eyes to the color of polished mahogany. He held her gaze, engaging in a silent battle of wills that stretched his nerves to the breaking point. The sharing of information went both ways, he wanted to point out, but she already knew that. She didn't trust him, why should he return the favor?

He kept his mouth shut, and she broke eye contact when she pushed away from the wall. "Let's go."

"I'd like to make a phone call before we leave for the airport."

"To whom?"

"My sister."

She didn't even bother to hide her disbelief.

"I didn't get a chance to let her know I arrived safely," he added to beef up the excuse. Neither Rachel or Halli even knew he was here, but he wasn't about to tell Evalina he was calling his convicted felon mother for answers. "I'll meet you downstairs—*if* that's okay with you?"

She hesitated, then crossed to the stairs. "Make it fast."

While counting the rings, he paced to the wall and saw Evalina had stopped at the foot of the stairs. Probably hoping to overhear his conversation.

His mother answered on the fifth ring. "Benjamin. I've been waiting for your call."

"Hello to you, too, Rach," he replied with a short laugh. "Sorry I didn't get a chance to call yesterday. I ran into a few…issues."

"*Rach?* Is someone listening to you?" His mother's initial confusion switched to suspicion in a heartbeat.

"Yes. How's everything there?"

"Am I supposed to answer that or are you filling time?"

"Good," he replied while moving away from the wall.

"I forgot how annoying this could be," his mother griped. "Just tell me if you got the Bible."

"No." He lowered his voice as he sat on the bed and angled his back to the stairs to keep his words from carrying too far. "It's in Rome. I've got a location and a key, but I've also got myself a police escort to the airport. Whatever the Fedorio Group is involved in over here got me flagged, and I've been ordered to leave the country."

"But you can't."

"I don't really have a choice in the matter."

"Benjamin, listen to me. You can't come back without that Bible."

Her voice had risen on a note of panic. Dread replaced anger and settled heavy in his stomach. He bent down, bracing an elbow on his knee while cupping his hand around the phone. "Mom, what the hell is going on? Since I got here, I've been drugged and robbed. The only thing they took was the coded address for the location in Rome."

An audible inhale traversed the line. "Someone else knows where it is?"

The little jab of pain from her words sharpened his voice. "I'm fine if you cared to ask."

"Of course I'm glad you're okay, but..."

*But.* From as far back as he could remember, there'd always been a *but* with his parents. A weary sigh escaped and he rubbed hard between his eyes. "But this Bible isn't just about righting past wrongs, is it?"

"No."

"Damn it, Mom, you swore to us this stuff was all over. That you changed."

"I have," she insisted, sounding like she was crying now.

He hardened his heart against involuntary sympathy.

"I'm so sorry, but it's not what you think. I didn't want to worry you."

The shaky apology was followed by a strangled sob. Dread morphed into alarm and stiffened his spine.

"The Bible your father stole thirteen years ago holds the key to a treasure. A priceless treasure that some men are willing to kill to possess."

He thought of Alisa and her brother Nick. She hadn't appeared to be a ruthless killer, but he hadn't actually met the brother. "Do you know who these people are?"

"They're here with me now."

He frowned again. That was impossible. "What are you talking about? You're still in Wisconsin, right?"

"Yes, but...*please*, Ben, I'm scared. You have to figure out a way to get the Bible."

Her fear resonated in the whispered plea. The chill that crawled up his spine stood the hair on his arms and neck on end. "Scared of what? Mom, what is going on?"

He heard more crying, and then a hard, cold voice grated across the line. "Your mother for the Bible, son."

"Who is this?"

"Don't concern yourself with unimportant details. Get that Bible and bring it back."

"You don't understand. I don't even know where it is—"

"Then find it. The terms are non-negotiable. Bring it back or she's dead."

The line disconnected, leaving him without answers. He sat in stupefied silence, thoughts whirling into one single conclusion. *Now* he didn't have a choice. Somehow, he had to get his ass to Rome.

## Chapter 13

EVALINA CROSSED HER arms over her chest, glanced at her watch, and summoned her dwindling patience to allow Ben one more minute. She got that he was punishing her by not telling her everything he knew, but if the stubborn man would come clean, this would be so much easier. Whatever the Marshall siblings were after, it wasn't Ben's identity. And if it had anything to do with the Fedorios—

The soft mechanical click of the lock on the suite door brought her head up a second before it swung open. Her first thought was that Antonio had returned. That idea was obliterated by the bullet that whined past her ear and impacted the wall behind her. She caught a split second glimpse of two men entering the foyer as she dove for cover behind the curved staircase.

"Eva—"

Shattering glass cut off Ben's voice.

"Get down," she screamed, praying he hadn't been hit. Her gun was in her hand without her being conscious of even having reached for it. "Stay there!"

Weapon extended in front of her, she kept low, hugged the half-wall on her left, and crab-walked up the stairs using her feet, butt, and one hand. They must be using a silencer because she hadn't heard anything more than a muffled report before the bullet.

They were speaking in Italian, arguing, the one on the left not happy with the other's actions. He shot back something about a diary and not caring who he had to kill to get it. She kept moving, scouring her brain for what they could mean. Her earlier search of Ben's belongings had revealed nothing more than new clothes in his bag. Had Alisa Marshall taken what these men were after? Is that what Ben had been so angry about?

Evalina was almost to the top of the stairs when one of the men spun into the opening in a standard defensive recon move. She fired a split-second before he locked in a kill shot. He went down hard, but she didn't relax in the sudden quiet after the loud report of her own gun. There was one more to deal with.

When she reached the top step, she scrambled around the corner so she could keep an eye on the stairway. Ben crouched behind the half-wall across from her. Her gaze swept over him, found no blood or apparent injury, and rose to his face. She raised her eyebrows in inquiry. He shook his head, a somewhat shell-shocked expression on his face. Assured he wasn't hurt, she trained her gaze back on the stairs.

Other than her heart pounding in her ears, silence reigned in the suite. The second man made no sound to give away his position, not even a shoe squeak on the marble floor.

After the gunfire, Evalina expected to hear sirens any minute. Hoped she'd hear them. Her damn phone was in her jacket pocket, on the arm of the couch downstairs, so calling for backup was out. The weight of keeping them safe fell squarely on her shoulders.

She watched the wall for any shadows indicating the second gunman was on his way up. Ben waved his hand for her attention. When she chanced a glance, he pointed behind her to a lamp on the bedside table. He made a motion with his arm, indicating she toss it over the side. Yeah, a distraction would be good, but he couldn't cross the opening to get the lamp, and she hated leaving the stairway unguarded.

Finally, she gave a reluctant nod. He turned to keep watch while she crawled across the floor to the opposite side of the bed. After unplugging it, she had to pull the table out to free the cord.

The plug scraped against the table leg and the wall, unnaturally loud in the dead quiet. No more than she grasped the lamp in preparation to head back to the wall, sound erupted behind her. She spun around to see Ben lunge at the man charging up the stairs. They fell against the corner of the railing, then stumbled and rolled down the curved staircase.

Abandoning the lamp, she skirted the bed and ran after them. Distantly, she registered the sirens she'd been hoping for. When she reached the first floor, Ben was dragging himself to his feet, and the second gunman was halfway to the door. She yelled for him to stop, but he kept running, and she wasn't going to shoot him in the back.

The man she *had* shot lay at the bottom of the stairs. He hadn't moved because she hadn't aimed to wound. Still, she scanned for his gun while kneeling to check for a pulse. Nothing. No pulse or gun. His partner had probably picked it up.

Certain the one on the floor posed no threat, she rose to pursue the second man at the same time Ben started for the door. She stiff armed him out of her way. "Wait here."

"With a dead body? Don't think so."

Insisting he remain behind would cost precious seconds she already didn't have, so she clenched her jaw and made sure he stayed at her back. Her own defensive training had her switching from one side of the hall to the next, only to find it empty. In the fifteen seconds she'd taken to check the dead guy, the live one had escaped.

She lowered her Beretta and rounded on her shadow. One shove put Ben's back against the wall. His only response was a slight lift of his eyebrows as she glared up at him. She almost wished he'd have fought back.

"What the hell were you thinking, jumping him like that?"

Now his eyebrows drew tight together. "I thought he was going to shoot you."

"He could've shot *you*." Memories of him lying on the boat surfaced once more. To combat the unwelcome emotions that accompanied the recall, she focused on her anger. "I'm the professional, here. Next time you let *me* handle the guy with the gun."

"Fine. If we run into any more psychos between here and the airport in the next couple hours, they're all yours."

His sarcasm only annoyed her more, but in the street below, sirens indicated the police had arrived.

Evalina kept a sharp eye on him as she dealt with the authorities. At her insistence, Ben had come back inside the suite, but didn't venture away from the entryway after they'd given their joint statement to one of the agents. Because her and Antonio's investigation was confidential, she'd kept all mention of Fedorio out of it and not surprisingly, Ben had followed her lead.

She snuck looks in his direction from a short distance away. One of the paramedics had bandaged the cut on his side while she filled out one final piece of paperwork. Any lingering effects of jetlag and the sleep aide were nowhere to be seen. In fact, he seemed to have been injected with a dose of caffeine she desperately craved. His shoulders and spine were rigid, his gaze sharp as it took everything in. Adrenaline, she reasoned, watching him fidget near the small foyer.

One of the crime scene technicians brought down Ben's items from upstairs and Evalina directed the tech to where he stood. He accepted the bag, then draped his jacket over the top of the bag while shouldering the strap. His hands were shoved in his pockets before he cast another all-encompassing glance about the room.

She bowed her head over the clipboard in her hands while continuing to observe his actions from the corner of her eye. He seemed more on edge than recovering from an adrenaline high. Which made sense, considering only minutes after claiming he didn't know what was going on, two men arrived, guns blazing. He knew more than he was letting on, and as soon as they finished here, she was going to sit his ass down for a long talk, airport be damned.

A moment later, she noticed his phone in his hand. His thumb scrolled the screen and as he stared at whatever was revealed, all color drained from his face. Her stomach dropped. The alarm caused by his expression doubled when he abruptly turned for the hall. Evalina scribbled on the clipboard and shoved it into the hands of the first person she passed as she rushed after him.

One glance at the busy hallway between the suite and the lift and she went the opposite direction. He wasn't too far ahead, but moving fast for the emergency stair exit.

"Ben! Stop!"

His stride didn't slow, and she broke into a run to catch up. The heavy exit door banged against the wall as she shoved through. "Where do you think you're going?"

She managed to grab his arm on the landing between flights, but he jerked free. A second grapple caught the strap on his overnight bag. It slid from his shoulder and hit the landing with a thump.

"Let me go, Eva."

After his pointed use of her full name since they'd come face to face at the café, the more familiar abbreviation was like a punch to the gut. Sucking in a deep breath, she renewed her determination to stop him. This time she was ready for his resistance and managed to get in front of him as he stooped for his bag. Short of pushing her down the stairs, he wasn't getting past.

He straightened, strap held in his hand with the bag still on the floor as she took her stance. "Get out of my way."

"Not until you give me some answers. Those men think you have something they want and were willing to kill you for it. *And me.*"

He dropped the strap to step closer. She tensed, but still wasn't prepared for the lightning fast move that swung her around and pressed her back to the wall while he crowded her close with the length of his body.

She sucked in a breath as his eyes locked with hers, brilliantly blue in the morning light flooding the stairwell. Tension radiated from his rough grip. Experience reminded her he was unpredictable and passionate, yet despite the threatening stance, she was shocked to realize she didn't fear physical harm at his hands.

As she stared, as they breathed together in the minuscule distance between them, a shadow of desperation darkened his eyes.

"Answers would be a good thing right about now," he agreed, his voice low and gruff. "You first."

"Me?"

"What are you investigating Fedorio for?"

The demand took her by surprise, and she stiffened. "I don't owe you any—"

"The hell you don't."

Increased pressure on her arms spurred her into action. She wedged her hands between them, intending to force some space so she could break free. Quicker than before, he caught her wrists and forced her arms above her head. Her knee jerk reaction was countered by the full weight of his body pressing hers to the wall. An instant flush of sensual heat, combined with helpless fury, added fuel to her adrenalin.

"I came to Italy to pick up a book for my mother from her cousin," he said, teeth clenched against her struggles. "Then you and Antonio show up to escort me around, and suddenly I'm getting shot at again."

Her indignation spiked, but she was unable to gain any leverage for an effective counter-measure against his superior strength. She'd save her efforts for when he let his guard down and settled for a glare as she caught her breath.

"You think what happened up there was *my* fault?"

"You tell me. I was never booked at the Armani, and I never told Fedorio where I was staying. How else would anyone know where I was except through you and your partner? As I recall, he wasn't so forthcoming with you on your last assignment, either."

She opened her mouth to object, but realized he might be right. Antonio had called in their location, as well as ran the checks on Alisa and Nicholas Marshall. She didn't believe Antonio was directly responsible, but had they somehow been the connection that led the two gunmen to the hotel?

"They could've followed you from your meeting yesterday," she suggested, monitoring his expression for any indication he was lying.

"If that was the case, they would've been the ones to steal my bag, and it would've happened a lot sooner than the piazza."

"How do you know it wasn't them?"

"I suspect I'd have gotten more than just a scratch on my side. And if it *had* been them, they'd already have what they wanted."

"Which is?"

Indecision flickered in those blue depths, as if he wanted to tell her, but couldn't quite bring himself to trust her. Doing so would prove he'd lied.

Then his gaze lowered to her mouth, and she realized the demons he wrestled were entirely different, but all too familiar. As he began to lower his head, the awareness she'd been desperately trying to ignore rushed forward to steal her breath and leave her light-headed. God help her, if he kissed her right now, she wouldn't stop him. Her eyelids grew heavy in the charged silence, and his grip on her wrists eased.

The break in his concentration registered in her mind with a distinct click. She held still one more moment, and then the second before his mouth met hers, she wrenched her arms free, bucked her body against his, and managed the space necessary to escape his physical control.

A quick spin protected her back and she faced him, ready for his next move.

## Chapter 14

BEN LET HER go. Palms flat against the wall, he leaned forward and barely kept from banging his forehead against the cold stone. He was a fool for even thinking about kissing her, let alone acting on the urge. His life was complicated enough and getting worse by the hour. Last thing he needed was to lose his head over this particular woman all over again.

He sucked in a deep breath and pushed away from the wall. Why was it, every time he came to this county, he got fucked? And not in a good way. Once this was over, he was never setting foot on Italian soil again.

When he turned around, the sight of her gun in her hand stopped him short and pissed him off. "Are you going to arrest me for assault, or just shoot me here?"

She lifted her hand from her side and the flicker of surprise on her face made him wonder if she'd even been aware she'd drawn the weapon.

Tucking it away again, she replied, "Neither. I've had enough paperwork for one morning."

The unexpected dry humor caught him off guard. When he remained silent, she sighed.

"I'm tired, Ben. And hungry. Can we just be straight with

each other *for once?*"

"Sure." He crossed his arms and waited.

"The Fedorio company, run by Dante and his cousin Este, has been under investigation for a couple years now." She turned and started down the stairs. "Fraud, money laundering, illegal weapons."

Ben scooped up his bag, hitched the strap over his shoulder, and followed. "And how exactly do I fit in? The only laundering I do is my clothes."

A brief smile touched her lips, but it wasn't until they were through the exit and on the sidewalk that she turned to answer. "Your name showed up in their phone records a few days ago, and then you booked a flight to Milano. My job was—is—to determine if you are setting things up for your father's upcoming release. Maybe working for Fedorio yourself."

He held her gaze without blinking. "I already have a job."

"And yet you were drugged last night and two men tried to kill you this morning."

"Yeah." That didn't look good. Lifting a hand to rub the back of his neck, he shifted his attention to the people out and about for the start of a new day. Whether on foot, pedal bikes, mopeds or cars, the streets and sidewalks were beginning to come alive.

He returned his attention to Evalina. She was a cop for crissakes. And she'd just been—as she put it—straight with him. After the text he'd received upstairs, he'd rather have her on his side than against him, which meant it was time to forget being raised to distrust cops and tell her everything for the sake of his family.

"I came to Italy for my mom, to get a Bible my father stole and sent to Dante Fedorio just before he went to prison."

"Is that what the Marshalls were after?"

He frowned. "The Marshalls?"

"Alisa and her brother, Nicholas." His initial confusion had her tilting her head in disbelief. "You were going to sleep with her without even knowing her last name?"

It sounded bad, but he forced a careless shrug since he hadn't intended to follow through.

Evalina shook her head, disgust evident in her expression. "I should not be surprised. Men are all alike, whether Italian or American."

Annoyance surged forward. "I was trying to get you out of my damn head," he defended. Once the words were out and he saw the glimmer of comprehension in her eyes, he went on offense. "It's not like your actions were all that honorable the last time we spent the night together."

Her face paled in the morning sunlight, then color rushed in. But when she lifted her head, her expression was shuttered. "You're right. I am in no position to judge. I apologize."

*For leaving me that night, or judging me now?* he wanted to ask, but this time managed to keep his mouth shut. He'd already revealed way too much to her on that front.

"Going back to your previous question, yes, that's exactly what those two were after. Only Fedorio didn't have the Bible. Just a box from my father, with an address and a key—which they took last night."

"What is so important about this Bible?"

He pulled out his phone and activated the screen to bring up his most recent message. The image that popped up made his blood run cold all over again. He handed his phone to Evalina, with its picture of Rachel inside her jewelry booth at a Wisconsin craft fair, talking to a customer. Her blond hair was tucked behind an ear on one side, its long length confirming the recent date on the bottom of the picture was true.

"This is your sister."

"Yeah."

She glanced at him, and then one upward sweep of her thumb revealed a second photo of Rachel taken through her patio doors, sitting at her kitchen table with her laptop and a cup of coffee. Dated today. Beneath that was a simple yet effective text: *Will add insurance if necessary.*

"You got this when we were upstairs," Evalina stated. "This is why you left."

"Yep." Though Rachel appeared fine, with his mom already in danger, he didn't like these men watching his sister, even from a distance.

"Insurance for what? Who sent this to you?"

"The men who are holding my mother until I bring the Bible back to the U.S." He took his phone back, but then held it up between them, guilt for having doubted his mother continuing to eat at him. "This is why you have to let me go. I have to find that Bible before the Marshalls do, or my family will get hurt. I can't let that happen."

"But they already have the address."

"It's coded, and I know how my father works, so I've got the advantage. All I have to do is get to Rome before they figure it out."

"Rome?" she repeated before a frown creased her forehead. "My boss is never going to agree to that."

"Oh, I think he will." Taking a deep breath, he forced his next words out after her earlier explanation. "Fedorio gave me one more thing on my way out."

Her amber gaze sharpened on his.

"It was an old diary from the late eighteen hundreds."

"*Diario*. That's what the men were arguing about upstairs."

"My father loves history, so Fedorio asked me to take it back as a gift to him. I agreed because I was in a hurry, but once I started looking through it, I realized there was some sort of code in the pages. Certain words, letters and numbers were traced over so they stood out."

Excitement flashed in her eyes. "Sounds like a record book. That could be the evidence we've been searching for to build a solid case against the Fedorios. Dante gave it to you to get it out of the country for safe-keeping with your father."

It wasn't an entirely implausible explanation.

"Did he say anything else about it?" she asked.

"No. And unfortunately, it was in my original bag."

Her enthusiasm dimmed. "The one stolen in the piazza?"

He nodded. "That's the bad news. Good news is, I'd bet my

life Nick Marshall is the one who took it. You get me to Rome to find the Bible, and I'll get you the diary."

She stared off down the street, uncertainty etched in her sunlit features. He did his best not to fidget while waiting for her decision. He had to go no matter what, but with her help, it would be so much easier.

A muted buzz had her reaching to answer her cell. "*Pronto, Antonio. Mi senti? C'è qualcosa di nuovo?*"

She spoke in her native tongue, too fast for him to pick out much more than her partner's name and a few other words. Not understanding her was enough to make him want to learn the language, until he reminded himself he was never coming back to Italy.

A few minutes into the conversation, she suddenly took hold of his arm and pulled him toward the street. He followed her across, and down the opposite sidewalk as she continued to talk. They wove past pedestrians and business men and women on pedal bikes at a rapid pace that challenged even his long strides.

As she continued to walk and talk, her restless gaze increased his tension and put him on full alert. *Roma, diario,* and *commissario* caught his attention and he waited impatiently for her to complete the call. She hung up a few blocks later, but maintained the military mission march.

"Care to tell me what's going on?" he asked.

"Antonio was calling to tell me to bring you in to the police headquarters."

That brought him to a dead halt on the sidewalk. "Why?"

She glanced back, saw he'd stopped, and returned to stand in front of him. "Because of what happened at the hotel. And…"

Impatience added bite to his tone. "What?"

"Dante Fedorio was murdered early this morning," she said quietly.

Shock rendered him speechless. Next came a flicker of sorrow for the cousin he'd met only yesterday. Though distant, he was family, and he'd seemed nice. Now, beyond their brief meeting, he'd never know the man. Then the full implication of

Evalina's news sunk in, and anger rolled through him fast and furious.

"I didn't kill him."

"No one thinks you did," she assured him. After another sweeping assessment of their surroundings, she urged him forward once more. "But with the obvious connection, no way they would send you home without bringing you in for questioning first."

He consciously forced his teeth to unclench. "We don't have time for a God-knows-how-long interrogation. The longer—"

"I know," she interrupted. "Antonio and I both agree recovering that diary is now our top priority."

"And the Bible."

Her solemn gaze met his in a sideways glance. "Yes, and the Bible. Since we need you for that, Antonio will clear things with our boss while you and I get my car. We'll meet him in Rome this afternoon. Now watch for a taxi."

Despite his relief to be heading in the right direction, Ben still wondered if Antonio was involved deeper than Evalina knew. How else would the gunmen have known where to find him, even down to the exact room number so they could get a key from the front desk?

He'd save those suspicions for when they were alone in her car, after he'd had time to think it through more. Right now, with a plan in place, he needed to hear Rachel's voice. He pulled out his phone and placed the call as they walked.

Evalina watched with a frown. "Who are you calling?"

"I need to check on Rachel."

"You didn't actually call her before, did you?"

"It was my mom," he admitted. "I needed to find out why someone else would want the Bible."

She nodded in understanding, but as the phone rang, he could almost see her keeping tally of his lies in her mind. He'd done what he thought he had to do at the time. It wasn't like he hadn't had good reason for each one.

His sister picked up mid-ring. "Hey, Ben, how are you?"

Coming to an abrupt halt at the sound of her cheerful voice, he demanded, "Are you okay?"

"Um...I'm fine. Why?"

He breathed easier. She didn't sound scared, or like someone was forcing her to act as if everything was normal. "Where are you?"

"At home. Why, where are *you*?"

"Have you heard from Mom?"

"Not since the day she was released."

"You don't know where she is?"

"No. She was going to buy a bus ticket and said she'd call when she got to Wisconsin. Now stop firing questions at me and tell me what's going on."

From the tone of her voice, he pictured her sitting up straight in her chair, eyebrows drawn together in a frown of concern. *She doesn't know.* He raked his free hand through his hair and blew out a somewhat relieved breath as he began walking again.

"I'm in Milan."

"As in *Italy*? Yeah, right." Rachel's laugh was full of disbelief, but when he didn't say anything more, it died. "What are you doing there?"

"Short version—Dad stole a Bible years ago, and shipped it over here before he went to prison. Mom convinced me she wanted to return it to its rightful owners, but—"

"A Bible?"

"Supposedly it holds clues to a treasure, so he sent it to his old college roommate for safe-keeping."

Alongside him, Evalina's head swiveled in his direction at the mention of treasure. He caught the suspicion in her eyes before she resumed her search for a cab. She better not add that to her mental list. If he mentioned it while she was listening, she should realize he hadn't deliberately withheld the information. He just hadn't gotten that far yet.

"You know," Rachel said thoughtfully. "I remember something about a Bible back then. I just can't...quite...put my finger on it."

"Yeah, well, someone else did and now Mom's in trouble. They're watching you, too."

"What do you mean they're watching me?"

Ben hated the note of fear that crept into her voice, but she needed to be aware of the situation. "Someone is holding Mom until I find this bible and bring it back. They know where you live, too."

"You're not kidding here, are you?"

"No. I have no idea who these men are, but this is one hundred percent serious, Rach."

"I can't believe this. Why is this Bible such a big deal now instead of thirteen years ago?"

"Good question. At first I thought mom might be involved, being so soon after her release, but she sounded really scared on the phone, and she was crying. Then some guy came on the phone and told me he'd let her go once I gave him the Bible."

"You think maybe all the digging those reporters did after Halli and Trent went public tipped off an old acquaintance of Mom and Dad's?"

"Maybe."

"Does Halli know about any of this?"

"No. I thought I was just picking up a book and coming home, so I didn't bother saying anything to either of you. But things have gotten complicated over here, and I think you should go stay with her until this is over."

"She's in L.A. with Trent for his new movie."

"I know."

"I can't just pick up and leave," she protested. "I've got orders to fill, plus a show in Minnesota this weekend. I can't afford to lose the table fee or commissions."

She put everything into her jewelry business, but somehow he had to convince her to get out of Wisconsin. The texted picture of her flashed in his mind. "You're working on your laptop, aren't you? Drinking coffee out of a red mug? Ponytail, black shirt, gray vest?"

"Um, yeah, how'd you…know." The sudden screech of her

chair legs sounded across the line. "Are you saying they're watching me right *now*?"

"Yes. They sent me a picture using Mom's phone. Rach, please. It's bad enough Mom's depending on me, I don't want to worry about you, too."

A loud click, followed by the scrape of metal on metal told him she'd flipped the deadbolt and drawn the curtains on her French patio doors. Next to him, Evalina stepped off the sidewalk to hail a passing taxi.

"Should I call the police?" Rachel asked.

"No—that won't help any of us."

Hearing his own words, he drew in a deep breath and blew it back out. Normal families would suspect a practical joke and tell him to come on in for a cup of java. Hell, *normal* families would insist their sister call the police. However, with their past, Rach knew the drill. If a cop showed up at her front door now, both she and their mother would be in even more danger.

Much as he hated to, he admitted, "Ah…I've actually got help on my end over here."

"Who?" She didn't even give him a chance to reply before exclaiming, "Oh my God, you called *Evalina*?"

"It's a bit more complicated than that, and I don't have time to explain right now." Holding up a finger to Evalina to indicate he needed a minute more, he said to his sister, "Just promise you'll watch your back and get out of there without it looking obvious. Tonight if you can, otherwise tomorrow morning. Text me when you're with Halli."

"Mike's home this week. I'll call him to go out for a beer and head out from there."

Good. He trusted her neighbor Mike to protect her. The guy had served ten years in the Marines and worked private security.

"When are you coming back?" Rachel asked.

"Tomorrow, *if* I can solve dad's codes in time and if the flights aren't full because of that damn volcano in Iceland."

"Good luck," she said. "And be careful."

"You, too."

"I'm not just talking about the Bible, Ben."

His gaze shifted to Evalina standing by the open door of the taxi. Sunlight glinted off her long ebony curls, and despite a night of no sleep, she was still gorgeous. Even from an ocean away, his sister was much too perceptive. "Thanks."

He disconnected the call and pocketed his cell while sliding into the back seat of the cab after Evalina.

Once she gave their driver the address and sat back, she asked, "Rachel okay?"

"Yeah." He leaned his shoulder against hers and spoke in a low tone so his voice wouldn't carry to the front. "Is Antonio still following Alisa and Nick?"

"He picked up the car on a camera from the A1 near Arezzo, but it was just Alisa. It appears the two split up somewhere after Florence. He tracked her as far as Rome, where she exited the Autostrada for the city. So far, he hasn't located her on any cameras there."

"Is there any way to track Nick?"

"Headquarters is monitoring the credit card he used for the Armani, but they've probably figured out the police are aware of them, so my guess is they'll use cash as long as possible."

Exactly what he'd do.

As they rode through the streets of Milan, the rocking movement of the cab shifted her shoulder against his. Her warmth seeped through the thin silk of his shirt, threatening monumental distraction and reminding him of Rachel's warning.

"What makes you so sure Nick Marshall has the diary?" Evalina asked. "And if he does, how do you know he won't assume it's just an old diary?"

Ben held back a wry smile. Apparently *she* had no problems concentrating. "Because this whole thing leads back to my parents, which means Nick Marshall is a con man. He'll recognize the diary is more than it appears."

"Takes one to know one?" she asked.

Her tone was casual, almost teasing. But Evalina Gallo didn't tease, and her question hit a little too close to home. He stared out the window as he mumbled, "Something like that."

## Chapter 15

AT HER APARTMENT, Evalina packed an overnight bag, some toiletries, her handcuffs, and extra ammo for her Beretta. After securing her tactical shoulder holster, she gathered the long strap of her duffle bag in her fist and returned to the tiny kitchen to find Ben searching for something they could eat. Unfortunately, her refrigerator was as empty as the rest of her life, so she kicked the door shut on her way past.

"We'll get something at an Autogrill on the way."

He followed her outside, through the inner courtyard of her apartment complex and past the fountain. "Is that like a McDonalds?"

"Not quite." The thought made her smile as they exited to the street and then both tossed their bags in the back seat. He added his jacket, but she kept hers on the middle console for easy access when they got out.

Twenty minutes later, she checked her mirrors and zipped across the slow lane to take the exit off the A1 for the highway café that served Italy's road warriors.

"Good, God," he muttered when she careened into the parking lot. "Can I drive when we leave? I'd like to get there in one piece."

She ignored him and pulled into the first spot she found. Then she sat for a moment, scanning the other cars entering the lot. Ben opened his door, but she reached over to grab his arm before he could get out.

"Wait."

"What?" He looked at her, then turned to follow her gaze. His arm muscles tensed beneath her fingers. "You think we're being followed?"

"I'm just being careful," she explained, releasing his arm.

After another minute, she was satisfied enough to don her jacket over her weapon and head inside. They were lucky it was late-morning on a Tuesday, or it'd be packed with her fellow countrymen taking weekend holidays. As it was, she still had to ease her way through the multitude enjoying their *café* at the counter. A tap on her shoulder brought her around to see Ben two people behind her.

"Get me a large coffee to go, please. I'll find some snacks for the drive."

She opened her mouth to protest, but he was already moving away. Well, he'd figure it out soon enough when he had to make do with what she bought. She placed an order for two *Rustichella paninis*, a couple *cornetti,* and two *caffés*. Instead of drinking hers at the counter as usual, she carried their items to one of the tall tables set near the stocked shelves.

Ben came from the checkout area with a full bag of purchases. One look at the small china cups and saucers sitting on the table and he dropped the bag at his feet with a thud. "I said large."

"This isn't America."

"Tell me about it." He scowled and reached for the cup that even she had to admit looked tiny in his large hand. His first sip brought forth a grimace. "Wow. I forgot how strong these are."

"If it's not enough, I bought you some pocket coffees." She slid a couple of the small, wrapped squares across the table.

He eyed them as if they'd bite. "What the heck is *pocket* coffee?"

"Our version of the *to-go* cup you Americans favor. It's chocolate infused with espresso. A shot of pure caffeine. *Molto buono.*" There were a few tucked in her own jacket pocket for later.

"And that's legal?"

She rolled her eyes, then took a bite of her *Rustichella* while handing the second bread pocket stuffed with melted cheese and cured meats to Ben. Once she finished, she dusted the crumbs from her fingers and leaned sideways to check out his bag. "You do know it's only about five hours to Rome, right?"

"I didn't know what you like."

Her arched brow challenged that explanation.

He swallowed his last bite of *panino*, downed the rest of his *caffé*, and shrugged. "Okay, fine. I don't know what half of it is, so I got an assortment to increase my odds of finding something I'd like. And it's a good thing, because I'm still hungry."

"Definitely more believable." She motioned to the pastries still on the table. "Have a *cornetto alla crema*. I remember you like them."

He hesitated mid-reach, his gaze rising to hers. Before he could read the ridiculous panic sweeping through her at the admission, she finished her *caffé* and pushed the empty cup to the center of the table. "We should get going."

She didn't wait for his agreement before escaping outside, away from his perceptive blue eyes. She might as well have told him she'd thought about him every day since she'd left that night. Maybe not quite every day, but awfully close.

That long stride of his caught him up halfway to the car. Still avoiding looking at him, she made a split-second decision and pulled the keys from her pocket. "Catch."

He made an impressive one-handed grab with the hand holding the hastily wrapped pastries. "You're letting me drive?"

"Yes."

"All right, that's it." He stopped and turned in a circle as if searching for someone. "Where's the real Eva? She'd never hand over control like this."

Again with the shortened name. Because she vividly recalled he'd used it in the height of passion, it did things to her that messed with her head and ruined her focus. Drawing upon every bit of reserve she possessed, she forced a smile while opening the passenger side door. "*Sapientone.*"

"Excuse me?"

"It means wise guy. Now, shut up and drive."

His deep, rich laugh threw her even more off-kilter. She hadn't heard it much and discovered she liked the genuine article way too much.

After a few adjustments of the seat and steering wheel, he took them back on the road. Part of the reason she'd let him drive was because she knew the *caffè* wouldn't sustain her for the entire drive. The other part was that even though she was pretty sure they hadn't been followed into the Autogrill, gut instinct had her on edge. She could keep an eye out better if she wasn't trying to concentrate on driving while she was tired. Keeping Ben's attention focused on the road was a bonus.

The first half hour passed uneventfully, but then she thought she spotted the same car that'd caught her attention earlier. It was too far back for her to match the registration plates, so she couldn't be positive, but after what'd happened at the Armani, she wasn't taking any chances.

Sitting up straighter, she took out her phone and brought up the GPS map application. After a bit of studying, she told Ben, "Take the next exit. It'll take us longer, but it might be better for us to stay off the Autostrada."

His attention shifted to the rearview mirror. "We got a tail?"

"Maybe."

A sharp nod conveyed his willingness to follow her direction. Off the highway, they cruised the back roads at a good clip. In between checking for signs of someone following them, more than once she found herself observing Ben from the corner of her eye. He'd rolled the sleeves of his black shirt to just below his elbows, revealing muscled forearms as his large hands gripped the wheel. He handled the car as if he'd been born behind the wheel, navigating the increasingly winding roads that took them through Lombardy and the Emilia-Romagna region.

She didn't spot any tail as they travelled along remote roads of the Apennine mountain range and through the occasional tiny town even she'd never heard of. Her map told her they'd crossed the northern border into the Tuscany region and were in the more localized historical area of Garfagnana. Located between the Apuan Alps, the main part of the Apennine Mountains that stretched along peninsular Italy, Garfagnana was an area she knew about, but of which she had very limited familiarity.

The spring-green scenery was beautiful, reminding her of why she loved her country so much. Earlier, fresh tilled farmland had given way to blossoming hillsides covered in olive groves and the occasional vineyard. Nothing near what populated the southern part of Tuscany, but enough to invoke the romance that epitomized *Italia*. Now, the rugged landscape provided breathtaking vistas around practically every turn.

Less than two hours ago they'd been in the fashion mecca of the world, but out here, they could almost be the only two people on earth.

She glanced to the left again, taking in the strong line of Ben's not-quite-square jaw. The man had certainly left an impression all those months ago, and it wasn't solely his good looks. He had fought for his family with a loyalty and determination she didn't often see in her line of work, unless it was for greed. He'd included her in that circle when he'd tried to warn her of Nino's betrayal and lunged in front of his gun.

It made her wonder what she might have lost by leaving him so many months ago. Could everything be different if it were just them, without life and fear and the past to get in the way? Would she *want* things to be different?

The small voice in her heart whispered *yes* so fast she should've known better than to even ask the question. Such thoughts were much too dangerous.

Shifting uncomfortably in her seat, she glanced at her phone and removed her jacket again while directing him to turn left at the next crossroad. Switchbacks carried them up the side of one mountain and down another. After she'd declined a *cornetto* earlier, he'd eaten both and now reached into the back for his food from the Autogrill. When the car swerved toward the shoulder, she pulled his arm back over the seat.

"I'll get it. You keep both hands on the wheel, please."

She lifted the heavier than expected sack onto her lap and took stock of his purchases. A couple liters of water explained the weight, and the rest consisted of packaged food he appeared to have selected at random from the shelves. "You really didn't know what you were buying, did you?"

He shrugged and gave a small grin. "I bought a bunch of stuff, figuring the odds are in my favor there's something close to potato chips in there. How'd I do?"

"Well, you have some *tarallini*. Similar to what you American call a pretzel. Though I'm surprised you found some this far north—they are more common in southern Italy."

"What else?"

"*Fonzies*. They are puffed, cheesy twists."

"No chips?"

She made a face and surveyed the other items. "No wonder so many people in America are overweight."

"Hey, you basically bought me donuts."

She shook her head while reaching for the package of *Fonzies* from the bottom of the sack. She pictured his body on the bed back at the hotel and silently admitted junk food wasn't something he needed to worry about. Besides, the lightly sweetened crème-filled *cornetti* were nothing like the sugary confections Americans favored. She remembered those from a childhood trip to Walt Disney World in Florida. It had been their last family holiday before her mother died.

Her hands stilled as a vision of her mother's grinning face filled her mind. The beautiful blond woman who'd flouted tradition and given her such an unorthodox name for an Italian girl, yet she'd loved her more than anything. In this particular memory, Evalina and her sister Carina had giggled like crazy as their mother took turns tapping frosting onto each of their noses. Then her father scooped up a big glob with his finger and returned the favor. They'd all laughed together when he kissed it off.

"You find some?"

Ben's voice startled her from the reverie. Sharp pain in her chest caught Evalina unaware. She hadn't thought about that time they'd all been together and happy in so long. Blinking away sudden tears, she lifted the item in her hand.

"Sorry." She cleared her throat. "Only the *Fonzies*."

He navigated around a sharp turn before glancing at the bag.

Evalina's heart leapt into her throat when she saw a group of wild boars charge out into the road. "Watch out!"

Ben jerked his attention back to the front. She nearly got whiplash when he yanked the steering wheel to the right to avoid the animals. Her foot reflexively stomped on the floor at the same time the the tires squealed, but the car didn't stop soon enough to avoid the shoulder drop-off that brought them to a bone-jarring halt.

As the angle of the vehicle registered, she watched the seemingly synchronized group of animals shift one way, then the other, before scurrying off into the woods.

"Are you okay?" Ben asked from his side of the car.

She blinked, registering the contents of his bag dumped at her feet. "I'm fine."

"Damn. I never expected *that*."

They opened their doors at the same time. Ben got out onto the road and circled around the car. She stared down at the couple foot drop before sitting back and leaning against the head rest with her eyes closed.

*Deep breath. Relax. Maybe it's not so bad.*

"*Son of a bitch.*"

Ben's angry exclamation echoed her initial thoughts, confirming it *was* that bad.

"Eva? Are you sure you're okay?"

She opened her eyes to see he'd returned to peer at her

through the driver's side door. "I'm fine," she snapped. "Much better than my car from the sound of it."

Concern vanished as his lips compressed at her annoyed tone. She didn't care. They'd just lost their only transportation in the middle of nowhere. After slamming her door, she climbed across the seat to exit on his side.

Reaching to brace her hand on the door, she saw him extend his to help her out. Last thing she wanted was his hand engulfing hers, but he was too quick to give her a choice. The moment his skin touched hers, she grit her teeth against that hot, ever-present awareness that flared to life. He released her before she could pull free, suggesting she wasn't the only one affected. Didn't matter. *That* road was not getting traveled again.

After a walk around the vehicle, she drew the same conclusion as Ben. The front right end of the car dipped down into the ditch while the back left sat up in the air, a good six inches off the ground. If she reached over and kicked the back wheel, it would spin free and clear. She gave a brisk rub of her bare arms, chilled in the cooler mountain air.

*Mannaggia. Siamo fregati.* Totally screwed. He knew it and she knew it, but standing there staring at the teetering vehicle, she still found herself asking, "Could you use a tree branch to leverage the front wheel up? If we could get some traction in the back…"

Derision added to his laugh made it much less attractive than earlier.

Ben opened the back door and reached into the car to toss out their bags. "I appreciate that you think I'm that strong, but really, I'm not Mr. Incredible."

She didn't have to actually know who Mr. Incredible was to get his point, the jerk. "Believe me, I'd never go that far. The most important word was leverage."

"It would take a *tree* to move that car. I can't lift that either, but if you want to give it a shot, by all means, leverage away."

His junk food and their jackets joined the overnight bags on the road before he shut the door.

Annoyed with his sarcasm, she bent to pick up her stuff. "So much for getting there in one piece. You should've just hit the damn pigs."

"You're the one who yelled *watch out*."

"You're the one who was worried about a stupid bag of chips," she shot back.

Taking a knee on the road, he made a show of packing the snacks and water in his leather bag, one by one. Just to piss her off, she imagined. She looked down at her duffle and realized she'd been moving on autopilot.

"What are you doing, by the way?" she asked.

He rose and lifted his bag to settle the strap diagonal over his head and across his chest. With his jacket fisted in one hand, he turned to face her as she put hers on. "Which way to the nearest town? Forward or back?"

They hadn't passed a town in forty-five minutes. Or even another vehicle for that matter. Heading back to the last rural community on foot would waste hours of time they didn't have.

"Neither. I'll call headquarters and see if they can send a car from the local *Municipale* or the *Carabinieri*."

He shook his head before she even finished speaking.

"You'd rather walk?" she challenged.

"Hell yes, I'd rather walk. We still don't know how those guys knew I was at the hotel. I really don't want to paint a target on my back and then call in the location."

Frustration tightened her fingers on the handle of her bag. He was right, damn it. They had to keep moving. If they were lucky, a car would come along and offer a ride. But until then, walking appeared their only option.

She pulled out her phone to check what would be their best route. The app showed their location with a little flashing red dot. As she stared at the map, she got a sinking sensation in her stomach. Using her finger, she moved the screen left, up, down, then back right.

Dismay mushroomed. *That can't be right.*

"Well?"

The impatience edging Ben's voice made her cringe. "Ah...I think we took a wrong turn a little ways back."

His arm snaked out to nab the phone from her hand before she realized his intention. She didn't bother to try to take it back and watched him scrutinize the display, resigned to what was coming. He maneuvered the map the same as she had, only slower, taking in every detail.

"*A little ways back?*" His gaze rose to hers. Blue took on a steely overcast, though his voice remained ominously quiet. "It's been fifteen miles. When do you think it might have dawned on you we were going the wrong way? Maybe after the next five miles, when the road *dead ends?*"

She swallowed hard and held his gaze with grim determination. Steely overcast became roiling storm clouds.

"Blame it on the chips if it makes you feel better. But this little screw up could cost us everything."

## Chapter 16

EVERYTHING FOR BEN was a hell of a lot more than a Bible or a diary. His mother's life was at stake—and possibly his sister's. Anger boiled his blood, but it wasn't solely directed at Eva. Yes, she'd royally screwed up the navigation, but he should've been paying closer attention instead of obsessing over the fact that she remembered those pastries he liked and then bought some for him.

They were nothing more than sweetened croissants, and he was thirty-one years old, for crissakes, not some virgin twelve year old with his first crush.

He wanted to smash the phone against the boulder he'd just narrowly missed with the car before landing in the ditch. Definitely his fault, not hers.

Once the urge to vent his aggravation with violence passed, he extended the cell to her with precise control. She took it, holding his gaze, remorse darkening her eyes. Yet, completely contradicting the emotion was an edge of defiance in the challenging tilt of her chin.

She didn't shirk from accepting her share of responsibility, but she also didn't apologize. He'd like to say not surprising, considering her track record, but guessed it had more to do with her recognition that the blame was not all hers to shoulder. The first realization piled on the guilt for his unfair accusation. Her failure to voice a simple "I'm sorry" reawakened emotions from nine months ago and pissed him off all over again.

He backed away a few steps before swinging around to start hiking up the mountain road, as much to get moving as to avoid the apology forming on *his* lips. To hell with going backwards. She owed him, not the other way around.

"Really?" she called after him. "You're choosing that way?"

"I don't look back, Eva."

"Oh, right, because a dead end is so much better."

He stopped and leaned his head back, eyes closed. After a deep breath he turned to face her. She stood by the car, arms crossed, hip jutting out at a belligerent angle. The afternoon sunlight glinted off her long, ebony curls and bathed her beautiful face as if God was trying to say *"Behold what I have made."*

His gut clenched and his pulse sped up. Good Lord, he was losing it.

Forcing himself to think rationally, he pointed in the direction they'd come from. "That way is fifteen miles of backtracking just to get to where we should've turned in the first place. Then it's another almost twenty miles to the nearest town."

He pointed behind him. "This way might be a dead end, but according to your map, once we reach that end, if we head due south approximately five more miles, we should come to a road that actually leads somewhere. Who knows, we might even be able to hitch a ride."

Extending both arms from his sides, palms up, he started backing up and finished with, "Feel free to backtrack if you want, or call your boss and sit here for all I care, *I'm* going this way."

He turned and kept walking, not bothering to wait for her decision. Didn't have to. If logic didn't work, she'd follow if for no other reason than she needed him to get that fucking diary. He did, however, shorten his stride the slightest bit so she'd be able to catch up.

When she drew even with him almost ten minutes later, he was still working on his anger when she shocked him with a quiet, "I'm sorry. I know you're worried about your fam—"

"Don't," he cut her off. He couldn't think of his family at the moment. He allowed a quick glance down and over, but returned his attention to the road as he admitted, "It wasn't only your fault."

She shrugged beside him, and they kept walking.

With each step they took together, he felt his resentment toward her fading. It'd been a long twenty-four hours, and the next twenty-four had no chance of being any shorter. He wasn't one hundred percent sure about everything going on, but he didn't believe she'd put his family in danger by giving him wrong directions on purpose.

"I texted Antonio," she said after a few minutes. "I advised him we are delayed until tomorrow."

Ben tensed. "You tell him where we are?"

"No. You made it clear you don't trust him."

He heard the resentment in her voice now, but didn't bother to deny her statement. It was true. "He doesn't trust me, either."

The look she tossed him said he shouldn't be surprised. And he wasn't surprised, just disappointed. Because she clearly agreed with her partner.

"So, have you two been working together since last July?"

"Since yesterday morning."

He turned his upper body, dipped a shoulder, and got a good look at her face. "*Real*-ly? Just for me?"

"Unfortunately."

"Careful. I might take that personally."

"Take it however you want. My point is..." She trailed off and her step faltered. When he paused, too, she moved forward with a look of renewed determination. "I've been working alone since Nino."

Ah, there was a name he'd managed to forget for awhile. *Nino Da Via.* Her previous partner who'd shot him, but the bullet had really been intended for Eva. After being betrayed by the one person who was supposed to have had her back, did she now find it difficult to put any faith in Antonio? An agent who'd also lied to her on that past case?

Before he could figure out a tactful way to ask, she said, "I was supposed to begin a two week vacation yesterday."

The quick change of subject made him wonder why she'd mentioned her dead partner if she didn't want to talk about him. But he went with it.

"Talk about bad timing. Where you going somewhere fun?"

"No. It wasn't really my choice to take the time off."

"Ah. Well, then this has got to be better than laundry, right?"

From the corner of his eye, he saw her smile. "Of course. Getting shot at has always ranked above laundry in my book."

The exchange reminded him of his thoughts upon first landing in the country. *The prospect of being trapped in Italy rated just above getting shot and well below a root canal.* Ironic he'd actually thought that, yet here he was, pretty much trapped in the country. It was not a good sign that a somewhat civil conversation with her now was totally changing his perspective.

They started up around the curve of another switchback. He glanced back at how far they'd gone. A flash of sunlight glinting off something below them caught his eye, further down from where they'd left her car. When he paused to search for the source, Evalina stopped alongside him.

"What is it?"

He pointed downhill as the glimmer of a vehicle became visible through the trees. "Think that could be a ride?"

"If we're lucky."

Her serious tone had him lowering his voice. "And if we're not?"

"We will both be very grateful you insisted on walking."

She tugged on his arm, pulling him into a squat so they could watch through the trees as the vehicle approached her car. It came to a stop and two men got out cautiously, arms extended, weapons in hand. Ben instinctively ducked further as he met Evalina's grim gaze.

*Not lucky.*

While one of the men stood watch, the other checked everything around and inside the marooned car. Then they conversed a few minutes and got back in their vehicle. When the car continued up the mountain instead of turning around, he and Evalina moved as one for cover.

A quick scan of their surroundings located a heavily camouflaged outcropping a good fifty yards off the road. He pointed it out and she nodded. It was impossible for the men in the vehicle to hear them, but the approaching danger seemed to require silence. Evalina motioned for Ben to go first. His instinct was to insist he protect her back, but when she drew her gun, he knew he'd be wasting his breath. She handled the men with guns.

Evalina followed his lead until they were behind the thick foliage, completely concealed from the road, yet with a vantage point that let them see their pursuers through the leaves. They'd set their bags aside and now she crouched to his right, shoulder braced against a tree trunk.

"Cover your shirt," he warned.

The sun reflected off the shimmery pink material and after a downward glance, she quickly zipped her black jacket. "*Grazie.*"

As they both settled into their hiding spot, the rustle of leaves and dry branches quieted. He absently fiddled with a twig while cataloging the wind in the trees above their heads and the melodic songs of birds as they flitted from branch to branch. In the distance, it sounded like a squirrel chattered, until the rumble of the engine drowned out the other sounds.

The car cruised past, giving them a brief glimpse of the two dark-haired men inside. Little snaps turned the twig in his hand into multiple pieces.

"Recognize either of them?" Evalina whispered, taking pictures with her phone before they disappeared.

"The passenger could be the guy from the hotel. I didn't get a good enough look."

"You'll get another chance in a few minutes."

The engine noise faded and sounds of the wilderness became

audible once more. Sunlight filtering through overhead branches created a dappled effect on the forest floor and the bushes surrounding them. During the wait for the vehicle's inevitable return, Ben spotted a small lizard on the sunny side of the tree Evalina braced a hand against. When she turned her head, the reptile scurried up the trunk, past her fingers. Her surprised squeak was cut short when she jerked back and landed on her butt.

After a moment of disbelief, his laughter escaped as a smothered snort. "What was *that*?"

She glared at him, but he couldn't stop grinning as he stretched out a hand to help her up. A shudder shook her shoulders. Her wary gaze searched the tree where the reptile had been.

Ben shook his head. "A man twice your size points a gun at you and you don't flinch. A little lizard crawls past and you freak."

"They're creepy."

"So are guys who want to kill you."

His smile remained until the drone of the engine alerted them to the return of their unwanted visitors. Evalina got her phone ready for more pictures and this time he caught a clear view of the passenger.

"I'm pretty sure it's the same guy from the hotel." Forearm braced on his knee, Ben flipped another little branch between his fingers as he watched the sedan head back down the mountain. "How do you think they found us this time?"

She scrolled through the photos on her phone as she answered. "I don't know. They could've followed us from the hotel, but then why not come after us at my apartment?"

"Good point." He dropped his gaze and deliberately broke the twig in half. "Have you been in touch with anyone where you work? Text, or email?"

"Only Antonio. And he only knows we were going to meet him in Rome and were delayed. Even if he relayed that to…"

When she didn't finish, he glanced over to see her staring down the mountain, her forehead furrowed.

"To...?"

"It's my car." She muttered a few words in Italian that needed no translation. "It's my personal vehicle, but it was equipped with GPS tracking for a previous undercover assignment."

Now that made sense. "Who can access that?"

"Only someone within the *Polizia de Stato*, or possibly Interpol," she stated, her voice flat.

Her expression hardened. He hated being right about there being an inside source, but at least they knew for sure. Which didn't necessarily rule out Antonio, either. Her face told him he didn't need to point that out.

The dark sedan had reached her vehicle again. After a moment of watching the driver maneuver his car into position, Ben realized they were going to pull it from the ditch.

"Why would they do that?"

"Maybe to lure us back so they can keep tracking us."

Another thought occurred to him and he cast a pointed glance at her hand. "Is that your personal cell?"

Realization dawned in her eyes and she flipped it over and removed the battery. Slipping it and the phone into a pocket on her duffle bag, she explained, "Without the battery, they're untraceable. You should do the same."

"Can they track mine?"

Her dark eyebrows arched skyward. "Do you want to find out?"

"Not particularly."

He checked to see if any messages had come in from either of his sisters or his mom, but found nothing beyond a spam text and his buddy Jim confirming the time and place for his bachelor party in two weeks. The message read a bit surreal given his current situation. Copying Evalina's actions, he slipped the separated phone and battery back into his bag and turned his attention back downhill.

Once her car had four wheels back on solid ground, the two men stowed their gear and drove out of sight.

"They aren't going far, I guarantee it."

Ben tossed the pieces of twig to the ground and reached over to grab their stuff before rising to his feet. "Time to start walking."

## Chapter 17

THE LATE AFTERNOON shadows stretched far to Evalina's left. They'd been walking for hours through the rough, wooded mountain terrain. They had talked at first, but by the third time he'd referenced one of his sisters, eventually they both fell silent again. The importance of his family was making it harder for her to keep her own painful memories tucked safely away.

On top of that, now she was beyond tired and felt every stick and stone through the fashionable soles of her leather boots as if she were barefoot. As comfortable as they'd been on the city sidewalks in *Milano*, they hadn't been intended for rugged, cross-country hiking. Ben kept a brisk pace, glancing back every so often to check her progress. She didn't complain about her fatigue or her sore feet as he moved further and further ahead. If she'd have had a good night's sleep and proper footwear, *she'd* be leading the way.

"Hey, check this out," he called back, not sounding the least bit winded.

When she caught up, he handed her his bottle of water before pointing through a break in the trees, across a shallow valley to the other mountainside.

"There's a tower over there."

Indeed there was. Tall and square, the gray structure had probably been standing strong against the elements for hundreds of years.

"If we head that way, we'd have shelter for the night," he suggested.

After taking a drink and handing the bottle back, she squinted through the trees at the setting sun. Once it was gone, they'd lose their light for navigation. Its warmth had already dissipated, and she shivered inside her lightweight jacket.

"Think we can make it before dark?"

"It'll be close."

She drew in a fortifying breath and squared her shoulders. "Then let's move."

He started forward, then stopped and retraced his steps to stand in front of her. "Gimmie your bag."

His fingers closed around the strap and he began to lift it over her head. Automatic protest brought her hands to his, but the warmth of his skin under her cold fingers startled her. His gaze widened, then dropped to their hands as he turned his over to grasp hers. Refusal died on her lips when his eyes met hers. Tension flared between them in a single, electrified heartbeat.

She twisted her hands free of his and ducked to remove the bag. "*Grazie.*"

He muttered under his breath as she walked away. When his heavier footsteps sounded behind her, she kept going with determined strides.

"You want my jacket?"

"I have my own."

He didn't offer again. They descended into the valley and started up the opposite side. The sun hung suspended above the next mountain over for those last few moments before it dipped below the peak. She could no longer see the tower above the trees, and after twenty minutes, she began to worry they'd veered off course in the increasing twilight.

"Hold up," he said behind her. "I think there's an old trail here."

She backtracked the few meters to where he squatted, forearm braced on one knee while his other hand swept the ground she'd tramped over. Faint parallel ruts appeared to be worn into the earth diagonal to the direction she'd been walking. Though overgrown, years of travel had packed the soil so as not to allow anything more than grass, ferns and short forest undergrowth to take root. That the path was still visible through the towering trees told her it was probably hundreds of years old.

"Good catch," she acknowledged. Silently, she berated herself for yet another detail missed, even though it wasn't as big a deal as the GPS on the car. If only she'd thought to disable it before they left, they wouldn't be stuck out here right now.

Ben rose to his feet and moved ahead, taking the lead once more. He increased his stride and her efforts to maintain the same speed got her blood pumping faster. It took another half hour to reach the tower, and by then it was so dark they almost ran smack into the brush surrounding the structure. She'd been hoping for some moonlight, but the promise she glimpsed to the east had since been eclipsed by a bank of dark clouds.

She vaguely recalled rain in the forecast. Wouldn't it be their luck.

Their bags landed at her feet with a dull thud.

"You find the door and I'll get some wood for a fire," Ben directed.

"There won't be a door," she advised before he could move away. "It's a lookout tower, used years ago by soldiers to spot and signal villagers of enemy attack. The entrances were built high above the ground to avoid infiltration by enemy forces and were only reachable by ladder."

His sigh sounded in the darkness. "And what are the chances we'll find one of those laying around?"

"They used rope ladders. Which would be—"

"Rotted away after all these years. I wasn't really expecting an answer," he informed her, moving out of her limited range of vision. "We're still going to need wood."

Another survey of the moonless, starless sky had her worried they'd also need a roof over their heads before the night was over. She stretched out her hands and fought her way through the underbrush surrounding the base of the tower. Once her fingers met the rough stonework, she worked her way around the outer walls, searching from corner to corner for sections of crumbling mortar.

She heard Ben drop an armful of wood near where she assumed their bags were, then the crinkle of dried leaves told her he moved off again. On the back side of the tower, she fought though a particularly thick area of brush to reach the far corner.

"What are you doing?"

His voice directly behind her made her jump about a foot and sent her pulse racing. She hadn't heard him with the rustling of branches and snapping of twigs under her own feet. Hopefully he hadn't noticed her startle. That'd be great after her embarrassing incident with the lizard.

"I'm looking for a way inside. Those are some dark clouds rolling in."

"You said there were no doors down here."

"I'm looking for loose stones."

"You're going to break through the wall?" Surprise rang in his voice. "This thing has to be hundreds of years old, wouldn't that be destroying a national monument or something?"

"I'm not planning to tear the whole thing down, just enough to get us inside," she retorted. "It can be repaired."

She found a small indent in the space between the rock bricks and dug with her fingers. A shower of weathered, crumbled pieces of mortar cascaded down onto her feet. When she applied some force, one of the stones on the corner gave about an inch.

"Right here. This one's loose."

Suddenly, his warm, solid chest pressed up against her back. She sucked in a breath, and held it in her constricted lungs as his fingers brushed against hers on the wall. His palm swept the surface, searching in the wrong direction. She grabbed his hand and placed it on the loose stone as she dared to breathe once more. The enticing combination of warm male and the earthy smells of the forest went straight to her head.

For a weak moment, she left her hand covering his and leaned back against his unyielding form, allowing the contact to freshen the memory of how his hard, naked body felt against her softer curves. It warmed her all the way through, and an anticipatory heaviness settled low in her belly.

"I feel it too."

He'd dipped his chin so the husky words were spoken right next to her ear. It took a moment to realize he was talking about the wall, not the heady sensations swirling through her body. His hand slid down to test another, and hers rode along.

"This one, too," he added.

"Do you think you can break through the wall?" she asked, her own voice now breathless.

His breath stirred her hair and tickled her ear. "I'm going to give it one hell of a shot."

Something had changed in his tone. His low voice carried a strange undercurrent that made her wonder if he was talking about more than the physical barrier in front of them. Desire began to pulse through her, moving beyond a manageable simmer. Taking a deep breath, she forced herself to pull her hand away while side-stepping from the heated half-circle of his arm.

His stance, hand braced on the wall, head bowed, reminded her of inside the stairwell at the hotel. Right after he'd almost kissed her. Her heart jerked, and she quickly turned away.

"Good. But only enough for us to get inside."

She left to retrieve the wood he'd gathered and bring it over to the opening, then went out into the dark to find more. When she returned, she discovered he'd had some success once he used a larger chunk of wood to ram the first stone free. A couple others fell. With a little more work, he had a hole in the wall big enough to fit through and disappeared inside. On her third trip back, light flickered through the opening.

Stepping past the displaced stones, she climbed inside to see their accommodations for the night. Ben glanced up from clearing the ground on one side of the fire and straightened to extend his arms.

"It's not the Armani, but we'll be dry. And not a lizard in sight."

It was dusty, and dirty, and musty-smelling, and probably full of spiders and tons of lizards they couldn't see. But she suppressed a reactive shudder because he was right, it would keep them dry. And hopefully hold some heat. She held out her hands toward the bright flames, noting he'd built the fire below and slightly to the side of a square hole in the stone floor of the level above their heads.

"How did you start this so fast? Do you have matches?"

"No, but there are a few things left over from my childhood that come in handy."

"Meaning?"

"I know how to start a fire without matches."

He turned away and went back to work. Clearly that's all he intended to share on that subject.

She ducked back outside to retrieve their bags. Dampness had crept in on a cool wind, swaying the tree tops overhead and blowing leaves at her feet. Ben met her at the opening and tossed their bags onto the cleared area. Then she passed the dry wood inside and he stacked it off to one side until he deemed they had enough for the night.

Relieved to finally stop moving once she was back inside, Evalina thought about collapsing on the ground and going to sleep. Training and tenacity kept her on her feet. Ben brushed past, removed his jacket, and spread it on the floor near the fire in front of their bags. Then he lowered himself to the ground *next* to it and dragged his bag to his side.

"You don't have to—"

"Just sit," he ordered without looking up. "If I'm tired, you've got to be exhausted, so just sit."

Too drained to argue, she sat on his jacket as he began removing food from his bag and placed the bottle of water between them. She hesitated, then unfastened her holster to place it and her weapon next to her duffle. The likelihood of anyone being able to locate them now was slim to none. Even her gut had relaxed over the past couple hours.

Once everything was laid out, Ben asked, "See anything you'd like for dinner?"

"Not really." She gave a weary smile and picked two items anyway. "These will do. *Grazie*."

"*Prego*." The corners of his mouth quirked when she tossed him a surprised look. "I've learned a few words, just not enough to buy groceries. What do you suggest for me?"

She handed over the package of *tarallini*, and *bauli cornetti alla crema*, a mass-produced version of the earlier fresh *cornetti* he'd devoured earlier. As they began to eat, the packaging crinkled, the fire popped and snapped every so often, and water sloshed in the bottle whenever they took a drink.

"I was thinking as we were walking," he said suddenly. "Do you know who killed Dante Fedorio?"

Shaking her head, she admitted, "That's a question I would've asked you during questioning."

"I just met him yesterday. He seemed like a nice man."

"All I know is what was in the briefing file I received Monday morning. The investigation has focused more on his cousin Este, but because of his position in the company, Dante was not to be overlooked."

"If the diary Dante gave me contains the evidence you need, that means Este could be responsible for the murder."

"That is a definite possibility," she agreed.

He nodded, staring into the fire and the silence lengthened. She remained quiet as well, too tired to think about the situation right now anyway. Instead, she was simply thankful that the stone walls around them blocked the wind, and the fire warmed their shelter enough to chase away the damp chill that had triggered her earlier shivers.

Ben finished eating, tossed his trash into the flames, and then got up to add a couple more pieces of wood to the fire. When he sat back down, he arranged his bag as a pillow before stretching out on his back, hands linked across his stomach. *Great idea.* She disposed of her garbage, trying not to think of her soft bed at home as she shifted on the hard ground.

While unzipping her boots, she snuck a glance over her shoulder at him. Other than that brief conversation a few minutes ago, he'd been so quiet, it made her wonder what he was thinking about. Only the second she wondered, she knew, and felt a rush of guilt as she set her boots aside.

"I'm sorry we're stuck here when we should be in Rome already. You must be worried about your family."

When he didn't reply, she twisted to see if maybe he'd fallen asleep already and found him watching her though slitted eyes. She avoided meeting his gaze by facing the fire again and absently began rubbing her aching feet.

"There's nothing I can do about where we are, so I'm trying not to think about it," he admitted.

A lump formed in her throat at the bleak emotion that seeped into his low voice. It was clear his family was everything to him, and she understood that particular method of dealing with issues. Pretty much lived her life that way. Running. Avoiding. His situation was different than hers, but the concept was the same. The survival tactic had kept her going since she was fourteen and lost both her parents less than a month apart. One to cancer, the other in the line of duty to that murderous bastard Alrigo Lapaglia.

Only the thing with running, she was discovering, is eventually you ran out of places to hide. Used to be, when ghosts of the past surfaced, she would banish them by refocusing on bringing her father's murderer to justice. Now that the man was dead, she had nowhere to run to escape the relentless thoughts clamoring for attention.

Like today, when that memory of her family ambushed her. And then she'd mentioned Nino to Ben—had felt the urge to explain to him she didn't think she'd ever be able to trust another partner, and she was worried about how that would affect her career. Her job was her whole life; without it, who was she?

She hadn't been able to voice that concern to a licensed psychiatrist, so why this man, of all people? The almost compulsive need to tell him long buried fears left her feeling vulnerable and exposed, as if she might take one wrong step and her whole brittle world would come crashing down around her.

Ben sat up beside her, any signs of restfulness vanished. His knee brushed hers, sparking a zing of electricity along her nerve endings that put her even more on edge before he shifted away.

He reached to pick up a twig and started breaking little pieces off to toss them into the fire. "So…to help me not think about it, how about you tell me about your family."

The suggestion caught her off guard. Her startled look had him arching his eyebrows as he reasoned, "You do know all about mine."

Cursing herself for having brought up family at all, she briefly considered distraction. Of monumental proportions. The attraction between them was undeniable, and if she made the first move…

*No.* She couldn't use him like that again. Even though—if she was being completely honest with herself—the mere prospect of distracting him *that way* made her pulse pick up speed.

"My parents are both dead," she stated bluntly, hoping to deter further questions and keep herself from moving forward with the completely self-destructive idea she'd just vetoed.

"Sorry," he murmured.

She shrugged and turned to arrange her makeshift bed for the night. She wouldn't even have to feign being tired.

"What about your sister?"

Her gaze jerked to his. "How'd you—"

"The villa, remember? Nine months ago you told me you have a sister."

She had. Because even then he'd been able to get under her defenses and convince her to reveal personal information that was better left unspoken. The irrational urge to get up and run nearly overwhelmed her, but in the next instant, she took a breath and the words poured out. "Her name is Carina. She's twenty-four and manages a flower shop in Rome."

"That's convenient." Completely unaware of her inner turmoil, he threw the rest of the stick into the fire before dipping his head to look at her. "You'll get to see her before you head back to Milan, right?"

She began to nod, as he would expect, but then to her horror, tears welled in her eyes.

## Chapter 18

EVALINA QUICKLY DUCKED, but not before Ben saw her tears. "What'd I say?"

She shook her head, lifting a hand to wipe her cheeks. Those whiskey colored eyes met his, only to fill up again. Dismay twisted her expression and she shot to her feet. His stomach clenched as he watched her cross to the opening in the wall, thinking she was going to leave. Wondering if he should follow.

When she simply stood there, back to him, hands lifted to her face once more, he rose and brushed the dust from his jeans and hands.

"I haven't seen Carina in almost five years."

Slow steps brought him to her side. Close enough to touch, and God knew he wanted to reach out, but he kept his hands to himself. She'd already pulled away from him twice today.

"Why so long?"

Her slim shoulders lifted in a shrug before she angled toward him and leaned a shoulder against the wall next to the opening. Shadows darkened one side of her face, but the side closest to the fire revealed she'd wiped all trace of tears away and regained her composure.

"She wants nothing to do with me," she said, her voice flat.

"When she found out I was going after Lapaglia, she told me if I did, she never wanted to see me again."

"That seems a little harsh when you were just doing your job."

"She was afraid he'd find out who I was and kill me. Like he did our father."

*Whoa, what?* "Alrigo Lapaglia killed your father?"

She nodded. "He was a cop, undercover, just like me."

Dumbfounded, Ben turned and sank down on the edge of the tower opening. He leaned his back against the wall, drawing up one knee for balance. He'd had no clue of her personal connection in that case.

"He is why I am who I am today." Her soft voice contained a wealth of choked emotion.

"That explains a lot about what happened at the villa," Ben said. "Even after finding out you were undercover, I never understood why you and Nino let things go as far as they did. Well, no, I understood Nino..."

The naked anguish in her eyes hit hard, her torment stabbing into his chest like a knife.

"I'd been chasing Lapaglia for three years. Spent endless months imbedded in that *bastardo's* organization, dealing with him and his men every single day."

Her eyes closed, and the ache in his chest intensified at the thought of what she could be reliving. When she opened them again, they glittered with desperate determination.

"There was a shipment of animals due that was going to give us enough to lock up our case and put him behind bars for the rest of his life. We were so close. When he brought you and your sister in, I didn't know what to do. Between Nino's insistence we needed the evidence on Halli's video, and the chance to avenge my father *right there* within my grasp..."

"Eva. Relax, it's okay," he assured her, wanting to ease her obvious distress. "We were strangers, and you had a job to do. You didn't owe us anything."

She turned away, but then swung back, her eyebrows drawn

together in a fierce frown. "My job is to serve and protect, and my father was already dead. I should've done more to help you and Rachel instead of putting you in even more danger."

His heart stuttered, then pounded hard. Somehow he managed a dismissive shrug. "It's in the past. We all made it out okay, and your father's killer got the justice he deserved."

She didn't like that answer—her frown remained as she seemed to weigh his words; her eyes narrowed in consideration. "What's done is done?"

"Yeah. Something like that." The first splat of raindrops on leaves sounded, drawing his attention to the darkness outside the tower. Now, if only he could get himself to heed that motto and move on from her.

"Is that another thing that comes in, how do you say—*handy*—from your childhood?"

He swiveled his head back at the odd note in her voice. "I don't understand what you're asking."

"You said you don't look back."

"I don't," he lied. Because clearly, he hadn't been able to forget about her.

"Is that a lesson learned from your parents when they stole from other people? Is that how they taught *you* to deal with your conscience?"

Her accent had gotten much thicker, and while he recognized she was purposely goading him, he still stiffened at her words. The realization that they were the truth sucked the air from his lungs, and he pushed away from the wall.

"How'd my parents get dragged into this?"

"You wanted to talk about family. Let us talk."

"No. I don't know what your problem is, but *my* conscience isn't the one that seems to be having a problem right now."

When he moved to brush past her, she grabbed his arm, her fingers gripping his bicep like a vice. The restraint snapped his tenuous control and he rounded on her. Grasping her shoulders, he backed her against the wall. Confusion surfaced when she offered no resistance. He knew from experience she could lay him out flat in one move if she wanted. So what was her game?

Hands flattened against his chest, she lifted her face to his. He swallowed hard at what he saw. Earlier she'd turned away from him. Now the heat in her gaze was pure invitation.

Closing his eyes against the temptation did nothing to stop latent desire from rising up to engulf him. Things had been explosive between them in the past. He discovered nothing had changed when his body hardened in response.

Desperation tightened his grasp. "What do you want from me?"

Her fingers curled into his shirt, nails scraping his chest through the silk material. "I don't know," she whispered.

Opening his eyes, he locked his gaze with hers and was surprised to see there was some truth to her words. Uncertainty was mixed with an intense hunger that matched his. Shallow breaths feathered his chin, raising his response level past rational thought.

He slid his hands up to frame her face and lowered his head. "Is it this?"

Giving her no chance to answer, he covered her mouth with his. He swept his tongue inside and there was nothing tentative about his possession or her response. She tasted better than he remembered; a unique blend of sweet and spice that could never be replicated.

Breaking the kiss, he rasped, "Tell me, Eva. Is that what you want?"

"Yes," she breathed.

"And what about this?" He dipped down for another kiss. As their tongues met and tangled with each other, he slid his hands along her spine, cupped her butt, and lifted her against his erection. She grasped his shoulders, grinding her hips against his with a sexy purr of pleasure that sent tingles along his spine.

Inhaling the exotic scent of her skin layered with the outdoor freshness of their hike through the woods, he kissed and licked and sucked his way from her mouth to that sensitive spot at the base of her throat.

"Tell me," he demanded.

She showed him by raising her legs to wrap them around his waist. He ignored the bite of pain from the bandaged cut on his side. With her back braced against the wall, she moved her hips up and down against his. The thought of her in that position without clothes between them nearly undid him. Uttering a low groan, he halted her movements and forced her to look him in the eye.

"Tell me what you want."

"I want you."

His heart kicked hard. "Are you sure? Because I don't think I'm going to be able to ask again."

A beat of hesitation put a vice grip on his chest. If she changed her mind—

"*Sì*. I want you kissing me. Touching me. Inside me."

Those words in her voice were the sexiest thing he'd ever heard.

"*Ti voglio dentro di me*. Right here, Ben. Now. No thinking, just feeling."

And that's just what he did—stopped thinking and concentrated on the feel of her smooth skin as he set her back on her feet and stripped off first her jacket, then that shimmery pink top that had clung to her full breasts all day. He cupped the creamy globes through her black, lacy bra and devoured the sight before him. Her nipples were hard, thrusting out, begging for his attention. The first swipe of his thumbs over them elicited a breathy moan that made his groin throb.

He massaged her breasts, then he rubbed his flat palms in circles over her nipples, loving how the hard tips tickled his skin. When he pinched them, she gasped and her hips jerked against his. He repeated the process until she made an impatient sound and reached behind her back. In seconds, her bare flesh was his for the taking.

When he lifted her, she wrapped her legs around his hips once more. Her breasts filled his hands, and he angled his body to allow the fire to bathe them in soft light before lowering his head. He worshiped one side, then the other, until the insistent movement of her hips made it imperative he set her back on her feet and shift his attention.

He swept his splayed hands up her bare back and buried his fingers in her hair to dive into another wild kiss that was a heady tangle of tongues and teeth. A particularly sharp nip on his lip made him wince until she sucked it into her mouth and laved with her tongue. He returned the favor as she went to work on his shirt.

The moment the buttons were done with, he helped her strip it off and tossed it aside while barely coming up for air. He guessed the shirt hadn't even hit the ground before her hands tugged at his jeans. For a brief moment, he saw her gaze linger on the bullet scar on his chest, but she quickly moved on. The button of his jeans popped free, zipper slid down, and she slipped her hands inside the back waistband of both his pants and boxer briefs.

Hot damn, she was eager.

His buttocks tightened when she dug in with her nails before pushing everything down. She broke the kiss to trail her lips over his chest and lower. Those full breasts brushed his erection when her tongue circled his navel. Her mouth continued its downward descent until she kneeled before him.

His heart lodged in his throat at the thought of her taking him in her mouth. When she did, he nearly came right then. He couldn't control the involuntary clench of his fingers in her hair as he fought not to thrust deeper. She swirled her tongue around the tip of his shaft, took him in all the way to her throat, and then pulled back.

He gave a deep, guttural groan. "My God, Eva."

She did it again before rising back to her feet. He instantly missed the warmth of her mouth, but knew better was yet to come. When he would've kicked off his jeans, it dawned on him that he was still wearing his damn boots. Swearing under his breath, he bent to untie the laces.

Before he could toe them off, she commanded, "Leave

them."

He glanced up and slowly straightened at the sight of her shimmying those tight jeans and matching lacy panties over the lush curve of her hips. Having removed her boots earlier, she easily stepped free of one leg, then lifted the other to pull the material off with her hand. Turning slightly, she draped them over the edge of the opening in the tower wall, right on top her jacket.

When she backed up and boosted herself onto the now-padded ledge, he thanked his lucky stars for the perfect height of the stones.

His shuffle-step brought a grin to her kiss-swollen lips and he matched it. Without an ounce of hesitation, she spread her legs for him, and he paused with his hands on her knees. Her complete confidence in her body, in the way she opened for him was absolutely breathtaking. She was perfect in every way.

He intended to take his own turn kneeling before her, but she leaned forward, hooked a hand on the back of his neck and pulled him close for another kiss. At his murmur of protest, she whispered, "I cannot wait. I need you inside me. Now. *Adesso.*"

*Damn.* Again, he found it hard to draw a breath. Every time she commanded him, he lost another thread of his control. Add in the Italian, and he was a goner.

She scooted to the edge at the same time her hand closed around his erection, guiding him to her entrance. She was wet and ready, and as she leaned back on her hands, splayed out before him, nothing could have stopped him from pushing into her.

Heat engulfed him. Her back arched upward, and she moaned when he reached the hilt. Needing leverage, he grasped her legs behind her knees and drew her forward.

"Yes," she gasped. "Just like that. *Sì, cosi`.*"

He held perfectly still. With her head thrown back, breasts thrust toward the sky, she was a vision he knew he'd never forget.

"*Ben,*" she urged, her voice and hips begging him to move.

He squeezed his eyes shut and grit his teeth. *Fucking A—not before her.* Drawing a deep breath, he pulled out to the tip and slid back in. A couple of slow, controlled strokes like that and he was able to open his eyes again. He wanted to watch her in the firelight.

"*Di piu`,*" she urged. "More."

He complied, and her soft sounds of pleasure became more vocal. She was so damn beautiful in every way.

"Do not stop. *Per favore, do not stop. Non ti fermare.*"

He gripped her legs tighter, more than happy to obey the combination plea and command. Each harsh breath he dragged into his lungs matched her gasps, and he felt his climax building. He prayed she was close, because he couldn't hold on much longer.

"*Eva...*"

Her muscles convulsed around him, and her scream pierced the night. A few more strokes, and his own release barreled through him like a freight train until his hoarse shout echoed in the tower.

## Chapter 19

EVALINA WOKE ONCE during the night, her head pillowed on Ben's chest, his heartbeat strong and steady in her ear. A sleepy smile curved her mouth at the thought of waking him up for a second round, but they'd dressed before laying down, and she was still so tired. While not exactly physically comfortable, she was content in his arms.

The next time she opened her eyes, she was alone. Memories flooded back, stiffening her limbs even as other parts of her body tingled. Turning her head from one side to the other, she saw he wasn't inside the tower, but had draped their makeshift blanket of her jacket over her upper body and eased her duffle beneath her head.

Covering her face with her hands, she squeezed her eyes tight. Oh, God, what had she done last night? Getting him angry enough to challenge her and then pretty much begging him to take her. How was she going to face him?

Another thought occurred to her—they hadn't used protection. She knew she was healthy, could handle the embarrassment of inquiring about his health, but what if she ended up pregnant?

To her complete amazement, the prospect didn't terrify her. Even more shocking was the tiny ripple of excitement that tickled her stomach.

*Oh, dio mio.* Had she lost her damn mind?

Now grateful for his absence, she sat up with a soft groan for the soreness in every inch of her body after their hike the day before and the night on the hard ground. Judging by the pile of glowing coals in their makeshift fire pit, Ben had been gone awhile. A glance toward the opening told her it was morning. Gray, no sunshine, probably very early yet. Maybe he'd gone out to go to the bathroom? Speaking of which…

Outside, though the rain had stopped, the sky remained overcast. Dampness hung in the air, suggesting more rain to come. *Favoloso.* That should make for a fun day of hiking. She hurried through the wet forest to take care of business and returned to the relative warmth of the tower. After adding a few more pieces of wood to the fire, she changed her clothes and packed the dirty ones in her bag. She freshened up as best she could with the toiletries she'd brought, then brushed her hair before pulling it back from her face into a long ponytail.

By the time she was ready, holster secured, boots zipped and everything in between, Ben still hadn't returned. Wishing she'd saved one of yesterday's pocket coffees, she slipped on her jacket over a long-sleeved black shirt she'd packed for today and turned to eye his bag. Her gaze swept over his jacket, spread out on the floor where they'd slept. The leftover items of food and one full liter of water sat off to the side, but she still didn't see the black leather bag he'd purchased in Milano. Her gaze scanned the entire room with a sudden numbing realization.

His things were gone.

He'd left her here alone and moved on without her. Suspicion crept in, undermining the sense of peace she'd experienced in his arms in the dead of night. Was the danger to his family real, or nothing but a ruse to get the police to take him to Rome legally? If the Bible held the clues he claimed it did, was he only after the treasure? Considering his background, that possibility seemed infinitely more likely.

Betrayal left a bitter taste in her mouth. She should've known better. After her partner Nino; after the indications that Antonio might also be a traitor; she should've known better than to trust anyone.

But the truth was, she *had* trusted Ben. The man had taken a bullet for her nine months ago and given her the best sex of her life. After last night, she'd expected...

*What? What exactly did you expect?*

She knelt and began stuffing the food and water into her bag. She'd need it for her God-knew-how-long hike this morning. In truth, she didn't know what she'd expected. Like an idiot, she hadn't thought that far ahead when she'd gone for the distraction to avoid further talk about her own family. But of all the scenarios she might have imagined waking up to, this was not one of them.

*Why not? You did the same thing to him.*

Guilt stilled her movements; anger spurred her to zip her bag with emphasis. She'd been protecting herself—with good reason, from the looks of it. From now on, she was on her own.

"Hey, you're up."

Evalina jumped, barely holding in a shriek at the sound of Ben's voice directly above her.

"Sorry, I didn't mean to scare you."

Heart still thumping against her ribs, she lifted her head to find him grinning down at her from the square hole in the floor above. Immediate relief that he hadn't left was quickly replaced by alarm at how happy she was to see his face. Getting to her feet gave her a moment to corral her chaotic emotions.

"I wasn't scared, I was just surprised. I thought you..." She abruptly snapped her mouth shut when she realized the rest of her sentence was much too revealing.

"Left?" he finished for her. "No, that's your move, not mine."

Even though she deserved it, she grit her teeth against the accusation in his words. Taking a deep breath, she fisted her hands on her hips and looked up again. His head poked through the opening as he lay on his stomach.

"What are you doing up there? And how did you *get* up

there?"

"I climbed the tower outside. The old mortar gave me plenty of handholds." He extended his arm down through the hole. "Come on up, I want to show you something."

She frowned at his dangling hand. "You can't lift me up there."

"Yesterday you thought I could lift a car."

"I did not. I said—"

"Oh, come on," he interrupted. "Just gimmie your hand."

She huffed out a breath. *Fine*. Let him make a fool of himself. She reached up, but their fingers barely brushed. When even that brief contact set off flutters in her stomach, she dropped her arm back to her side.

"I told you."

He ducked his head and pointed toward the opening in the wall. "Grab one of the stone bricks. We only need a few more inches."

"Is this really necessary?" she groused on her way to get the stone.

"If you're always this crabby in the morning, maybe I should be thankful you didn't stick around the last time."

She carried the heavy stone back to drop it beneath the hole. Stepping up, she met his gaze while raising her hand. "Keep it up and I will leave again."

His gaze narrowed. Emotion flashed in his eyes too quick for her to identify, and then it was as if a steel wall slammed down. He gave her a tight smile, grasped her hand, and hauled her off her feet. She barely had a chance to gasp before he had her head and shoulders above the opening. With a quick heave to the right, he deposited her on her stomach, legs still dangling. A firm grip on the waistband of her jeans preceded a jerk and her unceremonious landing on her hands and knees.

"*On three* would have been nice," she muttered as he pushed to his feet and let her do the same on her own.

"You're up, aren't you?"

He made a few swipes at his shirt and jeans, then left her in a cloud of dust that made her sneeze. Wiping her own hands, she glared at his back as he bounded up a set of stone steps along the wall that led to the next level. The man who'd brought her such pleasure only hours ago was nowhere to be seen. In fact, he gave no indication that what they'd shared last night meant anything to him, while for her, his initial easy grin had sparked thoughts of a quiet good morning, a soft touch, a long, deep kiss...

*No.* That's not what she wanted. And even if she did—which she didn't—they had no future together. As if being from two different countries with opposite cultures wasn't enough, his suspect background and her being a cop pretty much made it impossible.

*None of which matters*, she reminded herself as she dusted off her own clothes before stomping up the ancient steps. Her best bet was to take his cue and pretend like nothing had happened. If he continued to act like a *testa di cazzo*, it should be easy.

The stairs wound around the inside walls of the tower until ending at an extremely weathered door, four stories up. Ben had forced the rusted hinges just enough for them to squeeze through to the open lookout level. That he'd been able to move it at all should've been a surprise, but after the way he'd lifted her a few minutes ago, not so much.

She paused with her hand on the door. Through the opening, she saw him standing along the outer wall, looking out at the view. The cool breeze played with his already tousled hair, and even wearing the wrinkled silk shirt he'd slept in, a second days growth of golden-hued whiskers shadowing his jaw made him just about the sexiest man she'd ever seen.

Her nipples tightened beneath her bra when she recalled how those whiskers rasped against the sensitive skin of her breasts. If she'd have let him, they'd have scraped other places, too.

Her stomach clenched with longing. Desire throbbed deep inside, and a couple deep breaths were in order before she felt confident enough to step out and face him without begging for a repeat performance.

## Chapter 20

BEN HEARD EVALINA'S footsteps and turned to lean his hip against the waist-high wall as she crossed from the door to stand a few feet away. A glance sideways trapped his breath in his chest. He tried to think about the upcoming day, but it was hard with the image in his mind of her naked, spread out before him, head thrown back in the height of passion.

*"I will leave again."*

Her blunt warning echoed in his mind, bringing him sharply back to reality. It had been an eye-opening smack upside the head when he'd intended to come down and wake her with a kiss. Considering the fanciful road his heart had started down during the night, it was critical that he remember her exact words until they parted ways for good.

She glanced over, saw him watching her, and cocked one of those dark eyebrows at him. "What was so important that you had to drag me up here when we should be gone by now?"

His jaw tightened as he shifted his attention to the mountains. See? Entirely his problem, not hers. "I came up here to try to get a signal and figure out where we—"

"We agreed we weren't going to use our phones," she accused.

"Besides seeing where the hell we are, I needed to see if I'd gotten any messages from Rachel or my mom. I was willing to take the risk."

Her expression softened. "Did they contact you?"

"I couldn't get a signal." He turned away from her unexpected empathy. "Anyway, if you look over there, there's another tower."

Evalina squinted in the direction he pointed, but the low hanging clouds had closed in, diminishing the visibility. Hopefully she could still see the outline in the distance.

"It was clearer ten minutes ago."

"I believe you. These lookout towers were triangulated around a stronghold, or set up in strategic positions so enemies could be spotted well in advance to allow for maximum preparation to fend off an attack. Warning signals were sent using smoke and mirrors."

"There's a river down that way." He indicated left of their current location.

"If it goes past the other tower, a town could be on the other side of that mountain."

"Then you agree we should go that way?" he asked. "We'll still be headed south, and it'll only be a matter of time before we reach one of the roads I saw on your map yesterday."

More confident in his ability to focus on immediate issues, he waited for her nod of agreement. Instead, she looked back at him, and the hesitant concern in her expression struck him right in the chest.

"It's still very far. You realize if we don't find a road and a ride to the nearest town we could be out here another night?"

So much for focusing on immediate issues. His mind flashed right back to his earlier vision of her and he pushed away from the wall. "That's the last thing I want, so let's get a move on."

He grabbed his bag near the door as she stepped ahead of him. He'd brought it up so he could try to decode the address from his father. After some time studying it, he was pretty sure the numbers in the address indicated the letters in the street name, but without knowledge of Rome streets to help unscramble the letters and spell the correct street, that was as far as he'd gotten.

The moment they got to Rome, finding a map was top priority. He had to beat Nick and Alisa Marshall to that Bible.

By the time he reached the last set of steps, worry for his mother and Rachel had gained dominance over thoughts of Evalina. He wasn't sure it was an improvement, but wasn't really left with any other options.

Back on the first level, she sat on the edge of the square hole, legs hanging over the edge as she prepared to jump to the ground.

"Hold on. I'll help you down."

"I am more than capable."

"Damn it, Eva. I don't doubt you can handle it, but the last thing we need is for you to twist an ankle on that stone and slow us down."

"Then you may not want to toss me like a rag doll this time."

He paused. Um, yeah, he'd been a little rough hauling her up due to his reaction to her statement about leaving again. Kneeling opposite her, he braced a hand on the side, then offered his hand as he met her eyes in the dim light. "I'm sorry."

The annoyance in her expression eased a bit, and she dropped her gaze while reaching to accept his hand. He lowered her back down with a slight swing to land her in front of the brick, then tossed his bag down and dropped to the ground after her.

Since she'd already packed their minimal provisions, he picked up his things and spread the coals around from the fire to make sure they'd die out after they departed. Outside, he restacked the stone bricks to close up the hole in the wall as best he could, and they were ready to be on their way.

"I want to keep a fast pace, so if your boots become an issue, let me know."

After an initial look of surprise, she gave a brisk nod and set out ahead of him on the old trail that had led them to their shelter the night before. As if he'd challenged her, she remained in the lead, silent and aloof except when they each picked a few more of his snacks to eat and he shared the pocket coffees he'd tucked in his bag yesterday.

The espresso infused chocolate was bitter, but the jolt of caffeine cleared his mind. Except, with her in front, it was impossible to steer his mind away from her. In fact, the more he mulled over her cool attitude this morning, the more he began to draw similarities to how she'd been last night after they'd had sex. Physically, they'd joined in the most intimate of ways, and yet if he thought about it, he felt less connected to her now than when she'd admitted to buying those damn pastries for him.

If she hadn't snuggled close shortly after falling asleep, he might have thought she was just using him. Hell, she hadn't rolled toward him until *after* she'd fallen asleep, so maybe she had used him. Exactly like the last time.

*Don't look back.*

Yeah right. But thinking about the night she'd left nine months ago, he decided it was about time he followed his own advice. After last night and this morning, no matter how much his body craved her, he needed to keep his physical distance or he'd come out of this situation much worse off than the last time. Hell, the fact that he hadn't even *thought* about protection should clue him in to the danger.

Eva, and what happened between them, had to be put into the past like everything else.

They reached the next tower just before noon. This one offered hope in that it had iron bars pounded into the mortar on one side; steps leading to the second story entrance. He knew they'd made good time, but still felt a sense of urgency that propelled him up the side of the tower after testing the rungs were secure.

"Someone uses this tower," Evalina commented as she followed.

Which meant they were that much closer to civilization. Once they reached the top level, the door opened much easier than the previous one. Ben looked back the way they'd come and spotted the tower they'd spent the night in. In the other direction, another mountain peak, only this time, no tower and no signs of a town either.

Disappointment deflated his optimism that they'd secure a vehicle anytime soon. Hands braced on the waist high wall, he hung his head for a brief moment, then straightened with determination.

"Like you said, someone visits this tower. The steps, the door, it all means we can't be too far. We'll follow the river and it should lead us to something, right? A road. A house. A town."

"I agree."

"Good." Visibility had improved some, but the clouds rolling in told him it wouldn't last. They were going to get wet soon. He wasted no time admiring the various shades of spring greens spread out before them and headed down the stairs.

At the third story, he paused when he realized Evalina wasn't behind him. Her boots sounded on the stone steps a few seconds later, and she caught up by the first level opening. He moved aside so she could climb down the iron ladder first.

Once she was on the iron rungs, and he'd squatted down for his turn, she paused, looked up, and gave him a warm smile. "*Grazie.*"

His heart knocked against his ribs. Pure reflex returned the smile, but when she lowered her gaze to begin her descent, suspicion narrowed his eyes. What the hell was that?

He waited until she was almost to the ground before starting down himself. The rasp of a zipper reached his ears seconds before his boots landed on solid ground, and then the sudden, unexpected press of her warm body against his side caught him off guard. He hung on to the metal rung near his head for balance as he twisted to face her.

She moved in close, thighs brushing his, breasts against his chest. Heat spread through him. Left hand flat just above his thumping heart, she rose up on her tiptoes as if she were going to kiss him. He knew the smart move was to listen to the alarm bells ringing in the distant recess of his mind, but resistance was futile as blood raced through his veins fast enough to make him dizzy.

Then she spoke with that sultry Italian accent that got him every time. "Do you trust me, Ben?"

Completely off-balance in the face of her stunning one-eighty, he answered without even thinking. "No."

"Then we are even."

A metallic rattle startled him and he dropped his gaze toward the sound. With speed that defied comprehension, she reached up and slapped one handcuff on his wrist, the other on the iron rung he held onto.

"What the—"

A finger pressed firmly to his lips. "Shh. Don't speak."

Those serious whiskey eyes of hers held him spellbound for a heartbeat, then she pushed away and moved out of reach. The haze of lust cleared as she disappeared around the corner of the tower. Once he got past the humiliation of having fallen for her damn seduction act yet again, frustrated anger blazed hot enough to set the forest on fire.

## Chapter 21

EVALINA DREW HER weapon as she rounded the first corner of the tower and headed for the second.

"*Eva!*"

Ben's angry bellow echoed through the woods, making her cringe. She'd known he wouldn't be happy, but just for once, she wished the man would do as he was told and *shut up*. Moving as silently as possible, she focused on her goal in hopes of still maintaining some element of surprise.

Back to the wall at the next corner, she darted a look around the stone wall, spotted her quarry, and executed a spin that planted her feet as she leveled her Beretta.

"Do not move."

The man standing by the opposite corner froze at the sound of her low command. His back was to her, but with his wavy dark hair and tall build, she had a good idea of his identity.

"Put your hands on the wall, above your head," she ordered, moving closer, gun still extended. When he complied, she stepped up behind him, braced her gun muzzle against the middle of his back and nudged his legs apart. "You even think about moving and I *will* shoot you."

He remained silent and still while she patted him down and

confiscated a nine millimeter Glock. She did a quick one hand check to see it was loaded before securing it in the back waistband of her jeans. The cell phone in his jacket pocket she transferred to hers.

More shouting came from the other side of the tower. The guy turned his head slightly and one glimpse confirmed her first suspicion.

"Someone's not happy with you," he said, a hint of a smirk on his lips.

"*Sì*. Story of my life with that one." Satisfied he wasn't carrying any more weapons, Evalina backed up. "Now turn around, Nicholas Marshall. Nice and slow."

He faced her, surprise evident in his green eyes. "You know who I am?"

"I am *Polizia di Stato*. After that stunt you and your sister pulled in Milan, of course I know who you are." She jerked her head to the side. "Move. Ben will want to speak with you."

Ben's cursing came to an abrupt halt when Marshall walked into view. She followed, and he immediately turned his furious gaze on her.

"You ever fucking handcuff me again, woman, and I'll—"

"What?" she challenged. Withdrawing the handcuff key from her pocket, she then propped her hand on her hip and raised her eyebrows. "What will you do, Benjamin?"

This time, he wisely shut up until she tossed him the key. Catching it one-handed, he totally ignored their uninvited guest and turned to work the locks around his wrists. "Why the hell did you do this?"

"To keep you out of the way."

The moment he'd freed himself, he rounded on her. "I could've helped."

"Exactly what I did not want."

His frown deepened. "Because you don't trust me?"

"That, and you have a propensity to play hero." Nice in a romantic novel, but not always so much in real life.

"If you'd have told me what you were doing—"

"I didn't have time. You'd have argued and followed me and—" She lifted a hand when he started to shake his head. "—*yes*, you would have, and you know it."

"I'd be happy to leave you two alone if you'd like," Nick Marshall offered.

While sliding the handcuffs and key into his jacket pocket, Ben's jaw visibly clenched as he leveled his gaze on the man. When Evalina added her own glare, Marshall's humor vanished and he held up his hands in silent surrender.

"Where's your sister?" Ben asked.

His gaze held Ben's. "Don't worry about her."

"*You* should worry about her a little more instead of letting her attempt to seduce men she's just met."

The accusation clearly struck a nerve, but Marshall didn't respond.

"How'd you even find us?"

The guy shifted his gaze between the two of them. Evalina went on alert. She stepped closer, weapon raised from where she'd relaxed it by her side. When she'd spotted him from the top of the tower, he'd been alone, but that didn't mean his sister wasn't around. Possibly armed as he had been.

"Where is Alisa?" she asked. He still didn't reply and his continued silence tweaked her annoyance. "You can answer us here, *signore*, or I can arrest you and you can think it over in a jail cell. I have an entire list of charges. Robbery. Illegal concealment of a loaded firearm. Assault with a deadly weapon. Stalking—"

"Hey, whoa, hold on. I didn't assault anyone."

"You cut me when you stole my bag," Ben reminded.

"It was barely a scratch," Marshall scoffed.

"You arrogant sonofabitch."

Ben rushed the guy, grabbed his jacket near his neck, and slammed him back against the wall of the tower. Marshall fought back and the two wrestled for control until he twisted out from under Ben's hold and shoved free. When Ben would've gone in for round two, Evalina rushed between them. She pressed the barrel of her gun into Marshall's chest while holding Ben back with her other hand.

"Basta! Stop! *Vi state comportando come bambini.*" Her gaze drilled into Marshall's wary green eyes. "Where is your sister?"

With the gun poking into his chest, he didn't hesitate too long. "She's in Rome."

"Looking for the Bible," Ben accused.

Evalina lifted her hand to silence him and asked, "How did you find us?"

"We planted a tracking device on him in the hotel," Marshall finally admitted, jerking his chin toward Ben. The pressure against her hand eased a bit as Ben backed off, though testosterone still hung heavy in the air.

"Where?" he demanded.

"Your left boot. Under the tongue, bottom of the laces."

A quick glance behind her confirmed Ben had knelt down to check his boot. He found the device and rose to his feet once more as he slipped it into his front jeans pocket. "Why do you want the Bible?"

Anger flared in the man's eyes when he shifted his gaze to Ben. "It belongs to my family. Your father is a thief and a liar."

"Tell me something I don't know."

"He's also a murderer. My grandmother made the fatal mistake of trusting your father, and in return he destroyed her and everything good in my family."

Behind her, Ben's entire body stiffened. "And why would I believe you?"

"Don't believe me, ask him. Oh wait, that's right, he's in federal prison. Trusting him to tell you the truth makes as much sense as expecting an alcoholic not to drink."

"Even alcoholics can be reformed."

"Once a con, always a con," Nick sneered.

"Says the thieving jerk who helped drug me."

"And you're such a stand-up guy? I know exactly what you used to do, Sanders. You and I both know your whole damn family should've gone to prison."

"Used to. We've put that all in the past," Ben ground out.

"Really? Then why are you here thirteen years later retrieving your father's ill-gotten gains?"

Testosterone levels skyrocketed. Evalina decided to focus the conversation on something more constructive before they exploded. "The bag you stole from Ben in the piazza—do you still have it?"

Hard green eyes shifted back to her. "Why?"

"Is it still in your possession?" she repeated, injecting the question with calm authority.

After a moment of hesitation and a glance at Ben, Nick nodded.

"There was a diary."

"Ah, yes, the diary. It was quite interesting."

A calculating gleam had entered Marshall's eyes and Evalina's stomach shifted uneasily. Ben was right, the guy was smart enough to recognize there was more to the memoir that most would realize. Not good for them.

"We will need it back."

"I'm going to need my Bible," he countered.

Ben surged forward once more. "Listen here, you sonofabitch. My mother's life is on the line if I don't get that book back to the States."

"Sounds like poetic justice."

With an angry roar, Ben pushed past Evalina and punched Marshall in the face. The guy fell back against the tower until Ben hauled him back up. Evalina fired her weapon once into the air and both men froze.

"Release him," she instructed Ben quietly. He complied, but only after giving the guy a hard shove. Marshall stumbled over their bags and sprawled on the ground.

A light drizzle had begun to fall again and Evalina asked, "Do you have a vehicle?"

"Yeah."

"How far?"

He climbed to his feet, touching the back of his hand to his bloody lip. "About an hour out."

"Great. You will take us to Rome. Ben, put the handcuffs on him."

"Oh, *now* you want my help."

She cast him a quelling glance, but he'd already pulled the cuffs from his pocket. The guy resisted when Ben grabbed his arm to turn him around. She thought she'd have to break them up again, but after a short scuffle, Marshall backed down, hands held together in front of him.

"It's a rough trail, at least give me a chance to stay on my feet."

Ben glanced in her direction, and she nodded approval.

Marshall led the way along the route he'd hiked to the tower. Walking between the two men, Evalina kept her gun out, but down at her side. She pulled the guy's phone from her pocket and began thumbing through his most recent texts.

She let him get a few meters ahead, then in a low undertone over her shoulder, she told Ben, "They haven't figured out the address. He sent a text to his sister about an hour ago that he would follow us and see what we were searching for here."

Ben snorted. "If he only knew we were looking for the road he came in on."

The irony had not been lost on her, either. The cold drizzle was turning into a steady rain, so she slipped the phone back into her pocket as they drew closer to the rushing river. Wisps of fog began to form between the trees, and the terrain became rougher, steeper. It didn't help that the previous night's precipitation turned the ground into a squishy mess that sucked at her boots with every step.

More than once, she slipped, only to have a quick grab from Ben keep her on her feet. The first time, his touch sparked those tingles of awareness. By the third, she was too miserable to catalog any reaction other than thankfulness that he kept her out of the cold mud.

Ahead of them, Marshall fell on his side. When she saw how he labored to get back on his feet with his hands bound, she decided to uncuff him until they reached his car. They'd make better time, which would get them out of the blasted rain sooner. Looking back over her shoulder at Ben, she started to ask for the key.

Her next step came down on the edge of a rock buried in the mud and her ankle twisted under her full weight. She cried out as she went down. Ben's lunge was a second too late and she found herself on a fast slide down the steep bank toward the river below.

## Chapter 22

"*E*va!"
 Ben flung off his bag and slid down the bank after her. Twenty yards below, the river tumbled over boulders and fallen trees, probably twice its normal height after the previous night's downpours. The thought of her plunging into the cold water chilled his blood.

Suddenly, she jerked to a stop. He saw her bag had caught on a fallen tree limb and she'd managed to grab the strap as it slid over her head.

"Hold on, Eva!"

Heart in his throat, struggling to keep his own footing, he slowed his descent so he wouldn't wipe out and knock them both into the rushing water.

"Oh, God, I'm slipping..."

Her muddy fingers barely clung to the strap as she lay on her back, arm fully extended. A roll onto her side to reach with her other hand came up short, though she still clutched her gun. He made it to her bag and carefully moved closer. Her wide eyes met his.

"Ben—"

"Don't you dare let go. I'm almost there."

Seconds took a lifetime as he sought a firm anchor hold with one hand and reached for her with the other. In the next instant, he grabbed her slender wrist, wrapping his fingers tight on her mud-slick skin. He dug in his boot heels and dragged her up.

"You got her?" Nick Marshall called from above.

Ben collapsed next to the tree with Evalina half draped over his lap, clinging to his leg. He'd completely forgotten about the other man and glanced up the hillside to see he'd been on his way down with a long branch in his hands.

"Yeah, we're good," he hollered back. Relief leached the adrenaline from his system, leaving him weak-kneed.

Surprise registered a second later. Evalina stiffened at the same time he whipped his head around in time to see Nick drop the branch and turn around. *How the hell did he get the cuffs off?* In a flash of comprehension, he understood the reason the guy had resisted the handcuffs back at the tower. A quick check of his pocket confirmed it; he'd used the disruption as cover to lift the key from Ben's pocket.

"Marshall!" he bellowed as Evalina struggled to get to her feet. "*Nick! Wait!*"

The guy didn't slow down as he reached the top of the hill and disappeared into the trees.

"You have to stop him!" she exclaimed. "We can't let him go."

There was no way he could make it up the muddy slope in time to catch the guy. He reached to help her up, but she shook him off. "Go after him!"

"I'll never catch him."

"You could at least try," she accused. "He has the diary *and* he was our ride."

"He's gone," he bit out. "Let it go."

She spouted some words in Italian, gesturing with her gun. He smiled, then took a step back to bend down and drag her duffle from the mud. "Sorry. I was a little more concerned about you going for a swim than the stupid diary."

"That *stupid* diary is probably the only thing that will keep me from getting fired when this is all over."

"It wouldn't matter if you'd drowned, now would it?"

Her narrowed gaze met his as he shouldered her bag. "I can swim just fine."

"Oh, my God, I can't win with you." A disbelieving laugh escaped as he lifted his hands to rake his dripping hair back off his forehead. The move ground dirt against his skin, but he was past caring as he fisted his hands in his hair until his scalp tingled. "Instead of being grateful that I most likely saved your life, you're worried about your *job?*"

Dropping his arms back to his sides, he started to turn to make the climb up the steep slope. Just as fast, he checked the action and whirled back to face her.

"You know, I don't even see why the job matters so much to you when it seems you can't trust a single damn one of them. If you ask me, I've had your back more in the few times we've been together than any of your so-called collogues."

The look in her eyes told him he'd struck pretty damn close to home. She reached behind her with both hands, then did a quick turn and almost wiped out again. He made an instinctive lunge toward her, but she caught her balance and scanned her gaze over the ground.

"What the hell are you doing?"

"Looking for his gun. I must've lost it when I fell."

"He was carrying a gun?"

He'd known the guy was serious about securing the Bible, but hearing he'd been armed raised his determination another whole level. Would he have used it against them? Had he been coming down to help before, as Ben had first assumed, or had he in fact been looking for his weapon after her fall? The length of the branch in his hands had suggested he would've used it to pull them up, but after his lack of compassion for Ben's mother, Ben wasn't too inclined to give Nick the benefit of the doubt where Evalina's safety was concerned.

"We'll look for it on the way up. Let's move, we're wasting daylight."

She started to move past him, but by the second step, she drew in a sharp breath.

"Now what?" When he actually looked at her face, he quickly slid his arm behind her back to steady her, concern tightening his stomach muscles. "What is it?"

"My ankle," she said between clenched teeth.

His stomach sank at the thought she might have broken it, but then he realized even adrenaline wouldn't have been able to mask the pain this long. "Can you walk?"

She lifted her foot for an experimental rotation, her lower lip caught between her teeth. Her features were drawn tight, but she still nodded.

Glancing up in the direction they needed to go, he said, "We've got to be almost halfway to where Nick parked his car, so at least we know we're near some sort of road." Lingering resentment prompted him to add, "You'll be back to work before you know it."

Her back stiffened, but she didn't reply as he helped her until they reached the faint trail Marshall had been leading them along. Thankfully the rain had stopped, but now the wispy tendrils of fog were combining to form one thick blanket. Good thing they had the trail or they'd end up seriously lost.

There had been no sign of the gun, and he wondered if she'd possibly lost it when she first fell. Did Nick have it in his possession again? Not the best scenario, but at least he couldn't track them anymore now that Evalina had his phone.

Could Alisa? Ben dug for the tiny tracker in his pocket and then fiddled with it until he could remove the battery, just like they'd done with their phones. Evalina did the same with Marshall's phone, and as they resumed hiking, Ben's thoughts returned to Nick's accusations.

That the theft of the Bible had destroyed his family.

That Ben's father was a murderer.

Could it be true? As he'd said, he knew the thief and liar part, but *murder*?

Nothing was worth that, not even if it held clues to a treasure worth millions.

Not for the first time, he thanked God Halli had the sense to take a stand against their parents when she was just sixteen. Without her and Rachel, he very well might have continued down the same path as their parents—conning his way through life, ruining the lives of others. He owed much more than loyalty to his two sisters.

It was because of *them* that he'd come to Italy when his mother first asked. And despite Nick's reasoning for wanting that Bible—which Ben wasn't so sure he believed, anyway—now that he knew the stakes were much higher, he was twice as determined to secure it himself. If he could help piece everything back together, give Rachel and Halli the chance at a relationship with their mother again, maybe they could be the family they were meant to be before his parents made the wrong choices in their lives.

"Ben?"

Evalina's voice pulled him from his inner musings. He stopped to see if she was having trouble with her ankle, only to realize he'd gotten pretty far ahead of her. While she caught up, he took in her muddy clothes and wet ponytail hanging down her back. Even bedraggled and dirty, she was as beautiful as ever.

The thought of having almost lost her back there made his pulse race and his stomach lurched all over again. Thinking about his messed up family was actually easier than considering what had almost happened. He started to turn back to the trail.

"No—wait."

He looked back, eyebrows raised.

"Thank you."

Her eyes didn't waver, and he didn't need to ask what the thank you was for. He gave a brief nod, because he'd more so been pointing out her messed up priorities than seeking gratitude.

When he would've resumed walking, Evalina moved forward to stop him again with a hand on his arm. She didn't speak right away, and despite the fact the chill starting to set in, the hint of confusion clouding her eyes kept him from rushing her.

"What you said before..." She paused, dropped her gaze, and quickly moved ahead of him. After a moment of walking, she spoke while keeping her attention focused on the trail ahead. "I have been on my own for a very long time. I'm not used to anyone thinking of me, or putting me first, and certainly not rescuing me. So yes, I've lost practice in showing appropriate appreciation, but it doesn't mean I'm not grateful."

He nodded his understanding to her back. Another minute passed before she spoke again.

"In regards to my job...it's all I have. I don't...I don't know who I am without it." Her voice had gone quiet by the end.

"Well, hell, Eva, I can tell you that one. You are a smart, beautiful woman," he said with firm conviction. "You're also a sister. The job doesn't have to be your entire life. You have a lot to offer anyone who's smart enough to include you in theirs."

The drip of moisture from the leaves overhead and squish of their footsteps were magnified by the oppressive fog. Ben noticed her lift a hand to wipe her face. *Shit.* Had he made her cry? While he didn't regret his words, he now felt compelled to allay her concerns.

"Nick Marshall is not stupid, you know. He won't get rid of the diary, especially now that he knows we want it back. We'll figure something out by the time we get to Rome."

This time she nodded.

They continued in silence as the trail wound along the river, and he was glad to see that though she favored her ankle some, the pain didn't appear to be as severe. He was about to mention they'd been walking a lot longer than they should've been when she pointed to a bridge up ahead, barely visible through the fog.

Relieved anticipation faded when it turned out to be nothing more than a footbridge that connected the trail they were on to the opposite side of the river. Well built and sturdy, but nowhere big enough for a vehicle, and certainly not connected to an actual road.

Halfway across, she turned to him, pretty much hugging herself as she gave her arms a brisk rub. "We can continue to follow the river, or take this trail and see where it leads. What do you want to do?"

He wanted to hold her close and warm them both, but didn't expect she'd be too receptive. Since the fog obscured their view of what lay downriver, he crossed to the other side to see if he could tell which way Nick had gone.

"There are footprints over here. I say we stay on the trail. It has to lead somewhere."

After another thirty minutes of walking, chilled to the bone, weary, and hungry, he halted. She looked equally miserable as they tried to use Marshall's phone to locate their position, but still couldn't get a signal.

This time he asked, "Keep going, or turn back?"

Forging ahead could result in them spending a second night in the mountains, only without shelter and no dry wood for a fire. But going back wasn't guaranteed to avoid the same result. The helplessness of not knowing made it difficult to keep a tight rein on his frustration.

Evalina tilted her head and swiveled slightly to the right.

"What?"

She held up a hand. "Shhh."

Their eyes met. He found himself counting the seconds until finally the distant bark of a dog echoed through the fog. When a second joined the first, he frowned with a twinge of anxiety. "Are those wild dogs?"

She shook her head while removing her gun from her shoulder harness. "Hunting dogs. Or maybe even *tartufo* dogs. Either way, it means the owner is nearby."

"*Tartufo* requires your gun?"

"*Tartufo* means truffle. Dogs are now primarily used to locate the fungi because they do not eat them as pigs do. Truffle hunting is a very lucrative but dangerous business, because the *tartufi* are literally worth more than their weight in gold. The harvesters, or *trifolau*, are extremely secretive and protective of their groves from poachers, who are not always so careful to preserve the underground truffle-forming fungus. I do not know if whom we encounter will be a landowner, or a trespasser, or if there will be more than one. It is very important you follow my lead."

He nodded, as serious as she. "Got it."

They saw the dogs first. A smaller long-haired brown one that maybe stood about knee-high was a breed Ben didn't recognize. The second larger, black and tan animal he easily identified as a German Shepherd—which did nothing to alleviate his apprehension.

When the dogs spotted them and stopped, he sidled closer to position himself in front of Evalina. "I really don't like this…"

The Shepherd let loose a couple of deep, ferocious barks while the little brown one raised its head as if testing their scent. It seemed to make up its mind they were of no importance, because it spared them barely one more second before veering into the woods, nose lowered to the ground as it began a zigzag pattern. The Shepherd took a few steps, stopped to bark a few more times, then loped after its companion.

"Definitely *trifolau*," Evalina confirmed, her voice low. "Whoever they are, they will be suspicious of you simply for being American, but if they are trespassers and they discover I am *Polizia di Stato*, it will not be good for either of us."

Ben reached over and re-zipped her jacket above her breasts, completely covering her shoulder harness for the weapon she now concealed at her side. A glance up the trail revealed a lone figure emerging from the fog.

"What's our cover?"

"Lost hikers," she whispered.

The man that moved toward them cocked his rifle and raised it. Not quite pointing directly at them, but close enough to tell them he meant business. Evalina tensed at Ben's side and he wondered if she'd drawn the same conclusion as him.

Lost hikers was the oldest excuse in the book and wasn't going to cut it. Especially if there was more than one of them.

He slid his arm around her shoulders and drew her close. "Be my wife."

## Chapter 23

BEN FORCED A smile as she jerked her gaze up in surprise. Understanding registered in her amber eyes, and she gave an imperceptible nod before returning her attention to the man approaching them with a suspicious frown. She eased her hand beneath Ben's jacket and concealed her weapon against his back as the man spoke.

"*Questa è proprietà privata.*"

"*Ci scusi,*" Evalina began. "*Io e mio marito ci siamo persi. Lei parla inglese?*"

Though somewhat shielded by a hat and glasses, Ben felt the man's gaze shift to him. He only understood the end where she'd asked if the man spoke English, to which the man responded with a negative shake of his head.

"*Ci puo dire quanto dista da qui la strada?*" she continued.

Unable to follow their exchange, Ben took stock of the older man. He was probably in his late sixties, with graying hair and a number of lines around his eyes and mouth. His clothes were well worn in spots, but still probably much warmer than what he and Evalina wore. The legs of his pants were as wet as they were, but moisture dripping from the trees beaded on his coat and rolled right off.

By all appearances, he could be a hunter, though his tense posture suggested otherwise. Ben kept a watchful eye on his body language as well as their surroundings. Should the situation take a wrong turn, or a second hunter appear, he would protect Evalina any way possible.

She played her part to perfection, keeping her tone friendly while allowing a slight tremor to sneak in every so often, accompanying the occasional shiver against him. The Italian remained on alert, eyes narrowed and all-encompassing behind his eyeglasses as he responded. She flattened her palm against Ben's chest in a half hug before gesturing behind them with the same hand. The chill of her other hand against his back rivaled the cold steel of her weapon.

The man shook his head, and more Italian flowed between them. Ben hated like hell not knowing what was being said, but he took it as a good sign when the man's stance began to relax and the barrel of the rifle lowered to the ground. After a few more minutes, Evalina said her name, and then she pressed closer to Ben once more.

"*Mio marito*, Benjamin Sanders."

The intimate tone of her voice gave him his cue, so he caught her hand and smiled, curling his chilled fingers around her colder ones as he played loving husband.

The Italian observed the gesture as he nodded to them both. "Cesare Minimi. *Molto piacere,* Signor Sanders."

Evalina's tension eased significantly as she translated, "He is pleased to meet you. Tell him, *il piacere è mio*."

Ben repeated the words and the man's features softened into a brief smile before he spoke to Evalina again. Their conversation became quite animated, and after some gesturing, nodding, and a couple of *grazie*'s, she lifted her gaze to Ben's while lowering her hand with the gun from his back. Her eyes conveyed she'd determined the man was not a threat, and he trusted her judgment.

"We are still many kilometers from a road," she relayed in English. "As late as it is now, if we keep going we'd still be walking by nightfall."

"Can he give us a ride to the nearest town?"

She shook her head. "I asked, but he doesn't own a vehicle. He's offered his home to dry our clothes and rest for the night, but I know you're anxious to continue for your family. If you want to—"

Considering her trembling had progressed beyond any advanced acting ability, Ben didn't think twice before offering Cesare Minimi a heartfelt, "*Grazie,*" of his own.

Yes, he was anxious to get to Rome, but it did no good to dwell on what he had no control over at the moment, and spending a second night in the mountains without guarantee of shelter would be stupid. Once they were dry and had gotten some rest, they could start fresh first thing in the morning. With a full day of light ahead of them and some specific directions.

Cesare nodded in what Ben could only classify as fatherly approval. He removed his arm from Evalina's shoulders and stepped in front of her to offer a handshake to the older Italian. Appreciation for his generosity, and cover for Evalina to holster her gun.

Then he turned back and asked in a low voice, "Do we continue the ruse?"

Indecision flickered in her expression. "I recognize his surname, but I'd like to see where he leads us to be sure he is who he says he is."

"Okay." He bent to scoop her into his arms.

"What are you doing?" she protested. "I can walk."

He hiked her into a secure position against his chest. With his lips pressed to her forehead, he murmured, "Tell our host about your ankle, and how wonderful I am to carry my injured bride. It'll lend authenticity to our story."

"You are an idiot," she replied. "It's over a kilometer to his home."

Ben winced inwardly as she wound her arms around his neck, but turned to face the older man. Out loud, he boasted, "Piece of cake. Besides, it'll warm us both up."

Her eyes met his for a moment before her lashes lowered and she leaned forward to press a kiss on his mouth. His lips warmed beneath hers, but all too soon she pulled back and smiled at Cesare to sing Ben's praises—or so he assumed.

The man chuckled as he lifted a whistle hanging on a string around his neck to his lips. A bark echoed through the fog, and then Cesare turned to lead the way.

Suspicion prompted Ben to ask, "Why'd he laugh?"

"I told him you were sweet, but delusional, and predicted you'd drop me before we reached the halfway mark."

His ego took offense. "What do I get if I make it all the way?"

"The right to brag that you are a man."

She raised her eyebrows and gave him a challenging grin that warmed his insides as much as the press of her body against his.

"Real men don't brag," he informed her quite seriously. "Our actions speak for themselves."

She rested her head on his shoulder. "Then I suggest you do not drop me."

He didn't. Nor did he admit his arms were killing him by the time they reached the mountain residence Cesare Minimi called home. Holding her so close to him was worth the discomfort.

The trail ended at the backside of a clearing containing three smaller outbuildings and the house, which was actually more of a sprawling, gray stone villa. It was impossible to see how far the clearing extended in the fog, but even in the gloom of the dreary day, it was clear to see the outbuildings were well-maintained, with one of them sporting a number of dog kennel runs.

"Wow." Ben let Evalina slide from his arms until her feet were on the ground. "This is not what I expected here in the middle of nowhere. You sure we can trust him?" he whispered.

"The Minimis are big players in the Italian truffle market, so while I didn't expect *this* either, I am not truly surprised."

Following their leader across the backyard between the outbuildings and the house, Ben shortened his stride to accommodate her slight limp. The dogs had beaten them back from the woods, and now sat patiently at the rear door. Cesare took a moment to give each one a treat, a rough affectionate neck rub, and then opened the door. The dogs bounded ahead of him until an angry shout from inside sent the dirty animals scrambling back outside, tails tucked, heads low.

Quick footsteps preceded a petite woman's arrival in the doorway. She appeared about Cesare's age and non-stop Italian flew from her mouth. When she spotted Ben and Evalina, her tirade came to an abrupt halt. For about three seconds. Then her gaze narrowed, and she spoke rapidly to Cesare.

He moved closer and the two conversed in low undertones. Ben's questioning glance toward Evalina received a shrug, and he guessed she couldn't hear what was being said.

Whatever the man's reply, a moment later the woman motioned them inside while tossing a few more angry-sounding words at their host. As she turned, Evalina took a step forward, but Ben resisted her pull on his hand. The lady sounded really annoyed, and they must look like a couple of muddy vagrants asking to come into her home.

"We should at least take off our shoes," he said. The woman reappeared in the doorway so fast he blinked in surprise.

"You are American?"

"Yes," he confirmed cautiously. Her stare unnerved him, and coming clean about their lies didn't seem the smartest move right about now, so he put his arm around Evalina and searched his brain for the limited words he knew. "Ah, *mi...chiamo* Ben. And this is my wife, Eva."

"I am Ilaria." After a few more words for Cesare, she gave them a stern look and spun on her heel. "Come. Leave your belongings inside the door."

Ben bent to remove his boots. Next to him, he saw Evalina duck her head to hide a grin as she reached to unzip her own footwear and also took off her wet socks. "You should be more careful. You just put Cesare in the doghouse."

He looked up to see the man's frown as he turned to follow the dogs. "What? What'd I—aw, crap. How do I say sorry?"

"*Scusi.*"

Cesare glanced back as Ben repeated the word with an apologetic smile. He said a few words, grinned, and extended his hand for them to go inside.

"He says do not worry," Evalina told him as they deposited their things on a large plastic tray by the door for shoes. She unzipped her bag, rummaged inside for a moment, then withdrew a small zippered case. "They'll make up later."

Ben grinned at that, then followed her into a large, open great room. On the right side, a fire blazed in a massive stone hearth and the blessed heat hit his cold hands and face. A reactive shiver shimmied along his spine.

"Ooh, that feels good," Evalina murmured.

Leather couches and cushioned chairs were placed to take advantage of both the fire and what Ben imagined would be a breathtaking view through the large picture windows when the fog dissipated. Through a stone archway to the left was the kitchen and dining area, which looked out over the same scenery.

Hallways extended in both directions, and it was to the right that Ilaria led them in their bare feet. As she opened a door, she pointed inside and instructed, "Undress in here. You sleep in the bedroom through that door. I bring you clean clothes while I wash what you wear."

Evalina began to protest in Italian, but Ilaria's stern frown cut her off mid-sentence.

"We are close in size," the older woman said before turning her hazel gaze to Ben. "You are bigger than my *marito*, but same size as my son."

He limited his reply to, "*Grazie.*" The small, commanding woman scared him.

She pointed to the bathroom. "*Il bagno è di là.* I return soon."

"You go first," Ben told Evalina.

Ilaria paused and turned back, eyebrows raised. "You *are* married, no?"

He glanced at Evalina. In the face of their hospitality, lying to the older couple was starting to feel wrong enough that a twinge of guilt limited his response to a nod.

"You have made love, yes?"

Heat flooded his face at the woman's unapologetic candor. Though he didn't have to lie for that question, Evalina saved him from answering by pulling him into the room with her and closed the door. After tossing the small bag in her hand onto the white marble vanity, she removed her jacket, then unfastened her shoulder holster to place it on the counter along with her badge and Nick's phone. A towel from one of the open shelves under the vanity covered everything to maintain their cover.

She pulled her shirt over her head, revealing that sexy black bra. He thought of last night as she caught him watching in the oval mirror. She'd never been shy, so he wondered if the rosy glow in her face stemmed from awareness, or a reaction to the warm air on her chilled skin? He didn't even need the shower to warm up now.

"She'll expect our clothes when she returns," Evalina prompted as he stood there.

"Right."

Ben tore his gaze from her exposed skin above the bra and below, where her trim waist flared to sexy hips. After emptying his pockets, he stripped down to his boxer briefs that did nothing to hide his growing physical reaction to their situation. He leaned closer and lowered his voice as, wearing just her bra and underwear, she gingerly gathered up their dirty clothes.

"If you want to toss out your stuff from the shower, I'll hand everything out into the hall to her, and then wait until you're done." *Fantasizing the entire damn time.*

"*Grazie.*"

She avoided his gaze, depositing the items in his arms before stepping behind the wavy glass. He took the scraps of underwear she handed out, then forced himself to stop thinking of her naked body as the shower turned on. Ilaria would be back any moment.

He removed his briefs, swiped a second towel off the shelf, and wrapped it around his waist. Adding his underwear to the pile of clothes, he cracked open the door to see Ilaria coming down the hall. Perfect. He could give her their things without worrying about her spotting Evalina's gun.

They exchanged bundles, and he noticed he older woman's curious gaze fixed on the bullet scar on the left side of his chest. Shifting so the door blocked her view of that and the bandage on his side, he noticed she'd included a disposable razor for him to shave, and thanked her with a grateful smile.

Her hazel eyes twinkled. "Cesare tells me you are married very recent."

"Um, yeah. Yes."

"No hurry," she said quietly. "Warm your wife well, *signore*."

With that parting advice, she pulled the door closed. Ben swallowed hard. His gaze swung to the distorted silhouette of Evalina reflected in the mirror. Would she welcome him sliding open the door, stepping beneath the steaming spray with her, lathering soap all over—

He groaned under his breath and moved to stand against the tiled wall next to the shower, out of sight of the mirror. The seductive scent of vanilla and hazelnut rode the steam billowing from above the door. Leaning his head back, he closed his eyes and concentrated on the feel of the moist heat seeping into his skin.

*Aw, hell, not helping.*

## Chapter 24

THOROUGHLY HEATED IN more ways than one, Evalina slid the shower door open a few inches, willing her pulse to remain normal. "May I have a towel?"

Movement directly to her right startled her as Ben stepped toward the sink and retrieved the requested item. She couldn't keep her eyes from traveling down his bare chest and defined stomach muscles. The sight of his own tented covering told her their situation of forced intimacy turned him on as much as it had her. As she'd washed, craving built with every heartbeat, every swipe of the washcloth over her body until all she wanted was to replace her hands with his.

Now she saw no point in denying them both, and when he extended the towel, she grasped his hand instead. His gaze snapped to hers. She smiled her invitation, and smoldering desire in his eyes flamed high. The towel in his hand fell to the floor. The one around his waist joined it a moment later when she pulled him into the shower.

Even as he slid the door closed behind him, his mouth descended to devour hers. Need had built to an unbearable level and she wasted no time locking her arms behind his neck to lift herself up against him. A low groan rumbled from deep in his chest when she wrapped her legs around his lean waist and took him all the way inside her.

He sucked and nipped at her neck, then skimmed lower. His mouth closed over her nipple, and she rocked her hips urgently against his. Then she whispered in his ear how she wanted it.

"*Fammi tua.*"

When she repeated her desire in English, he abandoned her breasts and took her hard and fast against the shower wall. She encouraged him with every thrust as the hot water streamed between their bodies. As they careened over the edge of bliss, he swallowed her choked cry with another scorching kiss.

Evalina rested her forehead on his shoulder until he set her on her feet. He brushed wet tendrils of hair from her face with both hands, and their gazes locked. Water spiked his lashes, increasing the illumination of his amazing blue eyes in the overhead light. Her heart skipped a beat. Panic fluttered in her stomach. The tender emotion in his gaze was too much right after their physical union, so she pressed a quick dismissive kiss to his lips, and then twisted from his arms.

"Hurry so they don't wonder what we're doing in here."

"I'm sure they know," he said, a smile in his low voice. "Ilaria told me to take our time."

"Oh, God," she muttered, cheeks burning.

"We're newlyweds," he reasoned, pulling her back against his chest to nuzzle his whisker-rough chin in the crook of her neck. She closed her eyes for a brief moment, wanting him all over again.

Recognizing the danger in that, she shrugged away and slid the door open. "Not really."

"Eva." He caught her arm in a gentle grip. "What are you running from?"

A double skip in her pulse left her breathless. "I don't like strangers sitting out there thinking about what we might be doing in here, okay?"

He let her go with a quiet, "Yeah, okay."

While drying off and then dressing in the form-fitting gray

slacks and black sweater Ilaria had provided, she kept sneaking glances at the slightly fogged mirror image of Ben soaping his body in the shower. His tall, lean silhouette was almost as sexy as the real deal.

Combing out her hair, she knew exactly what she was running from and wasn't sure escape was even possible anymore. However, silently worrying about it and voicing those concerns to him were two completely different things. With a shaky breath, she gathered up her holster, her Beretta, and the extra ammo she'd dug from her bag. A few steps across the bathroom and she moved through the door into the adjoining bedroom they were to share for the night.

The room was as elegant and striking as the rest of the house. Beautiful furniture was made of the same kind of wood used for the massive beams supporting the ceiling. The cool blue bedspread matched throw rugs on the gray marble floor, enhancing the exposed stone of the outside wall and the room's private fireplace. The Minimis definitely did well in the truffle market.

A fire snapped and crackled in the grate behind the screen, presumably lit while they were in the shower. Another wave of embarrassment flooded through her. The emotion brought forth a frown of annoyance. Independent since her teens, and exposed to just about any scene imaginable while undercover, she'd never been a prude. And though she had very discerning taste when it came to the men she allowed into that area of her life, when she wanted sex, she'd learned early on not to let emotions enter the equation.

Her discomfiture now was completely unexpected and unsettling because with Ben, sex was becoming something much more than just...sex.

When she heard the sound of the shower door sliding open, she pushed the unwelcome thoughts from her mind. Checking to be sure the bed was already made up with sheets, she stashed her weapon beneath the top corner of the mattress. Even though they now knew Cesare wasn't a poacher, she worried revealing their true identities would be a mistake. They would wonder why an agent of the *Polizia di Stato* was hiking through the woods with an *Americano*, and she didn't want them viewing Ben with suspicion. Besides, the fabrication wouldn't tangibly hurt anyone, so it was probably better to play it through until they left.

Moving closer to the adjoining door, she called through the opening, "I'm going to see if I can help Ilaria with anything."

She didn't wait for his answer before exiting into the hall. The earlier pain in her ankle had subsided to a dull ache so her limp was barely noticeable as she walked toward the great room and the kitchen where Ilaria was in the middle of dinner preparations. After making do with Ben's Autogrill junk food for the past two days, Evalina's mouth watered at the succulent aromas of fresh baked bread, olive oil, and the savory scent of seared meat. An actual meal would be heaven.

Ilaria happily put her to work chopping carrots, garlic, and tomatoes that she then arranged in a pan around a glistening, browned roast of pork. She poured a liberal amount of red wine over everything, added fresh rosemary and thyme, sprinkled the top with salt and pepper, and finally covered it with a sheet of foil.

As she slid the pan into the main compartment of an old-style, wood burning oven, Ben entered the room. Evalina glanced up, then found herself taking a longer look while he crossed the floor. The pants and sweater might as well have been made specifically for him, and though it was only shortly after five p.m. she could've happily stared all evening.

He'd shaved the two days worth of scruff on his face, but with his damp hair finger-combed for a slight semblance of order, his confident, loose amble hinted at the rebel streak she knew lurked inside that sexy body, just waiting for any chance to break free. When his gaze unerringly found hers, the intimacy of the shower passed between them.

Her face warmed at the hungry look in his eyes, and she returned her attention to the new task Ilaria had given her of slicing bread for the *antipasto*.

The older woman turned from the oven as he passed through

the stone archway and approached the island counter where they worked. She gave him a once over before declaring, "*Perfetto.*"

"*Grazie,* Signora Minimi," Ben replied. "For the clothes and for sharing your beautiful home with us."

"Bah. Neither of you need be so formal. I am Ilaria."

He shared a smile with Evalina at the admonition before asking, "Can I help?"

"Your wife and I can manage. Go. Feed the dogs with Cesare," she suggested.

When Ben shifted his gaze to her again, Evalina thought he was checking to see if she'd be okay on her own. Then she realized he was probably uneasy about spending time with the Italian who only spoke the native language. She understood, but to refuse would offend their generous hosts, so she gave him an encouraging nod. He headed outside after one last lingering look in her direction.

"He appears a good man," Ilaria observed from beside her, speaking Italian once more.

Startled at being caught staring after her fake husband, Evalina directed her gaze back to the bread. "*Sì.*"

"You wear no rings."

She paused, staring at her bare left ring finger. "They had to be resized. Our marriage was somewhat…spur of the moment."

Ilaria nodded her understanding. "So romantic."

*If only she knew the truth.*

"How is it the two of you became so lost?"

Not entirely sure of the answer herself, she continued to play her part and let a sheepish smile curve her lips. "We were too wrapped up in each other."

"Young love. I can remember those days." The older woman chuckled. "It is easy to see the love between you two."

Evalina's heart swelled at the possibility. The sheer intensity of the resulting wish that it were true stunned her. Her walls were crumbling worse than the centuries old mortar on the lookout towers. Shaken, she quickly redirected the conversation.

"It's nice here. Quiet. Do you mind being so isolated from

civilization?"

"Not at all. Life here is simple, as it is meant to be. I have my best friend here with me, the countryside is beautiful, and we have this amazing home our son built for us. What more could I want?"

Indeed. "Cesare mentioned you have no automobile, so how do you get groceries and supplies? Surely you must go into town at some time or another."

"Our son Rafael brings his family to visit every weekend, along with any necessities we require. We adore our daughter-in-law and spoil our grandchildren rotten. We also have friends in Sillico, and on the rare occasions we want to venture out, we return with them for a few days."

"Do you mind if I ask why you don't drive yourselves?"

"Cesare is legally blind. He does not like to navigate the mountain roads, and I have no wish to learn."

Both statements shocked her. The first, because Cesare had made his way through the woods without any indication of sight impairment. The second made it impossible for her not to ask, "What would you do in an emergency?"

"We would handle it together, as everything else. We understand the risks we take to live the simple life we enjoy."

*To be so sure of the one you love and the life you live*, she thought as the older woman excused herself to go check on their wash. All Evalina knew was her idea of what her future would be—what it *should* be—seemed to become more uncertain with each passing day.

When Ilaria returned, they finished the food preparations and then spent some time cleaning her and Ben's muddy belongings.

Evalina found out the Minimis didn't own a television either, but did use a laptop computer to Skype with their grandchildren via a satellite internet system their son had installed. She wondered if she might be able to use Nick Marshall's phone to contact Antonio to throw off any traces executed by the traitor in her department, but then Ilaria told her the service had been down for the past day and a half because of the rain and fog.

Checking in the privacy of the guest bedroom a little later confirmed there was no signal.

Leaving their clean clothes and bags on the bed, she returned to the kitchen to set the table for dinner. The sound of the back door preceded the noisy entrance of the two dogs from earlier. This time they were clean, and after they sniffed at Evalina's legs, Ilaria gave them each a treat. The brown mixed breed was named Kira, and the larger male Shepherd was Masca. He reminded her of the dog she'd had growing up and still missed on occasion.

Evalina carried plates over to the table as Cesare announced he was going to get some wine and *prosciutto*. She was about to turn to look for Ben when he stepped up behind her, slipped an arm around the front of her waist and pulled her back against his chest. He used his other hand to brush her hair aside for a warm kiss on her neck.

"You smell good enough to eat," he whispered against her skin.

Ignoring the probability he was just playing the part of a smitten groom, she melted against him, soaking up his warmth, reveling in his hard body and effortless strength. Would it really be so bad if for one night she allowed herself to see what a life like this would be like before returning to her lonely reality?

After an audible inhale, Ben's soft, "*Mmmm*," vibrated against her neck, and she turned her head for a second kiss, on the mouth this time. His lips were warm and gentle as they caressed hers. He smelled of the outdoors—and vanilla and hazelnut, from the shower wash they'd both used. Sensory memory combined with anticipation for later and curled her toes.

Before the plates in her hands slipped from her grasp, she broke the kiss and quickly set them on the table. While turning in his arms, she cast a discreet glance toward where Ilaria had disappeared after Cesare. "Were you okay out there?"

He linked his fingers together behind her back. "Of course. I helped him move a few things from one shed to another, then played with their litter of German Shepherd puppies while he fed the rest of the dogs. How about you? I wasn't so sure about leaving you in here."

"Not only do I speak the language, but I *can* take care of myself."

"I know," he said with a brief smile. "And hey, we might be in luck."

"What do you mean?" she asked as the older couple returned, their arms full of wine and several cuts of cured meats.

After one more quick kiss for her, Ben stepped back and spoke toward their hosts. "Ilaria, when I was helping Cesare outside, I noticed a motorcycle in the middle shed. Perhaps we could borrow or rent it?"

At the mention of possible transportation, Evalina experienced conflicting emotions of hope and disappointment. She didn't relish more walking, but if he wanted to leave immediately, they'd be right back to reality before she had a chance to truly experience her current role. Selfishly, she wanted to stay the night.

Ilaria translated for her husband before answering Ben. "It belonged to our son, but does not run."

"I know a thing or two about bikes and motors," he countered. "What if I can get it running? I'd even purchase it, if you would agree. I don't want Eva walking on her injured ankle if she doesn't have to."

Her ankle wasn't so bad anymore, but she silenced an automatic protest. She had to put Ben and his family first. And her career. Personal wants and desires came last. Well, maybe not exactly last. Men on motorcycles had always been a major weakness for her, and the thought of Ben's muscled thighs straddling a bike made her flush.

After a moment of discussion, Cesare nodded, and Ilaria said, "If you can repair the motorcycle, it pleases us to offer it to you. But first, you must sit. Eat."

## Chapter 25

"DO YOU BELIEVE you can fix it?" Evalina asked quietly as she and Ben stood by the table. Ilaria was in the kitchen and Cesare busied himself pouring the wine.

"I'm sure as hell going to give it a try. It's an older model, but it looked to be in good shape. If I can get it running, it should get us all the way to…where we need to go."

"Good." And then they'd deal with the diary and the Bible…and soon say their goodbyes. She forced enthusiasm into her voice. "That would be great."

A slight frown darkened his expression, but then it cleared. "I'll take a look at it right after dinner."

Before she could warn him about the typical length of an Italian evening meal, Cesare plunked the pitcher of his homemade *vino della casa* in the center of the table and gestured for Ben to distribute the glasses around the table. Ilaria carried over a platter of *antipasto* and the bottle of extra virgin, truffle infused olive oil they'd brushed on the bread before toasting on the *brustolina* grill.

Once everyone was seated, Cesare said grace, and after the customary host's toast of *"Salute,"* or "to your health," Ilaria passed around the platter of food. Evalina pointed out the offerings of *bruschetta* topped with *prosciutto*, and the *crostini*, topped with thin slices of fresh roma tomatoes and *mozzarella di bufala*. When Ben took one of each, she grabbed the bottle of olive oil and drizzled it over his food and hers, explaining about the infused truffles and the earthy flavors the fungi added.

At Ben's first bite and appreciative nod, Cesare beamed.

"You are familiar with Italian cuisine?" Ilaria asked, her smile equally pleased.

"Very little beyond American versions that clearly do not compare." He glanced at Evalina after taking a sip of his *vino*. "But I look forward to many more delicious treats. My wife has made me excellent meals in the past."

His wording reminded her of when she'd delivered meals to him while he was being held for ransom by Lapaglia. He'd never voiced any appreciation for her culinary skills.

"Tell us how you two met," Ilaria requested.

Evalina set down her *crostini*. Before she could think of what to say, Ben reached over and covered her hand with his.

"It was a little over nine months ago that I first set eyes on her," he told their hosts before turning that striking blue gaze her way. "You've been with me ever since."

The declaration caught her off guard. Made her forget their audience. She tilted her head as the sensual effects of his low voice washed over her. "I have?"

"You have."

His serious expression touched off a tsunami of nervousness, compounded by the subtle caress of his thumb rubbing circles over the back of her hand.

"I've enjoyed being with you, Eva. Getting to know you."

She wanted to believe he spoke not solely for the sake of their cover. That he was telling the truth from deep in his heart.

"I have too," she admitted softly.

Emotion deepened the color of his eyes and his fingers squeezed hers. Happiness edged his smile, and she returned it as her pulse leapt.

As if suddenly remembering the other two at the table, he

returned his gaze to the older couple. "We first met when I was visiting Lake Como with my two sisters last summer. Eva resisted me at first, but I charmed my way into her good graces."

She reached for her wine glass with a laugh. That was so far from what had actually happened, and yet one hundred percent true in this particular moment.

"Now, you have years together," Ilaria declared, first in English, then Italian for her husband.

Cesare lifted his wine glass in a toast. "*Alla vita, all'amore, e a nuove amicizie. Salute!*"

Raising her glass, she couldn't help but meet Ben's gaze as she translated. "To life, love, and new friends."

He lifted his glass without breaking eye contact with her. "*Salute.*"

Dinner progressed past the antipasto, to the pasta dish, and then into the main course of tender pork and flavorful roasted vegetables. It was an interesting dynamic of Ilaria interpreting for Cesare, and Evalina doing the same for Ben. Ilaria had learned English from her daughter-in-law, who was an aspiring fashion designer. That explained the expert cut of Ben's borrowed clothes.

As they all relaxed, conversation and laughter flourished. The first pitcher of wine emptied, but the older Italian quickly refilled it, and their glasses. Every so often, he would raise his arm for another toast, and they would all drink again. Ben even got into the spirit and offered one of his own.

All the while, his touch remained constant. Whether it was the soft caress of his fingertips on her hand, the press of his knee beneath the table, or a lingering, intimate look accompanied by one of his pulse-revving smiles. Charming was one word she'd use to describe him; seductive was another. He had a laugh that warmed her insides and made her wish the evening would never end. She enjoyed his sense of humor, and marveled at his quick wit and the ease at which he picked up some of the more common words of her language.

After the main meal was finished, Ilaria rose to clear their dirty dishes. She waved Evalina back into her seat when Cesare launched into a tale about an Italian priest from the nearby town of Sillico being hunted by the Germans during World War II because they believed him to be an American spy. With the wine having loosened his tongue, the man clearly enjoyed his storytelling. Evalina translated as Ben traced little figure eights on her palm and idly toyed with her fingers.

"The townspeople refused to give up the priest, even though the soldiers threatened to kill everyone in the town, and searched from house to house. Convinced the priest had not been there after all, the head officer of the German soldiers decided to leave the town instead of following through on his threat."

Watching Ben listening to Cesare's animated voice, she saw his interest went beyond mere politeness and found herself equally enthralled.

"After the war, many years later, the priest received a letter. The man said he had been a solider for the German Army, and he saw him that night. He was the soldier who stood beneath the pergola the priest crawled across to escape the house where he'd been concealed. The soldier risked his own life by not revealing the priest's presence."

Chill bumps prickled along her arm.

"They later met and the priest thanked him for his life."

"That's just crazy," Ben murmured. "But in a good way."

"That's something you won't find in the history books."

Over glasses of *liquore di lamponi* and *limoncello*, Cesare took full advantage of his captive audience and continued his stories. Evalina savored the tart, fruity raspberry and lemon flavors of the dessert liquors as she interpreted another story from back during the war.

"One winter, there were so many Germans in the country, it was too dangerous to even go outside to find or hunt for food. Our countrymen would have starved had it not been for that fall's record harvest of chestnuts from the trees growing in the surrounding forests.

"To this day, those who remember that time do not recall a

year the trees bore so much fruit. My grandfather loved chestnuts because that is what literally allowed them to survive," Evalina translated for Cesare. "But he also hated them, because they ate them for breakfast, lunch, and dinner all winter long."

Ilaria smiled as she finished her glass of wine. "Bebbe tells that story every time I serve a meal with chestnuts."

"Italian dinners are full of stories," Evalina explained to Ben. "It is a big part of how our culture is passed from one generation to the next."

Cesare reached for the pitcher of wine, clearly intending to continue their education. But his wife beat him to it. "*Basta, caro. Fa tardi e i nostri ospiti sono stanchi. Lasciamoli riposare.*"

"She says enough. It's late. It's bedtime," Evalina whispered to Ben.

He glanced at his watch and his eyes widened. Clearly, he hadn't realized it was already after eleven. Evalina stood to help clear the table of their many glasses and he joined her. Ilaria shooed them away from the sink when Evalina would've started the dishes.

"I wash tomorrow. Go."

"I need to get outside and work on that motorcycle," Ben began.

"No," Ilaria stated in a firm voice. "To bed. Both of you. You work tomorrow."

His grimace prompted Evalina to shake her head in warning. Unless they wanted to explain why he was so anxious to work on the bike, it was necessary they respect the wishes of their hosts.

With a sigh of resignation, he stepped forward to give Ilaria a kiss on each cheek. "You're right, morning will be soon enough. *Grazie.* It was a wonderful evening I shall remember always."

"*Buonanotte*," Evalina murmured as the woman steered them toward the guest bedroom.

The room was cool, the fire having burned down to no more than embers. While Ben stirred the coals and added a few more pieces of wood, she took a quick turn in the bathroom to get ready for bed. No way would she have worn her skimpy tank top and shorts last night in the tower, but tonight, she slipped the sleep set on. Indecision hit when she grasped the handle to open the connecting door.

She'd packed what she normally wore to bed, never expecting two days ago that Ben would see her sleepwear. Now she wondered, would he view the scanty pajamas as an invitation?

Did she want him to?

*Yes.*

Taking a deep breath for courage she didn't normally need, she swung the door open and stepped into the room. His gaze tracked her movement across the cold floor to the bed. Just knowing he watched her heightened the delicious tingle of anticipation that had simmered beneath the surface all through dinner. Even considering the irresponsibility of continuing their intimacy without protection did nothing to dull the pulsing desire.

She drew the comforter back to slip between the cool sheets just as she heard the bathroom door close behind her. Ben exited a few minutes later, laid his clothes across one of the chairs near the fireplace, and turned for the bed wearing only his boxer briefs, making no attempt to hide anything. The snug cotton revealed his arousal and left no doubt his thoughts mirrored her own.

He pulled back the covers on his side and sat on the bed. Instead of lying down, he glanced back at her over his shoulder, his expression thoughtful. "*This* is the real Italy, isn't it? Not criminals with guns, but amazing food, great history, and wonderful people like Cesare and Ilaria?"

She rolled on her side to face him, arm propped on a pillow, head on her hand. "*Sì*," she confirmed, pleased at his perception of her country. "This is the *Italia* most people experience."

"I like this *Italia*." He leaned back against the pillows, covers bunched at his waist, fingers linked together across his taut stomach as he stared at the exposed wooden beams on the ceiling. "I feel bad lying to them."

His sudden switch caught her off guard. "I understand, but take consolation that we mean no harm by the ruse."

"Yeah."

He didn't sound comforted. Ironic that he, who'd been raised by con artists and had been one himself for who knew how long, and she, who made her living by lying to others in her uncover work, both felt remorse for the untruths they'd told the trusting couple generously sharing their home.

And yet, after the past four hours, she found herself wanting to ask, *are we truly lying about everything?*

For all her fearlessness, and even after the inhibition-lowering wine, the words stuck in her throat. Instead, she reached over and ran her palm along his warm, muscled forearm until she covered his hand with hers.

"Is there anything else in *Italia* you like at the moment?"

He turned his head toward her. His gaze tracked from her chest to her face while he lifted her hand to his lips. "I believe you already saw the answer to that question."

"I did." She gave a sultry smile and looked up at him through her lashes. "Which makes me wonder why you are still way over there?"

Rolling onto his side, he mirrored her pose. She tried to pull him closer, but his fingers tightened on hers as he resisted. "Because I realized something during dinner."

Afraid her mounting frustration would show in her voice, she raised her eyebrows in silent inquiry.

He placed her hand on his chest and then lifted his to brush her hair back from her face. His skin was so warm. Muscles firm, full of strength. While his heart beat steady beneath her palm, he traced the outer shell of her ear before trailing that feather-light touch down her arm. Tingles raced across her skin, chasing the tip of his finger.

His gaze connected with hers, and the intensity in his eyes made her heart skip. She suddenly found it hard to breathe.

"We have never made love."

She blinked, pulling back slightly. "Ah…what do you call

what we did earlier? And last night?"

"Sex."

Stunned at his perceptiveness, she simply stared at him.

"Don't get me wrong, it was great. *Damn* great," he assured her with the barest hint of a smile. "But it could be even better."

Alarm fluttered in her stomach. Her chest tightened even more, and she went for the distraction again. "I can definitely do better."

She swept the covers back, then leaned forward and pressed her mouth to his while rolling him onto his back. His token resistance and murmured protest died when she angled her head to deepen the kiss. While sweeping her tongue inside his mouth to caress his, she swung her leg over him and settled directly on his erection. The first slow grind of her hips drew a moan from both of them.

"See how good it can be?" she whispered.

"I know how good it can be, but this…"

Savoring the lingering flavor of fruity wine on his lips, she swirled her tongue around his, and mimicked the movement with another hip swivel.

"*Oh, God*…this isn't what I meant."

Through the barrier of their clothes, his rigid shaft throbbed against her core. His hands slipped beneath her tank top, fingers digging into her hips to hold her in place while he thrust upward. A smile curved her lips against his, and she gave a throaty sound of approval. She knew just how to play the man. Now to get him naked.

Placing soft kisses along his smooth jaw, she then moved down his throat to the firm muscles of his chest. Letting her sensitive breasts brush against his body, she flicked her tongue against his nipple, then sucked the hard little nub into her mouth. Did her mouth create the same sensations in his body as his did to hers?

His low, sexy groan told her *yes*.

She skimmed her lips to the other side, but froze when she encountered the disfigured skin where he'd been shot the last time he'd been in her country. Her heart jerked hard against her ribs. Realizing he'd gone still as well, she swallowed hard, then gave into temptation and tentatively traced the scar with the tip of her tongue.

He sucked in a breath, and she literally felt his heart punch inside his chest.

"Does it hurt?" She lifted her gaze to find him watching her, those blue irises of his the color of a storm laden sky. "I have heard of phantom pain that lingers."

"No." He shook his head, his voice choked. "That pain is gone."

She looked down again and brushed her fingers across the damaged flesh. Flash memories of how close she'd come to losing him that day bombarded her. After thinking of him constantly the past nine months and the past couple days by his side, she couldn't imagine the world without him.

He brought his hands up and raised her face to his. A softer, more tender emotion tempered the sizzling passion in his eyes. It constricted her lungs to the point she had difficulty drawing a breath. A lump formed in her throat, and the unnerving sensation of falling into an abyss created a feeling of lightheadedness.

*No.* That depth of emotion was much too dangerous. With her heartbeat tripping like crazy, she pulled free and focused on the physical. Whatever it took to restore her equilibrium. Shifting to lay beside him, she skimmed her hand down across his stomach.

"Eva..."

He reached to stop her just short of her goal, but she dodged his hold and slipped her fingers beneath the band of his boxer briefs. His second attempt locked his hand on her wrist with firm determination. "Slow down."

"I can't." She dipped her head to swirl her tongue around the flat nipple she'd neglected. "I want you, Ben. All through dinner..." She paused to nip at his flesh. "All I could think about is how good you feel moving inside me."

A strangled laugh accompanied the slackening of his grip.

"God help me when you say things like that with your accent. But..."

She circled her hand around his erection, and he pushed up against her palm. After a few sweeping strokes along the hot, steel length, she started to remove his underwear.

"No, Eva," he objected with another groan. His hand returned to halt hers. "Not yet."

"*Sì. Subito. Lo sai che mi vuoi.*"

"That is *so* not fair."

Confidence vibrated in her husky laugh against his stomach. Yes, she knew exactly how it affected him when she whispered in Italian.

She slid further down, intending to use her mouth to silence any further objections. Before her breath skimmed his taut stomach, he surprised her with a lightning quick roll that landed her on her back, hands imprisoned over her head. He loomed over her, his erection pressed into her hip, but he made no move to shift his body to rest between her legs where she wanted him most.

"No," he repeated. An unexpected hint of resentment tempered his low voice. "No sex, Eva. Tonight, we are going to make love."

## Chapter 26

HIS QUIET STATEMENT nearly stopped her heart in her chest. Then it pounded fast. Hard. She sucked air into her starved lungs and squeezed her eyes shut. Denial shook her head back and forth on the pillow.

"Yes," he countered.

Warm breath brushed her cheek, and with the next turn of her head, his mouth captured hers with forceful pressure.

*Yes.* A kiss. Hot and wild, it would push him back to the edge where she could take control once more. She surged up against him, straining her arms against his hold. Urgency pulsed through her. He alone could make the cold reality of her empty life fade away.

Only, instead of diving in with the passion she craved, pressure eased and his lips gently caressed hers before intensifying the kiss with deep, languorous, sensual laves of his tongue that stirred the butterflies in the pit of her stomach.

Then he lifted his head and commanded in a rough voice, "Look at me."

Trepidation wound through her as her lashes fluttered open. What was he doing? Why was he forcing this on her? Why wouldn't he just continue as they had been and help her ease the ache inside?

"I'm going to make love to you, Eva, because you deserve to have someone always thinking of you."

His tone had softened considerably, and even as she wondered if he'd read her mind, or if she'd maybe voiced her desperate questions out loud, she recognized the words she'd spoken to him after he'd saved her by the river.

"You deserve to be put first."

Almost word for word. He'd heard her loneliness and used it to blast through her weakened defenses. Unsure of his intentions, she anxiously waited for his next move.

"Let me love you tonight."

In the charged, lengthening silence, she realized he was asking her permission.

Her gaze searched his hopeful blue eyes in absolute wonder. She'd assumed he was giving her no choice, but in reality, he handed her complete control even as his own insistent arousal pulsed against her side. That right there captured her more than anything else. As much as the emotional intimacy terrified her, she was helpless to stop from falling completely under his spell.

All-encompassing warmth, different than desire, spread through her chest, and she fought that damn lump in her throat again.

"Eva?"

Unable to speak, she nodded.

Relief flashed in his eyes before he released her arms and dipped his head to kiss her again. Time suspended as she gave herself up to the heady sensation of his lips on hers. Exploring, caressing...loving. A girl could get drunk on kisses like that.

Heat rose when he slowly moved from her mouth to the thrumming pulse at the base of her neck, and lower. Her first attempt to touch him was gently yet firmly denied, and she didn't try again.

She instinctively recognized the difference between their previous fiery, frantic couplings and his avowal to make love to her this time. The emotion resonated in his touch, in the care he took to give her pleasure and worship every inch of her body as he literally and figuratively stripped her bare. The leisurely pace heightened the sexual tension strumming her sensitized nerve endings, and she had to clench the sheets in her hands at her sides to keep from reaching for him again.

Finally, he lay naked beside her, skin to skin, making her entire being yearn for his possession. He drew her sensitive nipple into his mouth as his fingers slid into the moist heat between her legs. She arched at the spine-tingling ripple of pleasure that shuddered through her already-humming body. When he withdrew his fingers and circled one moistened tip around her clitoris, her hips jerked in reaction and her breath caught on a desperate gasp.

"Oh, *mio Dio*."

"I want you to know, Eva...there's been no one since you." He punctuated the words with moist kisses from her breast to her lips. "Since last summer, I mean."

"I know what you mean," she panted. "For me neither."

He rubbed his fingertip back and forth, driving her closer to the climax hovering so close she was ready to beg.

"*Ben...*"

Between kisses, he murmured, "You've completely ruined me for other women."

The husky admission thrilled her, and deep down, she acknowledged it was sure to be the same for her.

He increased the pressure and tempo of his movements and the wave of pleasure she was riding exploded in a kaleidoscope of overwhelming sensation. His kiss muffled her cry of release, and before the delicious tremors subsided, he rose up above her. Opening her eyes, she welcomed him without reservation. Warmth from his blue eyes bathed her face as he joined their bodies together in one sure thrust.

Her chest tightened, shallow breaths barely providing enough oxygen. He withdrew and thrust again, watching her with each movement. Normally, the slow, deep strokes he executed would've sparked impatience, but the intense connection between them kept her from urging him faster as she moved her hips with his. The effort it took for him to hold back was evident in the slight tremble of his strong arms. She maintained the sensual rhythm he set, still holding his gaze.

She'd known love from her parents, but they'd been gone so long, she'd forgotten what the emotion actually felt like. In every way, Ben had reminded her tonight. It didn't matter slow or fast, how or where, sex with him would never be 'just sex' again. He'd completely seduced her, body and soul.

A burning sensation behind her eyes told her she was close to tears. *Dio, no*, she was not going to cry in front of him. Not again.

This time, when she swept her hands up his arms to reach for him, he let her pull him down to kiss him in a tangle of lips and tongues and heavy breathing that mingled with their joint sounds of passion and pleasure. When his strokes became faster, she rode another wave that carried her back to the heights of sweet heaven. He joined her with a hoarse cry before his arms gave out, and he collapsed on top of her.

His ragged breath stirred the damp hair by her ear. "God, I love you, Eva."

Completely sated, it took a moment for his rough, whispered words to sink in. Before she could clear her thoughts enough to react, he lifted his head and covered her mouth with his. The lingering passion in his kiss convinced her she hadn't imagined the words that packed enough power to change her life.

Initial panic was quickly replaced by unexpected joy, and she responded with all the emotions burgeoning inside her thawed heart. For the first time since her sister pushed her out of her life, she believed it was possible she could be happy again.

"*Mmm.*" Ben eased back and shifted his weight off her at the same time. "Damn that was nice."

*Nice?*

He planted a kiss on her forehead. "I'll be right back."

She levered herself up onto her elbows when he moved off the bed and crossed to the bathroom in the soft glow of the fire.

Confused disbelief didn't allow her to enjoy the play of light and shadow over his lean, sculpted body. Though not overly familiar with the emotion, common sense told her you didn't tell someone you loved them and then follow it up by describing an earth-shattering experience as *nice*.

As the sound of running water came from the bathroom, she wondered if maybe that's all it had been for him? Nice. Maybe she *had* imagined his declaration? Wishful thinking on her part. Or...had he spoken in the heat of the moment and not truly meant it?

The possibility pierced her heart with a shot of pain so intense she nearly gasped out loud. She thought of how he'd kissed her right after he'd spoken. The following casual comment, and how he'd quickly gotten off the bed—all the while avoiding her eyes.

*Diversion tactics.*

How easy to spot the strategy she was intimately acquainted with. She definitely hadn't imagined anything. He'd said the words, regretted them immediately, and now clearly wanted her to forget.

The hollow ache that remained with that realization prompted her to cover her naked body when she heard the water shut off. Ben reemerged from the bathroom, but didn't meet her gaze as he handed her a warm, damp cloth to wash. His consideration surprised her as much as him sliding close when he got back into bed. He aligned his warm body to hers, sliding his arm under hers and across her stomach to spoon her tight.

"Comfortable?"

Feigning exhaustion, she let her arm lay limp on his and murmured a soft, sleepy agreement. Then she stared across the room at the glowing coals in the fireplace, listening to his breathing deepen in sleep. Silent tears slipped onto her pillow, but not once did she give a voice to the forlorn words begging to be released from the dark recesses of her battered heart.

This is why she deliberately closed herself off. It hurt too much. The people she had loved either didn't love her back and left—like her sister and the few boyfriends she'd allowed into her life—or she lost them like her parents. If she were to one hundred percent open herself to Ben and lost *him*, she wasn't so sure she'd ever have the strength to recover.

Her best protection was distance. Each beat inside her chest deepened her resolve. Tomorrow she'd rebuild her emotional walls, and soon enough he'd be on his way back to the States, thereby solving the physical aspect as well.

Then she'd bury herself in her job once more. If she tried hard enough, some day she might even believe again that she was better off alone.

## Chapter 27

BEN LAY IN the predawn hour, wishing he could remain in bed with Eva into infinity, yet knowing it was impossible.

He hadn't meant to say, *"I love you,"* out loud. The moment the words had left his mouth, he realized laying his heart at her feet was just opening himself up for her to stomp all over it again. Panic ensued, and he'd smothered any reply she might have made with that kiss.

It'd taken a second for her to respond, but after she did, he murmured other things to distract her. Something completely inane he couldn't even recall.

Maybe she hadn't heard him?

Yeah, and maybe he wasn't an idiot.

No, she'd heard him. That she'd let the moment pass without comment confirmed he'd made a colossal mistake, and he was indeed an idiot. The best plan now was to continue to pretend it hadn't happened and hope everything would be fine.

Then he wondered exactly how to define *fine* when they were basically playing Russian roulette without protection, and he didn't feel even a twinge of panic at the thought of her becoming pregnant.

Evalina made a soft sound in her sleep. Her silky skin slid

against his as she rolled toward him. The faintest hint of moonlight through the windows kept the room from being pitch black, and unable to resist, he lifted his hand to brush her soft curls from her cheek.

A subtle change in her breathing registered. In the dim light, he sensed she now watched him.

"Good morning," he said.

He glimpsed her striking profile when she turned her head toward the window. "Still looks like night."

"It's a little after four."

"How long have you been awake?" she asked.

Her sleep-husky voice stirred the desire he'd been wrestling with for the past half hour. He wanted to stoke the fire across the room and see all her glorious hair spread out on the pillow as he made love to her in the morning light. Thoughts of starting off the day by sliding into her heat had him hard as a rock, but with the urgency of the day nagging in the back of his mind, he resolutely diverted his attention.

"Not long. I really need to get to work on that motorcycle, but I—"

"That's right, the motorcycle." Now she sounded fully awake, even annoyed as she shifted toward the edge of the bed. "I'm surprised you didn't go out the moment you woke up."

He took a breath. A voice in his head said *don't do it,* but he found he just couldn't help but take a chance. "I wanted to wait for you."

She fumbled her tank top in her hands, but then quickly pulled it over her head and reached for her shorts. "I don't know anything about motors, so I'm of no help to you."

Familiar distance resonated in her cool tone, and he injected a note of challenge into his. "We've never woken up together. Seemed this morning, of all mornings, we should."

When she continued to dress without a word, the tightness in his chest mocked his decision to deviate from the plan to pretend as if nothing monumental had happened. In an attempt to erect some protection around his emotions, he added somewhat flippantly, "And you can always hand me tools."

"Sure." She stood and scooped up her duffle on her way to the bathroom. In the doorway, she paused as he propped himself up on an elbow. "Get moving. As *nice* as all this was, we both have a job to do today if we want to get this over with."

The door banged shut, extraordinarily loud in the quiet room. His eyes narrowed. Get it over with? Is that how she felt after what they'd shared? A second later, his *other* words from last night flashed back. *Nice.* He flopped back on the bed with a groan and banged his head on the headboard in the process.

*Yep. Definitely an idiot.*

He swept aside the covers and quickly dressed in his freshly cleaned jeans and black shirt while she finished in the bathroom. When she stepped back into the bedroom ten minutes later, fully dressed and ready go, he was waiting for her, heart pounding.

"Eva..."

"Stop calling me that," she snapped as she brushed past.

He reached out to catch her arm, but she blocked him with her opposite hand. Her fingers twined with his, then twisted his hand upside down until just short of being painful. Growing up with sisters, he was well familiar with the move that could easily drop him to his knees.

Running his gaze over her face, he noted she'd tamed her mass of curls into a long, thick braid that trailed over her shoulder, ending just below her breast.

He took a step forward, testing her. Instead of holding her ground and applying pressure, she retreated. Another step and a smile from him fired up her resistance enough that he grit his teeth to keep from sucking in a sharp breath. When he continued forward, she backed up again, her frown deepening.

"Stop."

"Are you going to listen to me?" he asked.

She abruptly released him and crossed her arms over her chest. "You would have to say something I want to hear first."

Flexing his hand, a flicker of hope blossomed in the face of her defiance. He never meant to upset her with his insensitive choice of words, but anger meant she cared. *Right?* He was suddenly in a much better mood.

"Last night—"

"Is over," she cut in. "We need to focus on today."

"Not until we get a few things straight. Last night was amazing. That's what I should've said, and I'm sorry if I hurt you."

For a moment, he thought he may have touched on something when her eyes widened. But in the next breath, she squared her shoulders and lifted her chin.

"You're right—it was fantastic. But it always has been, so your words certainly didn't matter to me." She spun away and yanked the comforter from the bed. "*Nothing* you said last night matters when you consider we are wasting time that would be better spent figuring out a way to get to Rome so we can both return to our lives. Or have you forgotten about your family?"

It would've hurt less if she'd pulled out her gun and shot him point blank.

Spine stiff, he stalked over to gather up his own things while she finished stripping the bed. Behind the bathroom door, he figured out how to breathe again. Retreated behind the simple, mindless act of splashing cold water on his face and brushing his teeth. He shoved his things into his bag and then fought the urge to smash something against the pristine tile of the shower behind him.

With his hands gripping the marble vanity, he hung his head. After the past nine months of misery, how had he totally fucked up and fallen for her all over again? She didn't care for *him*, it was all about the job. The woman was running so fast there was no way she'd stick around, much less open her heart.

He lifted his head and stared at his reflection in the mirror. He hadn't forgotten about his family, only managed to set them aside for a brief time. But she was absolutely right—he needed to focus and put them first. Family mattered above all else.

Straightening from the sink, he reached to open the bathroom door and made his way along the hallway to go outside. The house was quiet except for the ticking of a clock somewhere in the great room, and the whisper of Evalina's movements behind him. Hyper aware of her presence, he purposely centered his attention on the little details.

A fire had been re-laid in the main hearth. It wasn't lit, and he knew the Minimis weren't awake yet when he spotted both dogs watching them from their blankets. The Shepherd, Masca, let out a low *woof*, but when Ben softly called their names, the ears went down and they came over, tails wagging. Kira even licked his chin as he bent to put on his boots by the back door.

Both dogs accompanied them outside into the cool dawn, trotting ahead as Ben led the way to the shed containing the motorcycle. The air was still damp, but the absence of rain or fog was a relief.

Flipping open one of the double doors, he told Evalina, "Once I dig the bike out, Cesare has a work area and tools over in the front part of the kennels."

She helped him move items out of the way until he could push the bike outside. When he turned back, she waved him out. "Go. I'll put everything back."

Sure. Great. He wished she was just being helpful, but knew it was more than that after the way she'd avoided getting too close to him the past few minutes. Because after all they'd shared last night, God forbid they actually touch in the light of day. He shoved at the bike to get it rolling again, funneling his resentment into his white-knuckled grip on the handles.

The five dogs Ben had helped Cesare feed the prior evening began to bark and whine when he first wheeled the bike inside. The yelps and yips of puppies joined the chorus. Their voices rose to a fever pitch a few minutes later when Cesare entered with Evalina. The Italian lifted a hand in greeting to Ben on his way past to care for his animals.

She started to follow, then hesitated and turned toward Ben.

"I don't really need you to hand me tools," he stated without looking up from his survey of what all needed repair. From the corner of his eye, he saw her spin on her heel and follow Cesare. Once the dogs were fed, the noise level quieted enough for him to hear the two of them conversing in their native language. Her voice speaking that language did things to him that should be illegal. And when she'd whispered in his ear last night...*good, God.* Even now he had to bite back a low groan.

Catching a subtle change in her voice and then her laugh, he couldn't help but give in to the distraction and glance over. A wiggling little ball of fur lay in her arms, trying to nip at the braid draped over her shoulder. She flipped it back with another laugh that tugged at his gut.

He quickly returned his attention to the job at hand and kept it there. Unfortunately, once he had a mental checklist of what he'd need, he had no choice but to head over and ask Evalina to translate. Her smile faded as he approached, reinforcing exactly where they stood.

"Can you see if Cesare has some items I'm going to need?"

She rubbed the pup's belly, deftly avoiding its sharp teeth and his gaze as she nodded.

"You might want to get a pen and paper," he suggested. "I have some in my bag in the house."

Her gaze lifted. "But you *can* fix it, right?"

"It might take a couple hours, but yeah, I think so."

The relief in her expression was like a punch to the gut as she bent to set the puppy down. He watched her leave, thinking he'd give just about anything to go back to their fun-loving companionship from during dinner the night before.

When she returned, she not only had his bag, but a steaming cup of coffee and a plate with some pancakes. He gratefully accepted the plate and coffee—espresso again—and then headed over to the workbench to start his list. As he printed everything out, he reached for a warm pancake, folded it in half and took a large bite. Flavor exploded in his mouth.

"*Mmm.* Damn that's good."

"*Fritelle di farina di Castagne.* Chestnut flour pancakes like Cesare's grandfather survived on during the war."

Ah. Yeah, they were good, but he couldn't imagine eating them three times a day for an entire winter. But then again, he totally understood doing what a person had to do to survive. Washing the rest down with a gulp of coffee, he finished writing and handed the paper to Evalina. He reached for a second pancake as she ran her gaze down the neatly printed list.

"Need me to explain any of it?"

She pointed to the second item.

"Carburetor cleaner. These first three, electrical tape, carburetor cleaner and brake fluid are essential. They may not have a car, but I saw a few other motorized machines, so I'm pretty sure he should have them."

"And the remainder of the items?"

"These others would just be nice..." He cringed inwardly at the poor word choice, but her expression remained neutral, so he continued, "But not one hundred percent necessary. If he doesn't have them, bring me something close and I can jerry-rig it." At her confused frown, he explained, "That means I'll make do with whatever I can find."

She nodded and snagged a pancake on her way to talk to Cesare. Ben rolled up his sleeves and set to work removing the gummed up carburetor. In less than ten minutes, he had his essentials and a few of the other items as well, including fresh gas and oil to replace the fluids that'd been sitting for years. Their host continued his search for the rest, but Ben was surprised when Evalina picked up one of the puppies and returned to play with it in the area where he worked.

The little dog gave a couple high-pitched yips, drawing Ben's attention as he tightened a hose clamp. Evalina sat on the ground, legs extended, smiling while she played with the pup. Her expression was lit with unexpected, carefree joy.

When she glanced up and caught him watching her, that smile dimmed. He rose and crossed to the work bench to locate the correct size ratchet wrench.

"I saw the news not so long ago," she commented on his way back to the bike. "That your sister and Trent Tomlin are now engaged?"

"Yep."

Almost a full minute passed, and then she asked, "Do you really think it will last between them? It's kind of crazy to think they found love in the middle of all that chaos."

His heart thudded against his ribs and his grip tightened on the wrench. Was she asking about his sister, or them? "Why is that so hard to believe?"

"High adrenaline situations intensify everything and falsely heightens the senses. Something like that can't be sustained in everyday life."

Is that how she saw their time together? The obvious skepticism sparked his annoyance. "Says you."

"It's highly unlikely," she insisted.

"I've seen them together, Eva, you haven't. They're the real deal."

Silence fell as he squatted next to the engine and made a few adjustments. The puppy had worn itself out and curled up on the ground between her legs. When Ben moved around to the opposite side, she picked up the pup and cradled him in her arms.

"I take it you're a dog person?" he asked, hoping for a bit of conversation and maybe even some peace.

"Is that not obvious?"

He shrugged a shoulder. "Well, everyone loves puppies."

"How can you not?" She rubbed the sleepy little canine's belly. "German Shepherds are my favorite. We had one when I was a little girl, and I always wanted another."

A wistful sigh reached his ears. Another sneak peak caught the longing in her expression.

"So get one."

"Dogs and undercover work don't mix," she said. "I am gone too much."

"Then don't be gone so much."

"Ha. It isn't that simple."

"It can be," he countered.

She seemed to consider his words, but then argued, "What you suggest is impractical. I can't change my entire life just for a dog."

"First of all, you could—*if* you wanted it bad enough." He shifted to rest his forearms over the seat of the bike and watched her while wiping grease from his hands. "But what I'm really suggesting is that you change your life so you can be *happy*. Maybe it involves a dog, maybe not. It should definitely involve your sister."

*And me.*

He swallowed the words before they could escape and abruptly pulled back to return his gaze to the bike. "And you should smile more. Like you do with those puppies."

*Like you did with me last night.*

She rose to her feet and returned the puppy to its mother, her expression impassive. So much for his advice. When she left the shed, he didn't try to stop her. As usual, he'd already revealed too much, and he gave himself a mental kick in the ass.

Why was he hell-bent on exposing himself to more pain? Did he really need a third rejection from her to get it through his thick skull?

Nope. Definitely not.

It was time to focus on what mattered most—the family she'd accused him of forgetting about.

He was going to fix the damn bike and then, she wanted distance? He'd give it to her in spades.

## Chapter 28

EVALINA STOPPED OUTSIDE the door of the shed, hands shoved in her pockets. So much for distance and puppy distraction, and Lord curse her attraction to men on motorcycles.

Ben's intimate familiarity with the bike didn't tone down the sexy one bit, especially with the sleeves of his black shirt rolled to the elbows, revealing those tanned, muscled forearms. While admiring his mechanical skills, it had been impossible to keep at bay the memories of his strong, capable hands so expertly tuning her own body.

Sure, she'd managed to push him away after his unexpected apology in the bedroom this morning, but further attempts for detachment had backfired when she'd asked about Halli and Trent only to have him vehemently defend their whirlwind relationship. He sincerely believed their love would last, and she had to fight a little seed of hope trying to take root within her own heart.

His quiet statement that she should smile more brought to mind their connection during dinner. She couldn't remember the last time she'd enjoyed herself and laughed so much. She had been happy—with him. Add in later, and it was a night she would never forget.

So why fight it? Why not take a chance that he'd actually meant those words spoken in the height of their soul-deep passion?

She leaned back against the sun-warmed wall and closed her eyes against the clear, crisp morning. Birds twittered in the trees as a vision of Nino flashed in her mind.

It caught her off guard, yet a moment later, she knew deep in her gut her former partner was the *why*. The bastard's betrayal still had the power to shake her confidence and mess with her head. As her partner, she'd trusted him with her life every day. But instead of having her back, he'd tried to kill her.

*What the hell kind of cop are you?* You *should've seen the signs.*

For the first time, she didn't run from the inner-voice accusations Nino's memory induced. She took a moment to consider the possibility that maybe this job she was so sure defined her wasn't *really* what she was meant to be doing.

A band constricted around her chest, threatening to cut off her air. She opened her eyes, focused on the bright forest twenty some meters away, and forced herself to breathe through the panic.

It passed, but in its wake, the vision of Nino was replaced by Antonio.

Face to face with the doubt surrounding her new partner, she pushed away from the building and paced in the slanted rays of the rising sun. She didn't want to believe Ben's insinuations, but the incidents at the hotel and on the dead end road made it that much easier to question Antonio's allegiance. The *ispettore* was a pro at working both sides of a coin; he could easily be doing the same thing now.

But why? For money? Did he have some sort of connection to the Fedorios?

She had no clue and didn't know the man well enough to even hazard a guess. Then again, maybe the reason it didn't add up was because it wasn't him. Maybe it was someone further up their chain of command, and Antonio was just a pawn, placed onto the chess board just like she had been.

And if that were the case, who was moving the pieces in this game?

Thinking of all the possibilities put a nagging ache right between her eyes. Sick and tired of the doubt and indecision, she made up her mind she would not go to Rome blind. Besides, if she found out what she could now, it would give her and Ben a better chance at securing what they both needed once they arrived in the city.

Evalina pulled her phone from her pocket, reconnected the battery, and powered it on to call her partner. Yes, it would reveal their location, but she counted on two things—Ben's estimation of a couple hours to repair the bike, and he'd already been working an hour, and the fact that anyone getting information from or through Antonio already knew their final destination. Given the amount of time she and Ben had been off the grid, she was taking a calculated risk that whoever had been in pursuit had continued south and was now waiting for them to show their faces in the capitol.

They wouldn't expect them to still be in the mountains of northern *Toscana*. Taking into account the winding roads, that gave them at least a four hour cushion from *Roma*, and about three hours should the bastards send someone from *Milano*.

With the rain and fog lifted, her phone picked up a signal right away. She almost ignored the voicemail chime, but then decided to listen to the four messages Antonio had left before calling him. The first one was from the evening she and Ben had spent the night in the tower. He wondered where they were, but would wait for her call.

The second was time stamped the previous morning. He relayed he hadn't located Alisa Marshall and there were no new developments on his side. The third message had been left yesterday evening, and the concern in his voice as he told her of the *Commissario's* rising displeasure prompted a frown. Was his worry genuine, or was he playing his part much like she and Ben had been at that same moment in time?

She was still debating when the last message from six-thirty-four that morning played in her ear.

"*Call me.*"

Not a request, but an urgent order tinged with apprehension. A chill crawled along her spine as she located his name in her contact list and then waited for him to answer with her heart pounding in her ears.

"My God, Eva, where have you been?" Antonio demanded in their native tongue. "Why haven't you reported in?"

The urgency in his voice ratcheted up her own anxiety. Checking to be sure neither Cesare or Ilaria were nearby, she explained, "We were stranded without a vehicle in the mountains. The gunman from the hotel showed up in the middle of nowhere, so we had to ditch my car, disabled our phones, and spent the last two days hiking through Garfagnana in search of a road. This is the first I've been able to get a signal." She left out the details of their wrong turn and dead end.

"You've been busy."

"Yes, and it's been fun," she said dryly. And not that she'd ever admit it to him, but she wouldn't trade the last two days for anything. Not even her job. The realization sent her heart into her throat while on the other end of the line, Antonio blew out a sigh.

"I didn't know what to think when I didn't hear from you. Especially after what I found out…"

The hair on her arms stood on end. "What did you find out?"

"Is Sanders there with you? Can he hear you?"

She glanced toward the doors Ben worked behind, and even though she reminded, "He doesn't speak *italiano*," she moved closer to the shed they'd pulled the motorcycle from.

"How has he been?"

"Anxious to get to Rome to secure the Bible for his family."

"Oh, I'm sure he is."

His muttered comment spiked her impatience. "Tell me what you found, Antonio."

"Since last week Wednesday, Este Fedorio has received a number of phone calls from the States. It's a burner phone, so no name to go with it, but the calls originated in Wisconsin."

She narrowed her eyes, considering the information. "Do you think the men holding Ben's mother are working for Fedorio?"

"That's one possibility."

The cryptic approach tested her patience. "And the other?"

"Did you sleep with him again?"

The unexpected question sent a flash of indignant heat from her head to her toes. She grit her teeth, then very calmly and distinctly replied, "That is none of your business."

"Dammit, Eva. The correct answer was *no*."

Her control snapped. "What the hell does this have to do with the case?"

"Everything when I can't be sure your integrity hasn't been compromised."

Oh, how ironic coming from him. "My loyalty is, and always has been, to *Italia* and the *Polizia di Stato*."

*Which is more than I can say for you.*

Silence broke on his expelled breath. "Interpol logged a call from the same number to Este late last night."

"And?"

"This time it originated in Rome. Which means, either the men supposedly holding his mother have traveled to our capitol, or…"

Ice cascaded through her veins. "Someone in his family is working with Este." *Possibly including Ben himself.*

"That's the more likely scenario," Antonio agreed. "The younger sister Halliwell is accounted for, but the mother and older sister are both off the grid."

"Rachel was supposed to be going to Los Angeles to stay with Halli."

"How do you know that?"

"Ben…called her." Her words faltered. She recalled how he'd lied about speaking to Rachel the first time. He could easily have lied about her going to L.A. as well.

*But I heard him speaking to her. He couldn't have faked that…*

She squeezed her eyes shut, shaking her head. Was she really so stupid? He'd disguised the first call to his mother by using Rachel's name. And during the second call, she'd stepped away to hail the cab. If he had indeed been talking to his sister that time, he could've said anything in that minute she was out of earshot.

Considering the way he'd grown up, the con probably came as second nature. He'd practically admitted as much in the cab when commenting about Nick Marshall—who also seemed pretty convinced the man she'd come to trust hadn't changed a bit.

Something else hit her in the gut. The men who'd burst into the hotel suite had shot at her without hesitation. Had *she* been the intended target in that hit? Get rid of her so he could complete the job he'd been sent to do?

"Eva?"

Antonio's voice brought her back to the present. Swallowing past the growing lump in her throat became difficult. "What?"

"When did he call Rachel?"

"Tuesday morning. Right after you and I spoke."

"Okay," he said thoughtfully. "I'll follow up on that. There is no record of either Lia or Rachel entering the country via customs, but Interpol is currently checking all known aliases. I'll have them review the flights to California, too. In the meantime, I'll text you the phone number from Este's phone records. I need you to check Sanders' cell to see if any of his contacts match the number."

Numb, she nodded, then realized he couldn't see her. "Okay."

After another beat of silence, Antonio's quiet voice reached across the line. "I'm sorry, Eva."

"Don't be," she bit out. "I'm fine."

She lifted her face to the sun, praying its warmth would thaw the chill that'd taken over her body. Antonio assumed Ben was guilty, that he'd been playing them—playing *her*—this whole time. Even she had to admit, it didn't look good.

She took a breath. Then another. And another.

Her brain began to catch up as blood flowed. Thoughts began tumbling over each other faster than she could sort them. Ben had insisted they walk away from her car instead of toward Este's men. He'd taken a bullet for her nine months ago. He'd tackled the man in the suite, and he'd saved her at the river when one little slip would've sent her into the water.

Yes, he'd lied more than once, but so had she.

If he truly wanted her gone, letting any one of those incidents play out would've given him the results Antonio's scenario claimed he desired. Instead, he was the man who'd had her back time and again. And last night he'd cherished her, intimately connected to her soul in a way she'd never imagined possible.

The warmth of the sun glowed on her cheeks, and her heart refused to believe *that* man could be so callus.

Alternate explanations whirled through her conscious, starting with the likelihood that Antonio was laying the groundwork for his own line of deceit. If that were the case—and even if it wasn't—she needed to proceed with her original plan and let the chips fall where they may.

"We're in the process of securing transportation to Rome," she told Antonio. "Let's plan to meet at the Coliseum at nineteen hundred tonight. West side, near the Arch of Constantine. I plan to disable my phone again as soon as we hang up, so if something happens that we are unable to make that meeting, the secondary time will be midnight."

"And what if you find a matching number on Sanders' phone?" Antonio inquired.

"I'll keep playing along. The diary is our top priority, is it not?"

"*Sì.*"

"Then let's get the job done," she stated firmly.

"*Bene.* Until seven, then."

She disconnected the call and sank down onto her heels, her back against the shed. She'd have an answer by tonight. When the muted chime alerted her to an incoming text, she memorized the number Antonio sent, and then removed the battery once more.

It would be an interesting day. She'd hopefully given her and Ben enough time to locate the Bible before meeting with Antonio to plan how to secure the diary. The secondary arrangements were her insurance that if she saw something she didn't like at seven, she could pull back and regroup without alerting him to her suspicions.

After the mental rollercoaster of the past few minutes, she sucked in and blew out a huge cleansing breath. Her gaze scanned the grass at her feet, then rose to encompass the trees. The rain of the past twenty-four hours left spring leaves glowing vibrant green in the bright morning sunshine. A jacket would be unnecessary by early afternoon, but for now, she crossed her arms and rubbed hard while debating how to handle what Antonio had revealed.

There had to be some truth to the information; he knew she could call into headquarters at any time to verify. The question was, how much, if anything, should she tell Ben? Protocol demanded she keep the information confidential. One never tipped their hand to a suspect.

Except she didn't consider him a suspect. She trusted him. She believed that *he* believed retrieving the Bible would ensure his mother's safety. He'd been genuinely worried for his sister, and deserved to know what she knew. Or thought she might know.

On the other hand, by his own words, family was everything. She knew what that kind of betrayal could do to a person, only for him, it would be another entire level deeper.

Before she could make a final decision, the double doors to the kennel shed swung open and Ben rolled the motorcycle outside. He swung one long, jean-clad leg over the seat, straddling the machine before shifting his balance to kick-start the bike.

After a few kicks the engine caught, but then died just as fast. She watched him reach down to make an adjustment before trying again. It started, chugging loud and unevenly. One more adjustment from Ben and then he revved the engine with a few jerks of his wrist.

The loud sound evened out, and when he raised his head, she caught a brief glimpse of the cocky smile on his lips. It faded as his gaze swept the area. He didn't turn his head far enough in her direction to see her, but before she could call out, he shifted into gear and swung the bike away in a wide circle. She rose to her feet as he shot down the dirt lane that Cesare had told them yesterday led out to the main road.

Insecurity swept in on the spring breeze as Ben sped out of sight. When the sound of the engine faded, she stared in astonishment.

Had he just left her?

Seconds became minutes.

She'd believed in him. Trusted him. Hell, if it had come down to it, she would have defended him at the cost of her own job. But he'd left without a single glance backward.

Antonio was right—he'd played her. All of them. How had she been so stupid to fall for his con? To fall for *him*.

Each cruel beat of her pulse magnified the pain and rising desolation ripping through her heart. Tears burned her eyes and a sob built in her throat.

Cesare stepped through the open doors of the shed, and she spun away, worried he'd see her expression—until she remembered he was legally blind. From the corner of her eye, she saw him continue toward the villa. Sheer determination allowed her to regain a firm grip on her emotions and thankfully shocked disbelief morphed into white-hot fury.

*Bastardo americano.* All his talk about finding happiness in her life, as if he actually cared about her, and then he screwed her like this? Hell no! When she saw the lying *gran pezzo di merda* again—and she did mean *when*, not *if*—she was going to arrest him.

Right after she kicked his ass.

## Chapter 29

BEN ACCELERATED UP the hill, relishing the feel of the wind and sun on his face when he reached the clearing. Circling around the buildings, he shifted into neutral and then braked to a stop outside the shed. Across the yard, Cesare and Ilaria stepped out of the back door of the villa.

He killed the engine as movement from inside the shed caught his eye. Evalina stormed through the open doors. Before he could lower the kickstand and get off, she slammed his bag into his chest with enough force to rock him back in the seat. He grabbed for the bag while struggling to keep the bike balanced.

"Whoa. What the hell was that for?"

"For leaving."

"I didn't leave." He frowned as she glowered at him, fists clenched, eyes flashing. *O*-kay, wow, she was good and pissed. He set the bag aside, then secured the bike and swung his leg over to stand in front of her. "I went for a test drive to make sure I didn't miss anything before we hit the road."

Her gaze narrowed. A flicker of uncertainty buckled beneath the weight of steel resolve. "More likely your guilty conscience got the better of you."

Clearly she was determined to think the worst of him. The

realization hurt, and at the same time, it ignited the anger that'd been smoldering beneath the surface of his civility. Fed up with her entire attitude since the moment she woke up, he reached for her. She wrestled from his grasp and then rounded back on offense. Instead of retreating, he lunged forward to capture her hands, twined his fingers with hers, and imprisoned her arms behind her back.

She struggled for freedom he refused to give. A firm jerk drew her forward against his chest until they were nose to chin. Her breath whooshed out in a tiny grunt.

He bent his head, forcing her mutinous gaze to meet his. "How many times do I have to tell you, Eva, *I don't leave.*"

Color rose in her face. He wanted to believe he read a flicker of hope in the amber depths of her eyes, but worried it was wishful thinking on his part. Even with that concern, he couldn't hold back the words of harbored resentment that spilled from his lips.

"See, I know how it feels to wake up alone and wonder what the hell you did wrong that the woman you just spent an incredible night with would disappear without a single word of explanation. No note. No goodbye. And when you can't answer that question, it lingers, through long, sleepless nights, for months on end, until you start to get really pissed off for being such an idiot to fall for her in the first place. God knows I should've been smart enough to avoid it a second time."

Her eyes widened and he heard her swallow. Voices registered and he realized Cesare and Ilaria were crossing the yard. Time to let her go, but…

The warmth of Eva's breath on his skin made it impossible for him to resist. He dipped his head and brushed her lips with his. Her shallow breathing matched his, and when her lashes lowered over those damn mesmerizing eyes, he blocked out the world and pressed harder. Releasing her hands, he splayed his against her back, keeping her close. She brought her arms up to lock them around his neck, holding tight as he angled his head to allow for a deeper, more intimate kiss.

The first sweep of his tongue along the seam of her lips picked up the lingering flavor of her morning espresso. Bitterness registered on his tongue, mirroring his emotions, and he immediately sought the exotic sweetness he knew she guarded deep inside. She opened to him with low, desperate sound of pure need that blasted through the flimsy defenses he'd erected.

Uttering a soft groan of frustration, he brought his hands up to frame her face while he withdrew from the kiss. She rocked back on her heels, fingers curled tight on his forearms, banked passion and confusion swirling in her eyes. *Good.* At least he wasn't the only one floundering in the deep end here.

"Grab your stuff," he said, his voice much too gruff for his own good. "I'll negotiate a price for the bike, and then we're leaving."

Her gaze shifted to the older Italian couple who now stood a few feet away. When it met his again, she gave a brisk nod, her cop persona firmly back in place to conceal all her emotions. "I'll be right back."

He couldn't help admiring her confident stride across the yard to the back entrance of the villa. As she disappeared inside, he realized Cesare and Ilaria were watching him with solemn eyes.

Before he could bring up the matter of price, Ilaria said, "We accept no money."

"Excuse me?"

Cesare began speaking in Italian, but his wife spoke over him in English. "We cannot accept money for assisting *la Polizia.*"

After a moment of surprise, shame and guilt mushroomed. "She told you?"

"No. But we are not fools, *signore.* You wear no rings. Your clothes, your footwear, your desire to buy transportation instead of retrieving your automobile. There is more than you tell us." She gave a soft smile. "I confirmed our suspicions when I searched the *ispettore*'s belongings this morning."

They hadn't fooled them one bit and after the lies, he couldn't even be offended at their snooping. "I'm sorry—"

Ilaria raised a hand to forestall his apology. "We understand the situation Evalina feared when the two of you met Cesare in the forest. He had equal concern, at first."

"Then why did you allow us into your home? How do you know I'm not a criminal?"

She laughed. "My husband may be near blind, Ben, but not everything is seen with the eyes."

He unsuccessfully fought a frown. Now he needed an interpreter for English.

"We may not understand your role in this story, but my husband can sense these things," Ilaria explained. "He believes, *we* believe, your feelings for her are true."

Was he that obvious? His heart began to thump in his chest, until he reminded himself they only knew he and Eva weren't married. Apparently they'd pulled off the being in love part quite convincingly. If only he actually *had* been acting.

A sideways glance revealed Evalina was on her way back. He really didn't want to continue this conversation with her listening, or at all, so he reached into his pocket and took out his wallet.

"I appreciate your understanding, but I'm the one buying the bike, not Eva. I have a couple hundred dollars—"

Cesare shook his head and rapidly crossed his hands back and forth. "*No.*"

"It is our gift to you," Ilaria insisted.

"You opened your home to us, gave us shelter and fed us. You've already given too much."

"It is the custom of Italia to help those in need. You insult us when you refuse our gift."

This was a first. The few times he'd been caught conning people in the past, the victims had always been angry—and rightfully so. For these two to remain so accepting and kind only doubled his guilt.

Ilaria moved forward and clasped his hands. "We ask for only one thing in return."

"What is that?"

She tugged him near under the guise of kissing each of his cheeks as she whispered, "Invite us to your wedding."

He reared back, head tilted, an uneasy smile twitching his lips. "Yeah, um...we're not..."

"All in good time, *signore*. All in good time." She patted the back of his hand. "Do not let something so special slip away."

What the heck did she know?

Evalina rejoined them as the perceptive woman released him. Her gaze dropped to the wallet in Ben's hand. "Everything settled?"

"Um...yeah," he said, returning it to his inside jacket pocket next to his passport. "We're good. I'm sure you'll agree it's better if you get the directions and then we can get going."

He took her bag and secured it to the bike along with his while she figured out where they were going. A few minutes later, Cesare leaned in to give her a hug and a noisy smack on each cheek. She grinned as she turned to Ilaria. The woman pulled her close and they did the air kisses.

"*Segui il tuo cuore*."

Ben caught Evalina's startled expression and wondered what the woman had said to *her*. Then he decided he didn't want to know. The older couple was much, *much* too insightful and now seemed to be playing wily matchmakers.

"Ready?" he asked Evalina when she stepped back.

She nodded, still looking a bit nonplussed as he shook hands with Cesare and thanked the couple for their hospitality and generosity. Then he swung his leg over the bike and started the engine. She braced a hand on his shoulder when she got on, but as her weight settled behind him, her touch withdrew. Turning his head to speak over his shoulder, he raised his voice above the rumble of the engine.

"Hang on. The road is rough."

This time she held onto his waist on either side. He reached down, took hold of her hands and pulled her arms around to the front of his stomach until her body rested snug against his back. It was going to be a long, torturous ride, and pretty much threw his 'distance in spades' vow right out the window, but *now* they were ready to go.

He gave the throttle a little juice and spun them around toward the dirt track. He nodded on his way past the Italians, while Evalina gave them one last wave goodbye. Once they were past the clearing and into the woods, he followed the route he'd taken earlier, bypassing his original turnaround spot.

Evalina's hold tightened as they travelled the bumpy track for a good five miles before reaching a deteriorated, paved surface that was no wider than a single lane. She directed him to the right and after a few more miles, the familiar freedom of being on a bike again eased into his psyche. With hours to go before they reached Rome, he gave himself up to the pleasure of the sun shining down, the wind in his face, and best of all, Eva's warm curves at his back.

Her body moved with his as he leaned into the switchbacks, and he wondered what life would be like if they could be the couple they'd been last night. *Man*, if that wasn't a dangerous road to travel. He'd be lying if he said a future with Evalina had never crossed his mind, but after what Ilaria had said, he wondered if someone else suggesting there could be one made it any more feasible.

He sat at the fantasy crossroads in his mind. Thought of the look in Eva's eyes after he'd kissed her back there, and made the imaginary turn.

They'd take rides like this all the time, exploring the countryside and rich, beautiful history of her country. Spend hours talking and laughing, and probably just as many arguing. Making up would be fun. He'd have her teach him her language, starting with all the sexy words she whispered while they were in bed together. Loving each other.

The possibility of a chance at that kind of happiness put an ache in his chest. Was there any way to overcome the obstacles between them? She clearly didn't know how to handle what was between them any more than he did. In the bedroom, she'd said one thing, but out in the yard, her eyes said another.

Words were spoken as lies all the time, but the eyes...*the eyes are the window to the soul.*

Would she ever stop running long enough to give them a fighting chance?

*Maybe*—if everything went as they needed it to today. Locating the Bible was crucial for his family, but no way Evalina would let him return to Wisconsin until they'd retrieved the diary from Nick Marshall. Common sense told him the only way Nick would give up the diary would be in a trade Ben couldn't allow.

If it came down to that decision, would Evalina back him up to save his family, or choose the job that she believed defined her life? The question settled like lead in his gut. Until he knew the answer, thinking, hoping, day-dreaming about anything beyond today was pointless.

Reality check firmly in place, he blocked out everything else.

A good twenty minutes into the ride, they came across their first vehicle outside the small mountain village of Sillico. The picturesque old town that Cesare had mentioned in his story the night before was staggered like steps on the steep mountainside, with many of the stone-paved passages between houses not open to motorized vehicles. It took a few wrong turns for them to navigate their way around to the main road.

They continued down the mountain, passing through Pieve Fosciana and into Castelnuovo di Garfagnana. He was surprised when Evalina directed him into the city, but she explained they'd need helmets or risk being pulled over and fined. Avoiding further police involvement was fine by him, so they asked for directions and quickly located a shop after topping off the gas tank.

Exiting the store about ten minutes later, Ben slipped on his new sunglasses and then hung his helmet on one of the handle bars. "I've been working on decoding that address from my dad and I think I figured out the key. Do you think any of these shops would have a map of Rome?"

Evalina's gaze surveyed the stores around them until she pointed across the street. "Check in there. They would be most likely to have one."

"You coming?"

"I'll wait here."

"Okay. I'll be right back." He waited for a passing car before jogging across. A shelf of maps were right near the door, so he located what he wanted and proceeded to the register. As he handed the girl some money, he glanced out the window to see Evalina digging into one of the bags on the bike. She pulled something out and cast a quick look toward the store before turning her back.

Returning his attention to the man across the counter, he accepted his change in one hand and grabbed the map in the other before suspicion snuck up and smacked him between the eyes. The coins went into his jeans pocket as he shoved out of the store. He moved down the sidewalk and then crossed the street so he could come up on the opposite side of where Evalina might expect should she turn to look for him again.

As he got closer, doubt eased when he saw she was just on her phone. Two steps later, his tension returned tenfold. "What are you doing with *my* phone?"

## Chapter 30

EVALINA COULDN'T CONTROL the guilty jerk of her hand at Ben's voice directly behind her. How the hell did he get back so quick? He stepped around to face her, and she took a deep breath to calm her racing pulse before meeting his cool blue gaze. Day and night compared to the look in his eyes after that earlier kiss.

"I—mine was dead."

He swiped the phone from her grasp. "Thought we weren't using our phones."

"Ah..." *Good God, get it together.*

His gaze rose from the screen and his eyebrows arched. "Find anything interesting in my contact list?"

*No. You didn't give me enough time.* She forced herself to hold his gaze. "I thought you might want to check for any messages from Rachel. Or your mom."

"You're not worried about anyone tracking us?"

"We can shut it off again right away, and we'll be long gone before anyone could get here."

"That's true. And you're right—I've been wanting to check." Suspicion remained in his expression, but he lifted the phone and maneuvered on the touch-screen. A moment later, relief eased his frown. "Rachel made it to L.A. yesterday."

Except Antonio had said they'd been unable to locate either Lia or Rachel.

"Why don't you give her a quick call," she suggested. "Just to be sure."

He glanced up, eyes narrowed, then looked back at his phone as he dialed. Lifting the phone to his ear, he raised his gaze back to hers. "Is there something going on I should know about?"

"I thought knowing your sister is safe would take off some of the pressure, that's all."

"Right." He didn't even attempt to hide his disbelief.

A slight alteration in his stance and facial expression told her someone must've answered on the other end, and a moment later he greeted his sister. Though he relaxed a bit, the fact that he didn't once move his gaze from Evalina's further confirmed he hadn't bought her unconvincing explanation. It appeared with this man, she'd forever be making rookie mistakes.

When he asked to talk to Halli, Evalina continued to watch his face for any signs he was attempting to cover something up. All those months ago, she'd noticed his nervous habit of fidgeting, but right now his nerves appeared rock steady. No tell-tale color in his cheeks, no shifting of his gaze. All indications pointed to him being on the phone with his sisters as the absolute truth, and nothing in his words suggested any type of code speak.

When he disconnected that call, she asked as casually as possible. "What about your mother? Anything from her?"

"No. I'd imagine the men holding her took the phone away."

As Antonio had said, men holding his mother was one scenario. It was the second possibility that she feared. She hated this. He deserved to know the truth, but she didn't even know what that was for sure.

Ben removed the battery and pocketed both it and his cell. She reached to put her helmet on, but mid-lift, he stepped forward and palmed it with one hand, forcing it back to waist level in one smooth, controlled move. His resolute expression made it unnecessary for him to speak out loud his demand for answers.

Resignation made her shoulders droop. "I called Antonio from the villa this morning."

The statement didn't seem to surprise him. "Do you trust him?"

"I don't know." She shifted her gaze down the street. "No. Not yet."

"That's progress. That'd you'd actually admit that, I mean."

Sighing, she looked back at him. "We're set to meet him tonight at seven outside the Coliseum. It's open, public, and we'll get there early to make sure he arrives alone. If I don't like what I see, we back out and figure out what to do from there."

Ben nodded, but she also saw a flicker of hesitation.

"We should have the Bible by then, so if we determine Antonio's clean, he can back us up when we go after the diary from Marshall."

Again with the indecision in his eyes. When his gaze wavered, dismay settled over her. He wasn't so sure about what would be required to obtain the diary. *No*, she realized. He knew exactly what it would take, but wasn't willing to chance the trade.

She tilted her head to catch his eye. "You won't lose the Bible, Ben. I promise."

His gaze searched hers before he gave a second tight nod. He removed his hand from her helmet and stepped back to reach for his own. Instead of putting hers on, she cradled it against her churning stomach.

"Can I ask you something?"

"What?"

"When you talked to Rachel...the other day, not now...you said you thought your mother might be involved in all this."

He stiffened. "That was before I knew what was actually going on."

"But—"

"Don't." He shook his head from side to side without looking at her. "Don't go there, Eva."

"I am simply trying to consider every angle."

With a fierce scowl, he pivoted, his hand gripping the edge of his helmet as he jabbed it in her direction. "You're trying to plant doubt in my mind about my mother so I will give up the Bible for the diary."

"No."

"*Yes*. But I talked to the bastard who threatened to kill her." He moved closer, nostrils flared as he glared at her. "Trust me, I heard the fear in her voice. It was as real as it gets."

"Okay." She held up a placating hand. "I'm sorry."

He stared her down for a few more tense seconds, then backed up and jammed the helmet on his head.

"Ben…"

"We're leaving. Now."

He swung astride the bike and started it with one forceful, downward kick. She secured her headgear and climbed on behind him. This time when she gripped his waist on each side, he didn't bother to pull her close. When he shot out onto the road, she had to clench her fingers in the material of his jacket to keep her seat.

Back on the road, the cities and miles flew by. Without the threat of being tracked this time, they made good time on the autostrada. And yet, as fast as the trip went, she still had way too much time to think.

Her gut and her heart told her he honestly believed his mother was in danger, but her mind wasn't convinced Lia Sanders' life was on the line. Convincing Ben of that without proof would be difficult. Even if the cell numbers matched, it didn't confirm his mother was the one making the calls to Este, and she knew Ben would do whatever he thought necessary to save her. His fierce loyalty was one of the things she loved about him.

*Love.*

*Yes.* She was past denying how she felt, even though the mere thought of the depth of her feelings had her simultaneously wanting to slide forward to hug him tight and leap off at the next toll to run the opposite direction.

Rationally, she knew the sooner she accepted they had no

future together, the better off she would be. He would return to his family in Wisconsin; she'd go back to Milano and attempt to figure out the mess her life had become. Irrationally, she wanted to gamble on last night, tell him what was in her heart as Ilaria had advised, and ask him to stay. However he responded, at least she'd know, and anything was better than the yo-yo currently jerking her emotions around.

Except the exits for Rome were coming up fast, and she still had a job to see through to the end. Ingrained dedication would not allow her to simply set the job aside.

Reaching under Ben's arm, she signaled for him to take the next right, and they coasted off the Autostrada into the city. It was noon on a Thursday in May, but being the most popular tourist attraction in *Italia*, there was no such thing as slow time in The Eternal City. At the first stop light, he turned his head to speak over his shoulder.

"Let's find a place to eat, and I can sit and work on the address with the map."

"We'll go to the Coliseum. There'll be many places in that area to buy food, and I can locate a good vantage point for our meeting with Antonio later."

When he agreed, she directed him through the congested city streets until the grand ruins rose up before them. He found a place to park and killed the engine. She got off, removed her helmet, and turned to set it on the seat. Ben still sat astride the bike, helmet resting on the gas tank in front of him as his gaze took in the massive structure before them.

"Wow. This is awesome."

From the look of awe in his expression, she knew he'd enjoy touring her country. Sharing the history with him, seeing it through his eyes, would be an amazing experience. *No, don't think of that.*

Tourists of every nationality crammed the sidewalks, and she waited for him to secure the lock he'd bought with the helmets back in Castelnuovo. She led the way to a tourist café and ordered them each pizza and bottled water; *frizzante* for her, *naturale* for him. He paid before she could dig out her money, and she thanked him as she handed over his food. When she turned to search for a place to sit, he called her name and started across the street toward the Coliseum.

Catching up, she pointed to the west side by the *Arco di Costantino*. While he deciphered the code, she could scout where they'd wait for Antonio later. They settled on a clear spot of grass in the sun, and as she began to eat, Ben wasted no time getting down to business. He took a huge bite of pizza, then withdrew his map and the pad of paper he'd used back at the Minimis.

She took a drink of water while he printed letter combinations from the address he'd written at the top of the paper. "Why did your father not simply leave you the correct address?"

"Nothing has ever been that simple with my dad," he replied, his cool tone indicating the miles on the road had only slightly softened his resentment.

Or maybe the emotion was directed at his parent?

He leaned closer to the map, gaze shifting back and forth before he wrote again. "As a con artist, he's suspicious of everyone because they might be trying to con him in return. The street listed is real, but the rest doesn't physically exist. The code is to protect the Bible in case the address fell into the wrong hands. Like in the case of Nick Marshall."

"You don't think he'll be able to break the code?"

"I doubt it. He doesn't know how Dad's mind works."

"And how does it work?"

"He usually buries a code within a code." Ben pointed to the numbers in the address with his pen and spoke around another bite of food. "The numbers indicate letters scrambled within the address. I need to figure out what street name the letters spell once they're unscrambled. Even then, I'm sure there'll be a twist."

She stared down at the maze of streets on the map of Rome. "It appears a bit like finding a needle in a haystack."

He shrugged. "I'm hoping something clicks from a previous

conversation. My dad is also notorious for dropping clues into casual conversation. He used to test us all the time when we were growing up."

Curious about how he'd been raised, she asked, "Code breaking one-o-one?"

"Yeah." His fingers tightened on the pen. "Something like that."

She noticed he had a habit of saying those words when he didn't care for the topic of conversation. And yet she couldn't help but comment, "You sound...resentful."

"No." He wrote a few letters, then paused and looked up. "Yes. I didn't mind it at the time, but I had nothing else to compare it to. We didn't go to school like regular kids because we were never in one place long enough. Halli insisted on going to public school starting in the seventh grade, but Rachel and I were used to being taught at home. It made for a lot of family time, though it wasn't until I got older that I realized we'd missed out on a lot."

"Yet you still have a relationship with your parents."

"There were some good times. Rare memories of all of us together and happy, even Halli." A brief smile curved his mouth before his expression sobered. "I can't help but hope someday we'll have that again. That we can be a normal family who gets together for holiday dinners and birthdays."

"Is that possible after everything they've done? Aren't you just setting yourself up for disappointment?"

"Maybe." He shrugged and started writing again. "Maybe not. Either way, for better or worse, they're still my family."

She swallowed hard, thinking of her sister, working ten minutes away at the flower shop Evalina had sat outside of a time or ten over the past five years. Carina had written her off, not the other way around. You couldn't force a relationship with someone who wanted nothing to do with you.

*You never tried.*

*I was protecting her.*

*You were protecting yourself.*

*No.*

*Yes.*

Yes, she had been protecting herself.

The truth sunk in, filling her with restless energy and stirring up annoyance. This wasn't about her and the fact she was afraid loving someone meant losing them. It was about Ben, and she hoped things worked out the way he wanted. Even more so, she hoped Antonio was wrong about everything else.

She finished eating and wiped her hands on a napkin before getting to her feet. "I'm going to check out the area."

His head tipped sideways as he glanced up without straightening. "You're not worried about me going after the Bible on my own?"

Instead of pointing out the fact that if he found it he'd never make it past airport security, she said, "I have it on good authority you don't leave."

He gave a short laugh as she walked away, but when she glanced back, he'd already returned his attention to his map.

She took almost an hour to scout the area around the Arch until she found her preferred vantage point to view all approaches to the ruins. Across the ancient grounds, she saw Ben had stretched out on his stomach, elbows on the map while he worked. Hopefully he was meeting with some success. They'd have to retrieve the Bible and return in time to catch Antonio's arrival so they could ensure he was both alone and not being followed. With the clock ticking toward one-thirty, she descended the steps and crossed back to Ben.

"Any luck?"

He made a noncommittal sound as she sunk down and folded her legs to the side. Frustration etched a deep furrow into his forehead. She wanted to reach over and rub the tension from his shoulders, smooth the ruffled hair off his brow, but wasn't sure he'd welcome her touch. Besides, once she started, she wouldn't want to stop.

"We could be here for hours yet." He buried his face in his hands, blew out a deep breath, and then rubbed his eyes.

"Can I help?"

"Be my guest."

The pad of paper landed in front of her before he rolled onto his back. He raised one arm to rest on his forehead, shielding his closed eyes against the bright sunlight. After a moment of staring, she shook her head and forced her attention to the address.

*6 Via di San Sebastianello, 178/179*
*00914 Rome, Italy*

She took a look at the numbers and letters and the three pages of scratched-out possibilities and…had no clue where to start. Readjusting her position, she stretched out next to him with the map spread out in front of them.

"Besides the obvious here on the paper, show me what you've been doing."

He blew out a sigh, then rolled back over and walked her through the process he'd applied. "Except I can't find anything on the map with all those letters."

Fifteen minutes later, she was as frustrated as he'd appeared when she'd sat down. Each alternate suggestion she offered he'd already tried. She rubbed her temples as she stared down at their notes. Her gaze narrowed on the numbers in the address.

"Maybe we're expecting it to be too hard."

"What do you mean?"

"What if the second line of the address is a secondary clue? Solve the first one before you can work on the second?"

His reach for the pad leaned his broad shoulder against hers and connected their hands. Electricity tingled up her arm. They'd been together for days now and still the skin to skin contact had a powerful affect. Especially when his touch lingered a moment longer than necessary before he drew back with the paper in hand.

"Can't hurt to give it a try."

He muttered under his breath as he began working the letters.

Every time he had a viable combination, he voiced it out loud and Evalina scanned the map.

"Tasinis...Astinis...Natisis...Sistina...Sitsina...Ista—"

"*Aspetti*—wait. Sistina...I saw that." Her visual sweep spotted the name top center. "Via Sistina—yes! Right here."

Ben turned his head, their eyes met, and he grinned. Her stomach flipped over as he lifted his hand to the back of her neck, drawing her closer as he leaned forward.

"You, my dear, are a genius," he murmured just before he kissed her full on the mouth.

## Chapter 31

SHE LEANED INTO the kiss, boldly dueling her tongue with his to ignite a firestorm of desire Ben had no choice but to suppress. They were too close to lose focus now. Reluctantly drawing back, he rubbed his thumb over her full bottom lip before lifting his attention to her darkened whiskey eyes.

"We should go."

Disappointment flashed as she lowered her gaze. "Yes."

He couldn't resist one more brief kiss, then released her to push up and sit back on his heels while gathering his notes and the map. She grabbed their water bottles, and they set off for the bike parked on the other side of the Coliseum. Threading through the tourists and occasional street performer dressed as a roman soldier, he was once again awed by the grandeur and sheer size of the historic site.

On the bike, Evalina navigated them through the misaligned streets that seemed to dominate every Italian city or town he'd been in. The maze-like narrow streets, some of them confusing one-ways, took them past more ruins and a palace with huge columns of marble. After a few more turns this way and that, the short street of Via San Vincenzo opened up into yet another city square filled with people.

The crowded piazza was dominated by a huge building, in front of which was a large fountain that stretched from one side to the other. As Evalina directed him to the right of the fountain, he slowed, switching his attention back and forth between the impressive attraction and the road.

"What is that?" he asked over his shoulder.

"*Fontana di Trevi*. The tourists call it the Trevi Fountain."

The name rang a bell. "Isn't there some thing about tossing coins in there?"

"Traditional legend claims visitors who toss a coin into the fountain will ensure a return trip to Rome."

Total superstition no doubt, and yet he had an irrational urge to pull over and dig a euro from his pocket. Instead, he continued driving until Via Francesco Crispi intersected Via Sistina. At the junction, all the traffic went in different directions. He couldn't go straight, because the street ahead was one way coming toward him. Via Sistina was also one way, but from where they sat, the street split traffic away in opposite directions.

He turned right and pulled off to the side to consult the map. Angling toward Evalina, he asked, "Could the nine-one-four in the second line of the address be a street number, or apartment number?"

She shook her head. "It's too high and the street isn't long enough. Number ninety-one is possible though. Or ninety-four. Fourteen, forty-one, forty-nine—"

"I got it. Any combination of two of the numbers." He looked at the building to his right and saw number thirty-eight next to the door. Next was thirty-seven. Glancing to the opposite side of the street, he saw one hundred ten. Unlike in the states where addresses tended to have odd numbers on one side and even on the other, these ones went right down the line and back up the other side.

"Except for fourteen, all the numbers we need are the opposite direction." He glanced behind them. "Think I can swing around?"

"I would not recommend it." She pointed toward two policemen across the street.

"Right—we'll check out fourteen first and then circle around."

He eased back into traffic until they reached fourteen. It appeared to be residential, but nothing about the entrance or surrounding area tripped any clues in his memory. He continued on and took the first street to the left. A few more turns brought them back to the Via Sistina intersection and this time he went right. As they approached the lower nineties on the right, the *Trinità Snack Bar Café* caught his eye.

A spurt of excitement quickened his pulse, and he braked while swerving into an empty parking space. Though the snack bar's name appeared to be the clue, its neighboring address of ninety-one is where Ben focused. The number matched his father's coded address.

"This is it."

"How do you know?"

He got off the bike and removed his helmet. "Last summer when I told my dad we were coming to Italy, he told me about a trip he and my mother made to Rome. They had tea at the *Trinità Café*. That can't be a coincidence."

Evalina stood on the sidewalk, her gaze raised to the sign attached to the first floor balcony. "This is a hotel."

When he saw the sign, his exhilaration evaporated as fast as it arrived.

"Would your father have sent the Bible where countless people would potentially have access?"

Hands on his hips, he lowered his gaze to the open doors and the stairs that he presumed led to a lobby. She had a damn good point, but seeing as it was the only location that currently provided any clues, he dropped to one knee on the sidewalk. "It's a place to start."

"On the *pavement?*"

The confusion in her tone made him smile while he fished out the key concealed in his right boot the past three days. When he stood, Evalina's perplexed expression prompted him to hold up the silver key that had barely escaped discovery at the *Armani*.

"This is what Nick and Alisa *didn't* get back in Milan. Whatever this opens should contain the Bible." He hoped.

Inside the lobby of the hotel, he did a quick inventory of the place before striding to the front desk. After exchanging greetings and establishing English with the check-in girl, he showed her the key. "Are there any rooms this key might open?"

A frown creased her brow as she shook her head. "No, *signore*."

Evalina joined him at the counter and extended her hand. "May I?" she asked Ben.

He put the key in her palm and watched as she looked at it, then flipped it over. He spotted the numbers etched in the metal the same time she did.

*43*

She turned back to the girl. "Do you have a room number forty-three, or thirty-four?"

Again, the girl shook her head. "We have only twenty-four rooms."

Ben turned away from the desk as he tamped down his frustration. He had to remind himself a place to start meant they were at the beginning with a ways to go. Evalina handed the key back to him as they returned to the sidewalk. His restless gaze took in the arched double doors across the street and then shifted to the street number *forty-nine*. With a quick glance to the left to check for traffic, he hurried to the other side and tried to fit the key in the lock.

Nope. Not it. He backed up and stumbled into Evalina. "Sorry."

His glance to the right was cut short when she pulled him left until they reached *forty-three*. It was a window. Forty-two had a door with a keyhole, and a call box off to the side. A brief perusal of the names gave no clues, so he moved to the door.

This time the key slid right into the hole and turned easily. A slight nudge unlatched the door. He removed the key and stepped aside for Evalina to enter first, then followed her inside.

"Now what?" she asked.

He thought a moment. "We try first floor, fourth door, or fourth floor, first door."

"The numbers from the postal code in the address."

"Yep." He followed her down the dim hallway to the fourth door. When he extended his hand to try the key, she quickly checked the action. Then she knocked on the door while reaching into her pocket.

Footsteps sounded on the other side and a moment later, a middle-aged man stood before them. Evalina flashed her badge, speaking to him in Italian as Ben listened. He recognized when she said his father's name, but other than the obvious negative head-shake the man gave, he understood little else.

After another minute, she thanked the man and he retreated back into his home.

"He has lived here for the past twenty-five years with his parents and says they do not know of your father."

"That much I gathered." He turned for the stairs. "Onward and upward."

On the fourth floor, he rapped his knuckles on the first door, then had to force himself to count to sixty. He lost patience at thirty and knocked with a bit more force. When no one answered, Evalina bent down and peered at the keyhole.

"Your key is too new for this lock," she announced as she straightened. "Even if this is the correct location, it will not fit."

Ben took his own look at the little metal plate with its old fashioned keyhole. Realization dawned and he fisted his hand until the key bit into his palm. "Sonofabitch, we need the damn skeleton key." He gave her a grim look. "Exactly like the one in my bag that Nick Marshall stole back in Milan."

"Ah. So he holds more than the diary."

He didn't bother to answer as he considered the door. Stepping forward, he grasped the handle and gave it a good shake.

*Damn.* Not one centimeter of wiggle room. He backed up because leading with his shoulder would get him nowhere. However, if he landed his boot right next to—

"No." Evalina cut off his thought as she moved in front of him. "Do not even consider it."

"Don't consider what?"

"Breaking in."

She knew him too well. "Come on. One good kick and—"

"Despite appearances to the contrary, I am still a cop, and I cannot condone breaking and entering. You're not even sure this is the correct place."

"It's not like I'm going to steal anything if it's not." When she didn't move, he proposed another option. "What if I pick the lock? We'd only be entering then. If it's not the right place, we close the door and move on."

Her indrawn breath had him expecting further argument, but then she released it on a resigned sigh. "I can live with that."

He patted his pockets for something to pry against the metal wards inside the lock that prevented just any key from opening it, but came up empty. When he turned his gaze to Evalina, he didn't even have to voice his question. She rolled her eyes and turned for the stairs, but not before he caught a slight smile on her lips.

"I'll return in a moment."

His own grin was directed to her back as she skimmed down the stairs. He leaned against the wall, his mind drifting back over the past few days. They'd been crazy, and yet when he managed to put everything else out of his mind, working with her to break the codes and figure things out was actually kind of fun.

He straightened as she came back up the stairs with both of their bags. When she extended her hand, he opened his and she dropped a hair pin, a tweezers, and a nail clipper onto his palm. He nodded approval; one of the three should work.

"Done this before, have you?"

She shrugged as he bent by the door and began to work the lock. "Undercover one-o-one. Fully sanctioned compared to the course taught by your father."

"Actually, this is mom's forte. They each had their areas of expertise and made a good team." He tilted his head to the side and glanced up at her. "We do, too, you know."

"I know," she agreed softly.

Warmth flooded his chest, and he smiled at the lock.

"About your mother..."

As if she'd flipped a switch, his good mood vanished. He didn't want to start this conversation with her again. "Not now," he warned.

"*Now* is the best time to do it," she argued.

He gave a little jerk of his wrist and heard the click he was waiting for. Ignoring her, he pushed the door open and looked around. His nose wrinkled at the musty smell that hung in the stale air, as if it'd been closed up for years—over thirteen, he'd bet. Evalina stepped inside, setting their bags on the floor before reaching back to close the door.

A glance confirmed her lips compressed in a tight line. Tough. He needed to focus on the Bible, not listen to her ridiculous accusation that his mother had somehow orchestrated this whole thing. She wouldn't con her own damn son.

*Wouldn't she?*

He fisted his hands, as if in doing so he could crush the seed of doubt Evalina had planted.

To discourage further discussion, Ben began searching the apartment for the Bible while she started on the opposite side of the living room. Dust floated in the afternoon sunlight struggling through the cloudy windows. Noise from outside was muffled, making the place feel like a tomb.

"Do you think your father owns this place?" she asked.

"He's never mentioned it." Neither had his mother, which made him wonder if she knew about it. All their assets had been seized during their trials, so this had to be under some sort of alias. For all their togetherness, had they kept such big secrets from each other? "If the Bible is here, someone had to bring it here for him."

"Do you think Dante Fedorio knew more than he let on?"

"Maybe."

Then again, if he had known anything, the man had maintained one hell of a poker face during their meeting in his office. Whoever killed him hadn't gotten the information out of him either. Other than the finger smudges he and Eva were leaving in the dust, the place was undisturbed.

So far, every drawer and cabinet he'd opened contained no sign of the Bible, or any books at all, for that matter. Their movements stirred up the dust. It swirled in the afternoon sunlight and over near the window, Evalina sneezed as she slid out the wide top drawer of an old writing desk.

Automatically, he said, "God bless you."

"*Grazie*," she murmured. A moment later, her indrawn breath drew his attention.

He turned at the same time she did, only she held a large brown package in her hands.

## Chapter 32

BEN STRODE FORWARD, meeting her in the middle of the room to take the unopened package. All it took was one look at the name on the address label for his excitement to surge. "My dad loves old movies. It's ironic, really, but one of his favorites is *To Catch a Thief,* and the name of Carey Grant's character is John Robie."

Plus, the return address was a post office box in Ohio. He backed up around a coffee table and dropped down on the couch. A cloud of dust billowed up and nearly choked him. Coughing, he tore into the packaging, ripping it off until he could open the mailing box. He lifted the lid to get a look at the book that had thrown his life into chaos and threatened his family for the past four days.

Evalina slowly sat beside him, silent as he traced his fingertips over the intricate designs adorning the Bible's ornate leather cover. It measured approximately twelve by fifteen inches, and a deep-set indent of a cross about the size of his hand dominated the center.

He lifted the heavy tome from the box, and Evalina shifted the packaging to the table in front of them.

"It is beautiful," she breathed.

Opening the front cover, he searched for the copyright date. *1827, Authorized King James Version.* Okay, that he hadn't expected. "It's almost two hundred years old."

The date, and the value it inferred, surprised him, though the fact that it did was even more shocking. His parents' background alone should've clued him in, but for some strange reason he realized he'd been picturing a basic run-of-the-mill tome, maybe with the words *Holy Bible, New Testament* printed in cheap gold lettering on black. This one had gold in the cover design, but he'd bet the odds it was one hundred percent real.

Beautiful color illustrations populated the delicate pages, still stunning even after all these years. He reverently turned a few of the pages, then closed the book with gentle care. His mother had said it held clues to a treasure, but clearly, the Bible itself must be worth enough on its own. The danger to her hit home a little harder, and when he turned to look at Evalina's reaction, understanding reflected in her expression as well.

He set the Bible back in the box and stood as he pulled out his phone. "Now, we'll call Alisa and get Nick here with the diary, and I can book the next flight home."

Evalina rose to grab his hand before he could connect the battery. "We need to meet Antonio first. We have a couple hours to get in place."

He shook his head and resisted the urge to curl his fingers around hers by pulling free. "I don't trust your partner. I think we should—"

"That's what the meeting is for, so we can be sure. So *I* can be sure."

"But we don't need him to get the diary. Nick will realize real quick he has no choice in the matter."

"And if he's still armed?"

"The guy isn't in this for the money. He's not going to shoot either one of us," Ben said with complete confidence.

"I still need back up," she insisted.

"I'll be your back up. You even admitted we make a good team."

Emotion flickered in her eyes. It grabbed hold of his heart and made him want to pull her close and convince her they could be a team in everything. Until indecision took over, and she spun away.

When she took a step, he made a desperate grab for her shoulders. They went rigid under his touch, and he flexed his fingers with the effort of not dragging her back against him.

He restrained himself to dipping his head right next to her ear. "We can do this, Eva. You and me. Let me make the call."

An infinitesimal softening of her muscles gave him hope. She twisted around to face him, and the determined glint in her gaze caught him off guard.

"You must promise to listen to me."

His pulse kicked up a notch, but he quickly accepted the condition. "I will." Raised eyebrows prompted him to add, "Promise."

She lifted her hand between them. "Then to be safe, use his phone. His sister is listed in the contacts."

He connected the call, and then wondered at her easier than expected agreement. Suspicion crept in with nervous energy. He stooped to pick up a piece of torn package paper off the floor as he waited for Alisa Marshall to answer. Instead, he got Nick.

"I was wondering when you'd call, Sanders."

"You in Rome?" he asked without preamble.

"I am. How about you?"

"Yeah, no thanks to you."

"I made sure your cop friend was safe before I left."

Ben would never admit to Nick he actually believed him, and instead, seized on the opportunity his word choice provided. "She isn't my friend, that's for sure. I ditched her the first chance I got."

She was watching, listening, and those delicate eyebrows arched skyward again.

"Right," Nick said, drawing out the word, completely unconvinced. "How'd you end up with my phone?"

"You're not the only one who can pick a pocket, Marshall. I

took it off her and split after I overheard her talking to her partner on the phone this morning." Ben infused anger into the words and Evalina's gaze flew to his. He hadn't really, but he had no time to dwell on her confused—almost betrayed—frown as he continued his tale.

"I was just their means to an end. A shill. Only they were starting to get greedy, and I realized once I'd located the Bible, and you showed up with the diary, well, neither one of us would be much use to them at that point. I may have been out of the game for awhile, but I'm not stupid enough to play those kinds of odds with a couple of shady cops in a foreign country."

Evalina's glittering amber glare conveyed she really didn't appreciate being lumped in the same category as her dead partner. She had to understand the importance of convincing the guy—and even she didn't know if he was lying about Antonio. Besides, it was working, because above her tangible anger, he could practically hear the gears turning in Nick's mind.

"You got the Bible?"

"Yes. And I must say, it's pretty damn impressive."

"What's the copyright year?"

*He wants proof I'm not conning him with a fake.* He fiddled with the piece of paper still between his fingers, folding it smaller and smaller between his thumb and forefinger. "Eighteen twenty-seven. Indented cross on the cover."

"Well, then, you got exactly what you came for." Disappointment resonated in Nick's low voice. "Why the hell are you calling me?"

The guy was definitely no amateur. Ben took a controlled breath to keep his voice steady as he cast the line. "To make the trade. Turns out that diary you have in your possession contains some damning evidence on some powerful people. That's why the cops were on me, and the man who gave it to me is already dead. If I don't get it back for them, my mother is next." He didn't have to fake the intensity in his voice with that statement. "These men have decided the diary is more important than the Bible, so I need to make the trade with you as soon as possible."

More silence. Ben unfolded the tiny square of paper and started over again.

"Nick, please." He subdued his impatience and added a note of desperation that wasn't entirely false. "I know you think you hate my family, but—"

"I *know* I hate your family."

"Okay, fine, hate us all you want, but *I* know that doesn't make you a killer. Help me keep any more blood from being spilled. This is the only way we both get what we want. If you and I do this before they find me again, the Bible will be back where it rightfully belongs, and my mother will be safe. We both win."

After a long minute, he actually thought the guy might have hung up. The digital screen told him he hadn't, and then a harsh breath rasped across the line. "Where and when?"

Ben rubbed his hand over his face in relief as he gave him the address. "As soon as you can get here. Just you and me, we'll make the trade and it'll all be over."

"I can be there in an hour."

Ben disconnected and faced Evalina to begin laying out a plan for Marshall's arrival.

"You are a very skilled liar," she stated, her normally sensual accent much more clipped and formal. "You almost convinced me, and I'm standing right here."

The remote tone constricted his chest even as he acknowledged her statement with a dip of his chin. "When the situation calls for it, I do what has to be done," he stated, tapping the phone against his palm. "I'm not about to apologize, either. Yes, there are things in my past I'm not proud of, and there are a lot of things left over from how I grew up, but the difference is, I don't use them for bad anymore."

Challenge practically vibrated the air around her body as she raised her chin and recited ten numbers. They sounded familiar. Almost like a phone num—

His muscles tensed, and he went still as a chill sunk deep into his skin.

"I see you recognize the number," she said.

"That's my mother's cell."

"It's also the number that has made numerous calls to Este Fedorio over the past week."

He frowned and absently stuffed the phone into his pocket. "Are you suggesting the men threatening her life work for her own cousin?" Here his mother was trying to right past wrongs and reconnect with her family, only to be betrayed by one of her own. He didn't doubt the man had probably killed Dante, too. *Bastard.*

"No," Eva said softly. "I think you know exactly what I'm suggesting."

Just like that, those whiskey eyes darkened with a strange combination of apology and sympathy. Then he connected the dots and his anger began a slow boil.

"I already told you I don't want to talk about this."

"You promised you would listen."

"About how to handle Marshall, not this." He paced toward the door, then swung around. "Why are you pushing so hard? What are you not telling me?"

"Fedorio received another call from that same number last night. The call originated from right here in Rome."

The sinking sensation in his stomach made him nauseous and he tried to reason it away. "That doesn't prove anything other than that phone is in Italy. Maybe they brought her here. Did that thought cross your mind while you were convicting her without any damn evidence?"

"You're right. There could be another explanation."

He tried not to get lost in her eyes as she moved closer. She countered his quick sidestep with one of her own, and then reached out to grasp his arms so he wouldn't move again.

"I hope I'm wrong. But if I am not...I thought you should be prepared ahead of time. Maybe it will lessen the pain."

"Whether you see it coming or not, betrayal is betrayal and still hurts the same." And as much as he didn't want to admit it, he knew what she prepared him for was entirely possible. It was a jagged-edged truth that plunged deep into his heart. "You of all people know that."

"I do." Understanding darkened her eyes. "So very much." Still holding his gaze, she slid her hands up his arms, a gentle skim that gave him a chance to move away if he wanted to. He didn't. And once her fingers touched his face, pulled him down to her tilted lips, the only thing he wanted was her.

He grasped her waist to pull her closer as he sunk into the kiss. Savoring her. Memorizing her taste. The feel of her. That it almost felt like goodbye scared him so much he allowed hunger and urgency to take over. He swept his hands up along her spine, fitting her body against his as he sought to stake his claim on this woman forever.

The exotic, spicy scent of her inundated his senses when he drew in a ragged breath. He mirrored her move and cupped his palms to her face. Staring into her eyes, emotions welled like the river back in Garfagnana—swirling and tumbling over the boulders strewn in their past, yet refusing to be contained. Amazingly, he saw what he felt reflected in her eyes.

Her lips parted on a shallow breath and her smile seared onto his soul.

*Say it. Say it now when there's no doubt she'll hear you and know the truth.*

"Eva...I—"

The rattle of the door handle cut him off and brought the rest of the world crashing back. As the door flew open, he spun around a moment too late. Nick Marshall stepped into the apartment, gun aimed at the both of them, his expression murderously dark.

"I *knew* it. Once a con man, always a damn fucking con man."

## Chapter 33

EVALINA CURSED HERSELF for losing focus. This was all her fault, and she deserved the weapon pointed at her. Only it wasn't, because Ben once again played hero and tried to shield her. The cop in her damned him for continually forgetting it was her job to protect *him*. The woman in her wanted to kiss him again.

Both feared he'd end up with another bullet in his chest.

"Move aside, Sanders," Marshall demanded, motioning with the gun as he kicked the door closed before reaching to lock it. "I want each of you to put your hands where I can see them."

"You aren't going to do anything," Ben predicted, seemingly unconcerned. "She's a cop."

"You don't know a damn thing about me, so don't presume to know what I am or am not capable of, you self-serving, lying sonofabitch."

Eva debated going for her holstered weapon, but couldn't risk forcing the confrontation with Ben in the middle. Instead, she stepped from behind him to face Nick, drawing the danger off her self-imposed protector.

"Threatening *la polizia* is a serious offense in Italy."

"In the States, too. I have no choice but to take my chances.

Now set your gun on the floor and kick it over here to me."

That's the last thing she wanted to do, but when she hesitated, he shifted his weapon from her to Ben. "I've got all kinds of reasons to shoot him. Seriously, don't make this more difficult than it has to be."

Like Ben, she didn't think he'd carry it that far, but when his green gaze held steady without a flicker of uncertainty, doubt surfaced. This was one situation she couldn't afford to misjudge. She removed her Beretta from the holster and slowly lowered it to the floor, laid it flat, then gave it a shove. The gun stopped just short of Nick's boot. Instead of bending to pick it up, he reached behind his back and brought forth a small black book.

"The diary," Ben confirmed before she could ask.

Nick gave a grim, humorless smile. "Don't look so surprised. I don't need this. I have no problem keeping my end of the deal so long as you keep yours."

And of course, he wanted the Bible. When Marshall lobbed the diary in his direction, Ben caught it, his clenched jaw barely holding in his obvious resentment. But Nick wasn't done. Next, he pulled out a pair of handcuffs—*her* damn handcuffs she'd bet—and tossed them to her. Then he bent to pick up her gun and tucked it into the back waistband of his jeans in place of the diary.

"Over there, by the water pipe. I want a handcuff on each of you."

He followed them across the floor and watched carefully as she threaded the cuffs between the wall and the pipe, then secured the metal bracelets on both her and Ben.

"I had a much different scenario in mind for the next time you put these on me," Ben said in a low undertone.

She lifted her gaze to his at that surprise flash of humor. With a wry grin twisting his lips, he turned to watch Nick make his way toward the Bible. No more than he leaned down to run his fingers across the cover, the doorknob rattled again.

He jerked upright, spinning around while raising his gun as a knock sounded on the door. "Who did you two call?" he accused.

Evalina met Ben's frown. His shrug said *no clue*. She stripped the diary from his grasp and tucked it against her back, concealing it beneath her jacket. His unease transferred through the metal to her. Or hers to him. Either way, this was yet another unexpected development she didn't like one bit—especially when they were pretty much helpless.

"Nick, it's me. Let me in."

*Alisa Marshall.* Identifying the voice did not ease Evalina's tension, especially when Nick's initial expression of relief went dark again. He strode over and yanked open the door.

"I told you to stay away—"

The redhead lurched sideways into the doorway, her arm held in a firm grip by Antonio. With his gun poking into her ribs, her hazel eyes were wide, bright with a telltale sheen of tears. "I'm sorry, Nick. He gave me no choice."

"Did you call him?" Ben asked in a low undertone as the *ispettore* forced the girl into the room.

Evalina shook her head. She didn't know if she was happy to see her partner or not. How the hell had he known where they were, and could they trust him? His dark glaze flicked to her and Ben before focusing on Nick once more.

"I am a police officer. Drop your weapon right now."

With his sister held at gunpoint, Nick extended his hands to the sides in surrender and readily complied.

"He has mine, too," Evalina advised.

After Nick had added her gun to his on the floor, Antonio motioned for him move. "Stand up and back away. Get the key for those handcuffs out—*slowly*—now go unlock Ispettore Gallo and put the cuff on yourself."

"Hey—"

"Shut up, Sanders," Antonio ordered.

Eva stretched her fingers between the wall and the pipe, touching Ben to stall his argument as she asked, "How did you find us?"

Antonio urged Alisa forward. "I located this one earlier today and followed the two of them here. She was very forthcoming when we met downstairs."

"I thought you were going to shoot me," Alisa complained, her voice still shaky. "I didn't know you were a cop."

As Nick approached Evalina to unlock the handcuff, Antonio walked the redhead to the back of the couch and instructed her not to move before he backed up to retrieve the guns from the floor.

"Hurry up," he told Nick. "We may not have much time."

Evalina glanced over from exchanging her wrist for Nick's. "What do you mean?"

Antonio was at the door, leaning back to look out into the hall before reaching to shut the door. "Este's men are probably already on their way."

The cuff clicked shut on Nick's wrist and she whipped around. "How do *they* know where we are?"

"I arranged for them to find out."

"You what? *Why?*"

"I told you we couldn't trust him," Ben muttered.

Antonio strode toward them, his jaw set hard, dark eyes glinting with malice. She fought an involuntary step backward while Ben surged forward as far as his restraint allowed.

"Don't touch her," he warned.

His towering strength at her back bolstered her courage. She met Antonio's eyes without backing down, but all he did was extend her gun, grip first. Her fingers curled around the comforting weight of the weapon, reinstating a semblance of control. He turned his back to her, paced toward the door, then whirled back.

Stopping a few feet away, he explained, "My job on this mission is not only to gather evidence against Fedorio, but to locate and expose whoever has been undermining the investigation against him from inside our own agencies."

Metal jangled against metal, and Nick's curse of protest went unheeded as Ben strained against the shackle. "You should've told her that upfront, you sonofabitch. She was almost shot at the Armani."

He'd pulled so hard the cuffs cut into the skin on both his and

Nick's wrists. Evalina eased him back to relieve the pressure. "I'm going to release you—can I trust you not to go all primitive while we figure this out?"

The burning gaze he transferred from Antonio's to hers revealed anger and frustration. Stormy blue eased into something closer to the color of a summer sky. "You can trust me with anything."

*How about with my heart? Can I trust you with that?*

"Eva, that's not a good idea," Antonio cautioned.

Ben's eyes darkened when he transferred his gaze back to Antonio. She unlocked the cuff, then refastened the metal ring around the pipe.

"Come on," Nick protested. He gave her a persuasive smile that she might have found attractive if he hadn't pointed a gun at them minutes earlier.

"Quiet. You're already in more trouble than you can handle."

Evalina stayed close to Ben, concerned the open animosity between him and Antonio would turn physical. They were evenly matched in height and build, but Antonio had his gun. She motioned Alisa toward her brother. "You stand over there with him and don't move, or we will charge you both with obstructing our investigation."

The girl readily complied, and then Evalina faced Antonio. "How does revealing our location help you find the mole?"

"It doesn't," Ben stated. He rubbed his wrist where the cuff had left deep, red indents while trying to cut the other man down with his glare. "*He's* the one responsible."

"And *you* were completely unaware of your mother's involvement?"

"My mother—"

"Not now." Evalina cut off Ben's aggressive move forward by stepping between the two men, her back to Ben. "Tell me about Fedorio."

After a long, tense moment, Antonio dropped his gaze from above her head. "Someone has been keeping him and his men one step ahead of us for months now, so we made use of the situation with the diary to obtain the proof needed to make an arrest."

"Who do you suspect?"

"My superiors have narrowed the potential suspects down to an *assistenti* to one of the magistrates in Milan. She began a relationship with the son of one of Fedorio's executives about two years ago."

"You believe she revealed where we were in Milan? And monitored the GPS on my car?"

"Yes, but I couldn't prove it since there were others listening to those communications. This time she alone received the information."

"So this should be done tonight?"

"Yes."

The confirmation set off conflicting emotions. She could return to her normal life, but with everything resolved here in Italy, Ben would leave with the Bible. Then again, what was normal for her? Another undercover assignment?

After the past few days, and the unrest she'd been trying to ignore weeks before that, it didn't surprise her that the thought of going undercover again turned her stomach.

"Did you recover the diary?"

Antonio's question combined with her inner conflict and ignited her anger. She moved closer to him and lowered her voice. "These men will shoot before asking questions. You should not have set this up with civilians present."

"You didn't give me much choice, did you? You should've called me."

"I wasn't sure I could trust you."

"Because *he* doesn't trust me." He jabbed a finger at Ben without shifting his gaze from hers. "You are way too personal in this case."

"*He* was right," she accused. "You should've told me what was going on instead of playing both sides—no matter how justified you think your reasons are. You are my *partner*. Partners are supposed to have each other's backs."

All her suppressed anguish of Nino's betrayal poured into those words, and there wasn't a damn thing she could've done about it. Antonio stared at her in the ensuing silence. Ben's hand offered support at the small of her back, but she held her partner's gaze, needing to see if he even cared. Remorse darkened his expression before he looked away.

"I was following orders."

Typical. He might feel bad, but no way he'd admit it in front of Ben and the others. "Now what?" she demanded. "How do we ensure no one gets hurt? Or anyone else in this building?"

"I have some friends here in Rome who've agreed to provide back up. They will be here soon."

"We should get them all out of here." She jerked her head in the general direction of Ben, Nick, and his sister. "Call in to headquarters that we've obtained the diary, and then we can deal with Este's men."

"You have the diary?"

"Yes." She returned to Nick's side to release him and looked him in the eye. "Ben will take the Bible—*and* if either you or your sister obstruct him in any way, you will discover *taking your chances* by kidnapping a police officer wasn't a smart move at all. Do you understand?"

All the arguments the man wanted to make swirled in his green eyes, but he nodded.

"I'm not leaving," Ben stated from behind her.

"You *are* leaving." When she turned to face him, the defiant look in his eyes prompted a sigh as she went to pick up the Bible. "We've been over this before—this my job, now let me do it."

"Then we need to talk first."

She glanced toward the door. Antonio was checking the stairwell while motioning Nick and Alisa forward. She pressed the heavy book into Ben's hands. "There's no time. You need to think of your family right now. You have what you came for, now go."

He resisted her push toward the door. "There's something I need to tell you bef—"

Antonio's body jerked backwards. He slammed up against the doorframe a second before his pained cry drowned out Ben's words.

## Chapter 34

"*Giù! Get down!*"

Evalina's frantic hand motions had Ben ducking to the ground. He dropped the Bible and twisted around to see Antonio fall forward through the open door, into the hall. A thick thump sounded when his head hit the floor, and then he didn't move. Eva crouch-walked toward the door, gun drawn and extended in front of her.

Alarm shot through him no matter how many times she reminded him this was her job. After a quick look back in his direction, she silently pointed toward a door on the other side of the living room that likely led to a bedroom.

Nick and Alisa followed her instructions, but Ben crawled across the floor toward her and the motionless Antonio. Urgent voices filtered up from the stairwell and hall below. Evalina had reached the door and now stood with her back pressed flat to the wall. When Ben reached the doorway, a deep frown creased her brow.

"*Ben*," she whispered in protest.

He started to move into the hall, but two more bullets impacted the wall near his head. Jerking back to the sound of Evalina's exclamation, he grabbed the *ispettore* by the ankles and dragged him back inside the apartment. Blood soaked the front of his shirt, spreading from a wound somewhere on his right side. Reaching blindly behind him, Ben searched for his bag while feeling with his other hand for a pulse.

*Still alive.* He lifted his gaze to Eva's and gave a tight nod. Relief flashed in her eyes before she returned her attention to the hall. She withdrew her phone from her pocket, and lowered her gun for the brief seconds needed to restore the battery.

"Here." Nick appeared and shoved a kitchen towel into his hand.

"Thanks." Ben ripped open Antonio's shirt, then folded and pressed the towel down hard over the bloody wound. The Italian moaned. Pain twisted his features as he started to regain consciousness.

More voices sounded from downstairs. Phone held to her ear, Evalina darted a quick look into the hall. Bits of wood flew as a bullet hit the doorframe directly above her head. She ducked, pulling back inside as she yelled something in Italian, maybe into the phone, maybe at the people shooting at them.

A female voice echoed from below. Ben jerked his head up and stared at the door opening. Voice recognition hit him like a fifty pound brick to the face. Ice froze the blood in his veins. His mother had just hollered at someone that her son was up there— and fear had not been the overriding emotion in her voice.

Numbly, he moved aside, making room for Nick. "Press on this."

The moment the other man's hand replaced his on Antonio's wound, Ben rose to his feet and flattened his back against the wall, opposite Evalina.

"Mom?" he called out.

"Benjamin! Honey, are you okay?"

*Honey?* She'd never called him that in his life. She'd moved up and it sounded like she was on the landing just below. He met Evalina's wary gaze across the open doorway as he replied, "I'm fine. However the cop that was just shot isn't."

"Do you have the Bible?"

Before he could answer, a low voice spoke in Italian. Ben caught the word *diario*.

"He wants the diary," Evalina softly translated, concern darkening her alert eyes. "He also doesn't want witnesses. I called for backup and emergency services. Can you keep her talking to give them time to get here?"

Ben shifted his gaze from Nick taking care of Antonio, to Alisa hiding behind the cracked-open bedroom door, and finally back to Eva. Each of them were here because of him or his family, even if in a roundabout way. If he gave these men what they wanted, they might remain safe.

"Benjamin?"

This time concern resonated in his mother's concerned voice, but it did nothing to thaw the block of ice encasing his heart.

"Do you have the Bible and the diary Dante gave you?" she called up.

Antonio tried to sit up. He collapsed back to the ground with a groan. When he tried to speak, his words were drowned out by a fit of coughing. Blood stained his lips; they were running out of time. Delaying his mother wouldn't remove the gunmen between the paramedics and Antonio.

"I'm going to need a minute, Mom. Don't let anyone shoot again."

Evalina frowned at his words, but he avoided her gaze as he retreated into the apartment. He retrieved the Bible, bent to pick up his bag, and then stopped in front of her. She looked up from where the bag rested against his hip.

"What are you doing?"

She wasn't going to like this. Hell, he didn't like it, but didn't see where he had a choice. He leaned out into the hall and saw his mother standing at the bottom of the stairs leading to the fourth floor. She smiled up at him and he turned back before any of the betrayal tearing him apart showed in his expression.

"I'm making it look like they're going to get what they want. Do you trust me?"

From the floor, Antonio made a noise from deep in his throat.

Hesitation flitted across her face as she glanced toward her wounded partner, and Ben held his breath. He remembered the last time they'd had this conversation. They'd both said no. He desperately needed the opposite right now, and Antonio casting doubt wouldn't help.

His fingers curled tight around the strap on his bag. "Eva?"

Still watching her partner, she nodded. "Yes. I trust you." A second later, she lowered her gun, took a breath and lifted her luminous gaze to his without flinching.

"*Ti amo.* I love you."

Oh, God, she broke his heart. His chest grew so tight, breathing was almost impossible. A lump formed in his throat and he closed his eyes against the pure emotion in hers. If only she'd said those words last night. He felt the warmth of her hand against his cheek and forced himself to step back.

Opening his eyes again, he saw her arm fall back to her side. Avoiding her gaze, he extended his hand. "Give me the diary."

She didn't hesitate to pull the book from behind her back. He took it with the one hand, and reached forward with his other to press Nick's phone against her palm.

"Keep this." Misery choked his voice to a whisper.

Confusion dimmed the light in her eyes as she looked down at the phone. Two sets of footsteps sounded on the stairs. Evalina went back on alert, pulling free from Ben to pocket the phone while raising her weapon once more.

"Easy," Ben warned everyone. Stuffing the diary into his bag, he turned his head to see his mother near the top of the stairs. One of the gunmen from the car stood with her, weapon trained toward Evalina.

"Time to go, Ben," his mother said.

He stretched his hand back to hold them at bay. "Give me a minute."

"Go where?" Evalina's narrowed gaze flicked to his, then returned to his mother.

The question was suspicion, dismay and accusation all rolled up in one. Gripping the strap of his bag to keep from reaching for her again, he lowered his gaze, unable to face her when he was about to do the same to her that his mother had done to him.

"*You're going with her?*"

"Yes." He cleared his throat. "Goodbye, Evalina."

His purposeful use of her full name made her flinch. "No. Don't say that. Backup is on the way."

*Exactly why I have to go. Before anyone else gets hurt.*

A shake of her head sent her braid flailing from side to side. From inside the apartment, Nick swore, and he was pretty sure Antonio did, too. Eva's aim with the gun waivered as her other hand rose toward him. He retreated another step.

"*Ben.*" Her voice commanded him to look at her. Fierce determination had replaced confusion. "You don't leave. How many times have you told me that?"

Those whiskey eyes implored him to stay. He hated this. Acutely aware of his mother behind him, it took every ounce of determination to summon a cocky smile. He lifted his hands, palm up, in a *what-are-you-gonna-do?* gesture.

His mother put a hand on his shoulder, her fingers digging in as she pulled him back toward her. "I see you haven't lost your touch with the love con after all these years. The girls never could resist you."

Evalina's eyes widened. Ben swallowed hard when comprehension obliterated any sign of the love she'd declared a moment ago. It tore a gaping hole in his chest, but he had to let her believe this had been his end game. He spun away from the look on her face and hurried down the stairs, the heavy Bible in his bag banging against his hip with every step.

Out on the street, he watched his mother climb into the back seat of a black sedan. He bent to peer inside, one hand on the door, one on the car. The driver stared straight ahead, but the older man in the back on the opposite side of his mother eyed him with cold, dark eyes. Reminded him of Alrigo Lapaglia, even though he bore a slight resemblance to Dante Fedorio. Had to be the other cousin, Este.

Instead of getting inside, Ben reached back, into the side

pocket of his bag. "I'm curious, mom, how'd you get away from your kidnappers?"

He caught the annoyed press of her pink lips a second before she curved them into a smile and leaned toward the open door. "Benjamin, I saw you at work in there. Don't pretend like you didn't figure this all out."

He glanced down the street, absently listening for sirens. "You're right, I did." *Only way too late for it to make a difference.*

"Good. Then get in, and let's see what you got for me."

Withdrawing his hand, he fisted it around the corner of the leather and swung the bag into the open space she'd provided for him beside her. "They're both in there."

As she looked inside, he took a mental step back. No longer his mother, she was simply the woman who'd given birth to him. Lia Maria Sanders. Prison hadn't outdated her sense of style, and hard-time had had no negative effect on her outward beauty. Inside, however, she was as dark as the devil.

She handed the diary to Fedorio and then lifted the Bible to place on her fashionable black slacks. A pleased smile stretched her lips as her hand caressed the carved leather cover.

"You and I can do great things together, starting with finding the cross that fits in this cover. It's worth a fortune." She lifted her light blue gaze. "You did well. I'm proud of you, Benjamin."

It was as if she'd reached in and fisted her greedy, malicious fingers around his already aching, bleeding heart. Only after hearing the words did he realize he'd been waiting for her approval his entire life. And five days ago, that statement would've meant the world to him. Now, the one person whose opinion he cherished most stood four stories up and probably hated his guts.

The cruel irony made him laugh as the sound of approaching sirens finally reached his ears. He slammed the door and backed away from the car.

She rolled down the window, watching him with a frown marring her smooth brow. "You're not coming with me? I thought you'd help—that we could hunt the treasure together."

"There's not a chance in hell that's going to happen," he declared, turning to walk away.

"Then why did you come down?"

The anger simmering below the surface whirled him back around. He jabbed a finger to the building behind him. "To protect those people up there!"

Understanding lit her blue eyes and she gave him a pitying smile. "Oh, my poor boy. Don't tell me you actually fell for your own con?"

"The only con is the one you ran against your own son."

"Benjamin, you grew up in this family," she reasoned with a slight shrug. "You knew what you were getting yourself into when I asked you to come here."

"Not quite, mother. A lot of things have changed since you went to prison. *I've* changed, and I believed you did, too, when you said you wanted to bring our family back together." Fists clenched at his side, he stepped forward. "I put other people in danger because I thought *your* life was at risk."

Alongside his mother, Este withdrew his gun to rest it on his lap. When Ben narrowed his gaze, Lia turned toward her cousin. She extended her arm to place her hand on the gun in a staying gesture.

"The missing cross is a priceless treasure, set with jewels to rival those of the British crown. Legend says it vanished in Venice hundreds of years ago and was lost forever. But every now and again whispers of its existence surface, and now is the time to finally discover the truth."

"*Truth?*" He gave a harsh laugh. "What do *you* know of the truth?"

"Enough. Besides, everything turned out just fine," she replied, a note of warning in her voice. "And if you can shake Halliwell's holier-than-thou righteousness, we could still be a family again. Don't screw this up like your father did, Benjamin."

He leaned in close to the car, his jaw clenched tight so he

didn't shout at the top of his lungs. "There is a man bleeding to death in there because of *you*. If you think I want anything to do with a family that considers that *fine*, you are delusional. I'll stick with Halli and Rachel, thank you very much."

The sirens screamed closer.

"You've got exactly what you wanted, so it's best you leave while you still can." He pushed away and walked behind the car to the other side of the street as the ambulance arrived. Lia Sanders and Este drove away as two police vehicles turned the corner onto Via Sistina and stopped behind the ambulance, emergency lights strobing.

The sirens went silent, then the officers jumped out, and a moment later Evalina met them at the door with a flash of her badge. Across the street, Ben moved into the shadow of a nearby entrance, listening to her bark out orders in Italian. The paramedics hurried inside and she turned to rush back inside after them.

Gone. Just like that.

*What? You expected her to look for you?*

Yeah, he had. He wanted nothing more than to bolt across the street and catch her. Ask if she'd really meant what she'd said.

Hell, he knew she had. She wasn't the coward he'd been last night. *He* wasn't the coward he'd been last night. Everything was different now, and yet his feet remained rooted to the sidewalk. He needed some time to sort through the jumble of emotions knotted in his stomach. Eva also had her own issues to deal with.

He hoped *she* uncovered the truth in the process.

## Chapter 35

EVALINA HESITATED IN the hall, then forced her feet to carry her through the open door of the hospital room. It'd been two days since the surgery to remove the bullet that'd collapsed Antonio's lung, but wires and tubes still snaked about the bed. The hiss of a pump sounded every so often, and machines beeped at regular intervals to a number of different cadences.

When she softly spoke his name, Antonio opened his eyes and turned his head.

"*Ciao.*" His voice rasped through lips too-dark against his abnormally pale complexion. He was alone in the room, and she noted the shelf by the window that had contained flowers and cards in other rooms she'd passed was bare. That he had no one to visit and bring him get-well wishes stimulated a little pang in her chest.

"You don't look so good," she said with a gentle smile.

His answering one was weak. "I feel how I look."

"Broken rib, punctured lung, concussion…" She propped one hip on the edge of his bed. "I'd say it serves you right, but you didn't quite deserve all this. Plus, a part of me does understand you were following orders. I'd have done the same thing."

"No." He shook his head as his eyes closed. "Not you. Because you were right. Partners are supposed to have each other's backs." His lashes lifted and his eyes met hers. "You deserved better. I should have been upfront with you—especially after Nino."

Emotion clogged her throat at the unexpected admission. She reached out and squeezed his hand in forgiveness. "What's done is done. The leak has been taken care of, and now Fedorio is in custody for all his crimes—including shooting you. We also expect to recover evidence that he was involved in Dante's murder. After all that, I've been taken off probation."

That last development should've made her much happier. Instead, she'd spent the past two days questioning everything she believed in. Wondering exactly what to do with her life. She'd sat outside her sister's flower shop this morning, but as usual, hadn't managed to quell her nervous nausea enough to walk through the doors.

Looking at Antonio now, her chest constricted with the realization this could be *her* someday. No flowers. No cards. No one but a co-worker. Maybe.

"I still owe you an apology," Antonio said. "And Commissario Marino stopped by earlier. He told me how Sanders helped out after all, so it appears I was wrong about him, too."

Right there was the main reason she'd waited this long to come see Antonio—she knew he'd bring up the American in one way or another. Pain sharpened the ache that hadn't eased in her chest since the moment Lia Sanders had uttered the words 'love con.' In stunned disbelief, she'd watched the man she loved—the man she'd just handed her heart to—walk away. All the while, she'd repeated the silent litany *he doesn't leave, he doesn't leave, he doesn't leave.*

Except he *had* left—and not looked back.

With a purposely careless shrug for Antonio, she stood up and paced to the window. It took concentrated effort to keep the anger and bitterness of Ben's betrayal from her voice. "Oh, I don't know. Yes, he activated the GPS tracker in his bag that Nick Marshall had planted on him and gave me the phone, but neither he nor his mother were anywhere to be found when we arrested Fedorio with the diary."

"Have you looked for him?"

"What would be the point, other than to find the Bible? But Nick Marshall has no documentation the Bible belonged to them, no proof it was stolen, and we have no other legal reasons to detain Ben or his mother, other than Lia violating her parole."

"Forget legalities, Evalina, and forget Lia Sanders. I heard what you said to Ben. Maybe I don't know you that well, but you don't strike me as a person who says *those* words without meaning them."

She glanced back over her shoulder, and the sympathy in his brown eyes stiffened her spine. There was no use denying it. "It doesn't matter, because he left. Clearly, he made his choice."

*Damn.* Despite her best efforts, her voice was loaded with wounded anger.

Antonio shifted in the bed, then smoothed the blanket over his stomach. "I can't believe I'm defending the guy, but you do realize he was most likely protecting you? Protecting *everyone*?"

She turned around and leaned against the window sill, staring at him as the explanation penetrated the thick fog of betrayal blanketing her thoughts.

"He probably saved my life by getting Este and his mother out of there before back-up arrived and forced a standoff situation that could've lasted hours."

*Oh my God.* Why hadn't she thought of that? With Este and his men gone, there'd been no delay for the paramedics to rush Antonio to the hospital.

She'd been too busy blaming Ben for leaving, she hadn't taken the time to think about the other reasons he might have done it other than he'd been conning her from the beginning. Considering Antonio's explanation, if she took her broken heart out of the equation, the con didn't add up.

Hope ignited like a sparkler on New Year's Eve.

*But why hasn't he returned by now?*

Her newfound optimism burned out rather abruptly, as sparklers are wont to do, leaving her holding ashes of wishful thinking once more.

Antonio gave a weary sigh. "Evalina, you're good at what you do. One of the best I've seen. But take it from me, don't let the job become your life. It's not worth what you give up."

---

SHE PARKED ON the narrow, one-way street outside her apartment building and leaned her head back against the seat with her eyes closed. She was exhausted after the five hour drive on the autostrada from Rome back to Milan. Her ceaseless, bouncing thoughts, and the stubborn tears that had fallen in the privacy of the rental car after she'd left the hospital, hadn't helped.

She'd hoped to fly, but found out the day she and Ben had cruised into the capitol on the bike, the ash cloud from Eyjafjallajökull had finally advanced enough to shut down the airports. Which meant Ben and his mother were stuck somewhere in her country. However, as she'd told Antonio, seeing as she'd retrieved what her *commissario* wanted from Fedorio, there was no official need to search for them.

*For him.* He had made his choice.

Fresh tears threatened, and she hated that she'd been reduced to being so weepy. With a shaky sigh, she lifted her head and grabbed her overnight bag from the passenger seat to exit the car. She slammed the door in a fit of temper and passed through the iron gates that led to the interior courtyard of her building. The damn man dominated just about every waking thought, not to mention, the past two nights, her dreams had been pure torture.

Somehow, she had to—

"*Arf.*"

The unmistakable high-pitched bark of a puppy snapped her to attention.

"*Arf, arf.*"

She turned toward the sound and saw a little ball of black and tan fluff running toward her. Dropping her bag at the sight of Ilaria and Cesare, she crouched down as the German Shepherd puppy attacked her feet with a ferocious little growl.

A smile replaced her initial frown of surprised confusion. She scooped up the pup as the older couple approached. "*Signore. Signorina. Buona sera.*"

"Ispettore Gallo," Ilaria greeted.

Confusion returned, instantly combined with a flush of guilt when she realized they knew of her lies. "You know who I am...I apologize for the deception. When we first saw you in the woods, we didn't know if—"

"Stop," Ilaria interrupted, drawing her gaze from Cesare. "There is no need to explain. In our business, we understand the position you were in. Safety first, and after that, maybe a little wishful thinking...no?"

Evalina looked down at the grunting, squirming puppy, humbled by their bottomless generosity, but unable to confirm the woman's suspicions without choking up. Once she sufficiently reined in her emotions, she lifted her gaze to the couple, wondering why they'd sought her out.

"You raise and train the dogs for *tartufo* hunting, correct?"

"*Sì*," Cesare replied. He reached out to rub the pup's ear between his thumb and forefinger. The little dog whipped its head around, nipping at his fingers.

"Is that what has brought you to Milano? Is this little one going to a new home?"

Ilaria smiled. "If you'll have her."

Evalina jerked her gaze up. "*Me?*"

"*Sì*. Benjamin requested we deliver her ourselves."

"Ben?" Evalina's heart pounded impossibly hard as she swept her gaze past the stone fountain and around the cobblestone courtyard. "Is he here?"

"No, *cara*, I am sorry. He visited us at the house yesterday."

"Oh." Disappointment settled heavy in her chest. Ben had driven all the way into the mountains to see them, but he hadn't made any attempt to contact her. Pain magnified with each beat of her heart, almost beyond endurance.

Sharp needle teeth latched onto her hand. As she stared down at a little bead of blood welling from her skin, Ilaria's words replayed in her mind.

*Benjamin requested we deliver her.* She raised her gaze in amazement. "She's from Ben?"

"A gift for you, if you're willing to accept her."

Her own dog. From Ben. What the hell had he done?

*I can't rearrange my whole life for a dog.*

*You could—if you wanted it bad enough.*

Cesare and Ilaria watched her, expectation in their expressions. She focused on the bundle of fur in her arms, thinking it'd be easier to gather her thoughts. But the longer she stared at the pup, the more confused she became.

*Change your life so you can be happy.* His voice echoed in her head. *Maybe it involves a dog, maybe not.*

Well, wasn't he just going out of his way to make sure it did. Did he really think she could say no with them standing right in front of her? They would be insulted. Not to mention, bright, chocolate brown eyes gazed up into hers. A pink tongue lolled from the side of the dog's smiling mouth, emitting sweet puppy-breath with every little pant and grunt.

How was she supposed to make a decision with so much unexpected pressure? "I told him I had no room for a dog in my life," she muttered, trying to be annoyed with him.

Ilaria smiled. "He predicted you would say that, which is why he made it clear, the choice is yours, Evalina. Do not be concerned about offending us if you choose not to accept her."

"We are staying at our son's home here in the city for a few more days if you need time to think about it." Cesare reached to take the Shepherd. "We will keep her until—"

"No." Dismay and alarm made Evalina's arms tighten protectively around the pup as she took a quick step back. "No. I want her."

The moment the words were out and the decision was made, the constriction in her chest eased. Not just from the past few minutes, but from the months since she'd caught her father's murderer. She smiled at the couple who'd become like family in such a short time it seemed impossible she hadn't known them a week ago.

"*Segui il tuo cuore,*" Ilaria had urged the other morning. *Follow your heart.*

Evalina lifted the little puppy until they were eye to eye. "I definitely want...her."

The pup gave a high-pitched yip, tossed her head, wiggled her butt, and then lunged forward to bite Evalina's nose.

## Chapter 36

BEN PICKED A blade of grass and propped his elbow back on his one raised knee as he ripped it into tiny pieces. The washed-out, gray tones of the cloudy sky matched the water, and his mood.

"You're going to strip the lawn bare with all this brooding."

He glanced sideways, then tossed the grass toward the lake as Halli dropped down to sit beside him. "Sorry."

She laughed and leaned over to bump her shoulder against his. "I'm kidding."

He bumped back, but kept his gaze on the rippled surface of Lake Como. "Any news on the airports?"

"Sounds like they'll reopen tomorrow. Trent has the plane and crew on standby if they do."

Guilt poked at him. "You guys never should've flown all the way over here last week. I heard him on the phone yesterday, and it sounded like he was dealing with some ruffled feathers in L.A."

Halli shrugged. "He said it's fine. They were able to rearrange the schedule and film some scenes he's not in. As an executive producer, he does have a little pull, you know. Besides, Rachel thought you might need us, and I agreed with her. Trent didn't even hesitate when he offered to rent the jet."

He reached over and pulled her into a one-armed hug against his side. "Thanks for having my back. All of you."

"That's what family is for." She leaned her head on his shoulder. "We'll always be here for you, Ben."

Unlike their mother. Halli hadn't been surprised when he told the story of what happened in Rome, but he'd seen the disappointment in their older sister's face. As foolish as him, Rachel had also hoped for them all to become a family again. That would never happen now—not with Lia anyway. They'd see how things went when their father was released next month.

"So...tomorrow. What are your plans?" Halli asked.

The question hit on the exact reason he'd been *brooding*. He dropped his arm from around her shoulders and plucked another blade of grass. It'd been five days since the Minimis should have delivered the puppy to Eva. Surely she'd figured out the meaning behind the gift, so if she'd wanted to find him, if she wanted *him*, she'd have been here by now, right?

*Right.*

His fingers fisted on the last little bit of grass. "I'm coming home with you guys."

Halli drew in breath as if she were about to say something, but then she let it out again, just as loud. Her mouth must be pretty sore with all the tongue-biting she'd done the past five days. He silently prayed she did it again.

"You sure? Because you're welcome to use the villa if you want to stay longer."

The tiny piece of grass fluttered to the ground between his legs. "Thanks, but no."

"You know—"

"Hal, I *really* don't want to talk about it." When she started to argue, he held up a hand. "I didn't push you last year, so leave it be."

"Maybe you should have."

His jaw clenched as he shook his head. Her frustration simmered as they sat in silence, but finally she sighed, rubbed his back, then braced a hand on his shoulder to get to her feet. "Come on. Trent and Rachel made a new antipasto to go with some wine we found in town earlier."

"I'll be there in a few minutes."

When she didn't move, he looked up to see her frowning down at him with a combination of sympathy and annoyance in her blue eyes.

"I get what you've been waiting for, Ben, really I do. But a piece of advice? If you love her, stop being so damn stubborn. Go fight for her with everything you have or you'll regret it for the rest of your life. Believe me, it's worth it."

His chest constricted so much he couldn't have replied even if he'd wanted to. But she stalked away, leaving him to stew on her advice. When he realized he was picking grass again, he tossed the cool blades aside.

Damn it, she was right. Eva had left him all those months ago, so he had it in his mind that she had to decide he was worth coming after. But maybe, he still needed to convince her. Fight for her the way his mother should have fought for her own family.

Wondering how fast he could make it to Milan on the bike, he shoved to his feet and turned for the villa. After only two steps, his step faltered as a little German Shepherd puppy barreled across the lawn.

Halting, he lifted his gaze and his pulse leapt at the sight of the woman who'd captured his heart. Her long, dark curls tumbled about her shoulders, and her black shirt and jeans accented each sexy curve of her body. That take-charge, confident stride of hers carried her across the yard as if she were on a mission.

A smile tugged the corners of his mouth until a sudden shot of nerves attacked. Was this Halli's doing? For days, she'd minded her own business, so it seemed awful convenient Evalina would show up minutes after she decided to speak up.

Unsure how he felt about that, he squatted down to intercept the puppy before she bee-lined into the water. Held captive, she nipped at his fingers as Evalina reached them.

He took a deep breath and raised his gaze. "My sister have a hand in this?"

Confusion clouded her eyes. " '*Scusi?*"

"Did Halli call you?" he clarified. Unsuccessful at keeping a note of resentment from his voice, he quickly returned his attention to the puppy.

"No one called me," she stated. "Not even you."

Her turn for resentment. The tension in his shoulders eased a tiny bit. *She came on her own.* The puppy plopped on its stomach, then started biting at the grass.

"You kept her," he said unnecessarily.

"Her name is Aida."

He closed his eyes for a brief moment. Her accented English never failed to hit him on a visceral level. The little dog rolled onto its back, kicking paws extra large for her chubby little body as he rubbed her belly. "Aida works." Anything worked with Eva's accent. "It's a pretty name."

"It means *happy*."

Her words stilled his hand, until sharp little teeth dug into his skin. Hope soared inside his chest like a kite on the wind, but he tugged the string to hold it in check. The implication of that statement needed confirmation. He scooped up the puppy and stood to face Evalina. "And are you happy?"

"That will depend on your response to my question." Those whiskey eyes held a surprising hint of vulnerability that squeezed her grip on his heart.

*Yes*, he wanted to shout without even knowing the question. Instead, he ran a hand over puppy-soft fur and held his breath while Evalina's gaze remained locked on his.

"Did you mean what you said that night in the mountains?"

They'd spent two nights in the Garfagnana region, and he'd said a lot of things, yet he knew exactly which words she referred to. His heart lodged in his throat, but he swallowed past the nervousness and gave her the truth.

"I meant it then, Eva, and I mean it now."

Warm emotion turned her eyes luminous. He stepped closer, cradling the wiggling Aida to his chest while lifting one hand to brush his knuckles against Evalina's cheek. "I love you. Probably since the first night we ever spent together last summer."

And what do you know—not even a hint of bitterness surfaced with the thought of that night.

Her smile defined the puppy's name. Ben slid his fingers though her hair to draw her in for the kiss he'd been dying for all week. Her lips were sweeter than he remembered. He memorized them all over again, and then needed more. He'd always need more with her.

When he leaned in to deepen their connection, the imp between them gave a loud, growling protest and squirmed for freedom. "*Arf.*"

Evalina smiled against his mouth. Easing back, she took Aida from him and set the puppy on the ground. Ben reached for her when she straightened, hauling her against him for a second kiss to bold, italicize, and underscore the three words from a moment earlier. She wound her arms around his neck and matched his passion without hesitation.

A wolf-whistle pierced the air. Ben opened his eyes for a quick glance toward the villa and saw Rachel, Halli and Trent watching from out on the raised pool deck. He couldn't hold back a grin, but waved them away with one hand while spinning so his back was to them. A round of applause and laughter faded as he continued the kiss until he and Eva both needed air.

He lifted his hands to her face once more, brushing her hair back as he drank in her beauty. With a smile on her glistening lips and love shining from her darkened eyes, she was absolutely stunning.

"What the hell took you so long, woman?"

She flattened her palms against his chest as her smile faded. "I had many things to determine in my life. Knowing I love you wasn't one of them," she quickly added.

"That's good to know." He lowered his hands to her shoulders and took a deep breath. "But we do still have a lot to talk about. I want to make sure you understand why I left last week." A wry grin curved her mouth. "Antonio set me straight on that."

"If he had anything to say, I'm surprised you're even here."

"It's not what you think. First of all, your mother planted doubt when she said you were still good at the love con. And then you left with her and never looked back."

"I'm sorry." His fingers tightened involuntarily on her shoulders. "It killed me to walk away with you thinking what we shared wasn't real."

"It hurt," she admitted. "More than I ever thought possible. And though I figured out the tracker, Nick's comments only reinforced your mother's words, and I still couldn't see past the fact that you had left. Your mother—your *family*—had won."

He would've argued that, but she spoke over him.

"Then I visited Antonio in the hospital. He surprised me when he came to your defense and pointed out that you most likely saved his life."

"It was the only way I knew to get Este and my mother out of there in time."

She nodded. "I understand now."

"Sounds like I owe him a thank you."

"I believe it's mutual."

"Is he going to be okay?"

"He returned home yesterday," she confirmed with a nod. "Should be back to work within a month."

"Good. And what about Nick and Alisa? After Este and Lia were arrested, did they get their Bible back?"

Evalina frowned up at him. "The Marshalls returned home to the States, but...your mother is not in custody, Ben."

He drew back. "*What?*"

"She was nowhere to be found when we tracked Este. Neither was the Bible."

"Oh, God." He shook his head. "I shouldn't be surprised, and yet..."

"It's okay." She laid her hand against his cheek. "I know how much family means to you, and you want to believe she has good in her somewhere."

Ben turned his head to press his lips against her palm. From the corner of his eye, he spotted Aida sprawled in the grass not far from them, her nose resting on her paws. Returning his gaze to Eva, he took both of her hands in his.

"You were right before, family *has* won. The way I grew up, they were the only constant I could ever count on. But I realize now, family consists of the people who matter most to me, and they're all right here. Rachel. Halli and Trent." He tightened his hold on her fingers. "*You.*"

Moisture filled her eyes. "You are my family, too."

"And what about your sister?" he asked, counting on love to negate the risk of the question. "Have you gone to see her?"

Her gaze fixed on his chest. "Not yet. I was...well, I had hoped...maybe you would be willing to come with me?"

She lifted her head, and he no more could've denied her than stop breathing. "Of course I'll come with you."

When a tear spilled down her cheek, he pulled her into a hug. Her arms wrapped around his waist as he rested his chin on the top of her head. "Anything you need, Eva. I'm here for you. Always."

"*Grazie.*"

After a moment, he held her at arm's length. "And after everything that happened with Antonio, and Nino, are *you* doing okay?"

A smile lit her eyes. "I resigned from the *Polizia de Stato.*"

His eyebrows rose toward the sky as her words registered. "Because of Antonio?"

"No."

"The dog?"

She laughed. "*That* would be a bit drastic."

"You quit your job—that is *very* drastic," he corrected. "Life-changing."

"Yes," she agreed. "And my life needed changing. Even you could see that."

"If you decided to accept the puppy, I thought you'd take a desk job. Or something that didn't require undercover work that kept you away from home for extended periods."

"I most likely could have. But for months, I've been struggling with everything, and I realized that for much of my adult life, I've been lying to everyone, including myself. I had no family, no friends, nothing but a job that I convinced myself made it all worthwhile. Except, the one thing I valued most—that defined me—was also based on nothing but lies."

"You fight the good fight," he protested. "Upholding the laws of your country for the good of the people. It's a hard job, but you perform it very well."

"I lost too much of myself in the process," she argued. "When Cesare and Ilaria brought the puppy, your words from the villa replayed in my mind. I saw the past years of emptiness and loneliness, only this time they stretched out in front of me, and I knew I could not continue to lie to myself. I needed to decide what I wanted more; my job, or a life worth living."

"You can have both," he reminded. Not to try to talk her out of the decision, but to let her know it didn't have to be such a leap off the cliff.

But she gave a vehement shake of her head. Aida was up and exploring again, so she bent down to clap her hands for the puppy's attention. The rascal looked at her, then took off in the opposite direction.

"I have never taken the time to figure out who I am without my work," Eva said as she straightened. They stood side by side, watching the German Shepherd chase a bug. "Ever since my father's death, I've focused one hundred percent on becoming and being a good investigator. But there's so much more out there, and thanks to you, I want *more*."

Coming to terms with such a heavy realization was not easy. He knew that from back when his parents had been sent to jail, and he'd re-evaluated his entire life. He wished he could've been there for her, but understood the importance of finding the answers on her own. Her strength of conviction made him love her even more.

She turned to him once again and lifted her gaze. "I wanted to come find you the moment I decided to keep Aida, but I also knew I needed some time to let that decision settle and become reality." She laughed again, the sound happy and carefree. "I have no idea what I will do now, but I don't even care."

He smiled at the excitement in her voice, but then her expression became serious again, and his heart thumped in his chest.

"I still owe you an apology."

"For what?"

"Leaving you last summer."

Did she have any idea how much those words meant to him? The contrition in her eyes said *yes* and swelled his already full heart.

"From the moment I met you at Lapaglia's, there was this connection between us like I've never experienced before. There was never a time you felt like a stranger, and I found myself wanting to get close to you. I worried it would jeopardize the case I'd spent years working toward, and then, after we were together that first time...well, *everything* was so intense. It frightened me. Running was the only way I knew how to deal with the unfamiliar emotions. Unfortunately, that goes back to not knowing who I was."

Apprehension skittered along his spine. She'd just admitted she still didn't know who she was. Instinct told him it would always be intense between them, so where did that leave him? Would she bolt again when she got scared? He stuffed his hands in his front jeans pockets and glanced toward the water, trying to fight the building trepidation. If she left him again—

"Ben."

Her low voice compelled his gaze back to hers. She pulled his hands from his pockets, then fit their palms together and intertwined their fingers.

"I love you."

He opened his mouth to say the same, but she gave a fierce shake of her head and gazed up at him through her thick lashes.

"I trust you with everything. My life. My heart. Loving you doesn't frighten me anymore, it makes me stronger. You don't leave, and neither will I. Never again."

Belief was his relief. He purposely waited in the breathless silence, then cocked an eyebrow. "Now may I speak?"

She grinned and nodded.

Using their joined hands, he drew her close and leaned his forehead against hers. "I want to spend the rest of my life with you, Eva. Marriage. Kids. How does that sit with you?"

"You ask odd questions, Benjamin Sanders, but the first part sounded wonderful." She rose on her tiptoes to press her lips to his. Before he could deepen the kiss, she pulled back. "Now, I have a question for you."

"Go ahead."

"What if I am already pregnant?"

He jerked back, eyes widening. "Are you?"

"I do not know, but we shall find out in about a week or two."

He tried to contain his smile, tamping down on the thrill that she could be carrying his baby right now. "Would you be okay with that?"

"I do understand the consequences of making love, *caro*. Do you think I would have seduced you if I did not?"

No need to hold back his grin any longer. "Oh, *you* seduced *me*?"

"*Sì*. And you were easy."

He laughed at that truth. "Only with you, Eva. Only ever with—"

His vow was cut short by her kiss. Their kiss was cut much too short by a splash. They turned to see Aida floundering in the water, halfway along the dock.

"Oh!" Eva pulled from his arms and ran for the lake.

Ben followed, but by the time they reached her, Aida had somewhat figured out the doggy paddle and was wading ashore. Evalina scooped the soggy pup into her arms. "*Ah, piccolino. Dovresti stare più attento, cucciolo.*"

When Evalina hugged her too tight, the dog wiggled for freedom. Evalina set her down, then grimaced as she plucked at the wet material clinging to her full breasts. The moment she let go, the snug shirt sucked right back to her skin. Ben gave a low groan when he saw the effect of the cold water. Movement caught his eye, and over Evalina's shoulder, he watched the Shepherd make her way back down the steps to the dock.

"You're going to need a dry shirt before dinner." A smile tugged at his mouth as Aida took a running leap into the air.

"*Sì.*"

Behind her, the puppy landed with a splash. Evalina whirled around, then threw up her hands amidst a torrent of Italian. Ben thought of Ilaria Minimi chastising Cesare and grinned at his future.

Aida ker-plunked her way back to shore. She shook, lost her balance, then climbed to her feet and bounded up the rocks for another round. Hands propped on her hips, Evalina tilted her head in resignation.

Ben chuckled and draped an arm across her shoulders. She reached up to link her fingers with his as the puppy played. A glance down at Eva's chest stirred his latent desire. He pulled her to him with the one arm, dipped his head to finish the kiss Aida had interrupted, and ended up wrapping both arms around her to lift her off the ground. Those luscious curves molded against him, getting him wet in the process. He didn't give a damn.

And *then,* she stoked the flame of passion into a raging inferno when her hot breath caressed his ear with sexy, whispered words he didn't understand.

"*God,* I love it when you do that," he growled. She gave a sultry laugh as he set her back on her feet. "Will you teach me to speak Italian?"

"Only when we are in bed."

That sounded wonderful, but he felt compelled to warn her, "I want to learn more than the dirty words you whisper, so it's going to take awhile."

She started toward the villa before tossing him a sassy smile over her shoulder. "*Sì, amore mio, lo sò.*"

All he needed to understand was the *yes*. As he retrieved the puppy who'd run out of energy halfway back to the dock, his tortured groan rumbled up from deep in his throat. "God help me with you Italians. Antipasto, dinner, and dessert are going to take *waaay* too long."

THE END

*Thank you for Reading!*

I hope you enjoyed Ben and Eva's adventure in BETRAYED. If you'd be so kind as to leave a review where you purchased the book, it would be greatly appreciated. Reader reviews allow us authors to continue to write the books you love.

## About Stacey Joy Netzel

I fell in love with books at a young age, and growing up, whenever Dad realized I'd disappeared when I was supposed to be working, he usually found me hiding out somewhere with a book. Writing evolved from reading, and the first story I ever finished was in high school, about my celebrity crush. I got an A on that creative writing 'assignment,' though I'm not sure my teacher ever read all 187 pages. I started writing again in my mid-twenties, and no matter the journey my characters take, the end result is always the same—Happily Ever After.

I'm an avid reader, and also a fan of movies with that HEA. I live in my native Wisconsin with my husband and kids, and in my free time, I enjoy gardening, canning, and visiting my parents in Northeastern Wisconsin (Up North) at the family cabin on the lake.

Check out my website at STACEYJOYNETZEL.COM to sign up for my Newsletter. Not only do subscribers receive new release updates, they also enjoy EXCLUSIVE contests, and bonus short stories to go along with my *USA Today* bestselling Romancing Wisconsin series.

## Find me online:

Website and Blog:
www.StaceyJoyNetzel.com

Facebook:
facebook.com/StaceyJoyNetzelAuthor

Twitter:
twitter.com/StaceyJoyNetzel

Hearing from readers is a very special thing for any writer, so pop in and say "Hi!" at any of the above locations. Or **subscribe to my newsletter** to keep up with my newest releases.
smarturl.it/BKSJNNewsletter

Again, reviews are always appreciated!

~Thank you, and happy reading~

❧ STACEY ☙

*Recommended Read*

If you enjoyed **BETRAYED**,
here's the first chapter sneak peek of:

CONNED

Italy Intrigue Series – 3

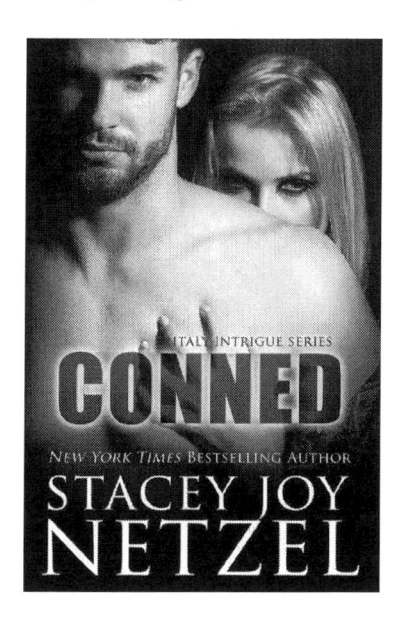

*She's looking for answers.*

One year after being shot in Italy, Rachel Sanders returns in search of the jeweled cross that triggered a heartbreaking family betrayal. Determined to keep the treasure from her mother's greedy hands, she's caught off guard by the interference of an irresistibly charming rival. His unexpected offer to help might be self-serving, but she's thrown into a precarious situation where she can't refuse.

*He has a score to settle.*

Nick Marshall has a family legacy to recover and a score to settle. Anyone with the last name Sanders is fair game—until he meets Rachel. She's gorgeous, smart, sexy, and doesn't buy one word of his cover story. When their attraction combusts, each kiss makes his deception burn like acid, and he begins to question his end goal.

*The cross is the key.*

But they're not the only ones after the cross. Ruthless players willing to do anything to recover the treasure first put Nick and Rachel's lives at risk. Despite all the secrets and lies, lines quickly blur between the con and the real deal. Can love survive a double-cross when the mystery is unlocked?

*"...a refreshing action-adventure filled with an intriguing mystery and sexy romance. Stacey Joy Netzel delivers a strong novel packed full of deception, intrigue, danger, and sexual chemistry so strong, it's palpable. She keeps you reading until the very last word."*

~ Erin, ByoBook Club

## Chapter 1

SOMEONE WAS WATCHING her. The unseen stare electrified the fine hairs on the nape of Rachel Sanders' neck, and touched her skin like a chilling physical caress. The light breeze coming off the Grand Canal was not enough to warrant the sudden bumps that sprung up along her arms in the July heat. Dusk had fallen, but the temperature had to still be close to eighty.

She lifted her napkin to wipe her mouth, then set the cloth on her plate to indicate she was finished with her meal. Pretending to search for her server, she sought out the source of her unease.

No one stood out amongst the dimly lit terrace tables clustered outside the doors of the restaurant. Though it was hard to see with the candlelight reflecting off the clear glass, nothing appeared out of place inside, either. The rest of the busy square—*campo*—seemed business as usual. No one paid her any undue attention as they enjoyed the warm summer evening.

The ring of her cell phone made her jump, bumping her hand against her plate and rattling silverware. Geez—she was letting her nerves get the better of her. Even though she had absolutely no reason to be nervous, past experience in this country lingered in the back of her mind. Past experience growing up magnified the disquieting sensations.

She quickly dug the phone from her bag and answered when she saw the caller ID. "Hey, Halli."

"Hi," her younger sister greeted. "How's Venice?"

Rachel casually shook her hair back, adjusted the sheer, black scarf that'd slid down one shoulder, and forced a smile so it would carry into her voice. "I've only been here a day, but so far the food is amazing."

"When does your convention start?"

Her smile faded. "In two days. I'm going to see about touring the island of Murano. I have some design ideas for glass jewelry, but I need to do a bit of research first."

"That Murano glass is gorgeous. I can't wait to see what you come up with. How long are you there for again?"

"I booked a week."

"You know, you should stay longer and get some sightseeing in, then meet us at the lake in a couple weeks."

She let out a relieved breath. Halli didn't seem to have any suspicions about her cover story. "Listen to you, Mrs. Tomlin. Much as I love *Lago di Como, I* can't afford a month off work."

"Ooh—nice accent."

"Thanks. I've been practicing."

"*Credevo che le vendite andassero bene dopo che ho indossato I tuoi design alla premiere di Trent. Non è cosi?*"

Rachel laughed. "I haven't been practicing *that* much, show off."

"I said, I thought sales were good after I wore your designs at Trent's premiere?"

"Which is exactly why I can't take off that long. Or shouldn't," she added to set the stage in case she *did* decide to extend her stay. "I don't know, I guess I'll see."

"I say take whatever time you can while you're there. If you overlook the dirtier canals, the bridges, squares, and shops are great. Trent took me for a weekend after the wedding, and I loved it. I can't wait to go back and explore."

She was thrilled at her sister's happiness, yet still acknowledged a little twinge of envy as the waiter arrived to take her plate. Welcoming the distraction, she smiled her appreciation, then frowned when he replaced the empty dish with a small ceramic glass of what looked to be limoncello. She reached out with her free hand as he began to turn away. "*Mi scusi*—I did not order this."

He shifted back alongside her chair and replied in Italian. "*Complimenti della casa, signorina.*"

*Good lord, what a voice.*

When she lifted her gaze to the server, her breath caught in her throat. Dark hair, dark eyebrows, and thick lashes made his green eyes all the more brilliant in the soft candlelight. There was a warmth in that gaze that made her think of whispered words of seduction, and deep, slow kisses. Heat that had nothing to do with her two glasses of wine unfurled low in her belly.

As she stared up at him, the man spoke again in heavily-accented English. "Compliments of the house, *signorina.*"

"Oh." And she could've figured that out if his voice hadn't short-circuited her brain.

A flash of white teeth through the shadowed stubble on his jaw increased her heart rate. His light touch grazed her elbow, sending a tingle along her arm at the same time she realized he wasn't the same waiter who'd taken her order, or served her meal. This one was much closer to her age, and so damn gorgeous she was in danger of turning into a drooling idiot.

She shook her head as much to clear it as to say no to more alcohol. Which only got her another charming smile and a dramatic bow. Her second frown formed as he backed away, picked up an empty plate from a nearby table, then disappeared inside before she could even think to murmur a hesitant, "*Grazie.*"

"Rachel? You still there?"

She dropped her attention to the glass. "Yeah."

"What's wrong?" Halli asked.

"Nothing, really." Her fingers tapped the chilled ceramic. "Just a drink I didn't order."

"Do you have an admirer?"

Humor colored her sister's voice, but Rachel didn't smile now that she was reminded of the sensation of being watched earlier. "No, I guess it comes with my meal."

She turned to scan the surrounding area again. Normal people doing normal things. The man who'd served the limoncello must've been a busboy, even if he had looked to be near thirty years old. It wasn't uncommon to see men of all ages serving in the restaurants and cafés of *Italia.* She searched inside, but couldn't distinguish him from the other workers bustling amidst the full tables.

"Limoncello?"

"Yep."

After casting one last glance around, she lifted the small glass and sipped. The distinctive, sweet, lemony flavor of the traditional dessert wine sang to her taste buds and slid down her throat. "Mmm, it is good."

As she sipped again, Halli's sigh came across the line. "Makes me want some, but I don't think I'll hold my breath at finding any here in the Montana Rockies."

"How is everything out in God's country?"

"Amazing. Long hours, but it's going great."

"How much longer are you guys there?"

"About two more weeks to finish filming. If we manage to avoid any major delays, we should be back in Italy by the time Ben and Evalina get back."

"Have you heard from them at all?"

"Hah—right. We're talking Ben and Eva here. On their honeymoon. In Hawaii."

"Yeah, yeah, I know." She shook her head with a grin. Knowing those two, they probably weren't venturing far from their hotel, even during the day. She wouldn't be surprised if they returned with news she'd be an aunt in nine months. Ignoring another twinge, she said, "I thought they might've called about Aida, that's all. How is the little terror?"

"Growing like a weed. And she's a handful, that's for sure, but everyone loves her. One of the handlers has been working with her, and she's actually starting to listen some. She's a very smart puppy."

"Aren't German Shepherds known for that?"

"Yeah. In fact, having her the past week has Trent dying for one of his own."

"Oh, boy."

"Yeah, I know."

"Well, if Ben does call, tell them I said hi."

"I will. And…speaking of hearing from family…"

The sudden drop in her sister's voice made Rachel tense. She wasn't going to like what was coming.

"Has Mom been in contact all?"

Her stomach plummeted. Maybe her cover story hadn't held up after all. The thing was, Halli always avoided talking about either of their parents. She certainly never broached the subject first, which made Rachel wonder what she knew now.

"No. Why?"

"I want to know you're in Italy for the right reasons." Suspicion laced Halli's voice. "Reasons that have nothing to do with those letters Dad sent you."

She hated lying to her siblings after all they'd been through growing up, and even more so after last summer. Through the thin material of her summer halter dress, she traced the bullet scar on her left thigh. They'd had each other's backs in everything, which made her betrayal of trust now seem even worse.

"I promise, I haven't heard a word from Mom." Not since right after the woman had been paroled in spring, anyway—nor did she want to.

She had, however, visited their father in the prison infirmary last month. Which Halli knew, because she'd told her siblings about him getting a shank in his gut. He was doing okay, but his parole hearing had been canceled because of the fight he claimed another inmate had started.

What Rachel hadn't mentioned was the conversation she'd had with their father. Ironically, this was one instance Halli would agree with him. Besides, she only intended to do some research here in Venice to satisfy her own curiosity.

*Liar.*

No—that was it. She'd see if there was any truth to the myth their mother had chosen over all of them, and then head home again. Which made a little white lie better than getting her sister and brother all worked up and worried for nothing.

"I just don't want you—"

"Hal, my check just arrived, and I'm still wiped from the flight. I'll talk to you in a few days, okay? Tell you all about the conference."

Guilt mounted when her sister gave a sigh of resignation. "Yeah, okay. And I can't wait to hear what you think of the glass companies. Take lots of pictures."

Translation: *Prove you're there for the reasons you claim.*

"I will. And listen, if I can figure out a way to swing staying long enough to meet you at the lake, I will."

"That'd be great. Love you."

"Love you, too. Say hi to Trent. Bye."

She slid the phone back into her purse and searched for the waiter to signal for the check. Sipping the last of the limoncello, she acknowledged she was tired, but only because she'd walked along a fair number of those dirty canals, seen many beautiful squares, and crossed countless bridges leading past amazing buildings. Reconnaissance somewhat complete, tomorrow she planned to visit the reading rooms at the Bibliotcca Marciana Library in St. Mark's Square.

She'd done online research prior to her arrival, and narrowed down what books she would request to see. With only four applications accepted per person per day for viewing of works printed prior to 1851, she prayed the first four she'd picked would provide the information she sought.

After paying her bill, Rachel left the *campo* in the general direction of the apartment she'd rented, and walked along the promenade bordering the Grand Canal. The city of Venice was comprised of six *sestieri*, or boroughs, and she'd found a somewhat reasonably priced location in the eastern *sestiere* of Castello. Reasonably priced in Venice in July was stretching it a bit, but business had picked up after her famous brother-in-law's premiere in May, so she'd splurged.

The heels of her sandals clicked along the cobblestones, across one bridge, then the next. They added yet another sound to the hum of activity along the city's still-crowded streets. The sun had set not too long ago, and street lanterns and lights spilling from windows lit the busier areas.

A dozen or so Venice blocks away, she turned from the water, toward the heart of Castello. Away from the Canal, she surmised many of the people out and about were locals, with only the occasional tourists mixed in.

Couples walked hand in hand. Others walked dogs. Friends stood in groups, talking in Italian and laughing. One or two single pedestrians strode with purpose, possibly ready to be home after a long day of work, or anxious to meet someone special.

Rachel soaked in the ambiance, enjoying the slower pace with no cars, or even bikes. Nine o'clock was still early enough that she wasn't in a rush to get back and shut herself off behind her apartment door. Maybe once she satisfied her curiosity, she would take Halli's advice and smell the roses, so to speak.

The closer she got to her rental, the less people populated the narrow streets. Away from the popular tourists areas, it was a much different atmosphere than when she'd left in the daylight hours. There was less light, too.

Surprised by an unexpected ripple of apprehension, she increased her pace while doing her best to not think about the strange sensation at the restaurant. When she reached the end of the shadowed street and took a left turn, she was relieved to see a tall, four-lantern light post at the end...until she realized the path dead ended at one of the countless smaller canals bisecting the city.

*Whoops—wrong turn in the maze.*

She glanced up at the street sign as she swung around to retrace her steps. From the corner of her eye, she spotted a dark shadow duck into an entryway up ahead. Her step faltered. Her pulse skipped, then revved into the red zone as she faced the deserted street.

Rachel pulled her sheer scarf closer about her bare shoulders. Muffled voices registered, and a moment later, an older couple exited the residence one door up and to her right. They offered a polite, *"Ciao,"* before walking ahead of her. She returned the greeting, then followed directly behind them.

Inching closer to the couple as they approached the entryway three doors farther along, she peered into the shadows. Relief flooded through her when she saw the dark space was empty.

Keeping her feet moving, she thought back over the past minute. Other than the couple's exit, there had been no other echoes of a door opening or closing—was it possible she'd imagined the shadow? Like she'd imagined someone watching her in the square?

A deep breath helped slow the pounding of her heart closer to normal.

One final glance back at the empty street convinced her she was being overly paranoid—once more letting bad memories get the best of her. What she needed was a good night's sleep so she could start with a fresh perspective in the morning.

As the couple continued on their way, she took a moment to get her bearings and continued down the next street toward her rental. The entryway to her building had a light, but the rest of the street was dark enough to get her heart thumping again.

"You're being ridiculous," she whispered, forcing her feet to walk, not run.

She entered the building and glanced up as she reached for the stair railing that led to her second floor accommodations. When she saw the door to her rental open inward, her foot froze on the first step. A man came out, his head turned away from her as he did a quick check of the immediate area near the door.

Rachel jerked back out of sight, then moved as quietly as possible to hide beneath the stairwell. Her pulse kept time with the thud of his feet as he rapidly descended the stairs. She held her breath, waiting for the sound of the door. It opened, but when she didn't hear it close again, she cautiously snuck a peek.

She bit back a gasp, as much for the identity of who'd exited her apartment, as for the bundle he held in his hands. Her father's letters. The very letters she was here to research in connection with the Bible that had almost gotten Ben killed.

Her father had told her to leave it alone, but his written words from almost fourteen years ago had been etched into her brain ever since her brother's wild trip from Milan to Rome four months earlier.

*The cross is the key.*

Unfortunately, the key to the cross had just walked out the door with her mystery waiter.

For one disbelieving moment, she stared at the closing door. Then she set her jaw and hurried after him.

---

**CONNED is available in print and ebook.**

Made in the USA
Monee, IL
02 September 2019